BETWEEN NEVER AND FOREVER

BETWEEN NEVER AND FOREVER

USA *TODAY* BESTSELLING AUTHOR

SHAIN ROSE

PAGE
&
VINE

Page & Vine
An Imprint of Meredith Wild LLC

Copyright © 2024 Shain Rose
Cover Design by Bitter Sage Designs
Editing: KD Proofreading, Salma's Library

Paperback ISBN: 979-8-9877583-6-6

Note on Content Warnings

As a reader who loves surprises, I enjoy going in blind with each book. Yet, I also want to give my readers the opportunity to know what sensitive content may be in my books. You will find the list of them here: www.shainrose.com/content-warnings

PART ONE

CHAPTER 1: KEELANI

"I'm not screwing you against a tree in the woods, Kee." Dex Hardy's voice was restrained as he pulled back to glare at me. His piercing green gaze didn't waver even when I frowned at him.

"Live a little, Dex." I ran a hand through my tousled waves and pouted in the moonlight. The cool breeze whipped between us, and he tightened his jacket over my long-sleeved dress.

"Live a little? You dragged me to this underage party in a dress that's two sizes too small for you—"

I looked down at the stretchy violet fabric that hugged every one of my curves. "You don't like it?"

"You know I like it. Too much. It's the only reason I'm here tonight." He grunted. "I don't need twenty guys also liking it and taking advantage of you when I'm not around."

I leaned against the trunk of the tree to stare up at him. "Then take advantage of me instead."

"Kee, I'm not indulging in your recklessness tonight. It's not happening here." His eyes were determined now, hardened dark emeralds shining brightly in his decision. Dex never wavered once he made up his mind.

"It's better out here than somewhere someone might catch us."

He sighed, and I saw how his muscles relaxed a bit under his dark T-shirt. "I don't really give a fuck if someone sees me with my girlfriend."

The way he emphasized the label made the butterflies in my stomach flutter and then immediately scatter from the *whoosh* of fear I felt. "Don't call me that when you know we can't be together."

He shook his head, his dark hair long enough that it fell over his forehead before he combed it back. "Then we shouldn't be out here in the woods."

I crossed my arms. "You agreed to keep us a secret while I figure things out with the record label, Dex."

"It's been a whole damn year, Kee. A year of me loving you, and a year of you wanting me to keep it a secret. For what?" The question flew from his mouth just as thunder rumbled in the distance. The clouds were rolling in for the night just as clouds were rolling in for our relationship too.

"Trinity Enterprises wants me to look like that all-American girl, okay?" Even as I said it, I hated the reason.

"Is Ethan the all-American guy?" He lifted a brow as he threw Ethan's name in my face.

"He's..." I didn't know what to say, honestly. Trinity Enterprises definitely wanted us to date. They had us perform together every chance they got. We attended award shows together, galas, magazine cover shoots, everything. "We don't want each other. It's just for the press."

His jaw ticked. "Imagine seeing another woman on my arm."

"I already have. Gabriella was all over you tonight." My stomach twisted in knots, the butterflies in it now curdling with the acid of jealousy flowing through my veins.

"Kee." He turned away from me and stormed off. Then he spun back and strode up to me to point his finger in my face. "You set us up. You wanted me to date her."

I squeezed my eyes shut, trying so hard to find the strength to keep this charade up. "You're right. And you should be with her. She's great." She had long auburn hair, a nice smile, and she was a good friend to all of us. She wasn't messy like me, didn't come with a million pieces of baggage that Dex shouldn't have to deal with.

"I don't want anybody but you." His dark eyebrows dipped low as he tipped my chin up and rubbed it with his thumb, back and forth, back and forth.

"You can have me here," I whispered. "Just not out there."

"I want you *every*-fucking-where."

"You have me. Here. In private. It's just for now. We'll have each other forever soon enough."

He just shook his head at me and tucked his hands into the pockets of his jeans. "In private. How is that supposed to be good enough? Especially when in public you'll have another man all over you?"

I took a shaky breath. "It's only for a while."

"Remind me. How long is your contract with Trinity, Kee?" He crossed his arms.

"Three more years." I sighed.

"Yeah." His square jaw worked up and down. "Exactly."

"Look, just... I'm not stopping you from being with others." I tried to be fair, even though the words felt stilted as I said them.

His jaw worked again, over and over. He stared at me like he wanted me to understand this wasn't a good idea, like he was trying to see if I knew it wasn't. When I didn't show weakness, he said, "Fine. You know what? Fine. Let's go."

We both stomped through the woods, branches under our boots cracking and breaking like I thought my heart might. We traveled back up the hill to our friend's home. Her parents were out of town, but the white ranch house was lit up with life. We saw Gabriella and Dimitri, Dex's younger brother and my best friend standing there.

Gabriella squealed as we approached them; she'd obviously had more than one drink in the time I was gone as she screeched, "Where were you?"

She'd been a good, longtime friend but one I kept at arm's length. No one had learned much about me in high school except Dimitri. I'd been a loner, throwing my songs on social media and running around the neighborhood with Dimitri and Dex as a freshman. My junior year, though, Trinity Enterprises had caught a video of me and signed me as an artist.

Suddenly, everyone at school wanted to be my friend, but Dimitri and Dex were the only ones I trusted. They were the only ones who'd been there before everyone else.

"Don't make it so damn obvious next time. Gabriella's been looking for you both for the past twenty minutes," Dimitri whispered, "I'm not going to cover your asses just because you're my best friend, Kee." Yet, his glare was softer than Dex's as he chastised me—nicer, sweeter. Dimitri would always be there for me even if the dynamic had shifted when I'd finally admitted to him that I had a crush on Dex.

Dex's eyes locked on mine as Gabriella gave me a hug.

"Oh, I was just taking a call from my agent," I answered fast.

She leaned into Dex. "Ugh. Isn't Keelani amazing? I'm waiting for the day that I get a call from a freaking record label."

I shook my head. "It's not all rainbows and butterflies, Gabriella." I might have been talking to her, but I held Dex's gaze.

"Right." She shrugged, and when the thunder rumbled again, she waved us all inside. We weaved through the crowded living room and found some space in the kitchen, where Gabriella continued on. "It must be nice, though, Keelani. You don't have to hang out with us all the time. Instead, you're hanging with celebrities like Ethan Phillipe."

That comment had Dex's neck flexing and the words in my throat catching. A silence that crackled with tension filled the space. Thankfully, Dimitri laughed right as Dex's friend, Kyle, meandered up to us. His lopsided smile was full of delight as he lightly slapped Dex on the back. "Slumming it at home when you're in college now, bro?"

"Just here to see my brother and apparently you." Dex shrugged and then leaned against the island countertop even though his eyes were on me.

"And me!" Gabriella snuggled close to him, their hips side by side, her head against his chest, and her hand smoothing the T-shirt that I knew was thin enough for her to feel his six pack.

Dimitri swung an arm around me and then whispered, "You need a drink."

"I need four," I grumbled and disappeared with Dimitri into the basement where I knew there was a whole bar.

Dex didn't follow me. I knew he wouldn't. I walked away from the love of my life as my friend hung on his arm like she belonged there.

That night, we all drank too much. I remember offering Dex drinks, but he continued to say no, continued to say that we should leave.

Instead, I turned back to the oak bar counter and hopped onto it. "Who's ready for a dance party?"

"You're being reckless again," Dex growled as he stared up

at me.

"I'm letting loose." I swayed my hips and smirked down at him. "You should try it."

"We need to leave," he said, but I ignored him. "You've had too much to drink, Keelani."

"I hate when you call me that," I whispered to him because he knew it was my formal stage name and I didn't want to be that here. I didn't really want to be her anywhere. The label was suffocating, the responsibility was draining, and the rules were binding. The last thing I wanted was a lecture from him now.

But I needed one. I was too stirred up in my emotions and too immature to think of the repercussions.

I poured alcohol down everyone's throats, was the life of the party, and tried to enjoy myself so much so that I wouldn't have to consider the realities of my situation. When Dex had finally had enough, Kyle offered to drive us all home.

Laid-back Kyle who'd drank just about as much as me. Kyle who was so sweet and genuine. He'd wanted to help.

Dex said no. Even Dimitri looked wary, but Gabriella and I were too far gone to listen to reason. We ran through the freezing rain and folded into his car without looking back at Dimitri and Dex, laughing like we were getting away with not obeying a parent.

We just wanted to have fun, but it wasn't as fun when Dex followed me into that car, unwilling to let me go on my own and gave me a look about as stormy as the weather.

"It'll be fine," I whispered to him because Gabriella was between us, giggling still.

Yet, the night was dark, the roads slippery, the rain heavy on the windshield.

How safe did you feel on a bridge in a vehicle going seventy on a highway in icy rain? Safe enough to text? To tell your friends in the back seat you're fine, you've got it under control?

"Kyle. You've got to slow down," Dex yelled right as Dimitri swore from the front seat.

But it was too late.

Kyle's confidence that night cost him his life. When he looked up from his text, he was veering into oncoming traffic. He overcorrected, yanking the steering wheel straight towards the railing.

The vehicle crunched all around our bodies in a way I never expected.

I vaguely remember the sound of the collision into the siderail. It was deafening, so booming it rattled our bones as the front of the car scraped, metal on metal, against the side of the highway. It all happened so fast.

And so slowly.

The car almost seemed to halt. The air was pushed out of my lungs at the slicing pain of the seat belt. But the sound I'd never forget was that of Gabriella's screams. They pierced through the air, filled with fear. She hadn't been wearing her seat belt, and the momentum carried her forward as we were jerked back.

The car flipped off the edge of the highway. Flipped over and over. The impact and her screams were loud, but the silence as the car fell and tipped upside down was louder.

Down, down, and down.

Into the dark depths of the water.

When we hit the lake, our fragile bodies jerked all around in the dark, and the lights of the car immediately went out.

It was probably only a second of us floating there, suspended on top of water before it began to sink, but it felt like forever before I heard Dex's voice, pointed, direct, and determined—"Do not panic, Kee. You hear me? Don't fucking panic."—but it held fear.

We were too young. None of us knew what to do in a life-and-death situation.

"I can't... I can't swim well." I wiggled as the blood rushed to my head. We were all hanging upside down by our seat belts as water crept toward our heads fast. I reached for the button but found it harder to press with the pressure of my body against it. "I can't get—"

He reached around me and undid my buckle as he yelled to his brother, "Unbuckle and get the hell out."

I hit the roof of the car that was now sinking and the water's freezing temperature immediately made me gasp. Dex was there to catch my gaze.

"I got you, Kee. I got you, okay?"

I shook my head, trying to glance around and see where everyone was. I saw Dimitri struggling with a door, but Kyle wasn't moving. Dark liquid was dripping from his head. Was it water or blood? And then I saw the hole in the windshield.

So big that a body could have fit through it.

Shattered.

Water rushed in, and my eyes widened.

"Kee." Dex's hands went to my face. "Focus. You're going to follow me, okay? I. Got. You."

"No. What?" I whispered before I screamed, "Don't get me. Get her! Get Gabriella! Where is she?" I tried to yank my face away in a panic, but he was pulling me forward. "Where is she?" I think shock was taking over as I started to shake, my clothes soaking in the inky black liquid that was rising faster and faster. The car was sinking, which meant we were about to be under water, under a sheet of ice in the dark.

No one heard about people surviving car crashes in freezing water. They heard about the tragic results, and we were about to be one.

"Fuck," he swore over and over as he pushed at the door. It didn't budge. "Get ready to swim. We're going through the windshield—"

And then his face disappeared as we went under. I don't remember taking a breath or grabbing back on to his hand. I don't remember how he and Dimitri somehow got the door open or if we went through the hole in the windshield once we were fully submerged by them pulling me through it.

I don't remember swimming out. I don't know if I even did. He probably dragged me the whole way. I saw how his eyes held so much determination, so much fear in that moment that he would have been propelled to do almost anything.

I put my life in their hands because a body shifts into survival mode and trusts who it must. Deep in my bones, I knew I could trust Dex.

He found the hole in the ice the car had broken through, and they maneuvered me up onto it. We were lucky it didn't break under our weight. Others weren't as lucky.

So fast a life could be taken.

So fast a person could become a hero, a victim, a survivor, or a villain.

Dimitri pulled me close as I shook from either the freezing temperature or the adrenaline coursing through my veins but he grabbed Dex with his other hand. "You're not going back in."

"I've got to find them." Dex's eyes were wild. "I've got to."

He dove back through that hole in the ice as I heard blood curdling screams all around us.

They were mine. Me, screaming for him to come back, screaming and crying and fighting Dimitri as he pulled me to safety and lifted me up to carry me away from the lake.

Lightning struck and thunder rumbled over the sound of sirens approaching. When the cops and ambulance got there, they had to sedate me.

I remember the icy rain on my face, the lightning in the sky, and the rumble of that thunder before I blacked out.

***

"Keelani." My dad's calloused hand was in mine as he took me home from the hospital the next day. I heard the disappointment in his voice. "I'm glad you're okay but the local news is starting to trend."

Right. He wasn't glad. No one sounded that dejected when they were happy. "Last night was—"

"A complete tragedy. You shouldn't have been..." He took a deep breath and pulled his hand out of mine to turn into the driveway. He didn't move to get out once he shut off the ignition, and instead, his hands tightened on the steering wheel. He put his forehead against it before he looked up at me with his tired brown eyes. "You're so lucky to be alive, Kee."

I glanced away when I saw the tears in his eyes. My father didn't cry much. He was too big of a man, too stoic in the collared shirts and flannel tees that he wore with his khakis every day. "I know I'm lucky."

"The town's reporting on you and Dex, though. I won't ever be able to thank him enough for saving you, but the media is painting a picture of the two of you as a couple now. He's the hero who saved you, then went back for his brother and his friends. Your manager... Mitchell at Trinity Enterprises thinks the narrative will spread to national outlets and hinder your brand if they don't intervene."

"Dad," I whispered, my eyes cutting to his fast. "You can't..."

"You all had a high blood alcohol levels. Kyle lost his life, and Gabriella is in a coma. If she comes out of it, she won't be able to walk for months, Kee. She was dating Dex, but he saved you?" He asked the question like he already knew the answer. My heart beat rapidly as my mind scrambled for a response. He tsked. "You're a public figure. You're contractually obligated to be with..."

It wasn't in writing, it was only a verbal instruction, but we all knew the truth. Trinity Enterprises wouldn't allow me to be with anyone other than Ethan.

Gabriella was supposed to be the one Dex saved. Not me. And because he did that, he'd outed us to the world. They painted him as a hero at first, as the boy who dragged the girl he loved out of that water to save her. They said he loved me, that he risked his life for mine.

"Trinity is working on changing the narrative," my dad concluded.

"Dad, what does that mean?"

"It doesn't matter, Kee!" He smacked the steering wheel in frustration and then put his forehead against it. "They get to do whatever damage control they want. And you need to agree because otherwise you're in breach of a very big contract that we can't pay back."

I stayed silent. The contract and record label were things I didn't want to work out, but I knew what the money meant for the family.

"I spoke with Mitchell." Of course he'd spoken with my

manager. "They're willing to give us a bit of a bonus if you move to Nashville—"

"Nashville?" I screeched. "Dad, I can't leave you and Mom. What are you talking about?"

"I'll take the bonus and work on some things. Get you back here as soon as I get a bit more money." He mulled over his options, but I knew what it would come down to. My dad always tried to save everything by going to visit the casino or by placing a bet with a bookie that never worked out.

"What if I just do more shows?" I asked even though I didn't want to do that.

He shook his head and looked out the window at our small house. "We need this for your mom, Kee. The stroke she had... She can't work anymore, and with the bonus, I can get her some medical care."

"Dad," I whispered, "please don't make me go."

"We've agreed that it would be best for you and your career. You're almost eighteen. It'll be great. Your image will be safer there. We'll have you paired up with the best in the industry. You'll give us some breathing room too for Mom to heal."

"Breathing room?"

"Keelani." He turned to me now, his eyes hardened to make the point. "You know the mental toll of all we've been through? And then you were at a party drinking with men you shouldn't have been with." His voice was cajoling but his words struck at my heart.

"*Men?* They're my friends. They're our neighbors, Dad. Dex and Dimitri—"

"They don't know about our financial struggles or how much your job means to our family, do they?" He lifted a brow. "They may be friends, but we're family. We stick together. This bonus will help. I can make it work."

His tone sounded so hopeful with that statement. Even though I knew time and time again that we lost money from his gambling, I still wished he'd win big one day, if only for the happiness it would bring for a moment. The times he'd come home with a few winnings this past year, he'd smiled so big. Yet, the rest of the year hadn't been so good.

"I'll get you back here in a few months if Nashville doesn't work out," he promised as if he could. My father had lost his office job years ago but had somehow stretched our money out since my mother's stroke. I knew he'd made some shady deals by just the looks of some of the men who now came around our house, but I didn't question it. We were family, just like Dad said.

"Dad, I was going to go to college here," I tried. "I really want to be close. Other kids' parents are—"

"If this is the worst thing I do to you as a parent, you can thank me, Keelani," my father cut me off, his tone hardening. "You can take online courses."

"That's not the point."

"The point is your plane leaves next week. Don't give a statement to anyone. Your new contract has an indemnity clause, which means you can't refute anything released from Trinity about this car wreck."

Had I fucked up that much that he sounded so disheartened, so disappointed? I hated that. "Dad, I just want this all to work out."

"I know, Kee. I know. It will. Your mom will get better." He said it with conviction, and I heard the love he had in his voice. "We just have to do this for her. You understand?"

I nodded because he was my dad, and I'd have done just

about anything to take away the pain I was causing.

"And, Kee, if you're sneaking around with that Dex who saved you, end it. End it now."

CHAPTER 2: DEX

Gone was the fire. Gone was the passion. In its place was the ice.

A coldhearted Keelani had taken possession of the love of my life. Numb. Frozen. Maybe full of fear. I didn't fucking know.

That car wreck changed us, and I couldn't seem to get her back, not even after hanging out with her every day at home, asking her what was wrong aside from the obvious, and visiting her family.

I knocked on her door a week later when I saw the large, black SUV outside her house. It was in my bones to keep tabs on her and her fucking reckless behavior. She went off the rails a lot when the label came to visit, and I knew today wouldn't be any different.

But when I saw suitcases being wheeled out, my walk turned to a run.

I pushed past her sleazy-ass manager and strode straight into her house. Her mother was at the kitchen table, humming a quiet song about a beach in Hawaii where she'd grown up. I knew it to be a favorite of Kee's because they would sing it together every now and then. Her and Kee's voices were so similar that I'd come to find comfort in being in that kitchen, hearing the joy they spread through a melody.

Today, though, the melody was sad as she wiped away tears. Yet, she smiled at me when she saw me. "Dex, come in! Did Dimitri tell you?"

Anela had never known about Keelani's relationship with me. She thought I came over to entertain her daughter when Dimitri wasn't around, to check in, to be a good brother and neighbor.

"No. What's going on? Dimitri has been acting weird."

Her mother tried to get up, but she didn't move as easily as she once had since the stroke. I waved away her effort and bent down to hug her.

"I know she's near eighteen and she's going to go off to college anyway, but I'm selfish, you know? I want my baby home."

"Of course you do." My heart thudded in my chest with confusion and fear now.

"You think Dimitri will go visit her? Keep her safe?" Her dark eyes were the exact same color as Kee's and just as full of life most of the time. Why did they look so damn dejected now?

"Safe from what?" I ground out. Dimitri didn't have to keep my girl safe from anything. That was my job. "Where's Kee now?"

"Her bedroom." She stood up to escort me back, but I loved that woman about as much as I loved my own mother.

"Sit down, Anela. Can I get you some water or something?"

"Of course not, honey." She chuckled and sat down at her kitchen table. Grabbing her phone, she pulled her glasses from her shirt and pointed to her screen. "I'm going to just do some internet warrioring for a bit. Tell these trolls to leave my Keelani alone."

"Mrs. Hale, can you not go on Instagram today?" Keelani's bald headed manager whined from behind me, having entered the room with Keelani's father.

Anela winked at me and tilted her head toward Keelani's

room before she started bickering with Mitchell. "Why shouldn't I go online today? Everyone has something to say about her. Well, so do I. I am her mother after all."

I took the opportunity to beeline down the hall of pictures that showcased Keelani smiling on stage, waving to crowds, dancing in skintight leotards. She was beautiful when she performed, but it was nothing compared to her standing in sweats at home without makeup.

Keelani's big doe eyes looked up from another suitcase she was packing, and she didn't race up to me like she normally did, didn't hug me like I was everything to her now. Her movements were stilted as she took a shirt, folded it deftly, then placed it in the suitcase.

"Kee?" I murmured, not sure what the hell was happening.

She breathed out a long sigh before glancing out the window and then back down at the suitcase. Suddenly that long dark hair that I loved served as a shield to block me out, hiding her features from me. Then she said the words that would gnaw at my soul for years to come. "I'm leaving."

"What?" I frowned, not sure I'd heard her correctly. "Wait. Now? Leaving for where? You don't have a tour for—"

"No." She shook her head and folded another shirt. "I'm leaving for good. Moving to Nashville."

"Nashville?" I glanced around her room like there might be some clue I'd missed. "But you have college here starting in the summer—"

"I'm finishing last semester of senior year online, Dex, and then I'm not going to college. Trinity wants me in Nashville right now before the tour and—"

"You're screwing with me," I cut her off, shaking my head. My mind couldn't comprehend what she was saying. She was the damn love of my life. Nashville was too far.

"I'm not." Her tone was clipped and stiff but that was her only indication of pain.

I stared at the girl I loved, willed her to look at me. "You're not leaving."

She finally looked up and those deep-brown eyes of hers filled with tears. "How can you honestly think there would be any way for me to stay, Dex?"

"What's stopping you?"

"The news! You... You shouldn't have saved me, Dex." Her voice was broken and full of pain as she said it.

"I'll always save you, Kee. Don't you get that?"

"But it's ruined us instead of saving us! I have to leave now." She threw up her hands.

"You don't. You can't. Gabriella's still in the hospital. Dimitri's all jittery as hell about getting in a car. You can't leave now. You're going to college here in the fall and—"

And me. You've got me here, I wanted to say.

"They're writing about us," she whispered, like I should care.

"So what?" I threw out the words harshly. It was the last thing on my mind. We were coping with trauma, trying to mend our bodies and minds. None of us should have had to worry about the public right now.

She spun around to grab her phone and then held it out to me, pointing her finger at the screen. "They're writing about us *together.*"

Her and her fucking secrets. "Let me get this right. You're leaving because the secret's out about us. Who the fuck cares?"

She shut her eyes like she was in pain, and it crushed my damn soul. Her pain was because we were out there in the world, not because she was leaving, not because we were imploding in slow motion. And even still, I wanted to hug her, to tell her it would be all right. I didn't step forward though. Not when she was breaking my heart.

She was trying to leave when all she had to do was stay. "I can't be with you, Dex."

"Fine. Don't be with me." I shrugged, acting as though the words didn't feel like a knife to my gut. Then, trying to temper my reaction, I rubbed a hand over my face before I continued. "But you can't leave. You're Dimitri's best friend. Your family needs you, and I..." I needed her too.

Didn't she know that by now?

"My family needs me to leave. I'm a mess here. I'm wild and reckless, and it's bad for my career and the record label and—"

"You're you here," I corrected her. "You go be fucking Goldilocks for a damn record label, then you're selling yourself short. They're watering you down. You should be singing the songs you sing in your bed to me. We go down to the lilacs in the woods, and you sing your heart out, Kee. That song you sing with your mom in the kitchen, the world wants that. That's what you deserve, and what your family—"

"My family," she emphasized and suddenly straightened, "wants me to go just like I want to go."

"What the fuck did that record label tell you?" Something was wrong.

"They told me I can make it. My dreams can come true. And that Ethan really does love me, Dex. And I..." She hesitated and looked out the window, her chin trembling as she said the next words. "I think I love him too."

That was the wrecking ball of destruction. Those words

obliterated the confidence I had in our relationship, the confidence I needed to keep her here. "You don't mean that," I said and walked right up to her to take her chin in my hands, to rub over it back and forth. "Don't lie to me, Kee. Not about that."

She lifted her chin and backed away out of my reach. Her eyes shut, and I immediately missed the dark chocolate color of them. "Why are you making this hard? This wasn't supposed to last, Dex. You know that."

"Of course it was," I whispered to her. "We were *always* going to last. You sang to me that you'd love me forever."

"I do!" she screamed and threw up her hands, but then she fisted them and brought them back to her chest. "I did. But Ethan and I work together and...maybe I don't love him now, but I could."

She uttered that part in desperation, like she was trying to make me comprehend.

I shook my head. "I don't understand, Kee."

"I could love him, Dex. I will. I can do anything I set my mind to. You told me that once, and I believe it."

"Don't play with me," I ground out. She was twisting my confidence in her, twisting my love. My emotions spun round and round, out of control. Sadness mixed with rage that burned so hot all I saw was red, vivid red that made me want to commit a damn crime against a man I didn't know.

"Just... You honestly shouldn't be here. I'm surprised my manager even let you through."

"Let me through?" I muttered through gritted teeth, rage pumping in my stomach, in my bones, through my blood. "No one is going to let me do shit when it comes to you. You're my girlfriend."

"Ex-girlfriend," she murmured.

"What?" I stepped back like she'd pummeled me.

"We can't keep doing this. It's not good for either of us. It's never going to work with me moving and..." Her voice broke, but she managed to get out, "You can't just be with me in secret for years. They have me under contract for three, and what if I re-sign with them? They'll want me with someone..."

"Someone who will propel your career? Someone like Ethan Phillipe?" I wrestled the words out now, knowing where this was going.

"It's not only about him, Dex. Do you honestly think it's healthy for you to see me flirting with him out there and then coming back to apologize to you in private?"

"Then tell the label about us." I said the words slowly because I'd never said them before.

She hissed, "What?"

"Tell them about us," I repeated.

"I... I can't, Dex." She shook her head, and her beautiful hair swung back and forth.

"So you're choosing him? That why you wanted me to keep this secret so badly for so long? In the end you wanted him and the fame and the money." I shouldn't have said it, but hurt people hurt people and all that shit.

"Screw you." She shoved me, but I saw the quiver in her lip now. "You know that's not what this is."

"What is it then?"

"I just... I don't love what the record label is doing either, but I signed." Tears welled in her eyes. Then she whispered again, "I signed. I had to."

"Right." I took a step away from her. "You need to stand up for yourself with them for once, Kee. You practically run around this town, free as a bird, causing havoc wherever you go, and you won't take shit from anyone. Why keep taking it from them?"

Crossing her arms over her chest, she put up a barrier between us physically and emotionally. "What if I want to take their shit, Dex? What if it's what allows me to get my music out into the world?"

My jaw flexed involuntarily. It was her dream. My dream for her too. Everyone deserved to hear this girl sing, even if I wanted to bottle up her voice and keep it all to myself. "You should be doing it on your terms." They'd already had her for a year and hadn't let her sing a damn thing she wanted.

"These are my terms. This is what I want, Dex. They gave me options." She took a deep breath and looked away. "This was the best one."

"Leaving all of us is your best option?" I blurted out because I wanted her to repeat it. "Say it out loud, nice and slow, and tell me if it sounds right."

"I'm leaving," she whispered. "I'm leaving you all to follow my dream, and I hope you'll support that."

I shook my head back and forth. "You leave this town, I'll never forgive you. You get that?"

"Dex, this isn't how I want it to end. We could be friends and—"

"I'll never be your friend." The words came out fast with fury. "I've told you I love you; I've promised myself to you. I want to *marry* you...not be your friend." She gasped at my confession, yet I continued on. "You've always been my girl, my girlfriend, my future wife. Nothing less. Don't you get that? I promised you forever, Kee."

"But forever can never be, Dex." She choked back a sob, but

this time I didn't pull her to my chest like I had so many times before. She tried to cover her mouth with the back of her hand to hide her turmoil.

"Yeah. You pack that bag and leave, you can bet it'll never be."

She narrowed her eyes then, glared through her tears, and said, "Maybe one day you'll overlook this, and we'll be friends."

"Never happening, Keelani. Never in a million years."

My girl was stubborn.

She still packed up that night and left me.

CHAPTER 3: KEELANI

THREE YEARS LATER

The way my name rumbled out of his chest caused shivers to erupt everywhere over my body, even after the years I'd avoided seeing him.

"Keelani?" I heard a sigh. "I know you're up there."

I tried to slow my heartbeat as I pursed my lips together. The sun was setting over my backyard, and Dimitri and I had been up on the roof all day, catching up, sharing nonsense and memories.

"I didn't know he was going to be here. I swear," Dimitri said, but his smile gave him away.

"You're an ass," I whisper-yelled. "You tell him all about my family drama too?"

Dimitri and his family knew about my mom's early onset Alzheimer's, but Dimitri had told me no one discussed my family situation with Dex.

"Babe, none of my family would tell Dex that. We know things between you two are hard enough. You should talk to him though."

I scoffed. He didn't understand that I'd tried over and over. Too many times to count.

"Keelani!" Dex bellowed from below.

I growled at his voice, at him using my whole name like I

was a child he had to chastise. I glared at Dimitri one more time before I stood up. I wasn't going to cower. "Can I help you?"

"What the hell are you doing up there? Get your ass off the roof right now." His tone was harsh, lacking any kindness toward me.

I frowned at him. This was how he greeted me after three years of silence? "I'm fine."

"I'm sure you are. I don't really care one way or the other, except knowing my parents, they'll be pissed if I let you stay up there and something happens. So, climb off the roof or so help me God, I'll come up there and drag you down." The words rumbled out vicious and condescending.

It's true that our parents were still friends. I knew from what my father told me that Dex's parents came around as much as my dad would let them, helping with bringing in the mail or asking if my mom wanted to walk their farmland some days.

Little things like that were big things for us. It was the best way to help when a family was experiencing the early onset of a degenerative brain disease. Not that Dex knew any of that.

"Whatever." I rearranged my bikini top with my back to Dex and sat down on the shingles so I was out of his sight. I glared at Dimitri. "You gonna tell him you're up here with me?" I whispered down to where he lay on the shingles.

"No way in hell," Dimitri whispered back. "He'll be pissed I was up here ogling your ass."

"You'd better not be ogling my ass, you dick." I'd give Dimitri hell only because I knew he was a shameless flirt, but I also knew he only had platonic feelings for me.

"Is my brother up there with you?" Dex bellowed.

I tried to ignore the flutter in my stomach, the way my heart jumped immediately. It could have been a hundred years since

I'd last seen him, and I would still react that way to anything regarding Dex.

Dimitri was already crawling away when he turned his puppy dog eyes on me. "Stall so I can climb to the other side and get down. I'm going to be late for my date if he catches me."

I glared at him, saying nothing.

He furiously whispered, "You know as well as I do there's going to be hell to pay if he finds out I'm up here with you. He's the most jealous of us all."

"He's not jealous anymore. We've been done for years, and he never answers me." I'd tried to apologize to Dex more than once for how I'd left. I'd gone to therapy, tried to work through the trauma of the car accident, how the label handled it, everything. Still, no response from Dex until this very moment.

I bit my lip and rolled my eyes before turning around and standing to catch Dex's gaze. My heart beat fast as I stared at him. The years had been good to him. His chest was wider, his gaze stronger, his hate for me probably strongest. I wouldn't let him see me cower though. "Don't be ridiculous. This is where I get the best tan."

"Kee." He breathed my name as his eyes raked up and down my body, and immediately my pussy clenched and my nipples hardened. *Damn him.* He was still sex on a stick.

He rubbed his chin before glancing around, probably trying to figure out how I'd scaled it. "How long have you been up here?"

"Long enough." I pointed to the corner of the house with the gutter drain and said, "Want to help me down?"

Dex hesitated now. Our connection had been broken years ago, and now we stood in our parents' yards like kids again. "Why are you here?"

"At my parents'? Where I come to visit them?"

"You don't come to visit often. Dimitri didn't say—"

I popped a hip. "Why would he say anything to you about me being home?"

"Because he knew I'd be home, and that fucker probably wanted us to talk."

I chewed on my cheek and glanced behind me. My lovely best friend was gone. Missing in action. "Maybe." I shrugged and walked to the corner gutter. "Not much to talk about. You helping me down or not?"

He didn't move forward. He actually stepped back like I was poison ivy or something.

So I scoffed and went to the gutter myself to swing my body over and loop my hand in the metal.

I was only half into my swing before his large, calloused hands found my bare waist. "Jesus. You want a broken leg? Is this how you take care of yourself without me around?"

His voice was deep, full of grit, and it sent shivers down my spine in a way it shouldn't. I forgot how intense the electric shock was between us, how the air shifted, how the world seemed to stop. It was my turn to step back right into the corner of the house away from his proximity. He smelled like cedar and spice. It was just another damn thing I missed that I couldn't get over.

"I'm fine," I ground out and tried to brush his hands away from my hips. His fingers dug into my skin, sizzling and burning an imprint. "I take care of myself just fine, Dex."

He narrowed the mossy-green eyes I was obsessed with and said through clenched teeth, "You come home just to tell me that?"

I hadn't. I'd come home to check on my parents, to make

sure my mother's health wasn't declining rapidly, that my father wasn't panicking and spiraling out of control. He'd spent another chunk of our savings just weeks before, and I needed to right the ship. Otherwise, he was correct. I didn't come home much. It was too painful, too full of memories and regrets.

Like the one standing right in front of me.

"Maybe I did come home just to tell you that," I shot off immediately. He was irking the crap out of me, acting like I should listen to him, like he wanted to take care of me when he couldn't even respond to my reaching out. "Or maybe my coming home had nothing to do with you at all because I barely even think of you."

His eyes widened at my statement, and I saw the hurt flash in them before it morphed to anger.

"You really think I believe that?"

No. How could I when I thought of him weekly, daily, hourly? But I wouldn't admit that.

He took two deep breaths as he looked down at my lips and his hands shook on me like he was trying to hold himself back. Then he whispered, "Fuck it," before he slammed his mouth hard into mine, his full lips moving with the purpose of dominating mine.

There was no passion in that kiss, only pure hate and the intent to show me he had the upper hand. His tongue expertly slid across mine, his hands dancing over all the spots he knew I liked. He squeezed my ass, bringing me close to him, and I whimpered at the feel of him against me.

Years we'd been apart, but instantly, my body remembered him. Every part of me wanted him. I submitted immediately because he was the only one who'd ever made me feel that way.

His other hand threaded through my hair, and he dug his

fingers into the strands of it, loosening the bun I always wore now. Once he had enough around his fingers to grip, he pulled my head back to gain more access, to tower over me as he tasted what he didn't even want.

I whimpered at that thought. He didn't even want me anymore. I felt it in how he kissed me with no appreciation or love.

Yet, I clutched at his shirt, trying to hold on to the moment as long as possible. He was still a comfort I couldn't deny myself, a home to me after all this time. He was the person I felt safest with even though I knew I shouldn't.

When he stepped back, he did it abruptly, and I stumbled forward before catching myself. He didn't even try to help me. "Feels like you think of me a lot, Kee."

"Dex." I needed to control the shake in my voice, manage how he was making me feel. I hadn't felt like this with anyone else. The only feeling that came close was when I walked on stage. Nerves and excitement and adrenaline all at once. Love was a scary thing.

Still, I had to be mature about what was happening. Therapy had taught me that. "I want to talk to you about what happened when I left. What I said about Ethan was untrue and if—"

"You sent texts after you left and called me. You left me voicemails. I know you want to talk."

He twisted the dagger in me by saying it out loud. That meant he'd consistently ignored me, that he didn't care enough to respond.

"So, can we talk?" I needed this, and he did too. How was I supposed to get over the love I left behind when I'd never wanted to leave him behind in the first place? I needed to tell him that at least.

But he stared at me with a look of anger, and then he blinked and it was gone. All the pain, all the emotion, all the passion we had between us was gone. He'd turned it all off. "Fine. Let's go to the garden then."

"The garden?" I squeaked out. I hadn't been back there in years, not since the last time I'd gone with him.

He lifted a brow. "You have a problem with the garden, Kee?"

"It's just, we used to—"

"You scared of a few memories?" He looked me up and down like my love for him had been some childish thing.

I wanted to scream at him for that and remind him that once upon a time, he'd loved me too. Instead, I pushed past him to make my way down the hill of our backyards and then onto the wood-chipped path that led into a little forest. Our family had acres of land back there, but my father had found an open spot where he'd planted lilacs for my mother and me. She never walked along the path anymore, but Dex and I used to always come down here.

When we were young, I could run out into the backyard, across our field, through some woods and into the line of lilac bushes my father had planted so long ago. Mom had set up a little gate that I'd unlock with a gold key and then leave open. If Dex saw it, he'd make his way down into the woods and find me. We'd spent hours there.

It'd been our spot where Dex brought a blanket to lay on and I'd play guitar for him. I'd sing songs, and he'd listen like he gave a damn. He'd bring a phone too, and we'd watch movies under the stars, make out for hours, and then he'd send me home even when I tried my best to take it further.

Now, we weaved along the path in silence, like we were supposed to wait until we got to our old spot to talk, but when we did, the lilacs weren't in bloom. Most of them had been overtaken by other plants, abandoned and not kept up. I think my mouth fell open at how badly my parents had let the spot get. "They must have forgotten..." I choked on the word, and Dex's eyes narrowed. I hadn't told him about my mom. It wasn't his place anymore to know. "They must have forgotten about this place," I whispered out.

There was only a small patch of grass left, flowers threaded through weeds and buckthorn. A remnant of how it used to smell lingered in the air. Before, when they were in full bloom, the smell was sweet, floral, and bright. They smelled of spring and sun and joy.

"Your parents have better things to do than keep up a little garden that means nothing, Keelani."

He was right, for reasons he didn't even know. And as the clouds rolled in, the lingering smell of them turned painful, agonizing. It filled me with sadness as he stared at me and our space with complete apathy.

"Dex, this garden meant something to me," I admitted. "It meant something to us."

His green eyes scanned the area. "A high school crush is barely something to fret over."

Flippantly, he dismissed all we'd had. "Is that all it was to you?"

"What more could it be? You left and moved on. So did I."

Why did I want him to not mean it? Why did I need him to hurt like I did? Because I still loved him. I still dreamed of this spot. I still held on to the taste of his lips, the feel of his hands, the way his heart beat with mine.

"I didn't move on," I uttered, my voice cracking under the weight of my emotion. "I called you and—"

He stepped close to me and put his hand on my cheek as one tear fell from my eye. His thumb immediately brushed it away, like he was taking care of me even while the words he said were cold. "I didn't answer, Kee, because I didn't care."

"So you don't care at all, then?"

He sighed like he was dealing with a child, then he tilted my head up so his lips were aligned with mine. "Do you feel something when I kiss you, Kee? Tell me. Do you get butterflies?"

This time he kissed me softly, so softly. My eyes fluttered closed to take in how featherlight his touch could be, how he could treat me like I was precious.

"I feel everything," I confessed because I at least could honor our relationship even if he wouldn't. I opened my eyes to search his. "I want you still, Dex."

Emotion of some sort was there now as he glared at me, irises deep green like a forest in the midst of a dark storm. "You're stunning, Keelani. Does the world know how beautiful you look after you've been kissed by me? How your eyes light up? How a blush paints your cheeks? Would they know what's under this bikini?" His finger dipped into the waist of my bottoms, and he dragged it along the edge before his hand disappeared underneath. I gasped as he swept his fingers over my clit to play with me, to test how aroused I was.

His mouth went to my ear. "Soaking already. Such a fucking good all-American girl. You built that brand so well, Keelani." He sneered the name. "Do you think they know you still get wet for me like this?"

His finger slid into my pussy, and I didn't stop him. Instead, I pulled him close. I wanted his masterful mouth even if it was venomous now, and he gave it to me. I pulled him down to the ground and stared up at him, the trees above us, their leaves as green as Dex's eyes. I'd like to think I saw hunger in them now, and when I lifted my knees on either side of his hips and rolled them into his hand, that jaw flex wasn't fake. He wanted me too.

"It doesn't matter what everyone knows right now. All that matters is we both know we still want each other." I rubbed my hand down his chest to his belt buckle and then his length. I whimpered at the sheer size of him, hard, thick, solid through his jeans.

"You like how I feel against your hand, Kee?" he asked, his head bent forward, his breathing coming faster now. Mine was too. I couldn't stop what was about to happen because I wanted him there in that grass, alone in our garden among the lilacs and memories we once had. Maybe I was lonely, maybe I was still torn apart from what had happened before, or maybe I simply still loved him.

No one forgets a regret as big as losing your first love. No one survives it without scars and pain. I wanted to heal us in that moment, and I wanted him to want that too. "You know I like how you feel, Dex. I always have. Please. I need you. Show me you need me too."

He chuckled in my ear as I bucked against his fingers. He slid another one in, and I gasped as he curled them at just the right angle. Up and down. Up and down. Soft at first, then harder and harder. "Are you sure I still want you?"

"Yes," I hissed, frustrated that he wouldn't admit it. He was fighting this, and we'd both been stubborn for years. I didn't want to be anymore. "You wouldn't be here if you didn't."

"Maybe I just want to fuck you once and for all, Kee. Ever think of that? Most men in the nation want to now, but you're so close with Ethan Phillipe." He sneered the name.

"He's good for the brand. You know that. If you read my texts and listened to my voicemails..." I took a deep breath and tried to move past the hurt of him ignoring them all. "You didn't respond, Dex," I whispered.

"I didn't respond because it was you who left," he said. "You chose to have me only like this. You're the heartbreaker here, Kee, not me."

"No. I did what I had to do. You know that nothing between Ethan and me is—" I cried out as he pinched my clit, then I shuddered under him as he moved his fingers faster.

"This pussy is still so tight. It's begging for me and only me to fill it up, fuck you into oblivion, and make this good girl be bad. No one else can do that like me, you know that don't you?"

His words pushed me closer toward the brink even though I hated us talking about it. And then he pulled away from my face so he could sit between my legs, his face not close to mine anymore. He was putting distance between us, yet he kept his hand between my legs and stared down at how he played with me.

"Spread your legs." His tone was much more commanding now, deeper, authoritative.

"Dex, someone could—"

"Want me to stop?" His hand froze, and I bit my lip to keep from screaming out my disapproval. Instead, my body immediately obeyed, legs spreading wide. "That's it. Now, should I call you good or bad for that? You shouldn't be here when you have Ethan Phillipe waiting for you, right?"

I hated that I wanted him to call me both, and when I didn't answer, he smiled like he knew exactly why. "I don't care what you call me, Dex. Just... I need this."

He rolled a thumb over my clit. "Untie your bikini top and touch those tits for me. Let me see how much you want it. Work yourself up."

Maybe this was where I rebelled, where I did what I wanted instead of listening to the record label for once. I'd moved away from Dex. I'd let Trinity control my every step in the limelight. They'd arranged an alliance with Ethan, dictated my fashion style, filled my calendar so fully I'd go for months on end without a single day off—so here at home, with the guy I still loved, I wanted one more moment.

I pulled the string slowly as I held his gaze, and the triangles fell to either side.

"Fuck." He dragged out the word. "You still look divine. Why do you have to be so flawless, huh?"

His words were laced with pain, threaded in regret and turmoil. I knew I'd feel those same emotions later, but I couldn't stop from listening to him. He watched me and I watched him. But my eyes drifted shut as he told me to pinch my nipples. The sensation of the wind over my nearly naked body, the birds chirping in the distance, the smell of those lingering lilacs, and Dex. Dex here with me after I hadn't had a chance to be with him in so long.

"Look at me when you come, Keelani," he commanded, and when my eyes shot open, his were on fire with hunger.

I whimpered for him to go faster. "I need it. I need all this. Just one more time with you, Dex."

He went slower instead. "Just one more time, huh?" He shook his head as his eyes darkened to something sinister in them. "Tell me why you need it, Kee. Ethan not taking care of you the way he should?"

My gut twisted at his words. We were suddenly back to that.

Talking to him wasn't working. We weren't solving anything, yet I'd missed him so much I couldn't stop trying to convince him. I needed him any way I could get him. But I'd lost him.

And I didn't know if I'd ever get him back. Maybe the Dex I knew was gone forever and this man was left in his wake.

CHAPTER 4: DEX

"Fuck you," she ground out.

She had always fought fire with fire. I deserved her swearing at me, but I didn't care, not after what she'd done, not after she'd left me for ruin. And then she asked for a *last time*. Didn't she know we'd never even really gotten started?

"I'm not going to fuck you here, Kee. You only get my hand. Want to know why?" I picked up the pace, and her hips rocked with me. Her body still knew what it needed from me, and I wasn't above giving her that.

We stared into each other's eyes until I saw hers drifting shut. "Just tell me, Dex. Get it over with."

"Because you don't deserve that part of me when you can't give me all of you."

"I want to, Dex. I've always wanted to," she whimpered.

"Look at me when you say that. I want to know you mean it."

Her eyes shot open, and her deep-brown irises were filled with pain. "I've only ever meant it for you, Dex."

"Is that so? Is this all for me too?"

And then I pushed her clit in and rolled it fast as I pumped my fingers into her again and again. It was the perfect rhythm. I saw how her skin started to glisten, how her breath hitched, how her whole body clenched in anticipation. Her pussy tightened on me, too, as she screamed out my name. Over and over.

It wasn't enough to heal the pain she'd inflicted, but the

anger and the turmoil stopped flowing through my veins for a second. She was here with me, and it was all I really wanted. I loved the girl even if she didn't love me enough to stay.

Her gaze turned hazy as she sat up and reached for my belt buckle fast, her movements jerky. "I want all of you here, where we always did everything. I want this memory with you."

Another memory. Not a present or a future, just a past. Did she realize it felt like a dagger every time she talked about us this way?

I stood up and stepped back away from her.

She looked ravished in the sun's setting rays that poured in through the trees. Her long hair had fallen from its bun, and tendrils of it floated in the wind while all the birds chirped around us. The lilacs brought out a hint of violet in her eyes even though they looked devastated as she realized what was happening.

"I don't want to fuck you in the middle of a garden, Kee."

"Dex—"

"I don't really want to fuck with you at all anymore." I said the words aloud so we could both believe them.

"I want to talk. I can explain—"

"There's nothing to explain. Neither of us lives here anymore. You're not a part of my life. And I never want you to be."

"Dex." Her body shuddered at my words, and then she wrapped her arms around her chest.

Fuck, I wanted to hold her. I wanted to tell her we'd be all right. I took a deep breath and grabbed the strings of her bikini instead. I tied them back around her neck as I knelt down to look her in her eyes. "Stop calling me. Go live that glitzy life you always wanted." I needed this closure, and so did she.

"But that's not why I'm doing this—"

"I don't care why you're doing it, pretty girl. I just don't want any part of it. It's why I don't pick up when you call, why I don't text back. I barely even read the texts, Kee. I'm living my life."

Yeah, I'd ignored all sixty-five texts. I hadn't read them each twenty-five times over. I hadn't figured out a way to ping where they were coming from. I certainly wasn't obsessed with her twenty-four-seven. That would have been unhealthy.

"How can you say that?" One tear fell from each eye, but she swiped them both away.

How could I keep the cycle of our hell going? We were broken, and we kept breaking each other. One of us had to stop.

"I'm letting go of a childhood love, heartbreaker."

"Don't call me that." She said it with venom but the nickname fit.

"Whatever, Kee. We went through trauma together, but it doesn't mean we can't move on."

"That's what you think it was? Just some childhood crush?" Her eyes narrowed now as I sat back on my haunches.

"What else would it be?" A love so profound that I'd never get over it, but I couldn't share that. My pride had already been lost to her once. Now, I was graduating college, getting opportunities of a lifetime to work on patented software. And she was soaring in her career.

"And what are we now?"

"Well, you seem to be settled into that pop star status, huh? I'm just working on getting through college."

"I want whatever I can have with you."

"You can't have anything now," I said and stood back up. "You look pretty in a garden, Keelani. You should tell your record label you want a garden on your next album cover."

"Is that all you think I care about?" The question was uttered in pain.

I lifted a brow. "Isn't it?"

The way she looked at me with dejection, I swear it made the air shift around us. That garden would haunt me for years to come. "Do you really think I don't love you?"

What she didn't understand was that this whole town had turned on me. Even my parents questioned how much I'd given her to drink that night. And her parents, well, I couldn't face them after the PR stunt that was pulled. I distanced myself completely, compartmentalizing it all in order to survive. I came home, I engaged with my family, and then I left.

Kyle's death, Gabriella's injury, and Keelani's safety were all on me. My heart was calloused over after years of the town's questioning, after years of interrogating myself also. Never again would I lose control like that and let love steer me into something that wasn't right.

So, I shut her down. "I don't know, Kee. All I know is that you said you didn't love me once."

"I didn't mean it."

I stepped back and away from her. "Yes, well, I mean it when I say I don't love you now."

I didn't mean it either.

PART 2

CHAPTER 5: KEELANI

Twelve Years Later

"Do I have to look at your sad face for the next six months every time I bring up my brother? Because I can't handle it. I hate when women cry." Dimitri sighed and sat down on my hotel room's couch next to where I was getting my makeup done.

"I don't look sad. And I'm not crying." I looked up from the book I was reading to stick my tongue out at him in his stuffy navy blue suit. My best friend had grown into a successful businessman over the years, just like each of his brothers. The Hardy Elite All-Access Team, HEAT for short, had expanded globally as a hospitality and real estate empire. They now even had a technology brand that rivaled the best in the world. Each of them were billionaires and well-loved. Yet, when it came to showing me any manners that people claimed Dimitri had, he failed miserably.

My overly ambitious intern-turned-PR strategist and hairstylist, Olive, pulled my thick dark hair into a bun as she wrinkled her tiny nose and snorted. "You look like a sad little seal who got stranded out of water even while you're trying to disappear into another book."

"Olive, seals don't get stranded out of water." I turned off my phone's reading app so she couldn't glance over my shoulder to see exactly what I was reading. The romance novels were my escape and mine alone. I frowned into the mirror at her but ended up smiling because Olive was too sweet to get mad at. Her bouncy curls and the pink little plumeria flowers she always put behind her ear brightened my day along with her personality. "I think they can wiggle their way back in, maybe?"

"You *think* they wiggle?" Dimitri lifted a brow.

"They probably shimmy or crawl or whatever." Olive tried to help me out but then Dimitri gave her a look. He'd officially labeled us the dummies of our group.

"Why don't you go back to working on whatever you do." I rolled my eyes in the mirror.

"I invest money to make people more of it, Keelani. And your ass needs to let me start investing for you."

I would if I had money to invest but I wasn't going into details about that with him. Ever.

"Maybe one day." I glanced up at Olive who was now brushing my hair. "How's class, by the way?"

"Online classes suck and I hate them. You know I have that one professor. He's great but other than that, I just want to work," she blurted it all out, her dark curls dancing around her face, as her wrist shoved her glasses farther up the bridge of her nose.

"Probably because your online classes aren't teaching you shit," Dimitri grumbled, but the new makeup artist who had been brought in heard him.

Although she'd been working quietly for the past twenty minutes, she scoffed loudly as she pushed her razor-straight pink bob out of her face. "Like you learned so much more from sitting your ass in a college seat?"

Interesting. The woman seemed quiet, but her tone had

bite. Her tan skin seemed to shimmer, and her pixie-like features made me glance more than once at her ears to confirm she wasn't an elf.

"Pink." Dimitri didn't even look up from his phone as he sighed. "I'm not saying we learned anything from college at all. I learned from practice and from getting my feet wet."

"That's what I'm trying to do with Keelani," Olive pointed out as she smoothed my hair bun. "And because of that, I know that unfortunately Dimitri is right, Kee. You're only performing for Dom and Clara's wedding tonight, but they'll have media coverage obviously. You can't start your Vegas residency being mopey. It'll kill your vibe."

"Okay, but I'm contracted for a month of rehearsal starting after tonight and then five months of real performances," I pointed out. I wanted extra time for rehearsals to get everything right before I got on stage. It'd been stipulated in the contract I'd been on site at the Black Diamond or in the city for those next six months.

"Yes, but they'll still write about it on socials. I can already see the comments," she whined, because as the person who was basically handling my PR at this point, she was going to have to put up with it the most. "Maybe if we talk about—"

"There's nothing to talk about," I snipped out. My dress started to constrict over my chest at the thought of what they wanted to discuss.

"So, what you're saying is we'll all be drinking and talking for hours later tonight?" Dimitri muttered.

"You're buying," Olive said, and then they waited silently for me to cave.

I wouldn't. Not even if a whole hour of quiet passed.

After one minute though, I blurted out, "I mean, I'd hoped

to never see him again, but instead, tonight I'm walking into his ridiculous resort."

"That's a very luxurious, state-of-the-art casino and resort that is one of the best in the country, I might add," Dimitri finished for me because he was part owner of the Black Diamond Resort and Casino.

"I know it's the best, Dimitri. You Hardy brothers did it again." I waved my hand around theatrically, and the makeup artist—who I didn't know very well—snickered while Olive laughed outright. The HEAT empire grew every second of every day. I was proud and happy for Dimitri. As for Dex, well, I avoided any news regarding him.

"Stroke my ego some more tonight, and I'll forgive you."

I scoffed at his meaningless flirting. Dimitri and I had never so much as kissed. He was a manwhore, and I was the damn good girl of the century.

"Honestly, I do love this resort and casino." There wasn't a thing not to love. The casino had high ceilings, crown molding, beautiful views, crystal chandeliers with dim lightning, not to mention world-famous celebrities better known than I who didn't give a damn what I did. It felt freeing to disappear in a crowd and only be wanted for what I did best, which was sing.

"I know, Keelani." He grabbed my hand and squeezed it, rubbing a thumb over my knuckles. "You okay?"

"Fine, just trying not to focus on what is bound to be a shitty night." I glanced around the suite that he'd provided for the night. The plush cream fabrics that draped over the furniture along with the abstract artwork adorning the walls in the living area showcased how much Dimitri was spoiling me. I knew the bedroom had an unparalleled level of comfort and the bathroom was a sanctuary with luxury stonework, expensive toiletries, and a rainfall shower full of buttons with nozzles from every side. "Distract me. How much did this ridiculous room cost?"

Dimitri wrinkled his nose. "It cost less than you'll be paid for a night of letting people listen to your voice for an hour, that's for sure."

"In my defense, I don't see all that money."

"I know." Shifting in his seat, he narrowed those green eyes that looked so much like his brother's at me. "That's why I asked to see your contract."

"I have it handled." I didn't need him knowing that I barely saw any of it.

He hummed like he didn't believe me. Rightfully so since it was well-known my record label had me doing dodgy shit all the time. "And I've got you here for the next six months for assurance. Dom and I did good work with that." He smiled big.

Dimitri didn't really push where he didn't need to. He handled things with a soft hand, one where he manipulated things before they were a problem. I'd finally admitted to him that the record label was a stressor for me, and I could still picture the way his face dropped in disappointment that I'd kept my pain to myself. The next thing I knew, I was offered a residency in Vegas, with creative control to sing anything I wanted, at the Black Diamond, which was now partially owned by HEAT. No one had made that happen other than Dimitri.

He knew I only had six months left before my contract with Trinity expired, and he'd built a bridge that I could be protected on with a contract that lasted exactly that long with his resort in Vegas.

"Months at the Black Diamond Resort and Casino under your—and Dex's—watch. What could possibly go wrong?"

"Not much." Dimitri wasn't going to hide his viewpoint though. "Unless you decide to sneak around with him again."

My gaze cut to him. We didn't bring up the past so easily. He knew that. "I would never. I'm with Ethan, and we both know your brother hates me."

"I wouldn't use *hate*. He's just pissed you broke his heart."

"I didn't. That was all a silly mistake." I gave Dimitri a look because I had no idea who the woman doing my makeup was. No one was supposed to know about us. We'd buried that story long, long ago.

Dimitri patted her head and smiled at me. "Don't worry. Pink doesn't talk to anyone outside the casino."

She stopped doing my makeup and squinted her smoky-eyelined blue irises at me before she turned her ice-cold gaze on Dimitri. "Pat me like that again and I'll talk to everyone, including Bane, about how you're petting me like a fucking dog."

Dimitri held up his hands like he was being held at gunpoint. "Duly noted." He started to back away. "You look drop-dead gorgeous, Kee. Come say hi before you go on stage, okay?"

"I don't want to," I whined.

"I know you don't." He smiled big and winked. "That's why I'm telling you to. Call me if you need me."

"Not if, always when," I recited the line, and Olive mouthed it because she knew it was our saying by now.

After Dimitri exited, I let Pink work in silence while Olive tried to pep talk me. "It's going to be fine."

"It's going to be a disaster."

"Well, okay." Olive wiggled the frames of her green glasses and nodded. "Probably, but I can have ice cream and drinks waiting after the show."

"You know it's bad when that doesn't even sound good." I blew out my dark-red painted lips.

Her honey-colored eyes widened. "How dare you? What if it's turtle sundae?"

"Then I amend my answer, damn it. Still, this is going to suck."

"It's only one night. And maybe he won't even be listening. I bet he doesn't even know half the songs are about him." What a pep talk.

"Olive!" I tried to correct her as my gaze flicked to where Pink stood. "They're not about him. They're about—"

"Don't lie on my behalf." Pink straightened. "I don't care about your love life," she deadpanned, brushing powder on my face.

"Sorry," Olive squeaked. "Her love life is very much only about Ethan."

"Ha," Pink barked out. "I mean, you and Ethan are only seen together before an album hits. It's obvious that the on-again, off-again relationship you have is for the media. If I don't believe it, I wonder how much of your fan base does."

I slouched in my chair as I stared at the girl who now held back a smile. She was abrasive but in a sort of loving way, like she might hate the world, but she'd fight the whole world for you too. "If I'm being honest, I bet like thirty percent believe it."

"Probably more like ten," she said back.

Olive's mouth made an O, and there was a whole beat of silence where we tried our best to be professional.

And then we all started laughing. Hard. Tears were in my eyes because my record label had pieced together this sham of a relationship so abysmally over the years that I couldn't even feel bad that it wasn't looking great. I needed that laugh, too, because I was about to endure what would most definitely be months of torture.

"Don't you dare blink and have those tears fall over onto my work of art." Pink pointed at my face, trying to stop her giggling.

I took deep breaths. "Okay. No more jokes about my terrible career and dating life."

"It's not terrible. It's fantastic considering you're performing in a HEAT and Black Diamond resort. Artists kill to get these contracts," Pink told me, showing she knew a bit about who had performed here in the past. "You get rehearsal time correct?"

"Yeah, a month." I shrugged. "And then five months of performing every weekend." It wasn't the norm, but again, Dimitri had pulled the strings to make it happen.

Pink nodded as she moved to finish up a deep-violet eye shadow on me. "Perfect. You can survive that. Especially looking like this. Stand up and let's see if the dress works."

I sighed and got up to straighten my deep-purple dress. Although I had dark-brown eyes, the purple of the dress made them seem violet, and my hair up in the bun accentuated my high cheekbones. My eyes were now as smoky as Pink's. My lips glistened. Everything was in place. I smoothed my hair again.

"You should wear it down." Pink chewed her cheek, and when I glanced at her, she shrugged. "You've got beautiful hair, and you look uptight with that bun."

I turned to the full-length mirror now and frowned. "I always wear it up."

Olive held up her brush. "It's her brand."

Pink pursed her lips and then shrugged. "If your brand is you and you love it so much, then keep it up."

"What's that supposed to mean?" I said softly, trying to hold back my irritation.

"That good-girl act, the all-American sweetheart thing, has got to be a load of shit." She turned to my friend. "Am I right? No one can possibly doll up like a cute Hawaiian Barbie all the time and say *yes, please,* and *no, thank you* twenty-four-seven."

Olive didn't even hesitate. "She's got the sweetheart down pat for about as long as the cameras are rolling and not a second longer."

"Olive, what the hell?"

"What? You already told her you and Ethan are fake. What's the point in lying now?"

"I knew it." Pink clapped her hands together and smiled big. "I was nervous I was going to have to do boring makeup for a half a year."

"Well, that is my brand, and I—"

"You've got the casino backing you now. Do you know what that means?"

"Well, no, because—"

"It means you can do whatever the fuck you want. Bane and Dex aren't going to let anything happen to you."

"You know Bane?" I asked with a bit of hesitation. The man was ominous. He had dark hair, piercing blue eyes, wore black, and seemed to have a dark soul. Even when he talked, it seemed the whole room quivered. Yet, he was equal partner in the casino deal with HEAT. I knew his last name was Black and that he had enough money to stand beside the Hardys.

I wasn't sure how he came about that money, but I was sure I didn't want to find out.

"Yeah, I know him." She rolled her eyes. "Don't worry about

him. Or the Hardys. You know they take care of what's theirs. So, show them what you're made of. We should have some fun."

She said the word with vigor, like it was the only way to live, and I remembered the days I felt the same. The days back before I'd sold my soul to a devil named Trinity Enterprises. "Um..."

Olive was supposed to be my sidekick, but she nodded along with Pink. "She might be right. Maybe it's time to show them what you're made of. You know, for after your contract is up."

"What?" I whipped my head to look at her.

"I'm just thinking"—she wrinkled her nose like she hated what she was about to say—"maybe it's time to start putting a little more of yourself out there, sing some of the songs you *want*, be a little more yourself, and —"

"Definitely screw Dex once or twice. See if the dick still fits," Pink finished for her.

My jaw dropped. "Wow."

"I know." She stared at me with those eyes, no shame in them at all. "I'm a lot. It's fine. Love it or hate it."

I glanced at Olive who whispered, "I kind of love it."

I turned to look back in the mirror and sighed. "I have a good brand."

"That you hate." Olive nudged Pink, like they were a team.

"Right. You need to show him and everyone that you're more than a brand. Plus, sounds like you loved little Dex at one point or—"

"I... Honestly, Ethan is—"

"Oh, for God's sake, I'm not an idiot." Her eyes lit up with fire then. "Don't waste time treating me like one. I get that enough. You're here for a while, so don't lie to the crazy makeup artist who will be doing your face every night."

Silence descended on the room, heavy with questions from me and judgment from her. Yet, I immediately envied how direct she was with nothing to hide, and part of me wanted it.

"Fine," I whispered and glanced at Olive. "Redo my hair. Add more eyeshadow too."

Pink laughed almost maniacally, and Olive whooped.

"Please make me look amazing. I want him to salivate even if he hates me." I admitted it quietly, worrying my hands over the fact that I had to sing the love songs I'd written about him in front of him tonight. Some songs were ones I'd literally sung to him years ago in the lilacs, where I'd begged him to do more with me when we were just kids. And he'd always said then, "You want to keep me a secret, you can wait to do more with me until I'm not one, Kee."

The problem was that I never wanted him to be a secret. I just needed him to be. My songs were apologies to him, love notes to him, heartbreak about him. He'd hear the words and know. He'd *have* to know, and all I would have tonight would be my looks for armor.

CHAPTER 6: KEELANI

I stood behind the curtain not much later, waiting for the moment that it lifted. We let the violins build before it happened. I took deep breaths, closed my eyes, and reminded myself what this was all for.

Then, as the curtain rose, I stepped onto the stage, letting the spotlight find its mark. The light blinded me and was weighted with expectation as the crowd seemed to quiet. Was he watching me? Did he care that I was there? I worried about him out there only for that second.

But the violin's notes moved me, the music guided me to what I loved most, and I turned my focus to the bride and groom as I let out my first note. This was their night, their love, and their happily ever after.

Tonight wasn't a concert of my own but my entrance into the Black Diamond Resort and Casino as a private show for a Hardy. Dom Hardy and Clara had married Clara Milton. I sang and felt the words for them. The love song I launched into was one of my biggest hits, routinely played around the world at weddings.

The cameras that were on me would capture a childhood neighbor supporting her lifelong friends. It was well-known that the Hardy brothers lived next door to my family, that Dex had saved me in that car wreck, and that he'd been painted as the bad boy in my hometown.

Everywhere else, though, that narrative had no legs.

He'd buried that story over the years with how he'd become a ruthless arm of the HEAT empire. He controlled the security and technology, bought up real estate, and now owned this resort. When he'd implemented security software with Cade Armanelli, a genius hacker who'd worked closely with the US government, he'd catapulted his career to new heights. Since partnering with the Black Diamond Resort and Casino, their systems would now protect billions of dollars.

Social media and news outlets were about to have a field day with me being a part of it all. So, I gave them what they wanted. I sang about forever. I sang about a love that would never be lost. I sang about him.

About forever with Dex, even if I couldn't have it.

I'd been a songwriter first, and I'd written it for him before we broke up. He knew this song as well as I did. Music moved the soul in a way that sometimes a mind couldn't. The mind was too practical, too logical for the gravity of our emotions. And I knew in my head I should be singing for the bride and groom, but somehow the music and my emotions moved my gaze right to the man I was supposed to be avoiding.

Dex stood there in a three-piece suit, taller than most and more in control than anyone. He'd aged well too, so well my knees practically went weak as I got to the chorus.

His gaze was cold, though. His green eyes sliced through me like I was a weed in his path. And maybe I was. I was an obstacle, a disturbance for him, one he definitely didn't want.

In that moment, the only anchor I had was the mic in front of me. I gripped it like a lifeline and let the words flow out of me. I bled my emotions out onto that stage because my music did that for me every time.

I hoped the newlyweds felt as much a part of it as I did.

Dom and Clara deserved it after agreeing to let me sing on the night of their wedding, knowing it would make the news. My record label had been ecstatic. So, in turn, I made sure I delivered on each note with a soulful and emotional message, trying to invoke love into every word.

The next song, I sang swaying with my eyes closed so I didn't have to look at his. I wanted to get lost in it, not him again.

Yet, as I held the last note, I knew I'd have to meet his gaze again. One last song before the band would take over was what I'd promised. When I opened my eyes, he glared at me with his arms crossed, and I hated how I wasn't immune to those deep-green irises, his dark wavy hair, and how his strong jaw seemed just a bit sharper than his brothers'.

People had lost interest now, were mingling with other wedding guests, and I took a breath, stepped back from the mic, and let my fingers move over it for a second, letting the familiarity of it comfort me.

The event coordinator had made sure the mic was the exact right height on the stand for me. The chandelier lights overhead had been dimmed, as had the spotlight. I was certain Dimitri had made sure all my requests were taken care of.

And Dex would make sure to unnerve me all the same. He'd probably find a way to get me out of here by the end of the night. I could see his mind working on it already.

But then Pink's words came back to me. *Do whatever the fuck you want. Bane and Dex aren't going to let anything happen to you. They take care of what's theirs. So, show them what you're made of.*

This small, intimate audience size was the kind I'd always dreamed about, the kind I wanted to sing my own personal songs for. Fear and adrenaline coursed through me. This was either going to be the place I healed or the place I was completely destroyed. Suddenly, I *wanted* to be healed or destroyed. I wanted the closure.

For the first time in years, I looked out at him and felt peace.

I silenced the violins so I could sing the next song a cappella. It was fresh, it was new, and it was real.

I wanted to finally show them who I was. And it wasn't the sweetheart I'd been pretending to be.

HEAT

CHAPTER 7: DEX

Keelani Hale shouldn't have been on that stage. She shouldn't have been in my resort, on my property, or even in this city. She wasn't fucking welcome. I'd left behind our hometown, my life, and my damn heart to move on and away from her. Hadn't I made that clear?

Yet, my brothers were meddlers. "We needed a band." My new sister-in-law, Clara, smiled at me, her face bright with joy and love. They were trying to cajole me after they'd dropped the bomb she'd be here. "Dominic said she's close to the family and he loves her voice."

"You love her voice, asshole?" My blood was already boiling, red-hot with jealousy and rage and probably a little fear. I was in tune with what I felt when it came to Keelani, and I knew it wasn't good. They wanted to play matchmakers, but they were playing with matches and dynamite instead.

"I'm fucking married, Dex. Get a grip." My oldest brother's jaw ticked. "She's singing our first dance song. Then, she's singing at this casino. Then"—he glanced at all of us and smiled like they'd come up with the best plan ever—"I put her in the same apartment building as you for the next six months. You know how Keelani is. She gets a bit crazy when she's somewhere new. So, keep an eye on her. Mom and Dad love her, and you don't want her parents thinking we didn't take care of her while she was working in our—"

"I don't need anyone to take care of me," I heard from

behind me. Her voice had changed over the years. It had more rasp, was distinctive and low in a sultry way that traveled straight to my dick.

She was stunning with dark-brown hair, tan skin, and eyes that were so dark you couldn't tell the color.

"You don't need to be in Vegas trying to take care of yourself," I said to her through clenched teeth.

"Dex, honey, what could you possibly be worried about?" She smirked at me, but I saw the wobble in it before she turned to Dom and hugged him. She made the rounds hugging most of my family and then beelined away from me to Dimitri.

My fucking little brother was her safe haven. He had that spot in her heart, and I hated that I was jealous of him for that.

My date, Seanna, arrived back at my side with a flute of champagne. "She's very pretty."

She'd wanted to accompany me here tonight probably more for appearances than anything. We had a great relationship in that it was convenient. She climbed the social ladder by being on my arm, and we'd both relieved each other's sexual frustration. It'd been a nice arrangement over the years.

But it wasn't exclusive or emotional. I'd been clear about that.

I shook my head. "I don't want to talk about her. You know this."

She smiled. "That's fine. You intend to talk with her tonight then?"

I growled and left my date in the dust to go confront Dimitri and Kee. These two weren't going to do this. I couldn't be around it for months, couldn't stomach seeing her for that long. Yet, when I made my way around the corner, I just saw Dimitri at the bar. So, I confronted him right then. "D, I don't want her here. Not at all. I'm not doing it after tonight."

He turned to me as he scratched the back of his neck, which he only did when he was uncomfortable. "You are doing it, because we signed a contract with Trinity Records to have Kee singing here, bro."

"So, dissolve the contract. Pay them off. Take a hit on the investment then," I ground out.

"You're forgetting that we've grown this empire because Carl Milton gave it to us with stipulations, right?" Carl Milton had given us all a shot years ago by letting us invest in his hotel chain.

"Stipulations for..." My words drifted off. Both my older brothers knew Carl better than I had. When he passed away, Carl hadn't burdened Dimitri and me with much, but he had required in his will that we not go back on any contracts we signed in the next ten years. "You motherfuck—"

"I did it for you and her. So get your head out of your ass and get on board with six months. You haven't seen her in years, and you're both still not over the relationship you had. Either end it here or start it over." He walked off; left me at the bar, alone in my thoughts.

A week after Keelani and I had our last rendezvous in her family's lilac garden, my phone pinged me her location. She was with Ethan Phillipe at a fucking event. She'd gone back to singing and hanging on Ethan's arm with my little brother as her best friend.

I'd deleted her contact out of my phone, stopped practically stalking her whereabouts then and there. Before that, I'd basically built software to track her every move. So, I cut it all off. I left behind my heart, closed the door on my life with her, and focused on work. I excelled at that.

My closure consisted of avoiding everything about her—news articles, my brother seeing her, my family discussing any of the Hales. Nobody brought them up for good reason. I'd been fine until now, until my brothers bombarded me with my past.

CHAPTER 8: KEELANI

"Being engaged to Ethan for six months won't be that hard, Keelani," Mitchell's irritated voice ground out over the phone.

I'd planned to disappear into my hotel room and curl up with a good book, but my manager called to lecture me. So I sat at the penny slot machine, instead, as I listened to him.

"So, you need to do it."

He hadn't called to ask how the performance went. He hadn't congratulated me on getting through it either. He'd started the conversation with business, as always, and his business was mostly telling me what to do.

"I think me getting this deal with the casino is good enough for PR. Ethan and I don't need any more publicity."

"Yes, you do. And the label needs it too. We'll get sponsorships and news articles. It will boost both of your sales. And I'll remind you that you need to look your best right now. Your friend is helping you out by letting you sing in his resort."

I closed my eyes tight for a second, trying my best to listen to his reasoning after how much that performance emotionally drained me. He was right. Dimitri had gotten me this deal, and even if I didn't want it, it was the thing that would get me out from under the record label's thumb once and for all. My manager didn't know that, but he knew Dimitri was a friend— my best friend—and I didn't want to let him down.

Only six months.

Still, bile rose in my throat. Neither Ethan nor I wanted

this. It was the last thing we wanted. "He'll say no. He's got other plans."

"He's already said yes."

Motherfucker. "What? Why?" I whispered out, thinking of the late nights I'd had with my friend over the past few months. We purposely hadn't been seen together. People speculated we'd already broken up. We were going to let the relationship fade to black.

"Because no one says no to opportunities of a lifetime, Kee."

I rolled my eyes and stared at the machine. No matches across any lines. Typical. I hit the button again. "I'm saying no."

"Record label says yes, and you've got six months. Plus, your dad already agreed. I just sent you the screenshot of how happy he is about this. I included extra care for your family while you're at the casino and then making appearances with Ethan."

My phone pinged, and I saw my dad's texts to Mitchell. I hated that he hadn't asked me, hated even more that his paragraphs to Mitchell were so genuine and heartfelt that I felt slighted.

Still, it was my family.

My mother.

I sighed. "Send me the addendum then. We'll need to get Black Diamond to sign off on this too."

"Yes, yes. Do that for me tonight. Tell Dimitri this is needed and you want it. Ethan will be there within an hour." He hung up.

Then my phone pinged with a contract listing out all the public events I would now have to make with a new fiancé.

I couldn't bring myself to go back to the Hardy wedding,

even if Dimitri said he'd stand near me the whole time. I sat at the penny machine for nearly an hour instead trying to win money. If I did, I'd at least think my luck was changing. And I needed a change.

But I didn't win one single time.

***

Ethan showed up with his wavy blond hair and lanky frame and stupid perfect smile on his face. I'd hoped no one would pay attention, but he'd brought a literal cameraman with him. He pulled me in for a hug and said, "Mitchell called him. It's go time, babe." Then, he kissed me so theatrically, I was surprised the paps even took a photo.

All for show. All a facade. Still, I smiled and said quietly through clenched teeth, "I'll cut your balls off if you do that again. I'm saying yes, but I'm freaking mad at you, Ethan."

His eyes widened, and he chuckled before he got down on one knee.

Was this how women felt during a proposal? Like their life flashed before their eyes? Like, how had I gotten here, and how the hell could I get out? It's how I knew I wasn't meant for love, for forevers, and for marriage. I was abnormally sickened by this charade.

"My love for you has been the biggest secret to have to keep from the world, Keelani."

What a lie. We hadn't been seen together these past few months because we'd planned to let the relationship fizzle into the wind. Now, he was claiming we were in love in secret.

"Marry me and make me the happiest man alive? I want to share with the world how well we harmonize together."

Was he for real? That was so cheesy, especially when I knew his biggest secret wasn't that. Yet I worked up tears, and my chin wobbled before I whispered, "Yes." Honestly, the tears might have been a bit real since I'd agreed to marry a man I didn't love.

There was no kiss after the proposal, and the cameraman thanked us before he left like he was on a deadline. Most likely, he wanted to get that picture everywhere quick.

Ethan murmured apologies in my ear while a few people came up to congratulate us, but none of them were people I knew. The people I knew stood back watching. Dimitri had that look in his eye, and Olive shoved at his shoulder. They were disappointed. I knew they were going to give me hell. And the cherry on top was seeing Dex across the casino floor, standing there with a beautiful woman on his arm. His date was tall, stoic, and fit next to him perfectly as she turned to him to whisper something in his ear.

My gut shouldn't have twisted in pain, but it did. I took a deep breath and closed my eyes before I whispered to Ethan, "You can go home now. Show's over, right? I'm going back to my room."

"You okay?" He frowned at me, but what could I say?

I combed a hand through my hair, and he touched one strand of it. "I like your hair by the way. New look?"

"It doesn't matter," I sighed, looking back to where Dex had been standing and not seeing him there anymore. "I guess our teams will be in touch about the news, right?"

He nodded and straightened his black tie. He looked the part tonight with his hair slicked back, and I could tell he'd even had his eyebrows plucked like he knew the cameras would be capturing the moment. "Yeah. Maybe I should come up there and—"

"Not happening." It wasn't my voice but Dex's, from behind me, that cut through Ethan's proposition.

I whipped around, surprised to see him standing before us with a scowl on his face.

"Keelani, we have business to discuss."

His date was gone, but mine didn't get lost so easily.

"It's almost midnight," Ethan retorted.

"And she's still working. She's contracted for this wedding."

At that point, Dimitri made his way over. "I'll take Keelani back to her room."

"Nope." Dex shook his head. "Kee's coming with me."

"Dex—"

"Dimitri, I'm *this* close." His voice shook, full of emotion. I didn't know if it was anger or disgust.

How could I when I didn't know anything about him anymore? Yet, Dimitri glanced at me like he was asking my permission, like he knew his brother well enough to give him this. When he searched my face to see if I could handle it, I nodded. This wasn't my place to make a scene. I had too much respect for the Hardys.

"Tonight is about Dom and Clara. Your older brother just got married. So, let's not have a therapy session during his reception, guys. Ethan, go home. I'll call you tomorrow. Dimitri, I'll call you later. Dex, is business necessary at eleven o'clock at night?"

He crossed his arms. "I don't wait to talk business with anyone, Kee. Especially not you."

I scoffed but wasn't surprised. A lifetime ago, this man may have appeased me, but that had changed. Now, I was sure he wanted to make my life hell.

"I need to change, then. This dress is a lot."

He eyed it once, then twice for good measure. My stupid body tensed the whole time. "I expect you down here in twenty minutes."

"I'll meet you by the penny slots. You should play a few. They're fun and you look like you need a bit of that in your life," I said as I pushed past him.

I left them all there. Those men wanted to control the narrative, and tonight, I couldn't be bothered with much more of it. I was getting engaged to a man I didn't want after years of acting like I did just because a record label told me to. I felt stuck, caged, bound up. Most of all, I felt like a fraud. How had I let things go for so long?

I called home, and the phone rang twice before my father answered. "What's wrong, Keelani?" He didn't sound sleepy at all.

"I'm sorry to be calling so late."

"Ah, you know how it is. I'm up anyway." He sighed into the phone. "What's going on? You at the casino tonight?"

My father knew about the casino deal. Well, he knew what the money meant for our family, and he'd agreed to this phony engagement now too. I wanted to scream at him for it, accuse him of pushing me into something I didn't want, but then I thought of him with my mother.

He cared for her, loved her, would do anything in his power for her.

"I just needed to check in. How's Mom?"

He sighed. "Oh, she's good, honey. She got on the new medication last week, you know? And having a nurse around is helping. The addendum to your contract will help too."

I sighed. It was his way of smoothing the waters. "I didn't

want to agree to that. You're supposed to call me and discuss these things with me."

"Ach. You know I'm not good at that. But it'll be fine, honey. You don't have to marry him. Just be seen a few more places with him."

I nodded. He was right. I didn't say that, though. He wouldn't get an affirmation from me tonight. The wound was too fresh. So, I changed the subject. "Mom awake with you?"

"Yeah...she's here with me. We're watching television."

I had to hold back from asking to talk to her. "Did she have a good day?"

"Yeah, the new nurse is great. Her name's Maggie. She understands your mom probably better than I can."

Tears sprang to my eyes. "That's good to hear."

"It is. You did that with this Vegas thing, honey. You did great work." He cleared his throat. "Maybe I can come visit you there for a day or two, and—"

"That's not a good idea."

"I've been good with the money, Keelani. A few slots here and there aren't going to—"

"Mom needs you," I reminded him.

"Right." He sighed like he knew it was best. "She's doing well. I want you to know that."

I needed those words at that moment, and I blinked once as a tear ran down my face. "Can you tell her something for me so I can hear her voice, Dad?"

He cleared his throat and then I heard, "Keelani's sleeping at her friend's tonight, love."

"Hm. She staying at Gabriella's or she sneaking off to hang out with those Hardy boys?"

"Well, there's no telling." My father chuckled. "Want her

to come home?"

"They're all good boys. Let her live." Her words were like a knife to my heart because she didn't remember much further, didn't remember the turmoil we all endured, didn't remember me past that point. There was silence for a minute and then, "Who are you on the phone with? It's too late."

"Just Keelani. She's sleeping at a friend's." My mother just hummed that time. "She's back to watching the television, Keelani."

"Good," I whispered out. "Good. I might not be able to call for a few days, but hug her for me, okay?"

"Of course I will. Get some rest, sweetie."

I sat on that bed for way too long, staring at the wall. Missing her. Longing for a mom who hadn't been lost in the same memories for ages now.

I took my time peeling off my dress, getting rid of my makeup, and throwing my hair up. I contemplated standing him up and staying in to read. I'd found my safe escape for years with the books I could download and get lost in. Yet tonight, I knew even they couldn't save me. I'd have to face Dex sooner or later. So, I slipped on a maxi dress and a baseball cap before going to meet him.

I was armed now. Ready to endure whatever I needed to for the sake of my family.

CHAPTER 9: KEELANI

I told him I'd meet him at the slots, and now I regretted that because of course he wasn't there. Granted, I'd made him wait an hour instead of twenty minutes, but I'd obviously needed to decompress or maybe build up the courage to face him again.

I sat down at the machine. Betting a penny and pulling the lever was supposed to add a bit of a thrill and a little hope. But I didn't hope at all now. I'd lost more than once tonight and knew I'd lose again and again.

Going up against Dex Hardy would be a colossal mistake too—whatever he wanted to discuss, our conversation was long overdue.

Rightfully so. Our past had ruined us. Ripped our hearts apart and left the destruction for us to clean up. We'd mended ourselves in the only way we knew how. I didn't text or call him after that last day together in the woods. I tried my best to move on. But when someone breaks a person's heart, their words echo around them forever.

I don't love you. He'd said it so easily as I sat in the grass at his feet years ago. And then he'd walked away. I hadn't moved that night. I'd slept there with the lilacs around me, crying for hours.

Luck hadn't been on my side then. And it wasn't now either. I pulled the lever again.

A penny lost.

I pulled it again.

Another penny lost.

I sighed and kept on. I still had twenty bucks to lose before I left for the night.

I'd wait as long as I'd made him wait. But he showed up sooner than I had.

"So, what exactly is this?" I heard from above me, and the rumble in that whisper of his had my heart lurching. Not away from him but toward him, like it was waking up from hibernating away until its long-lost love came back.

"What exactly is what?" I asked without looking up at him. I kept my eyes on the slot machine screen, hoping he would elaborate without my eye contact.

Dex waited in silence, practically forcing my gaze his way. When I scanned his face, I saw he wasn't looking at me but the ring still on my left finger.

That stupid heart of mine picked up speed and raced much too quickly for what I was used to. It'd been in hibernation for a freaking long time. I was trying to get accustomed to its erratic behavior around the man I was supposed to not care for anymore.

"You think I'm going soft, Kee?" I frowned in confusion. I never said any such thing. "I know I agreed to your presence at the casino for six months." He'd argued with Dimitri, I knew that. "Yet, you can't possibly believe I'm going to allow you to accept a proposal here, under my roof, the first night of this fucked-up contract."

I shook my head and focused on the slot machine in front of me. Another penny lost, another pull on the stupid lever. This time, my eyes filled with real tears and not because I'd lost another damn cent. Dex Hardy's voice somehow still had a hold on me. He wanted a truth I couldn't give him right then. He'd wanted the truth for years.

He'd never get it, though, and he'd never forgive me. I'd left him behind even though I'd always looked back, and he'd never known it.

Dex set his drink down slowly on my slot machine and walked up behind me before he bent down so his mouth was close to my ear. Then, he whispered, "You come to my casino, my resort, have your fuckboy of a boyfriend propose on my property. And you're wearing his ring like it belongs on your finger. Tell me it's a joke. Say. It."

Dex had aged beautifully, and his mouth had become much more lethal too. Each word sliced through my flesh and cut me straight to the bone. Still, I chewed my cheek rather than start the war I knew was brewing between us and pulled the lever again.

Another freaking loss.

He grunted out a sound of disgust near my face and said, "You're doing it wrong."

I turned to see his forest-green eyes assessing the machine before he pressed a few buttons. He maxed out my bid and pulled the lever as I immediately glared. "That's too much money!"

As I finished saying it, though, the machine slowed and lit up like a Christmas tree. The earnings flashed on the screen with sirens going off, doubling, tripling, quadrupling the twenty he'd just gambled.

"You know, Kee, without a risk, you don't get a reward."

I scoffed and jackhammered my finger into the button that brought my bid back to a penny. "It's no risk at all when it's not your money."

He hummed. "Technically, since I own most of this place,

I'm paying you, heartbreaker."

I hated that he still remembered the nickname he gave me. Screw him. "Great." I yanked the card out of the machine and stood abruptly. "I should go cash out then."

He stepped in front of me, and I bumped into his chest. "You didn't do as I said, Kee."

"What did you say to do again?"

"Tell me that all this is a joke," he reiterated.

"Dex, let's not do this." I shook my head at him. It was one in the morning. I was tired, emotionally drained, and ready to tap out. I needed to, because it was that or I was going to unleash every emotion I had on him.

"Do what?" He tilted his head, and I couldn't stop myself from taking in how good he looked. He'd always cleaned up nice, but he filled out the suit he wore perfectly, his broad shoulders and large chest showcasing that he'd stayed in shape over the years. His hair probably had been combed nicely to start the night, too, but I could tell he'd put his fingers through it more than once now.

"There's no reason to act like there's something between us when there isn't."

"We've got more than what you have between you and Ethan Phillipe." He rubbed his jaw. "The chin wobble was top notch though. You lie to every guy you're with, or just him and me?"

"You know what? Fuck you, Dex," I grumbled and tried to walk past, but he caught my elbow.

"We've been damn close to you fucking me, Kee, and I'd bet if I allowed it, you'd take me up on the offer to get close again. Maybe even go all the way."

I spun on him, pissed that he had the audacity to goad me

when I'd tried to be the bigger person tonight. "If you allowed it? If I gave you the chance, you mean."

He stepped close then. Too close. My breath hitched, and I licked my lips instinctively. My body knew this stance, knew how it would feel to have him, and immediately I wanted to give in, wanted to rake my nails over his skin and claw at every part of him the way the memory of him tore at me.

"And look at you. Those pretty eyes are full of hunger, heartbreaker. Want to give me the chance tonight?"

I jerked back at his words and stepped out of his orbit. Long ago, my body had gravitated toward Dex Hardy but I couldn't get caught in revolving around him now. "I'm engaged."

"Not for long."

"Excuse me?" I glanced around, but it was late. The people in the casino didn't care about us. Our friends and family were all off celebrating a real marriage.

"You think I'm letting the headliner at the Black Diamond Resort and Casino marry a man I hate?"

"You don't hate him. You don't even know him," I sputtered out as he slid his phone from his pocket. Was he for real? "Don't you dare call my record label, Dex, or I'll—"

"Or you'll what?" Each word came out pointed.

What was there to even threaten? Dex had it all. He had the money, the casino, my stupid contract, and now even my record label in my pocket. "What do you even want from me? I'm not harming you. Just stay out of my way, and I'll stay out of yours."

"Stay out of your way? This is my place. I don't go home— back to my hometown—just to ensure I don't see your venomous ass."

"*Venomous?* Are you kidding me right now?"

"No. You poisoned that whole town against me. And then you came home acting like you loved me when really you were going back to hang on Ethan's arm a week later. Now you're here doing the same."

"I did no such thing." He made what I'd done sound so evil, so calculated. He didn't know how I'd cried, how I'd suffered, how I'd barely been able to get out of bed.

He barked out a laugh and then bent over and laughed his ass off. "Did you read the news when you left? They practically labeled me a murderer, and I didn't even want you in the car that night."

"I..." I shook my head and stepped back. I hated talking about that night. It haunted my dreams and then the news after tortured me. "I didn't control the news, Dex."

"No. But you damn sure didn't rebuke it, which was tantamount to an affirmation coming from the shining star of the town, Ms. Keelani Hale, who could do no wrong."

"Oh, don't act like they all hate you. You've done just fine since then." He and his brothers owned a whole freaking empire.

He narrowed his eyes. "Have I?"

"You know you have. So, just let things between us lie. Ethan and I will—"

"You won't be engaged to him here in this resort. I won't allow it."

"You're kidding." I stared at him. This was ludicrous. I mean, no one could demand something like that. The way he thought he ruled the world bubbled up inside me, and I now burst out laughing. He didn't control what I did. I laughed and laughed, probably because I was too tired to do any different. Then, I looked up and saw he wasn't laughing with me. I waved my hands at him. "You're funnier than I remember."

"I'm not joking." He crossed his arms, and the expensive smart HEAT watch on his wrist flashed in front of me as if to mock my position in this situation. "Call your record label and let them know."

He searched my eyes for far too long. I squirmed under his gaze, straightened the baseball cap on my head, and tried to back away. "Look, I appreciate the residency here, and I know I'm of benefit to the casino in turn, just as you all are a benefit to my bank account. Ethan and I are truly—"

"There's no Ethan and you."

"Of course there is." I rolled my eyes.

"Bullshit. You didn't even kiss him after he proposed."

"Well, I did before, and we were in public and—"

"Public? You scared of PDA?" He smirked now. "Your good-girl image too pristine you can't dirty it up when you feel like kissing your fiancé?"

"That's not it." Honestly, that was always part of the reason I never indulged in PDA, but he didn't have to know that.

"Right." He rubbed his chin and said without much emotion at all, "Call your manager and let him know."

"They own me, Dex; I'm not going to tell them no. It doesn't work like that. They want me engaged for publicity and to push sales here at the resort. It's a win-win."

"So you *want* to marry him?" He said it louder now, with emphasis.

"Dex, I'm not... I don't want to marry anyone, and—"

He leaned against a slot machine and crossed one ankle over the other as if he had all the time in the world. "So you *don't* want to marry him? Which is it?"

I sighed, so done with the back-and-forth as I rubbed at

one temple, willing away the stress headache that was coming on. Then I asked softly, "Does it really even matter?"

His eyes widened and he combed a hand through his hair as I saw his jaw dance up and down. "Yes, it fucking matters, Kee. What type of question is that? Do you seriously have that little of a backbone after all these years?"

"What?" I straightened at that. He had no idea why I did what I did. "You don't know me. Don't you dare toss insults my way like that." I stepped close to him and poked his shoulder.

"If you don't want to marry someone—"

"It doesn't matter what I want. That's not the point," I almost screeched. "And my marital status shouldn't matter to you." I glanced around now, irritated that he wanted to talk about who I was with when I knew he'd been with a woman earlier that night. "Shouldn't you be worrying about the woman you were here with tonight?"

He rubbed at the stubble on his chin before he admitted, "I sent her home."

"Why?" I asked, but his eyes burned into mine, communicating all I needed to know.

"Because I could only look at you all night." He combed a hand through his thick hair. "I've been with her for two years, and it's been damn near fifteen years without you," he said, and his voice suddenly held all the pain I felt. "And yet I hear your voice on that stage, look at you singing, and I still only want you."

"Dex—"

"It's downright shameful at this point that I even consider it. And you can bet I don't enjoy feeling like I can't think of anyone else."

Don't say it, Keelani. Don't you dare. But the words squeaked out anyway. "Two years?"

He put his hands in his pockets. "Yep. Coming up on two and a half."

Jesus, why did that hurt so much? "Is she your girlfriend?"

"Does it matter?" He lifted a brow.

"No." *Yes.*

"Then why ask the question?"

"I don't know. You brought it up."

"Bullshit." He rolled his eyes like he still knew me. "You're as jealous as I am."

"You can have whoever you want," I whispered.

"Can I really? Do you have whoever you want?" He narrowed his eyes at me in challenge.

I met him head-on. "Not that it matters to you, but yes, I do." I was standing up to him, and we both knew it. One of us needed to draw the line in the sand after all these years.

"I'm sure you do." He clenched his jaw. "But when I'm with someone else, I still picture you...and I'm sick of it."

My heart pounded. I wanted to tell him he didn't get to be sick of it when I had to endure it too. Yet, I couldn't. This conversation needed to be over. So I moved to brush past him, but he caught me at his side and pulled us over to a corner where he could lean in and whisper, "You picture me every time you fuck your fiancé, too, Kee?"

The anger that bubbled up inside me was overwhelming when normally I just tried to ignore my emotions, tried to suppress the irritation I had throughout the day. With Dex, he always had a knack for pushing me too far. "You don't get to ask me that after you left me in the lilacs, Dex. You left me to become who I am today, and you don't know a thing about that person."

"That's probably true. But I remember who you were, and I want to stop remembering, Kee." His voice cracked, and I hated that I still wanted to soothe it, that I felt myself breaking too. "So, you're going to get rid of that fiancé of yours. I'm too jealous to see him here with you."

I glared at him. "I'm sorry. You're jealous of what exactly? I didn't have a date hanging on me all night, whispering in my ear—"

"You accepted a proposal from the guy you've been dating for fifteen fucking years."

"You've known from the very beginning it's fake for the media! I don't even want to marry him," I blurted out before slapping my hand over my mouth.

He smirked like he'd goaded me there, like we were in a chess match and he'd won. I even caught a hint of the dimples I used to love flash across his face. I had to admit he still knew me enough to piss me off. He continued on in his stupid chess game, moving me around like I was a game piece he could control. "Then don't. Don't get engaged to him. Call your record label right now and tell them no. Kill the story." He sighed. "I don't want that shit in the papers tomorrow, Kee."

The way he used my nickname pulled at every fiber of my being. I was Keelani the Singer, Keelani the Sweetheart. Keelani Hale was a brand.

But here, in front of him, I was just a human, and a vulnerable one at that. "I can't do that," I told him quietly as I shook my head.

His stare hardened. "Still chasing that fame then?"

"That's not—" I took a breath so I didn't fall down the hole of pain and fury with him. "I have contingencies in my contract. I don't care about the fame, but the time and money are valuable."

He chuckled and rubbed his five o'clock shadow. "Money and time? You're here for six months, and we're paying you plenty."

I hated that he acted like he knew everything. "You're paying my record label plenty, sure."

"So, what? You want a few more shoes in your closet?" He looked me up and down. "Fine. I'll double it."

"Double it?" I squeaked.

"Not good enough? Triple it. What do I care? And it can be outside the label's contract so you can keep it all to yourself."

That money would let me pay for my mother's care for years and give me an opportunity to do what I wanted for once. I'd be free finally.

Still, the deal was too good to be true. I, more than anyone, knew what that looked like now. I stepped back and shook my head. "They won't agree. They need me to look like I'm going to marry someone. They want the publicity. Without the engagement, there's no story and—"

"Then you get engaged to me."

"What?" I hadn't heard him right, surely.

"Get engaged to me. Give them the story of a lifetime."

My heart galloped in the way it should have when Ethan got down on one knee. My heart wanted this to be a real proposal when it absolutely wasn't. "I'm not getting engaged to you! Are you— You have a girlfriend, Dex. How much have you had to drink?"

He rubbed his jaw again, looking me up and down, somehow studying every layer of me even though I wasn't giving him a single part willingly. "Yeah. It's time."

"Time for what?"

He frowned at me and then pulled his phone from his pants. "Time for me to stop trying to get you out of my system without having you here to actually do it."

I scoffed. "It's not happening, Dex. I'm not marrying you."

"You either marry me, heartbreaker, or you don't get married at all." Without another word, he spun around and put his phone to his ear. "Yeah, hi, Seanna. You make it home?"

I narrowed my eyes on him. He was calling his girlfriend after just proposing that sort of deal to me?

"Yes, I'm still here with her." He nodded and then looked directly in my eyes. "I wanted to let you know, I intend to marry her...if she'll have me."

The galloping of my heart stopped. Everything did. Dex was here in front of me, promising himself for six months, and suddenly all my anxieties and worries ceased. This was a disaster waiting to happen, but it was also the place I knew I wanted to break apart. Beside him. For him. Because of him.

If I couldn't find myself with the one man I'd always loved, I could destroy myself at the very least. And I'd still be me.

He paused again. "Seanna, I don't know, and it won't matter. I don't expect or want you to wait." He sighed. "Sure. Friends." Then he clicked off his phone and slid it back into his pocket before his gaze caught mine, determined now. "Your turn." His tone was commanding and authoritative. "Call your fiancé." He sneered the word, grating on my every nerve.

"Just..." I took a deep breath. "Stop calling him that."

"Why? That's what he is." Now he was goading me. "You gonna marry another man when you belong to me?"

"I don't belong to you. I never did!" I scoffed. "Even when I wanted to, the label owned me. I... My life is more complicated than you think."

"Try me."

"Have you been home lately, Dex?" I whispered.

"My home is here." His jaw flexed, and I saw the haunted look in his eyes. "I don't go back there unless it's for family."

I wanted to ask him to elaborate and share everything he'd been through. But it wasn't my place. "Right. Well, things are different for me now. I have responsibilities there."

"We all have responsibilities," he corrected, and he was right, so I just shrugged.

"Well, I'm sorry for how things—"

"It doesn't matter," he cut me off. "Especially when we can make all that go away with you following through with my plan."

"Does everyone do what you want around here, Dex?"

"It's my resort. Of course they do."

"You think me being with you is going to fix everything?"

"It'll be a start." He crossed his arms and stared down at me with disgust.

"If you think that, you're living in a fantasy land."

"A fantasy?" He lifted a brow and then leaned in close. "You're real, Kee. Maybe the all-American *Keelani Hale* isn't real, but you here in front of me is. I still feel you next me. I still hear your laugh. I still smell how sweet you taste—"

"Stop." Too late. He already saw the goose bumps rise on my skin.

He slid his finger across them on my arm, and we both watched how my body immediately reacted to him. I licked my lips and met his eyes right as he looked at me. "I won't stop until I have you. You know that, Kee. I won't stop till I get you out of my fucking system."

"Out of your system while you infect mine?" I shook my

head at him. To anyone else, this conversation may have been dramatic, but I knew how Dex could ruin me. I'd never love another man like I loved him. Leaving him had broken not only my heart, but my soul and my spirit.

"Tit for tat, heartbreaker. You ruined my whole life when you left."

"And if I don't?"

"You want to risk what I'll do if you remain engaged to someone I hate while under contract with me?"

"So...what? You're going to make my life hell if I'm engaged to another man?"

He stood there staring at me as I glared at him. Somehow the background noise around us fell away, the lights seemed to spotlight on him, all my thoughts quieted. "Absolutely. So, you ready to be done with his ring on your finger, Kee?"

"Dex." I almost whimpered his name now. And then I said softly, "Honestly, why?"

Dex Hardy, in a three-piece suit and all grown up, stood in front of me, ready to take over my world. And then he leaned in close and whispered in my ear, "Because your ass knows. You're not marrying anyone but me."

He took my fast-paced, always-moving world, grabbed it, and caused it to come to a screeching halt. I jerked back, stumbled over my own footing, and almost fell before he righted my stance. I didn't thank him but wiggled out of his grip again as I stuttered, "L-Look. I already agreed to be with—"

"If you say you're with Ethan Phillipe one more fucking time, I'll bring him here and make him admit to everyone your engagement is a fuck-up of a sham. Maybe I'll make him admit how many times he's fucked you too."

I rolled my eyes, because I could only tell him we were fake so many times. "What if he says it was a million?"

He growled and paced away from me before he came right back and said, "You want him to die, don't you? He must have been real fucking annoying over the years if you're willing to goad me into punching him a million times."

Well, Ethan was annoying sometimes, even though I loved him as a friend. I couldn't stop the smirk that crept out. "That's not what I'm saying, and you know it."

One side of Dex's mouth kicked up. "I don't know anything, Kee. But I'm going to learn. I got six months to learn every part of you."

I sighed, looked around to make sure no one was paying attention to us, and then grumbled, "I'm not saying yes yet. I need a drink or time or something to think this over."

He chuckled. "Careful. Can't have anyone hearing their sweet Keelani saying she needs a drink."

I scoffed and brushed past him toward the bar. I hated that he caught me glancing around and that it was true. My reputation controlled me. I'd been trapped far too long.

"You do realize the fact that I have to act like sweet Keelani all the time in front of people makes me less sweet behind closed doors."

He hummed. "I think I might enjoy the sour version of you after all this time."

"Is that so?"

"Sure. But even if I do enjoy you, I'm still going to fuck you like I hate you when we get back to the room."

My stupid, traitorous core clenched in response to his comment. This was going to be the longest six months of my life. I already knew it.

I ordered two shots and downed them both.

CHAPTER 10: DEX

"There she is," I said as I watched her swallow the hard liquor without wincing.

She slammed the small glass back onto the bar, pulled that silly baseball cap down over her forehead, and then narrowed her eyes at me. "Another."

I tilted my head and gave her a look. "Probably time to slow down."

"Why?"

"Well, I don't want you too drunk." She knew exactly what I was insinuating, but I didn't give a fuck. That was the point of this whole charade anyway.

"Oh, please. It's not like I'm hooking up with you tonight... or any night for that matter."

"Harsher than you used to be." I chuckled, but my dick jumped. It was how I already knew we were going to have problems and that my plan to get her out of my system was shit.

Keelani wasn't a woman I could get out of my system. She instead got in there, rearranged it all, and rewrote my DNA. I knew it the second I saw her on that stage tonight, singing a song that wasn't on any of her albums. I was ashamed to admit I knew them all by heart.

"We'll have two more shots of tequila." She pointed to the glasses, and the bartender obeyed immediately. I liked to think it was because she stood there with me, but most men would have given into her the second she pouted out those soft lips.

"Actually, just leave the bottle."

He frowned and glanced at me. "Sir?"

I nodded and waved him away.

She swiped the bottle off the counter and said, "Your room or mine?"

"We moving that quick?" I raised an eyebrow.

"Dex, I know you can barely stand me, and I've had the urge to stomp on your foot more than once tonight, so we both know this isn't going down that rabbit hole. That said, I can't be seen out here in the middle of the night drinking with you when I just got engaged."

"Most people in this casino are celebrities or want their own privacy. My security systems won't allow for anything to go out without our consent. When I put together the system, I made sure videography within—"

"Dex." She cut me off and took a breath to probably calm herself. "I've been promised privacy all my adult life. People always find a way to get around it."

"Not around me. If anyone's going to get footage in my resorts, it's going to be me."

She chuckled. "I wish it was only you. At least you used to know me."

"As opposed to...?"

"As opposed to a stalker here and there. Obsessive fans. Men with too much time on their hands. Women ready to tear down other women in any fashion. Someone looking to make a quick buck. The list goes on and on."

"I'm happy to control some of that when you're with me."

"You can't."

I hummed. I didn't think Keelani was aware of how powerful I'd become. "We'll see."

"You think you can control everything, Dex." She shook her head at me.

"Are you saying I can't?"

"You've never controlled me." Her eyes were so dark, I could never classify them as chocolate or violet. I couldn't see exactly what emotion she felt, either, as I stared at her. She wasn't like most people I dealt with now who I could put specifically into one box. Instead, she jumbled the way I lived, the way I categorized my life, the way I survived in it.

"And yet, here you are, in my resort, under my contract." That meant she was mine. It had to mean that now.

"Technically, you *and* your brothers *and* Bane own this—"

"They're going to let me handle your contract, and we both know it."

She couldn't argue with that, so she changed tactics. "It's not worth us getting involved when—"

I sighed at her circling a drain. She knew she was going to go down it with me. "Stop arguing with me and say yes."

"No."

"That answer will change by the end of the night." I nodded at the bottle the bartender had left. "Take it and let's go."

She took a deep breath before she stood in that flowy dress that still somehow showed all her curves when she walked and swiped the bottle off the counter before walking past me. I loved that she wanted to lead the way, even when she didn't know which elevator we were going to. Still, my hand found the small of her back and steered her in the right direction. Even after all these years, our bodies worked together and complemented each other.

On the elevator, we were silent as I swiped my watch to get us onto the restricted level where few people had access.

High-profile clients, Bane, and myself. We were the only ones who had penthouses on this floor. We went down the hall to French doors, and my fingerprints unlocked them as I turned the handles. Keelani gasped when I pushed them open.

The view out of the hotel was that of the Vegas Strip, lit up, alive, and beautiful. She flung her cap off her head and tousled her long hair out before striding over to the floor-to-ceiling windows. They allowed for the city lights to pour in, shining light on the sleek furniture within the living room space. She saw how the world was still alive out there, dancing in the night and giving us a show. "It's beautiful what people can make sometimes," she murmured.

"Dom helped design that building over there." I pointed to one of the big skyscrapers.

"I'm sure he did. And I'm sure you endorsed it." She hesitated, brushing a small hand against the windowpane before she continued. "And I'm sure your brothers have profited off it."

I couldn't tell if her tone was angry or not. "Should I be ashamed of that?"

"No." She shrugged and turned to me. "I'm ashamed I can't control my life the way you all seem to control the world. The way Mitchell has controlled me. The way you all morph it into what you want, no matter the casualties."

I hummed and stared out at the city lights. Getting a glimpse of how she saw the world was tragic. "We're not all monsters."

She narrowed her eyes at me. "I'm not so sure about that."

"Well, you'll have to find out."

"If I don't?"

"I'll be the monster you think I am. I'll dissolve your

contract with our resort. You going to sing somewhere else?"

She chewed her cheek. I knew she didn't want to do that. If nothing else, Dimitri had helped her get this deal and her record label wanted that for her.

"I don't have all night, Kee."

"If I do this..."

Who was she kidding? I scoffed and said, "You're doing it."

"If I do this, you let me sing what I want and do what I want on stage... Let me change my brand here."

"Change it into what?"

"Not the all-American sweetheart I'm sick of being."

"Interesting. Don't want to be a good girl anymore, huh?" She'd shown me her hand. I had her dreams and hopes in mine to hold over her head. Her brand was important to her obviously, and she wanted more control than she'd ever had before. I could offer her freedom, and in return, I'd hopefully find a way to be free of her.

"Oh my God. You know what? Just figure it out with the record label if you want this to happen, because they'll balk. I was with Ethan a few hours ago, and their all-American sweetheart should never be seen jumping from guy to guy."

"No one will care." I shrugged.

"No one... No one..." she stuttered. "You realize I'm a woman? I'll get slaughtered for breaking Ethan's heart, and they'll claim I cheated on him with you."

"Maybe you should admit it was the other way around." Saying that one out loud hurt, but it was true.

Her eyes widened as she gasped and then stepped back like I'd hit her. Her face contorted in pain. "You can't honestly believe that."

"What else should I believe?" Fuck, I hated to admit that

my palms were sweating as I waited to hear if she'd lie.

She shut her eyes hard, squeezed them so her long lashes curled up on her beautiful skin and then opened them with tears glistening. "I need to finish out this contract, Dex. I'm not going to change your mind about me. So, believe what you want. I don't care."

I stepped close to her. I did it so fast, my chest came to her chest, and immediately, she whipped her head up to meet my eyes. "You don't care? You don't care that for years I've had nightmares about you with him? And then dreams of fucking you away from him? You don't care that I'm about to make that happen now?"

"Just because I'd get fake engaged to you doesn't mean I'm going to sleep with—"

My hand went to her neck, and I practically pulled her off the ground so I could reach her lips more quickly. I didn't kiss her. I fucked her mouth. I destroyed it, took what I wanted and longed for. It wasn't nice or kind or subtle in need. It was a kiss full of fire and hate and vengeance. I branded her with the emotions we'd probably both felt for years.

My tongue still commanded her, thrusting around her mouth, claiming every part of it. My length hardened against her stomach, and she whimpered as she clawed at my shirt. Tonight, we were both being reckless. Her probably more so. She had a reputation to uphold, after all.

It was dangerous.

Defiant.

And exactly what I wanted us to be.

She pulled back, breathless, to glare at me and make her point known. "I hate that I'm doing this. Hate you for even pushing us here where we don't belong."

"We've always belonged together, and you know it."

She shook her head. "You'd better make this worth it, Dex."

And then she dove back in.

CHAPTER 11: DEX

She dominated the kiss, and it showed me the spark I'd missed in her. Keelani Hale was bold, defiant, and absolutely stunning when she let herself be who she really was. They'd caged her for long enough.

Her lips were still pillow soft and full as we tasted each other. She wasn't gentle or cautious with them, though. She bit at me and thrust her tongue over mine like she needed me to know who was really in charge.

Then she stepped back, and we both came up for air. Looking at her standing there in my penthouse felt dangerous but necessary, like she was a siren that had lured me in, waiting to have me try to devour her again. Instead, I was sure she'd tear me apart in some way.

And I was going to let her. I wanted her to feast on me, ravage me, and leave me all used up so I would never want her again. Six months with the woman I couldn't get out of my head. Six months of hell...and maybe heaven.

She tasted like tequila and citrus but still somehow smelled like lilacs. It reminded me of the year I lost everything. I'd lost my reputation, my friends, my heart. Most importantly, I'd lost *her*.

I dug into my pocket and handed her my phone. "Call your label."

She hesitated. "It's pretty late to be—"

"Now."

Her eyes narrowed. "They don't just pick up when I call. Mitchell is probably sleeping."

I shrugged. "Let's see."

Her gaze darted to her phone and then to me again like she was looking for an ounce of sympathy or understanding. She wouldn't get it. The quiver in her hands as she dialed the number was enough to show me she was scared, that she didn't push back with them even when she felt she needed to. She never had.

Good.

"Hi, Mitchell." I lifted a brow, and she rolled her eyes as she turned away from me. "I'm sorry to be calling so late, but with the whole proposal and everything, well, there's been a situation."

I heard the guy grumble something over the line. I followed her to the window, where we stood next to one another, looking out at the city lights.

"No. I accepted the proposal. Of course. But the guys from the HEAT Empire aren't happy about it."

HEAT had become big enough that no one ever wanted to hear that phrase. My brothers and I inherited the hospitality empire and made it our own. We dominated the resort industry, the technology and security industry, too. And, as of late, the food service industry with high-end restaurants and bakeries thanks to Clara, my sister-in-law.

Kee flinched at her manager's loud response. "Yeah, I do know them, Mitch." She glanced at me, and instantly I knew that fucker was leveraging our relationship. "But I sang during Dominic's wedding tonight. The resort just opened and—"

I snagged the phone from her hand. He wanted to leverage the relationship, then he could discuss the game he was playing directly with me. "Mitchell, correct?"

The man stuttered, and I instantly remembered his slimy voice from years ago. "Y-Yes, hi. Who do I have the pleasure of speaking to?"

"It's Dexton Hardy."

"Oh, it's a pleasure to talk with you again!"

"A pleasure? You used to ignore me most of the time, Mitchell. Let's not forget."

"I... I don't recall that." So quickly a man could forget when his ass was on the line. "So sorry if you felt I did that in the past. Probably was pretty busy. You know how it is when you're working and—"

I didn't have time for this, and I didn't waste my time on things that didn't matter anymore. "Kill the Ethan-proposal story."

He chuckled at first, like he wasn't sure I was serious, and then he floundered over his words. "Well, we can't. Keelani already signed onto being engaged and has committed to attending events with a fiancé. It's good for the brand. You understand?"

"I do. It's why she'll be engaged to me instead. The PR will be better anyway. You can figure out how to spin that story since you figured out how to spin the car wreck when we were kids."

He huffed and puffed with that comment. "I— Dex, that was never my intention."

"What wasn't your intention?" I asked. He could flounder like a damn fish out of water for all I cared.

"Let's not rehash the past. You said you will get engaged to Keelani? That... That could work well potentially. We can say you've both been keeping the relationship quiet for a while." I heard his excitement, the way he stumbled when he asked if I was sure.

"Who is to say we haven't?" I asked him with irritation. I didn't care to enlighten him on all of the details of this fake engagement. He could wonder if we were real or fake for all I cared.

"Oh, is that so?" He laughed nervously over the line but I could tell he was also thinking he'd struck a gold mine. He didn't realize I would probably end up being the ruin of him.

People didn't seem to understand that when they signed a deal with the HEAT empire was that they didn't only get one Hardy brother, they got all of us.

Dom was the big brother to all of us and tried to set an example. Declan had been in the public eye for so long that he knew how to maintain an image, and Dimitri was easygoing, handling problems before they even occurred. but he had a temper just as bad as mine and was secretive about a lot of shit.

I was a middle child, in between Declan and Dimitri. I'd accepted that it meant I was unhinged. I felt every single thing more because I related to each of them, and I felt every slight deeper than all of them too.

Something was off about her contract with him and about the record label in general. That wasn't my problem, but he had better not disrespect the HEAT name by not disclosing every single thing he could. And, if I was being honest with myself, I was interested in what the hell he had on Kee that ever made her leave me.

"I'd like her contract sent over to my legal team." I held Kee's eyes as they grew into saucers while she shook her head vigorously.

"I'm sorry, her contract with the casino?"

"No. The one she has with Trinity. I'm sure she'll

voluntarily give it to me as I'm now her fiancé, but you sending it to my legal team will be beneficial. I don't want any secrets between us when you're working with my fiancée. Do you?"

So, maybe I wouldn't wait for her to share, considering she looked like a deer caught in headlights.

"Oh, well, that's confidential—"

Did he think I was an idiot? "My future wife is either going to share with me or you are. If she shares it with me and I find something I don't like, Mitchell, the problems you encounter will be much worse. You understand?"

Somehow, he'd snuffed out her drive to be independent and had practically brainwashed her into thinking this was what she wanted. It's why even when I started to consider whether or not this would be a bad idea, I'd doubled down when she'd mentioned changing her brand. Something was amiss, and I was keen on figuring out what. Not to save her. Not even to help her. To get closure for myself.

I clicked off the phone before her manager could rattle off any more bullshit to me and handed it back to her. "Now...call your fiancé."

"Ethan?" she squeaked. "What the hell for?"

I put my hands in my pockets and rocked back on my loafers as I looked her up and down. "I'm not fucking you while you're engaged to someone else. Call him and end it." Then I spun around and walked to my kitchen. I grabbed a glass of water as I waited for her to blow up.

It was coming.

I'd seen her face redden, watched as her breath came faster, how her hands clenched at her sides. Then she stormed up to me in the kitchen and poked my shoulder hard as she glared up at me. "You're not fucking me either way." She said it defiantly enough that my cock jumped at the challenge. "You need to realize you're not going to control this whole situation, Dex. I am. This is my life. And I'm going to do what I want."

I took a deep breath, not because I was angry but because Kee scolding me was something I missed getting turned on by. I had to go slow here. I had to be strategic on how I was going to get her out of my system. My body wanted a moment to remind her of something though, and I took the opportunity.

I set the glass of water down and turned to stand chest-to-chest with her. I pushed up against her so she'd step back and then back again, until she hit the counter. My hands went to either side of her, and I leaned on them so I was close to her ear when I said, "Do me a favor, then. Let me touch you while you're on the phone with him."

"I'm sorry... What?"

I spun her toward the counter and moved close, caging her against the granite. "If I don't affect you, prove it. Wouldn't you rather show me once and for all you don't want to fuck around during our engagement?" I already had a hold of her maxi dress and was lifting it slowly.

"This isn't a good idea," Keelani said. But she was panting. Her ass wiggled against my length, giving her away. I pulled the flimsy fabric higher so I could stare at her smooth upper thighs.

"It's only a short call, Kee. Dial the number, and let's just see how you handle me." I nudged my cock against her then, let her feel what she'd missed over the years. I peered over her shoulder to catch her biting that pout of hers as I asked quietly, "Scared you can't?"

She flicked her gaze down to my mouth and dragged her teeth across her bottom lip. "I'm not scared of anything with you, Dex. We don't have anything between us anymore."

"Interesting." My hand gripped the back of her thigh and then massaged it as she gasped. "I seem to remember you promising me forever when you whispered you loved me."

"I was a kid. Like you said, it was a childhood crush."

I hummed. I'd used those words to hurt her, and I guess they had. Her saying them back at me years later stung badly.

"So, then, I won't affect you when you call that fiancé of yours. Go on." I egged her on. "Dial the number. Tell your fiancé you're done with him so I can fuck you into oblivion."

"Not gonna happen, Dex."

I sighed. "Kee, I think you misinterpreted what this is. I will rip your contract apart and throw your ass out on the street if you don't listen to me. Do you understand? We're not kids anymore. You won't walk all over me like—" I stopped. Fuck, I was still mad at her, and I wanted to punish her for it, make her feel it, make her suffer like I did.

"Dex—" Her voice was soft as she started to say something and set her phone down beside her. Maybe it was an apology. A reason. An excuse. But it was nothing I wanted.

I pointed to the phone. "Call that asshole if you want this deal. Right. Now."

She picked up the phone, her eyes holding a challenge now too. "You might control this whole city—they might be scared and listen to you—but you don't affect me at all. Go on and try to prove otherwise."

With that, she pressed Ethan's number, and I ripped her dress up her hips so I could see the thong she had on underneath. I leaned close to whisper in her ear, "Bend over the counter and face the window. Look out at the city I rule and feel how I'm going to rule you too."

CHAPTER 12: KEELANI

I could only keep up this facade for so long because he was about to find me soaked through my panties. Dex Hardy against me wasn't something I could ignore. His length alone caused my body to quake in anticipation. And his signature smell of warm spice and cedar was all around me. The vibration of his growl weakened me as his hands squeezed the globes of my ass. And the way he kneaded them so close to my pussy, well, I almost whimpered.

He knew how to tease a woman better now than he had before. Practice made perfect, I guess. And the thought of him with others curdled in my stomach as I tried to hold my ground. I may have loved him once, but we were adults now. He had turned into a colossal dick, one who wanted to seek some sort of revenge on me through this contract and get me out of his system. I had to remember that.

He'd left our hometown, I'd moved on, and we weren't really going to revisit what we could have been.

His hands smoothed over my ass cheeks and traced my panty line as I hit the call button. "Put it on speaker."

I glared over my shoulder, but he simply lifted a brow. The man was a masochist, I swear. Still, I did as I was told and placed the phone on the counter.

"Hello?" Ethan's voice was groggy over the line. "Babe? It's late as hell."

"He's answering pretty fast for a fake fiancé," Dex grumbled.

I shushed him. "Yeah, hi, Ethan." I cleared my throat because I sounded much too breathy for the call. Yet, as I did, Dex's finger hooked around the string of my thong. He then dragged it down into my pussy where I knew he felt how wet I was. He chuckled but I spoke loudly over him. "Did the record label happen to call you?"

"Now?" he grumbled. "What time is it?"

"Sorry. It's extremely late." Dex's finger curled up and into my core slowly, and my hands slammed down on the counter.

"Kee, have you been drinking?"

"No. Well, yes." I shut my eyes as he thrust in another and curled them up against my G-spot. "That's not why—"

"Babe, you okay? Give me a sec. I'm with someone."

There was rustling on the other line as Dex whispered in my ear, "Seems your fiancé is fooling around on you too."

The comment was ridiculous. "You *know* we're not really together," I seethed for the millionth time.

"What was that, babe?" Ethan asked now. "Sorry. I've got Janey in the other room."

I narrowed my eyes at Dex, ready to put this ridiculous narrative to bed. "Right. Ethan, I have Dex here." As I said it, the man had the audacity to brush a finger over my ass, and I gasped but kept talking, my voice strained. "He's convinced we're in a real relationship."

"Are you two together right now?" Ethan hesitated and then chuckled. "You finally making up over there?"

"Ethan," I ground out as Dex pumped his fingers faster in and out of me. My tone was breathless. "Can you just tell him that's not true?"

"Hm." My friend always had a knack for causing drama and now was no exception. "Well, we are engaged, Keelani."

102

"Ethan Phillipe. Don't even start. You know our relationship is a sham. The record label isn't running the story of our engagement anymore. I'm getting engaged to Dex instead. So, just tell him—"

"Well, that's unfortunate. I had the whole story about that one night we stayed up at my place and you..." I heard the mirth in his voice but lost focus when Dex pulled his fingers from me as he growled, spun me around, then lifted me onto the counter where he ripped the thong clean off me.

"Jesus," I gasped.

"I know. That was a good night." Ethan kept on. The fucker knew I wasn't talking about him. He knew exactly what he was doing. "When you let me go down on—"

"Do not even, Ethan. Freaking tell Dex we're not a real thing," I said as I saw Dex's eyes darken.

"Yeah, sure. We aren't real, Dex." Ethan chuckled because he knew he'd planted a few seeds already. "You can hear me, right?"

Dex's jaw was working over and over as he stood between my legs in that kitchen, his hands on either side of me but not touching me now. He finally answered, "I can hear you."

"Oh, good. She likes soft touches on her inner thigh and when you blow on her neck. We might not have been exclusive together, but I guess I should help you out since you abandoned her for years to let her hang on my arm."

The anger and jealousy ricocheted silently through that penthouse at Ethan's words. I felt how they shook the walls and my soul as Dex held my gaze. "You seem to know the whole story. Did Keelani tell you she left me first?"

It was then he took his time dragging a finger over the inner part of my thigh and I gasped.

"Seems you're right about her inner thigh though."

"Oh my God, seriously, Dex?" I reached for the phone, but he pushed it just out of my reach before he brought his hand up to the spaghetti strap of my dress and yanked it down so my breast spilled over the material.

"Want me to stop, Kee?"

I bit my lip because I couldn't bring myself to say no. I wanted him, I wanted this, I wanted a new path away from Ethan, away from the label, away from what I'd been.

"Yes or no?"

"No."

"That's what I thought." He chuckled darkly.

"You into hearing your ex-fiancée scream someone else's name, Ethan?"

If that man said yes, I was going to kill him later. Of course Ethan wanted to push boundaries, though, and said, "She still wearing my ring? If so, she's technically still my fiancée."

My eyes widened at his boldness. Ethan wanted to torture Dex. Rightfully so. We'd grown up in the industry together. He'd let me cry on his shoulder. We'd experimented together, too, but nothing ever came of it. He was in love with someone else, and so was I.

Dex glared at the ring like it was the kryptonite to his Superman. "I'm going to fuck that ring off you, Kee. Ethan can listen to you scream while I do it if he wants."

Ethan chimed in, "I'm into that sort of thing if you are."

I watched Dex's face redden, felt his grip on me tighten. "I'm not. Nor will I ever be. She's mine. You come near her again, and I'll ruin you," Dex ground out before pressing the End button. He took two breaths before he asked, "Now, want me fuck you nice, like this means something, or fuck you rough, like I hate you for all you've done?"

I shook my head at him, not really knowing the answer. This night would change me and change us forever. We'd never gone this far. But he didn't seem to care. This was his way of closure. We both knew that. "Just do what's real, Dex. I want the real thing with you."

He didn't wait another second to grab me from the counter and spin me around so that he could bend me over it. The counter felt cool against my stomach as he lifted my skirt. Then, he got on his knees to taste me.

He lapped at me like he was starved and sucked on my clit like I could quench some unsatiated thirst. I let him. I had zero restraint left when it came to wanting him. I'd dreamed of him for years. It was inevitable. We were bound to end up here, and I wouldn't have wanted to be with anyone else.

He stopped tasting me to murmur against me, "Take his ring off, Kee. I can't fucking stand you wearing it for another second."

I did as I was told.

CHAPTER 13: DEX

Her pussy tasted like heaven, hell, accomplishment, and failure all wrapped up into one perfect fantasy. I'd grown accustomed to being able to compartmentalize my life, fitting every feeling or person or task into a certain category. With Kee, though, my emotions shot off like damn fireworks in different directions. I'd craved her for so long. Yet having her right then, I knew, was going to ruin me.

Hell, she'd just removed an engagement ring from her finger. It showed me she wanted this as badly as I did. Sure, she was as sweet as I remembered, but now she'd matured into knowing what she wanted as she rocked against my tongue.

The thought of her learning her desires with Ethan fueled my jealousy, my pace, my need to have her. All this time, I could have had her, but instead I'd let another man be with her instead.

I flicked my tongue over her clit and watched her body jerk in response to me. Only me. I still owned a part of her when we were together here like this.

She whimpered and then breathed out, "I only want the real you throughout all this, Dex. Only you."

That statement had me faltering. Didn't she know I was colder now? Fiercer. Meaner. She'd done that to me. I undid my belt buckle and pulled my length free. Then I let her feel the cold metal against her pussy.

She gasped and looked over her shoulder. "Is that— You're

pierced?"

"Yeah, Kee." I felt her slickness drip over my cock and groaned, trying to contain myself.

"Is that going to hurt more?"

"Hurt?" I questioned, shocked all of a sudden by the thought of someone hurting her while screwing her. "I'm going to fuck you so good. it's going to hurt when I stop, Kee." I rubbed her clit again.

"Do it, then. Make this real again." She clawed at the counter as I gripped her hips, not sure if I was pushing her away or getting ready to dive into her.

I wanted this. I needed it. Yet my soul was scared of it. I was scared of having her once and for all. "We were always real, babe. This pussy of yours is so soaked, I'm guessing you've been dreaming about having me since the beginning." I wouldn't shy away from a fight anymore, and I controlled most everything in my life. I could control this too. I gripped her hair and pulled her stomach up from the counter to spin her around. I made sure she was sitting on the edge, so our faces were just centimeters apart. I wanted to see her when I finally showed her who she'd walked away from. "Keep your eyes on me, Kee. I want you to watch who can fuck you so hard you forget about the good-girl image you've built for yourself and see who you always truly belonged to."

And with that, I plunged into her.

Hard.

She gasped loudly and then whimpered as her eyes widened on me. It wasn't a sound I was expecting and not at all the sound I wanted. She slapped a hand over her mouth, and her whole body tensed. Her look alone would have had me freezing, yet her body language was even more of a signal to me.

"Kee." I froze, my cock still in her, bare and throbbing, but I was distinctly aware now that I was in unmarked territory. Fuck. She was breathing hard but not looking at me at all. "Kee, please tell me I'm stretching you because no one has ever come close to being as big as me." I shifted so I wasn't holding her so tight, and her eyes shut as a blush rose over her chest and her face.

"No one has come close to being inside me at all, Dex."

Her whispered confession had me swearing under my breath again even as my cock swelled like it was damn proud. Slick but so tight, the walls of her fought my cock. Suddenly the anger I'd felt before, the jealousy, the rage was gone. All that was left was my concern. "Kee, fuck. Please tell me I didn't just ruin this. Please tell me you're..."

"I'm still a virgin. Well, I was. Much more of a good girl than you thought." She cracked open an eye. "Fuck me like I'm not one though?"

"You're out of your damn mind." I started to shift back so I could slide out of her, but her hand shot out to grab my ass behind her.

"Don't you dare leave me now, Dex."

"We're not doing this." I shook my head, trying to tell my cock that too.

"We are. Just...take me to your bed."

"If I'd known—"

"If you'd known, then what?" she asked, her eyes burning with anger all of a sudden. "You wanted to fuck me like you hated me. Who cares then, right?"

Both of my hands were on either side of her on the counter now. "Babe, I'm not going to fight with you right now. My cock is so far inside you, I'm scared I'm going to break you, okay?"

She was still holding on to my ass tight though, and when I shifted, she whimpered again. Yet she said, "I'm not going to break. Just carry me to your bed. And don't pull out of me. Because that will hurt."

"Keelani, you realize the act of sleeping together requires that I—"

She smacked my shoulder. "Obviously, Dex. I want to lie in a bed and hopefully do it a little less...abruptly."

My forehead fell to hers and, for a moment, all the tension between us left. "Wrap your legs around me."

She nodded and bit her lip as she did. I carried her, legs wrapped around my hips, like she was my most fragile possession. I didn't care about most things other than working and keeping my family proud. Most of my hopes for making the rest of the world a better place died when our town turned its back on me.

"How did we get here, Kee?" I murmured in her ear as her arms wrapped around me.

Tomorrow, I knew we'd be back to arguing, to the awkward conversations, to our separate lives, but tonight, we were connected.

"Well, we got like this because I didn't tell you."

"I didn't ask, either. For some odd reason." His tone was sarcastic. "I had the idea you'd done this before."

"Ethan and I never slept together because he didn't want that and neither did I. He's been in love with someone for a very long time."

"With the person he was with tonight." It made sense. I turned the corner and passed the guest bedroom and the spare office space.

"Yes," she said softly. "Seems a lot of people found the

person they wanted to be with over the years."

Her eyes searched mine, and I knew she had questions about Seanna and me. With the fact that I'd just stolen her virginity, I offered up the honest truth. "I don't commit well to anyone. Seanna knows that. She's fine with it. We've... I keep my relationships casual but she's been casual for a while now."

Her chocolate eyes searched mine without judgment but I saw confusion too. "How do you not get attached?"

Easy. Someone breaks your heart into such small pieces, you have no attachments left. When I didn't answer her and kept walking, she changed the subject. "Enough rooms here?"

"It's a penthouse suite. You'll feel comfortable."

She rolled her eyes. "I'm not staying with you, Dex."

"Of course you are." I got to the bedroom and shoved open the oak French doors to a room that was all warm tones. "Where else would my fiancée stay?"

"I was actually assigned a lease at an apartment your brother got me near the resort for—"

"My fiancée is going to stay at my place." I held her ass to me and then turned to sit down on the bed.

"Wait." She gripped my shoulders and her eyes were wide as she looked around the bedroom. She chewed her cheek before she pointed to the soft, tantric chair in the corner. It had curves and angles I knew how to enjoy. "Maybe we should just sit on that chair? It looks soft and..."

I shook my head. Jesus, she didn't even know what it was. No way in hell was I having her on a tantric chair for her first time. I breathed out, trying not to imagine her bent over it. I stepped back toward the bed, my cock now throbbing with the feeling of her walls around me. "Trust me. The bed will be easier. I'm going to sit down, okay, Kee?"

She blinked a few times and took a deep breath before she nodded. "You're very big, Dex. Go slow."

"Baby, you're stroking my already large ego with that comment." I chuckled, but I felt her body start to tighten up. I'd wanted to torture Keelani with the idea of my fucking her being so good, she could never think of anything else; but instead, I feared how rough I handled her would be the way she would remember her virginity being taken. "Heartbreaker, you're going to have to relax into me and trust me, okay?" She bit her lip, but her legs stayed firmly around me even as I scooted us backward to where she could have moved away. "Can you look at me?"

"I feel like right now isn't the time for us to stare into each other's eyes. Let's just get this over with."

"I'm not stealing your virginity or *getting it over with*. Jesus, how am I even your first?"

"Did you honestly think it would be someone else?"

"Yes, Kee. When we walked away from each other, I wanted to walk away for good."

CHAPTER 14: KEELANI

He would have danced on my shattered heart if he could have. It was the difference in us when we broke up. I saw his hate, and he saw what I painted on my face as apathy. I still masked my pain and love for him very well.

And maybe these six months would help me overcome it. If he wasn't going to fall in love all over again, I wouldn't either. We'd learn from each other here. We'd grow. We'd move forward, and then we'd move on. Leaving the past behind once and for all was necessary to a person's survival.

"Well, I guess you decided to walk straight into me instead. So, please, just fuck me, Dex."

His jaw worked a few times before he ground out, "You're on top of me. You're doing this first. Nice and slow."

I rolled my eyes and shoved him down. My hands were on his clothed chest. I immediately started working at the buttons. "I want this off."

He brushed my hands away quickly, like he wanted to keep the shirt between us or like he had something to hide. Then, his hands were back at my hips, telling me, "Heartbreaker, forget about my shirt. Can you move on me?"

I bit my lip but kept my gaze on the buttons, focusing on that task instead of the big one. "I'll move when I'm ready."

He didn't confirm or deny whether that was okay. Instead, his fingers massaged my hips like he was trying to soothe me. I went back to working on his shirt and undid the last button. I pulled it apart just so I could stare at his chest.

Intricate tattoos weaved all around it. Yet, I didn't take much time to look them over before I anchored myself on his pecs and said, "Maybe we should flip over?"

He didn't say a thing until I finally glanced up at him. He had a sheen of sweat on his brow, and I could see how his neck was tight and coiled, like he was bracing for impact. "Kee, you're going to move your ass up and down on my cock. You. Not me. I don't have the control right now."

I saw that his pupils were dilated, the green of his eyes burning bright. Even if we'd been apart for years, my body knew immediately that this man wasn't going to move until I did. So, I took a deep breath and arched my back slowly to lift my pussy from his cock. Centimeter by centimeter, I felt all of him. The ball of his piercing rubbed against my tight walls before I brought myself back down on his cock again.

He hissed and then swore, but I was too lost in how the pain morphed to pleasure, how his hand immediately went to my clit to start rolling it again, how he massaged my ass like he was working me and molding me to take him again. And again.

I moved up, down, up, down, again and again. And every time, my breath hitched, my body quivered, my blood pumped adrenaline and need through my veins. Pain mixed with pleasure was like a drug of some sort. My nipples tightened, my pussy clenched, my body ached for just a little more.

I rocked onto him harder. One of his hands slid up my stomach to my breast and pinched the nipple, worked it like he worked my clit. My pussy wept around his cock because of it, and I whimpered and moaned for him.

"Starting to feel like you like it, Kee. Does it feel good having me inside you?"

I hissed out, "Yes." I couldn't have said no even if I should have. "We needed this. We needed to see how the other felt after all these years."

He hummed like he might agree but didn't say the words. "You know I'm stretching you, baby. I'm stretching you so only I fit you just right. This pussy is mine. You understand?"

I didn't answer right away, and he pinched my clit and my nipple hard. I gasped but my hips were working on their own now, grinding my pussy around his cock like I enjoyed how he wanted to dominate me in the bedroom.

"Look how you like fucking me, Kee. Might as well say you'll do it for six months, huh? I'll let you come then."

My eyes cut to him fast and there was a twinkle in them. "Dex, what the hell?" I wiggled on him but the pressure on my clit let up. He was teasing me, and I hadn't even known.

"Just say you like it, Kee. Tell me how my cock feels in you."

I felt the blush rising to my cheeks. His cock jerked in me, and I knew he was getting more turned on.

"Fuck, your tits even turn pink when you blush, heartbreaker."

"Dex, please," I whimpered out because I wanted to hit the high more than anything at this point.

"How does my cock feel, Kee?"

"It feels so good," I whispered, and he rolled my clit hard. "Jesus, it feels so amazing when you do that."

"Yeah, I know, heartbreaker. You want to come?"

I nodded over and over, and he took over then. He was gentle when he moved his hands to my hips and lifted me up and down, but it was to a perfect rhythm, and he rolled his hips to exactly the right spot. I felt his cock everywhere, in every place that I needed, as I brought my face down to take his mouth in mine. He kissed me soft as he fucked me slow. He didn't fuck me like he hated me, but instead treated me like glass, like he wanted to be gentlemanly with my first time.

When I pulled back to look at him, he ran his hand over my clit again and twisted it in rhythm with our movements as he whispered, "Come, Kee. Come for your fiancé."

His words shouldn't have pushed me over the edge, but they did. I screamed his name again and again as I unraveled on top of him.

He smoothed his hand down my back and let me shudder out each aftershock. I felt him drawing on my back as if to soothe me. His body was still so tight and rigid under mine. I finally looked up. "Dex?" I asked wiggling against him. His dick was still rock solid. "You didn't get off yet."

"Right." His jaw worked. "You want to shower?"

"No," I said slowly and pushed myself up with the little strength I had left. "I want more. I want..." I bit my lip.

"Kee." He said my name in warning.

"I want you to get off too."

He started to lift me off him, but I bared down and he grumbled, "Shit. Kee, I only have so much restraint."

"I'm asking you to not have restraint," I said. "This is an agreement between us. We're getting each other out of our systems, right?"

He finally took a hand from my hip to rub his jaw and shut his eyes in frustration. "I don't fuck nicely, heartbreaker. You need to get off me."

"Seriously? What if I don't want nice now?" I murmured. "What if I want more? Because I do. I want more, Dex. I want you like before in the kitchen."

"Jesus, Kee." He combed a hand through his hair and

shook his head one time, then two. "You realize what you're asking for? I'm not the boy I was. I'm not considerate or soft anymore."

"You never were truly any of those things, Dex." I rolled my eyes, and then I leaned in and tried to seduce him by biting at his ear. "Fuck me like you hate me, if you really do. Please."

He growled, and I knew I'd triggered the bomb within him. "I can't take it anymore," he ground out before he gripped my hips much harder than before and flipped us over.

He pulled out and hovered over me, his shirt still hanging from his sides, his forearms on either side of my face. I was cocooned by him, enveloped, swallowed up by everything he was in that moment as he stared at me with an intense gaze. "I want to hate you, you know that? And then I want to feel nothing for you. I'm still furious with you, Kee. I still want to hate you with every fucking bone in my body for how you left. How you came back, too, and fucked with my head."

I chewed at my cheek. "What are you going to do about it?"

"Remember you asked for this." He said it softly as he ran a finger along my cheek, and then he teased my clit with his piercing.

"Please. Please. Please," I said, moving my hips to get him closer.

And then he grunted, his hand going up to my neck where he gripped me. "Remember when you can't walk tomorrow, it's because you fucking begged for it." And then he squeezed my neck with force as he thrust into me.

I couldn't even gasp because his grip was too tight, but the sensation was overwhelming. My pussy was ready for him. I was ready. I wanted it—the punishment, the pain, the other side of being good. I wanted it all, and he pounded it into me.

His cock was huge, inches upon inches of solid, thick muscle, and he speared me like he wanted to brand me, wanted me to be stretched exactly for him, and I was. Still, I wanted more. "Harder, Dex. Let me feel it all."

"Jesus. You were never a good girl, Kee. Doesn't the world know that about their precious Keelani Hale? You were *always* a fucking bad girl," he ground out as he slowed down to let my pussy stroke him. "Look at how you take my cock, legs spread like you've done this a million times. You were made to be fucked by me. We should have told the world that from the very beginning. This pussy was always mine. Always will be."

He squeezed my neck harder as he fucked me faster and faster. His head fell to the side of mine as he pumped in and out, and I felt him panting rapidly. I watched as his muscles bulged and tightened, the veins on his neck popping out and swiveling like all his emotions were fighting to come out any way they could. There was so much between us. Pain, pleasure. Hate, love. Hell, heaven. We chased that heaven as he fucked me, both of us close now to getting off.

"You're on the pill?" he said, and I nodded, clawing at his back, wanting to feel him empty in me as much as he wanted to.

His other hand went to my clit and pinched it as he thrust the deepest I'd felt him go. As he did, he let go of my throat, and I gasped in oxygen, gasped in pleasure, gasped in the euphoria of an orgasm that was out of this world.

Every color flashed before my eyes, every feeling pumped through my veins, every thought flew through my mind and then flew out. I felt everything and nothing but pleasure at the same time. Dex's body tensed above me, and I felt the low growl deep in my bones as his cum shot into me.

I pulled him close, feeling his heart beating rapidly

with mine, in sync and harmony together. The feeling was overwhelming but also calming, like I could stay that way forever.

But then he got off of me, moving away fast like I could burn him, like I was poison in his sheets.

He was mostly clothed as he stood over me, his cock softening but still looking thick and formidable in the dim lighting. I saw the piercing glinting in the moonlight, and my mouth watered at how attractive he was.

He sighed before he tucked himself in and grumbled, "Don't look at me that way unless you want to fuck again."

"Where are you going?" I hated that I asked the question.

He buttoned up his shirt and then murmured, "Stay there."

He disappeared into the bathroom and came back with a damp white cloth. He told me to lie back and tapped my inner thigh. "Spread your legs, Keelani."

He wasn't calling me by my nickname now, and even though it'd been one given in pain, I was tied to it for some reason. My heart felt a stab of pain that he'd resorted back to Keelani. So I closed my legs and tried to swing them off the bed to get up. "I can clean myself up."

His other hand shot out to grip my arm. "Lie down. Now."

I turned to glare at him. "This was a fuck-you-and-leave-you situation, Dex. Let's not make it more than that."

"It was until I fucked you and figured out that I was taking your virginity."

"I don't need special treatment because of it! I've been wanting to get rid of it—"

"Why me?" He threw up his hands.

"Because I still trust you!"

"Well, you shouldn't," he ground out and then commanded,

"Now lie down."

I crossed my arms and threw myself onto the bed. "You're infuriating. Why even do this?"

"Because I'm not having regrets once these six months are over, Keelani. You might, but I won't." He dragged the warm cloth up my thigh, and I bit my lip at the sensation. Then he smoothed it softly over the middle of me and I whimpered. "You're going to be sore for a few days. Don't walk around much. I'll cater in food for you if need be. And—"

"I have rehearsals starting on Monday, Dex." I reminded him. "In a month, I need to be ready to perform multiple nights a week. Tomorrow, I'll have to do mic checks and—"

"Tomorrow you're off," he interrupted and then hummed. "So, it'll be the perfect time to move all your things here."

"I'm not moving in with you." His only response to that was to brush his hand softly over my pussy with the cloth, like he cared, but he rubbed a thumb over my clit too and I hissed, "Dex!"

It was the first time I saw a genuine smile whip across his face in years. His eyes sparkled, his dimples showed, and then he bit the corner of his lip like he didn't want me to see happiness at all between us. "Just reminding you who's in charge. You're moving in."

"I'm not. I'm going to go home after..." I waved down. "Are you done? I'll clean up and leave—" He didn't let me finish. He stood and scooped me up fast after he threw down the washcloth. "What the hell, Dex!"

"You'll stay in the guest room." He glanced back at the sheets, and I did too. I saw blood where I'd laid, evidence of what we'd done together bright red against the white sheets and shut my eyes in embarrassment.

"I'll replace those," I whispered out.

"Kee, look at me." He was walking now, cradling me like a baby on the way to his spare room, and there was no way for me to fight him, so I gave in and peeked open an eye. "Those sheets are now a prized possession of mine. They have your innocence all over them. I might even frame them."

"Don't be ridiculous. At least let me take them home and wash—"

"I'll take care of it."

"You don't have to take care of it. I can do it myself," I told him.

"You could, but you're my fiancée now." He frowned like he wasn't sure of our status all of a sudden but he still said the label with conviction. "You won't take care of anything."

I knew my stomach shouldn't have erupted with butterflies, but it did anyway. The problem with what I'd just done was that I didn't know if it was going to ruin me to have him be my first. I had now etched him into my memories, the man who not only stole my heart but now my virginity.

I did know, though, that it would probably ruin me if he wasn't my last.

CHAPTER 15: KEELANI

I was snuggling into his scent under the weight of his arm curled around me the next morning until I realized what the hell I was doing. He'd laid me down in the spare bed last night, and I'd fallen off to sleep quickly. I tried to shoot out of bed, but he cranked his arm tighter and grunted before pulling me back down.

"Shit." I shoved at him. "Dex, are you kidding? Wake up."

He rolled over and stared at me for a second, hazy with an old look that reminded me a lot of the boy he used to be. The fog eventually cleared from his eyes though, and he lifted his arm away. His tone had no emotion as he asked, "You in a hurry to get somewhere?"

"What time is it?" I tried to jump out of bed again but winced from the ache of the night before.

"Sore?" he murmured in my ear.

I chewed my cheek and nodded.

"Good." The word rumbled out of him as he dragged a finger along my bare arm with a look of damn pride across his features.

"You should feel bad for me," I pouted.

"Why? Because every time you walk around there will be a reminder of me making you feel good?"

I would have narrowed my eyes at him, but I was rubbing away the sleep from my eyes and considering how I'd never gotten dressed last night. I sighed at the idea of going to find my clothes. Yet, Dex rolled over to the nightstand and handed me clothing stacked atop it. The dress was folded neatly, like he'd prepared for the moment.

"Here. Get dressed. I have a car outside if you need it. And"—he turned once again to grab a box that he held out— "try this on."

I assessed how he had all this ready and realized he must have done it after I went to bed last night. He liked order and was already putting our situation in place. It was easy to succumb to it but maddening that he already had his mind set.

The proposal wasn't what I wanted. Not that I wanted one at all. Even still, the callousness of it was like rubbing gravel into old wounds. "No sweet words?"

He looked down at a ring box that wasn't there yesterday and cleared his throat. "I have nothing sweet to say, Keelani. I'm doing you a favor, and in turn, I'm closing a chapter of my life."

He was drawing a line in the sand. I'd stated that verbal sentiment a few times the night before too. Still, somehow, in the light of a morning next to a man I'd once loved, it felt like he was slicing that line through my heart rather than drawing it in the sand.

I stared at the box, trying not to be hurt. "What if I don't like the ring?"

"Did you like Ethan's ring?"

I glanced at my naked ring finger and was reminded of how he'd made me take that ring off in the kitchen. "I'm sure Trinity just sent him the one they thought would look best." I groaned, thinking of our phone call to him last night. "I need to call him."

"What for?" Dex's tone was instantly harder, lower. The man never hid his jealousy well.

He didn't get to ask those questions if this was all he wanted our situation to be. "Ethan's a friend, Dex. He literally got me through some of my roughest years. He's going to want to know what's going on."

With that, I pulled my dress on and then snapped open the box. A solitaire diamond stared back at me. It was massive. Two or three times the size of Ethan's. It was a statement, but it was generic, boring, and cold. It meant nothing to Dex. I could tell right away. "You pick this out?" I asked, trying to keep emotion from my voice.

"Of course not. My assistant had it sent over earlier this morning. It'll work for six months, right?" He stood to get out of bed and kept his back to me as he grabbed his watch off the nightstand. The muscles in his back moved fluidly, showcasing that pretty much every part of his body was in perfect shape. I saw a hint of the tattoos on his ribs but didn't catch much more as he hurriedly threw on a shirt. "Does it fit?"

I glanced down again at the ring, took it from the velvet lining slowly, and slid on the cool metal. Of course it fit. "Perfectly."

"Great." His tone was clipped. "Obviously don't wear it until I propose publicly. And go make your call. Then, let's work out the logistics of this quickly. I need to get to work."

"It's Sunday."

"And I work on Sundays, Keelani." He said it with condescension, like I should already know this. Then, he walked off in his boxers towards the bathroom.

This engagement was an agreement, a contract for financial security for my family. For starting my life over. I had to remember that; needed to tell myself that over and over. If it was closure for Dex, great. He could have that too. I knew with the way he was treating me, I couldn't be falling down the rabbit hole of investing emotions, though. I wiggled my dress into place, slid the ring off my finger, and placed it back in the box. It snapped shut with finality. Backing away from it, I went to find my phone.

After pacing back and forth in the living space while talking things over with Ethan, I told him, "You know I love you. It'll work out for both of us, and this is your chance to see if Janey is ready for something more with you."

"She isn't," my friend groaned but I knew he didn't know that for sure. He'd never told her how he felt.

"Tell her how you feel, Ethan." I sighed. "And then call me to tell me how it goes because I want to be the first to congratulate you."

He said he would think about it all. I wouldn't push him. Our careers were complicated enough without pulling in those we loved. He was protecting a relationship, and I honestly didn't know if it would be best for him to make it public anyway.

"Love you, Ms. Keelani," he said before he hung up.

"Love you back, boo," I told him just as Dex walked into the living room and made it known he was checking his watch. I could tell the band of it was expensive, as it flashed gold and it held one of the best smart watches made, a HEAT tech one.

I ended the call and stood staring at my fiancé as he leaned against the doorframe, looking me up and down. He had showered and was put together in his signature suit and tie, ready to conquer the world. His hair had been combed back, he had on loafers, and even his cuff links were in place.

"Took quite a while to finish that call," he said softly.

"I was smoothing things over for the both of us. You should be happy."

"Why would I be happy when it seems my fiancée loves another man?" His eyes held madness, but I met it with my own.

"I said 'I love you' to him because he's a friend who's been in my life for a very long time," I immediately argued, but then I caught myself. We weren't here to bicker with each other. "Do you really care?"

"The media will care."

For some reason, I wanted him to say anything but that. "Right." This was the life I lived, and I had to do it for more than just myself. "Well, we're going to have to figure out my rebrand today. Maybe slowly launch into my dating you."

He hummed. "Is that what you want?"

"I want to move toward rebranding as soon as possible," I grumbled, aware we couldn't simply push an opinion on the public.

"What does the new Keelani look like to you exactly?" He squinted at me as if trying to picture me some other way. "You need stylists and a new PR firm helping with that sort of thing? Would the record label have contacts for—"

"They won't help." I stopped him. "No one is going to rebrand who I am if what I've been doing is already working for them." I took a deep breath. "It just doesn't work for me now. I'm not a kid anymore."

He stared at me for a few more seconds before he said, "What does that mean?"

"I'm not the all-American girl. I'm singing to an intimate audience of a thousand people every weekend here in a month, right?"

"That's what you agreed to do, yes. The Orpheum Theater holds that."

"Right. That's extremely intimate. I want them to feel me and feel what's raw in my heart. I want to write my own stuff, have my own look, be..." I shrugged. "Me."

He studied me for a few seconds as he rubbed his chin. "Don't you think over the years you've become what you faked for so long?"

It was a slight, but I didn't stoop to his level. "Maybe parts of me are that way, but I know not all of me is, Dexton."

"Then call Olive and Pink and tell them to change your look." He looked like he couldn't be bothered with any of it as he pushed off the doorframe, making his way to exit the hotel.

"How do you know about Olive?" He hadn't been introduced to my best friend.

"I know just about all there is to know in my casino, Kee." He didn't elaborate further but instead changed the subject as he glanced at his watch lighting up. "Utilize HEAT's PR. It's at your disposal. Do what you need to do, but I need to be at a meeting regarding staff within the casino in about ten minutes. So, my assistant will send you information on events we can attend. Our PR schedule will be drawn up by her too. She can propose it to Trinity Enterprises, and we'll have your image all changed up with a neat, tidy bow in just six months. Perfect for you and that important brand of yours."

He said it all without looking at me as he texted away on his phone. I wasn't on his radar anymore. Instead, this had turned into business for him.

"What about your image?" I asked softly.

"Why do you ask?" He didn't look up.

"I don't know if you've considered what being engaged to me might do to you. My fans are used to Ethan and sometimes cruel—"

He frowned at his phone then didn't even blink as he said, "You ruined my image once, and I survived. You think I'm concerned about it again?"

"Dex..." I started, but what could I say? He was right that my omissions and silence in the past had ruined him at home.

"Again, there's a car waiting outside when you're ready. Grab some breakfast on the way to pack up what's left of your apartment that you want. We already have a team doing it, but they'll only be grabbing what I feel is necessary. Which, quite frankly, isn't much."

"Do you have someone in my apart— Wait." I combed a hand through my hair. "I'm not living with you."

That finally got his attention. His green eyes snapped up to glare at me. "Don't be ridiculous, Keelani."

"I don't want to live with anyone until I'm married, and—"

"Now you suddenly have a conscience about your damn marriage?" He scoffed.

He knew that was going to rub me the wrong way. His ass wanted to. "Of course I have a conscience. I always have. So, don't even start with that. I made an agreement with Trinity Enterprises, but I was never actually going to marry—"

"So what? My fiancée is going to live next door? I'm here all the time. Your belongings need to be moved here."

"The apartment is fine for—"

"Get real. The press is going to be following us everywhere as it is. We don't need them writing more shit about our separate living situations. This is supposed to be believable."

I shut my eyes and whined at his logic. "I cannot live with you right now."

"Why not?"

"Because we're completely different people than we used to

be, and we don't seem to get along at all."

"I don't need to get along with you, Keelani. I need you to stay out of my way during the day and come to my bed at night." He looked me up and down, his words cruel but I was sure truthful.

"Oh, that sounds so good. I get to fuck an ex I have to beg for an orgasm." I could be cruel too.

Those green orbs lit with fire. "You begged for it, and then you screamed in ecstasy when you got it," he reminded me, and I hated that I blushed. "You must realize I'm not trying to welcome you? I'm trying to make this shit believable. For your sake and mine."

"You think it's unbelievable that I wouldn't move in with you? I'm literally in a magazine that has a poll on if I'm still a virgin or not. Eighty percent said they thought I still was."

"I can answer that one with certainty for them," he threw out, and my eyes widened at the fact that he was making a joke right now.

"Are you kidding me?"

He tried to be serious by pursing his lips and then shrugging. "It was the perfect opportunity. Plus, this isn't a big deal. I promise. It's easier for us to handle press when we're here at Black Diamond. My security is much better here. And this way, they'll probably stop voting you Most Likely to be a Virgin."

Wow. "So, you still have a terrible—and rude—sense of humor." I tried to be mad and serious about this. I really did. And it was a serious matter, but the fact that he'd taken my virginity the night before was pretty fresh on the brain. I thought of how I was still sore because of how big he was, how he'd taken me, how he hadn't been gentle, and I glanced down to where I knew he was pierced.

"Fuck me, Kee." His voice rumbled out low as he swore and rearranged his slacks suddenly. "Keep your eyes above the waist if you want to be able to walk out of here today."

I snapped them up, but I knew my cheeks were hot with the embarrassment of being caught. "Right. Just processing everything that happened last night."

He hummed. "You can process all you want when you're moved in here later. We're both here *together* tonight. And remember, most everyone around us is going to believe this engagement is real—"

"Minus most everyone who knows us because they're never going to believe this is real."

"Fine. Shall I wire you your paycheck for being my fiancée now?"

I rolled my eyes at the fact that he was discussing it with me. "You know what, Dex? Why don't you pay me at the end? That way," I said it with all the sarcasm I could muster, "If I'm not good enough at following your directions, you can keep your money."

"Great. I'll set a reminder." He truly did set one because my phone beeped almost immediately. "And keep the circle small. It'll make for less chance of a leak in the media."

With that, Dex turned on the expensive heel of his shoe and left me completely overwhelmed with what I'd agreed to.

CHAPTER 16: KEELANI

I could have fought him on the whole apartment situation but being at the Black Diamond was much easier. His penthouse suite would allow me to take an elevator down to the Orpheum and be ready to practice right when I wanted. There was ample space in the guest room, plus an office, the sauna, and the gym, along with two more bathrooms and a huge tub in the primary en suite bathroom that I wanted to indulge in daily.

It's why I went to pack my apartment and then spent the afternoon talking with Dex's assistant, who I decided was much too nice and beautiful to be his assistant. My mind was already full of unwarranted jealousy when it came to him.

She showed up asking about where all my belongings should be placed. I told her the primary suite was perfect and that we should move some of Dex's clothes out of the closet. "You know how it is. I'm having more clothes brought in, so he's giving me the closet."

She peered into his closet. "He's quite particular about where he puts things in here—"

"I'm guessing he's quite particular about a lot with you, huh?" I waited to see if she would indulge in telling me anything about him.

Her blue eyes widened as she stopped straightening a statue on one of the shelves of the dresser. "Yes." She said it hesitantly at first but then smiled at me. "As his fiancée, you know his quirks, I'm sure. All watches in a particular order in their case, cuff links placed together in their respective boxes, all his shoes polished after each wear and aligned perfectly with toes facing out. Just as he runs his business, he runs his house."

"Right. It's why he still wants his own space. In the guest room." I emphasized my point, and she chose not to argue.

"I'll be honest, he doesn't like anything moved. Or tampered with. Or, well, I'm sure you know." She eyed me suspiciously now. She was catching on like she may have had reservations when he'd called her to acquire a huge diamond ring. She even glanced at the box on the nightstand and then my bare finger.

"Did Dex give you all the details on this arrangement?"

"Nope." Her eyes narrowed on me and I saw her straighten her small frame though, like she wanted me to respect her in some way. "I can put two and two together though."

"I don't doubt that." I took a breath and took a leap of faith. "We're old friends. This benefits us both."

She nodded, but I caught the small gasp from her lips like she couldn't believe I was divulging anything personal. Then she smiled and I saw how her eyes crinkled at the corners before she said softly, "Thanks for trusting me with that. I'll do my best to be discreet and accommodate you both."

Before she left, she let me know that movers would be coming soon.

I sighed. Taking a bath in that tub overlooking the city would have to wait. I wouldn't risk people I didn't know walking in and out of the suite while I wasn't on full alert. Instead, I walked around my new home and realized Dex's resort and casino, as well as the design of this penthouse, was everything I wanted. He had splashes of color through every room, clean lines of granite countertops mixed with dark wood floors and chandeliers above. It was classy, chic, and luxurious.

Even with the perfect furnishings and decor that I loved, it occurred to me I had to make this living space mine for the time I'd be here. The primary bedroom was as much mine as it was his. Plus, he had an office, a workout room, and a damn sauna down the hall. He would be just fine. This was an equal partnership. So, I was going to get equal treatment.

Although it didn't feel that way. He could abandon this deal at any second, and my world would crumble. If I walked away from him, he'd probably be better off.

One of the movers grumbled that they needed to hurry. He didn't want to be here when Dex got home. Clearly, Dex had a reputation around this resort. People were afraid to mess up the order he created, and I saw it more and more around his house. His fridge was stocked with drinks all lined up perfectly. His cabinets held mugs with the handles all turned the exact same way.

I was going to mess up all his order, and a part of me knew it would make him mad enough to lose control. A part of me wanted that. The fact that I was looking forward to it clearly showed we were heading toward having a super healthy relationship.

Even still, I felt lighter than I had in months, maybe years. We'd weighed each other down, and we were going to be able to shuck that weight off one way or another.

I called Olive to share the news, then Dimitri. I shared the reality of it with them because there was no way they'd believe I'd actually gotten engaged. When I tried to tell Dimitri I'd see him tomorrow for a meal, he balked. "We're discussing this now. Where are you?"

"I'm...well..." I plopped down on the plush white couch and

glanced out the window at the city before I breathed out, "We decided to move in together."

"What? You're absolutely not doing that." His tone sounded final. "That's never going to work."

"It might actually work just fine, Dimitri." I brushed at the plush fabric so as not to get concerned that I was making him worry too much. "You know, because then I'll be at the resort all the time and—"

"You're staying at the Black Diamond? Are you in his fucking penthouse right now, Kee?"

"This isn't a big deal."

"It is a big deal," he grumbled. "My brother's gone completely off the deep end. And you know what? I dealt with the damn breakup last time. With *both* of you."

"Did you not want us to work things through?" I countered as I got up to pace. Then, I speed walked to my room and plopped down on the bed and then straightened as I watched another mover breeze by. They didn't seem interested in me at all, but I'd been wrong before.

"I'm coming up," Dimitri grumbled and then clicked off the phone. And honestly, I'd feel better with him here anyway.

It wasn't long before Olive, being more of an assistant than hairstylist, had rounded up our makeshift fashion designer, Pink, and was on her way over with her too.

Dimitri bickered with me for all of five minutes before succumbing to the fact that initially this had sort of been his idea, and he didn't want many more details about it. I didn't want to share them either.

Instead, I tried on the clothes Pink had brought with her from the entertainment dressing rooms, and we all stared at my outfit in the mirror. I was in a yellow pleather skirt that stopped just below my butt and a yellow pleather bralette that tied in the back like a corset.

"That's not going to work," Olive announced, glaring at her fashion friend.

"It will." Pink flipped her bangs and came over to me to wiggle the top more into place over my chest. There really wasn't any helping the fact that my boobs were spilling out.

"Well, it would work for a school bus look. Like a sexy school bus driver that shouldn't really be sexy because you're driving kids to school and—" Dimitri stood there grumbling in his three-piece suit like he was important.

"Stop," Olive cut him off. "It doesn't work, Pink. This is what you see as sexy chic?"

"This is what I could round up quickly," she corrected. "The designers are behind on getting Kee's clothing in, okay?"

"Of course they are," I grumbled, because what else would go wrong during my stay here.

"It'll be fine," Pink reassured me. "But right now, this wardrobe is what we had for casino performers. We'll have everything we need in a month, and now we can make changes. Who cares if they're behind on the old designs when you need new ones anyway? So, for this week in rehearsal, we're going to need to improvise. Plus, pop stars are supposed to show a little skin."

Olive shook her head. "Not that much skin. I wanted a Marilyn Monroe classic, not Big Bird from *Sesame Street* at the club."

Pink turned to assess me again, and we all saw the small smirk on her face as she tried her best to sell us a look that would never be received.

I slumped, looking at the mirror. "If I wear this at rehearsals, is it going to set a tone? And I shouldn't just be changing my whole wardrobe when designers are already working on outfits. I'll be overwhelming everyone, especially if we announce my engagement to Dex. I don't want them to feel like all eyes are going to be on us."

"Okay, well, don't announce it, then. I still think it's a terrible idea," Dimitri jumped in to add.

"We already finalized the agreement with the record label."

"We can get out of it." Dimitri shrugged like he'd do anything for us and it wouldn't cause a burden.

"Dimitri, it's done." I sighed and tried not to think about the fact that the Hardy's legal team would most likely be looking over my contracts soon enough too.

It was only a matter of time before Dex saw how little money I made and how even that small amount was whittled away by my father claiming he'd spend it on my mother. I hoped to at least keep that part to myself.

I'd signed away most of my life. It was detrimental to agree to every little thing the record label asked of me but I'd done it for my family. We all did stupid things for family. And I'd do it again.

That was the hardest part. If Dex somehow found out everything and asked me, I'd tell him that I'd do it again and again. I did it for my mother and father. It's what you had to do for family.

Now, I wondered if I could make it on my own and support them both, too, because I was going to try. I couldn't stay with Trinity for a second longer.

Olive must have seen my despair because she offered, "How about we allow for a costume change at the end of the show, where you can sing new music, okay? We'll fade the lights. It'll be organic and low-key. Intimate—just the way you want. The dress can be low-key too. Maybe just a black one. It's raw. It's you in your bedroom at night, belting out your broken heart anyway, right? That's not glamorous. And we want your emotion to showcase the songwriting, not the costumes."

I took a deep breath and held my hand to my bare stomach. We could do this. I had to believe in myself. It would be hard and tiring and extremely fast-paced backstage to get this all worked out, but we could shift the performance structure and my brand.

"Or how about none of this is a good idea right now? It is fucking ludicrous to take this on, Kee." Dimitri groaned and then pinched the bridge of his perfectly straight nose. I hated that every time I saw him, I was reminded of how good-looking he and his brothers were.

"Are we back to this?" I rolled my eyes and studied myself in the mirror, trying to understand how I could communicate a rawness and vulnerability, how to build that into my brand, and how to make it mine again.

"Yeah, because you rebranding and then trying to do it while being engaged to my brother, living here? It's— I think you and Dex might kill each other."

"Be realistic." I waved away his concern.

"You realize my brother is going to come through that door and flip the fuck out when he sees you moved all your stuff into his room?"

"He wanted me to move in." It's exactly what I was going to say to him too. I then pointed to my purple bedspread. "I'm just making myself at home."

"Did he say to do that?"

"I don't care what he said." I fluffed my hair in front of the bralette.

"It looks like a purple bomb went off in here."

"Purple's my favorite color." I even had got my nails painted purple for Dom's wedding. I didn't have a problem showing it off. I had a purple painting hanging over the bed. It was abstract but sort of reminded me of a sad face. A purple throw pillow was nestled into the armchair in the corner. I'd arranged my favorite purple vase on the dresser.

"You don't need this right now." He had his hands on his hips.

"Whatever. Did you have to come over dressed like you were on your way to a meeting? Why are you fully dressed in a suit?" I pointed to Dimitri and curled my lip as I plopped down on the soft king-size bed.

"I was at work."

Olive sat next to me and scoffed. "You look stuffy."

"You look homely," he countered, crossing his arms and staring down at us. "How do you even have the job of doing her hair when you can't do your own?"

Olive just laughed, straightened the little Hawaiian flower in her hair, and brushed her curls out of her face at Dimitri's barb because she had to have known it didn't mean anything. They threw insults back and forth like they were playing ping-pong most days. She crossed her legs and leaned onto my shoulder. "Let's be honest. I'm the only one who will put up with the ridiculous hair styles they ask me to do with Keelani's hair."

"Hey! My hair is easy."

"You have about the same amount of hair as three horse manes. You think it's easy tying it up in a bun every time you go on stage?"

"Yeah. Well, I don't expect I'll be tying it up much anymore." I glanced at Pink. "You said it's a new look."

She shrugged. "It's necessary. Let your hair go free along with your brand."

"See!" I spun to wink at Dimitri. "Everyone agrees this is a good idea except for you."

"That's because you've surrounded yourself with delusional friends."

"Ones who believe in me."

"Delulu is the new you-you," Pink singsonged, and Dimitri groaned. "By the way, let's see the engagement ring. Where is it?"

I shook my head. "I'm not wearing it until we're actually publicly engaged."

Olive chimed in. "Smart. Also, I'd like the record to state I'm not sure I'm all for this engagement, but I'm all for your new look."

Dimitri's eyes narrowed on Olive's. "Look. I wanted her and Dex to work through their past, but get engaged? You think she's capable of handling all that along with a rebrand?"

"What's that supposed to mean?" I interjected.

"You want me to spell it out for you?"

I frowned at him because I highly doubted he would. "Please do."

"Why do you need this rebrand now? Why not in a year or two or even three?"

"I don't know. There's a lot of reasons," I said. Yet, I looked away from my best friend, and he caught me immediately. He knew as well as I did there were only a few reasons I kept singing my songs to the masses. It wasn't for the fame. I hated the press. Hated my record label even more. And the money hadn't been good until this Black Diamond deal with Dex.

None of that mattered though. It was for my family. For my mother. For her comfort. For her love. And maybe, hopefully, one day for her recognition.

"Why don't you give us one big reason?"

I pushed off the bed and paced back and forth. "You want me to say it?"

"I want you to know that's not what you should be doing this for."

"Why?" I shrugged. "So what if it's a little about my mom? I just want her to be comfortable and to maybe see—"

"Kee." He sighed out my name, and I hated the sound because I knew what would follow. "Do you realize her comfort isn't something you can fully provide and that she may not ever fully know you again?" That stopped my pacing. Those words hit me like a semi going seventy on the freeway and obliterated my optimism.

"It's not about what we think. It's about what's possible. And it could be possible. You have no idea." Olive was up and going toe-to-toe with Dimitri, mad he was trying to be realistic.

I stepped between them and shook my head, my hair swaying back and forth and covering up how I felt in that moment. They were both looking out for me in different ways. "Neither of you are wrong. It could go either way. But who would I be if I didn't try?"

"Trying to push yourself through all this is asking for a breakdown. You want that on your image?"

"I'm capable of handling this, Dimitri."

"Yes, I'm not arguing that you're incapable. I'm arguing whether it's healthy or not. You have to take care of yourself for once."

"I am. I always do." I crossed my arms.

"You have never put yourself first. And if I have to make sure to protect you from—" He was cut off from a voice behind us.

"Protect my fiancée from who?" Dex said.

I jumped and whipped around as Olive murmured, *"Jesus."*

Dex had the uncanny ability to sneak up on anyone when he wanted to, but Dimitri didn't seem surprised. He turned to confront his brother. "You had her move in? What are you playing at?"

"It was a mutual decision between me and your *best friend*, Dimitri." He sneered the label. "I'm sure she told you, considering you're the one who forced us into such close proximity in the first place."

"Don't put that shit on me." Dimitri took a step toward him. "She's not doing this. You need to reevaluate what you're asking of her, because she's going through too much right now to—"

"Stop," I blurted out abruptly. He knew I didn't share my mother's condition with anyone unnecessarily, and I knew that was what he was about to do.

"You gotta be honest," Dimitri practically pleaded.

"Honest about what?" Dex questioned.

"Nothing." I glared at them both. This was my life, and I was going to make my own decisions about it for once. "This is about my wardrobe. Nothing else. If you're here for that, feel free to stay. If not, I'd like my room to myself because I have work to do."

It took that moment for Dex to realize the room's changes. The colors. The bedspread. The few pillows and vase.

My name came from deep in his chest, low in warning.

"*Kee.*"

"Oh, look at the time," Pink said suddenly. "I have another client. I'll be leaving now."

Dex didn't take his eyes off me. "You can all leave. But, since I'm sure Kee told you, the engagement is real to anyone else and don't spread the news until PR does. See yourselves out."

"Whatever," I grumbled and went to unpack a box with a purple lamp in it.

"No." Dex pointed at it.

I intentionally set it down hard on the dresser. "It looks beautiful here."

"Beautiful? I had interior designers from around the world come in to decorate this place. You're going to drive me insane moving everything around."

Olive and Pink waved from behind Dex then abandoned me, leaving me with the two Hardy brothers. They stood there bickering over me, and I tried my best not to have a moment of *déjà vu*. They were bigger now but still argued like boys, and I stood there like a girl totally enamored with both of them in different ways. Dimitri would protect me always, and Dex would push all my buttons to see me spiral into oblivion with him.

"Exactly. She will drive you insane," Dimitri emphasized. "It's why I didn't tell you to have her move in with you. I didn't even tell you to get engaged. I wanted you two to work things out, not blow things up."

"Trinity required her to have a prominent partner and be seen with him. And Keelani signed without a single protest, I guess." He rolled his eyes, showing he didn't agree with me just signing things either.

I popped a hip out now to interject. "Do you think I don't have a backbone or something?"

"Not with them." Dex shrugged and then looked me up and down. "Would you disagree?"

"Don't say that shit to her." Dimitri shoved Dex, and Dex looked down at his chest where Dimitri's hands had just been and smiled. No dimples this time. Just teeth that he ran his tongue over.

"You want to fight this fight now?" He cracked his neck, and that's when I knew things were getting out of hand.

"There's no fight to fight. What's wrong with you two?" I shook my head and stood between them, still with my hands holding my bralette up. "I have rehearsal tomorrow. We need to prep my wardrobe, and I have voice lessons. So, this is fine. Everyone's fine. Let's all just be fine." Both brothers stared at each other over my head. So I stomped a foot. "Knock it off."

"This is a bad idea," Dimitri stated one last time.

"We'll make note of your opinion," Dex retorted.

Dimitri took a deep breath and then his light-green eyes were on me. "You good?"

I nodded and patted his chest. "It'll be fine, promise. Now help me out of this top." I tried to be lighthearted as I lifted my hair so he could untie the pleather crisscrossing of the bralette.

His hands unthreaded the strings while he said, "Sure."

But Dex stepped up behind me. "I'll take care of undressing my fiancée."

"Dex—" I sighed.

"You gotta be kidding me," Dimitri grumbled. Yet, his hands were already pulling away from my back like he knew that was a line his brother wouldn't allow to be crossed. "Let's get one thing straight right now, brother. You're not going to make rules about Kee and me. You lost that privilege."

"Did I? Interesting. It seems the title of fiancée—"

"Doesn't mean shit when it's only for appearances," Dimitri finished for him.

"She's still my fiancée." Dex said it like it was a clean-cut statement, no argument for anything else.

"Fake fiancée," I corrected and sighed. He had to realize his brother was protecting me. And then I leaned my head on Dimitri's shoulder. "D will always be my best friend, Dex."

Dimitri kissed my forehead and sighed. "If we all come out of this alive, you both owe me a damn dinner."

Dex cracked his knuckles. "Let us get through it then."

Dimitri stared at him before looking back at me. I shrugged because, honestly, it was just another thing I needed to add to the list to get through in my life.

"You're a masochist. Or a genius. Or both, Keelani." He squeezed me before he let me go and murmured, "Call me if you need me."

I replied back, "Always when, never if."

"She won't need you," Dex announced.

"She most definitely will. It's why I'll be here the whole six months, Dex. Watching to make sure you don't fuck this up." Then, he said, "You hurt my best friend, I break your face, Dex, even if you are my brother."

"Wouldn't have it any other way, Dimitri," Dex said, but he was staring at me now, a look I couldn't quite read on his face.

I guess it was a sibling bond. I was an only child, so I didn't quite understand it. It was like they needed to get it out of their systems and draw the proper lines.

Dimitri clapped him on the shoulder and then kissed my cheek. With that, my best friend left his brother and me standing alone.

"I'm going to ask this once, and I know I shouldn't. Did you have something with my brother?"

CHAPTER 17: DEX

The question about her past relationships shouldn't have mattered, and I shouldn't have asked it. Yet, it literally took everything in me not to sock my brother in the face for kissing her forehead in front of me after he'd offered to undress her.

"You're a dumbass, you know that?" she said with a face of disgust.

It was a fair assessment. I felt disgusted with myself, not only for the question but for the jealousy. "Do you intend to answer the question?"

"I mean, you want to know if I've kissed him? Because you know good and well I never fucked him."

"*Did* you kiss him?" My blood was starting to boil.

"So what if I did?" She shrugged and then turned around. "Help me get out of this bralette since you're so ridiculously territorial you won't even let your brother do it. As if he hasn't seen me naked already."

I practically choked on my own saliva as I tried to work through her confession. I grabbed at the string, but it tangled more as I cinched it this way and that. "Why the hell has he seen you naked?"

"Dex, literally most of the nation has seen me naked. I've posed for Vogue naked. Don't get me wrong, it was classy but it happened. And Dimitri has taken me to model shoots and sat there working through some of them. I don't know what he does on his computer."

"Probably nothing because he's staring at you," I grumbled.

And then she wheezed because I pulled the string the wrong way. "Oh my God. You're done helping with this. And we're done talking about this." She tried to take over the strings.

I shoved her hand away. "Who else has seen you naked?"

"Do you even hear yourself?"

"I do. I sound deranged." At least I was admitting it out loud.

"Exactly." She turned and smiled at me. "You sound like a man who cares."

"And I shouldn't." I took in a deep breath, and she nodded. We were aiming for the same goal.

"It's okay. I was jealous of your girlfriend last night too." She chewed her cheek. "We need to work through that."

"Want to work through some of it now?" I asked, looking down at the strings. I unthreaded them with purpose, and the scrap of clothing finally loosened enough that she could get it off.

She glanced over her smooth shoulder and licked her lips. She knew exactly what I meant by that statement, and my cock hardened just staring at her. Keelani wasn't only beautiful. She stood in my room half naked, and it made my damn knees weak with how fast and hard her appearance in the light of day struck me. She was fuller in the hips and breasts than I remembered, but her skin had stayed perfectly sun-kissed. Every curve of hers was mouthwatering, every facial expression distracting, and every movement mesmerizing. Whatever God was up there had blessed her and cursed and condemned me with the sight of her.

"I don't think screwing around is going to help us, Dex," she murmured.

"It's the one thing that helps me always."

"Right." She gulped, and her eyes seemed so innocent as she asked me, "How?"

"How what?"

"How does it help you?" I saw the blush rising to her cheeks. And then she cleared her throat. "I haven't... Well, I haven't experienced any of this before."

Jesus, I wanted to corrupt the fuck out of her. I wanted to be the one to stain the blank canvas that she was, make her my own and only mine. It wasn't healthy though. "I'm aware you haven't," I ground out.

"So, well, maybe you could help me." She offered up the idea like it was a good one.

"Help you how?" I asked even though I shouldn't have. I should have left the room right then, backed away from her and saved my sanity.

"Well, I don't know. I'm trying to... I want to change. I've been this person who hasn't done a thing, Dex. I've been doing what the record label wants me to for years. I was a freaking virgin. And what if I can find out who I am and experience all this while I rebrand. Become who I want to be with you helping me. You could...teach me."

"Teach you?"

She sighed and shrugged her tiny shoulders before walking over to her rolling wardrobe rack and pulled at some of the fabric with one hand while the other held up her bralette. "I'm inexperienced, Dex. If I could figure out who I am—"

She might not have been saying it outright, but I was going to end the idea right then and there. "We're definitely not maturing you so you can sell fucking sex with a rebrand and the type of voice you have," I ground out. She could have done that for sure with the rasp in her voice. She always had a rawness underneath all the bubbly music she sang. "You have more to give the world than that."

"You think? I seem to recall you saying I am what I've been faking to be."

"You couldn't hide the gift of your voice under anything pretend, Kee. When you sang down in that garden to me, you came alive. I fell in love with..."

"With what?" she whispered.

The words clogged in my throat. The heartbreak and pain of losing her, seeing her here, remembering what we'd been and what we'd lost all stopped me from speaking the words.

I cleared my throat. "It doesn't matter. The past between us can't matter. Just keep the damn room," I said, stepping back and away from her, away from the honesty between us.

"But Dex—"

"And if you want me to teach you something, learn something about me first. I'm not here to help you any more than I already have. I don't want to help you at all." My voice held finality, and I walked away like I didn't care.

I wanted to not care. I needed to try. I'd try everything to rid myself of her.

CHAPTER 18: KEELANI

He wasn't giving me a compliment, but it felt like one. Dex was being honest.

I went to bed that night in a new place with Dex's smell all around me even though he wasn't there.

He wasn't there in the morning, either.

Our first night together was a sort of haunting fluke I knew I'd have to get over. Yet my body still ached in places it hadn't before, and it was because of him.

He left me a text early the next morning—at 6 a.m. to be exact—like that was a normal time to be up.

> **Dex: You have a HEAT watch programmed on your nightstand for accessing most areas of the resort, including the penthouse. Use it.**

> **Dex: Also, Penelope can cater in your dinners if you want. Send her any dietary restrictions.**

It was already quite apparent he wouldn't be eating with me, but his text drew an even bolder line.

> **Me: I have it handled.**

I went to my rehearsals that day. I worked with my techs. I kept busy.

That night, I called Olive and ate at a resort restaurant with her, too nervous to sit around the penthouse waiting for him. Still, I was home early enough that night to see him working in his office, and although I was sure he heard me too, we didn't talk. I holed up in my bedroom and read through a whole romance novel because I couldn't sleep, knowing he was just a room away.

For the rest of the week, I felt my anxiety build. I had a team there now—backup singers, bandmates, dancers. The management was present, and Dimitri stopped by with Bane to confirm everything was working the way it should.

"Dex check the security for the theater?" Dimitri asked. I said I didn't know. Olive said she'd discussed it with my management team.

So many people helping to run the show allowed for Dex and I to not communicate at all if we didn't want to. And I didn't think he did. He'd agreed to this sham of an engagement, but that was all it was to him. Yet having him so near without any words exchanged felt wrong, foreign, and uncomfortable.

Mitchell called to talk about my next album, told me I should talk with Dex about looking over our contracts too. "He saw the addendum regarding you associating yourself with a prominent individual. You know, regarding the engagement. So, that's all he needs to see, don't you think? Him seeing your past contracts with us or the one you have for the next six months really isn't necessary. He shouldn't ask for that."

But of course Dex had, because he was organized, efficient, and structured. I had started to notice he was gone every morning and then home at night in his office working. At the same exact time every day.

I was surprised when the night before, he wasn't home in his office typing away when I arrived. So, I took my time getting ready for bed, waiting to hear the door open, waiting to just feel his presence. I meandered around and realized his penthouse suite was very organized. His food was in compartments in the fridge, his toiletries lined up in the bathroom perfectly like his closet had been.

That night, I wondered where he could be that he would have gone off his structured schedule, and then I told myself I didn't have a right to know. He lived a neat life where everything had a place, and he wouldn't mess it up with a contract he didn't know anything about.

Unless I pushed for it.

"Everything's going to be changing anyway. Let's leave the past in the past," Mitchell summed up.

I sighed. I wanted that too. I didn't want Dex to know why I'd given him up. My father had squandered so much of our money, and I'd never been strong enough to tell him how much that hurt, that he needed to find help for his gambling problem, that he was hurting the whole family. How do you tell the parent you always wanted to make proud that they weren't making you proud?

How did you stand up for yourself when all you wanted to do was stand with them?

I wasn't only ashamed though that I hadn't stood up to my father, I was ashamed that I hadn't handled my family's situation. My father reminded me time and time again that we kept our family issues private, that he didn't need any help with finances, that we could handle this ourselves.

I continued to believe him. Or just hold on to hope that

I could and would figure out how to take care of them on my own.

Dex didn't need to know anything else about it.

No one did. "I'll make sure we leave the past in the past, Mitchell."

"Should we start looking over the contract for next year? Ezekiel stopped by and he's got a great offer—"

"Not today." And not ever. This was the last time I signed away my brand to anyone, but I'd hold off telling him I wasn't resigning. "Let's not bring attention to that with Dex right now. I don't want him being a part of that. Do you?"

"No. No. Of course not." Mitchell was quick to rethink it.

I ended the call with a new mission of keeping the contracts from Dex and more determination to make my career work without Trinity Enterprises.

Swimming out in open water on my own was frightening, like I'd drown and potentially take my father and mother with me. It was easier to feel invincible on my own. Yet, when I considered my family, the idea of professionally failing, drowning, or dying was much more impactful.

So, I worked hard that week, and as I finished up a vocal lesson late one evening, I looked over at Olive to ask if she wanted to eat at one of the resort's restaurants again and have a drink too. "It's late, but I'm feeling like I need to do something."

Or I just needed to not be in that penthouse with him, knowing he was on the other side of a door working and not talking to me.

She looked up from her laptop where she was answering my emails and said, "God yes. Absolutely. Let's eat at the Italian restaurant tonight."

Dex: Press release is in two weeks.
You have a PA I should inform?

Wow. Not a "hi," "how are you," or a "was your rehearsal good?" That was fine. I didn't need it from him. I never had before, and I wouldn't expect it now.

Me: Send everything to Olive. Here's her contact info.

Dex: Great. Are you eating out?

I looked at the time and realized it was about an hour after I'd normally have walked in the door. I rolled my eyes. He didn't care to be around me but wanted to know where I was? We hadn't talked all week, and I sort of hated living in his space where the ghost of him was all around me. What was the point?

Me: I'm eating at the restaurant downstairs.

Then, I took a deep breath and tried to extend an olive branch by inviting him. Why couldn't we talk and at least try to be cordial during all this?

Me: Want to come eat?

Dex: Not particularly. There are four restaurants down there. Which one are you at?

He brushed off my invitation so easily that I put my phone away without responding to avoid feeling hurt. Yet, when I tried to pay for dinner later that night, the waitress handed back my card. "Sorry. Mr. Hardy has it covered."

"Wait. What?" I eyeballed the blonde woman who stood there in an all-black dress with a tight smile on her face.

"I can't take your card here. Mr. Dex Hardy said you shouldn't be paying for anything within the resort."

"Oh, really?" I narrowed my eyes at her.

Olive squinted at her glass for half a second before she said, "We probably want another glass of champagne, then."

"I have an extra rehearsal tomorrow, Olive," I snickered.

"Oh, right," She agreed with me. Yet, I suddenly felt infuriated that he'd avoided me all week just to text me, brush me off again, but then take the time to make sure my meal was paid for.

Who did he really think he was anyway?

"We'd like a whole bottle of champagne. The most expensive bottle you have." I added, feeling a bit liberated now. It would serve him right for declining me when I was just trying to be nice.

The waitress didn't even hesitate to rush off for it.

Olive laughed before saying, "Well, a bottle will be nice considering we have to get through all rehearsals with Frankie. We're going to need all that champagne." She curled her lip because Olive hated my creative director about as much as I did.

"You're a great personal assistant." I nodded and assessed her jokingly. "Really helping me propel my career with Trinity by drinking down here with me."

She smiled because even if I was joking, she had to know I

meant it. "Honestly, if it wasn't for my college classes and your residency, I'd say we drink through your whole damn contract."

I couldn't help the giggle that bubbled out of me. "'A Drunken Keelani Nuclear Bombs Her Career.'"

"Wouldn't be the first childhood star to spiral and want out." She shrugged. "At least we'd get you out of your hell."

I sighed. "But then we'd have launched your PR career off a cliff."

She looked down at her nails. "I'd find other clients. Once I finish this master's program, hopefully, I'll get more." Olive was younger than me and working on her master's degree in journalism or media management. I couldn't remember at this point because she'd jumped around one too many times from major to major. All I knew was I'd met her at a party a few years ago and she'd been kind enough to help fix my hair, saying she went to beauty school for a year too.

I asked her to do my hair again the next night, and the rest was history. "Did I tell you that Mitchell and Ezekiel are pushing for another contract?"

"And you're saying no. Jesus. *Ezekiel.*" She shivered. "I don't know how you deal with that weasely creep."

She had no idea. None of my friends knew. Sometimes, being a friend meant shielding your friends from the pain your life could inflict on them.

"He's not around much." I glanced up and grabbed the bottle the waitress had just brought. I poured us both a generous helping of the bubbly champagne. "Anyway, I'm holding him off as long as possible. So, cheers to that, and cheers to us being here on their dime for six months."

She clinked her glass and drank a healthy gulp. "Technically it's your dime, Keelani. You've paid your dues ten times over to that record label. And I know you fought for me to come with."

I hadn't told Olive, but I was sure she'd gotten wind of how I insisted on bringing my own personal assistant. The fact that the record label tried to control even who was around me, including my closest friends, infuriated me. Yet, I tried my best not to become bitter about it.

Instead, I wiggled in my little black dress that I'd thrown on before we came out. The fabric was thin, but it bunched up when I sat and exposed much more of my leg than I wanted to. I pushed it down one last time and glanced around to make sure no one had seen how it rode up.

"Kee, we're in a HEAT resort, remember?" Olive lifted a brow. "You don't have to worry about paps. They need a pass."

People paid hundreds of thousands to become a part of the HEAT's exclusive empire. Everyone here wasn't as concerned about my status, and somehow that made me breathe a bit easier. Even still. "Yeah, I don't know. Should we leave?"

"We're sitting in the corner of the restaurant in a very secure resort." My friend grabbed my hand and squeezed it like she could steal away a bit of my anxiety. "Breathe, girl. We're good here."

"So, you want to stay out?" I still worried for her safety or anyone's with me even more so than my own. We'd been bombarded a time or two before. "We could go back up to the suite if you want?"

"The penthouse with Dex?" She chuckled and then shook her head. "No thanks."

My phone buzzed right then, and I murmured for her to give me a minute while I stared at the text that had come in.

Dex: When will you be home?

156

Was he serious? I frowned and then glared at the screen. Like he should care.

> **Me: I don't know. Does it matter? You weren't home last night when I went to sleep.**

> **Dex: You could have texted me.**

> **Me: I didn't see the need to.**

> **Dex: Where are you?**

> **Me: I'm enjoying the company of my friends.**

> **Dex: Are you with my brother?**

> **Me: Seriously? Your jealousy is showing for literally no reason.**

> **Dex: It'll show more if you don't answer the question.**

> **Me: You know we're not really engaged. I don't answer to you.**

> **Dex: Kee, I'm not in the mood today. I had a long day at work. Answer me.**

> **Me: Go to sleep and stop worrying about your fake fiancée.**

Dex: Won't feel fake when I punish you for being out with my brother.

Dex: Tell me when you're going to be home. We need to discuss the press release.

I growled at my phone, at how he thought he could command something from me so easily, how he thought this was about the press.

"Trouble in paradise?"

"He's such an ass," I grumbled.

"Dex is texting you?" she inquired, but I was too busy to think about her questions as I silenced my phone, consciously and deliberately not responding back.

"He thinks I'm at his damn beck-and-call because he agreed to this with me. And yet he hasn't been around ever since we—" I stopped myself. I hadn't told a soul about us sleeping together.

Olive's honey-colored eyes widened. "Ever since you what?"

"Nothing."

"You're blushing." She pointed to my cheeks. "Did you— Are you still—?"

"Don't talk about it!" I shook my head at her. And then I knew—because she was such a close friend and I needed someone to confide in—that I was going to blurt out everything. So, I said, "If we talk about this—"

"Oh my fucking God, you lost your virginity to Dex Hardy and you didn't tell me. Spill it right now."

So, we drank champagne. Too much. And I told her all about that night.

"He's still in love with you."

"If that's true, why isn't he taking the opportunity to sleep with me and teach me everything he knows?"

"Because he's protecting you from yourself." She threw up her hands when I squinted in confusion. "Hello. He said he wouldn't help you turn into a sex symbol, that your voice was better than that."

I rolled my eyes. "It's not what he meant." And why did that make my heart ache? "Anyway, he barely talks to me. It's just us figuring out how to exorcise each other, I think."

"If you say so," she singsonged. "Let's get you back to your suite."

I'd lost the concern I normally had when it came to people watching me. I'd had too much champagne and let go of my worries since I was with my friend. We giggled all the way up to the penthouse, and she squealed when I swiped my watch into the elevator.

"Fancy."

"Silly." I shrugged.

"Honestly, it's probably necessary. You're both big names. Take the privacy and enjoy it." She nudged me and then wrapped her arm around my waist. "I'm happy we got here, Kee. This is going to be good for you."

Somehow, even if Olive didn't know everything, she knew enough to know a weight was lifting from me. "Yeah, I think so."

"You might not share everything with me, but I know you're struggling. You're strong enough to get through it. You got this. Don't let anyone tell you you're not strong enough. They don't know the strength of a woman."

I tried not to turn into a blubbering mess as I hugged her.

"I'll see you tomorrow."

I waved her on and was about to use my fingerprint to let myself into the penthouse but the door swung open before I even tried.

"You intend not to answer your fiancé when he texts you about when you're going to be home?"

CHAPTER 19: DEX

She'd been gone for hours. I knew she'd gone to dinner with friends. Or at least that's what she'd said. How people were supposed to blindly trust the person they were with was beyond me. Funny thing was, I'd never cared before.

I only did with her.

And I knew I was spiraling, because I'd considered calling every restaurant of mine to see which one she was at. I'd already informed them all that she wasn't to be paying for anything but now I wanted them to keep damn tabs on her? I hated to feel my control slipping, hated that I wanted to pull up the damn cameras and check. And I'd almost done so more than once. Instead, I'd been mature. I'd texted. Then, I'd threatened.

And she'd ignored me.

Thankfully, I got an alert for her spending over ten thousand dollars on my tab at one restaurant and I knew then where she was. It still didn't stop me from watching the hallway cameras while waiting for her ass to show.

It had taken hours.

"Have you been waiting up for me?" She stepped past me in her little black dress. The fabric was so thin I could see her nipples raised underneath it immediately. When I followed her to the kitchen where she set down her little clutch, her ass swayed so fluidly. It was like she didn't have a damn dress on at all.

"I was working."

She hummed and bent at the waist so she could put her elbow on the counter and rest her chin in her hand while she stared at me. "Do you work literally twenty-four-seven?" Her eyes sparkled with a hazy glaze, and I knew from how she questioned me, she'd drunk more than enough.

"A Vegas resort and casino won't run itself," I reminded her. "I can't go around mingling with friends every night. I need to make sure HEAT members feel safe and secure. Guessing you did if you were out there drinking fifty thousand dollars' worth of booze, right?"

Her eyes widened. "Fifty thousand? What? There's absolutely no way. We need to go down to the restaurant right now."

She turned toward the door but I stopped her. "What were you drinking?"

She spun back around. "Well, I just said the most expensive bottle..." Her eyes narrowed on me now. "Do not tell me you have bottles worth over fifty thousand dollars here, Dex. Do not."

"Of course I do."

"That's ridiculous!" She threw up her hands theatrically, wobbling on her heels. Then, she crossed her arms over her chest and bit her lip before she started giggling. "Well, I'd say sorry but it's your fault for having such a ridiculously priced bottle in your restaurant."

Her giggle turned to a laugh and I had to stop myself from joining in. She was obviously tipsy and felt liberated enough to give me some of that snark she used to always have with me long ago. "We have important guests here—"

"Not that important." She took a deep breath and tried to sober, wiping tears from her eyes from her laughing fit. "Fine.

Maybe you do have important guests. Should I apologize for drinking their bubbly? As for the bill, you can take it out of my salary if you need it."

"Need it?" Who the hell did she think I was? Did she even get why I was upset? "You think I need fifty thousand? Jesus, it's not expensive for me and who is a more important guest than my fiancée? Spend what you want. I don't give a shit. But I do give a shit when you don't text me back."

I saw how she straightened her spine. "Well, I was too busy having fun while you were too busy to come down because you needed to work all night to keep us safe, I guess."

"And did you feel safe?" I don't know why I even cared to ask at this point.

She squinted at me, like this was some sort of quiz. "I felt somewhat safe."

It wasn't what I wanted to hear. I wanted praise and trust like I would have gotten from her fifteen years ago. "You do realize people have to scan IDs just to walk the premises, right?"

She shrugged like it was nothing.

"The camera system has facial recognition embedded, a software I patented, just to be able to play the slots."

"I played the penny slots the other night."

"You think your face isn't in my system?" I scoffed. "It's been in my system since the damn moment I built it."

"Why?" she whispered.

"Because, Kee, if you were going to walk into one of my resorts or my buildings, I was going to be informed, but they weren't going to stop you. They would have left that job to me."

She rolled her eyes and her whole body swayed with the movement. "Of course you built a system just to make sure you could spite me. How does it feel holding on to that hate from so long ago?"

"Feels like I'm moving toward getting over it." I didn't offer more because I was sure I wasn't moving in the right direction.

"Well." She waved off the tension between us and straightened so she wasn't leaning against the counter anymore. "With you saying all that, I guess I feel a little safer in your resort then."

"Then I have more work to do because 'a little' isn't good enough."

"That's my—" She stopped like she was working through her tipsy haze to tell me something. "I get paranoid sometimes, you know? That has nothing to do with you."

I'd already seen her the other night in the hallway checking her surroundings. "Want to explain that further?"

"Your hotel is secure." Her eyes drifted to stare out the window at the city. "You have it all figured out, I'm sure."

I wanted to think so, but Bane and I were dealing with glitches that shouldn't have been happening, and they were too coincidental—which meant they weren't coincidental at all. I rubbed at my temples because the day had been much too long already. "What I don't have figured out is how you'd like to release the statement of us together. It's why I texted you tonight."

"Of course there's no other reason you'd have texted," she grumbled, and her bottom lip pouted out.

"Should there be another reason?" I had a million reasons. I'd flipped through them all mentally before I'd landed on that one for texting her tonight.

I wanted her home at the time she'd come home every night this week, I'd made a mental note she should be walking through the door then. I didn't want her with anyone else but me. She was my fiancée, and my fiancée should be having dinner with me. None of them were logical, considering she wasn't really mine anymore.

"Nope. We need to think through the media angle, sure, but it's probably best for the PR teams to handle it." She seemed resigned to it.

"It's your brand." He lifted a brow. "You don't want a say?"

"Dex, normally what I say is passed over by layers and layers of public relations and—"

"I'm asking you now. What do you want the statement to be? How would you like us to be seen?"

"You want me to make the choice? We're not capable of running the data points on how it will be received and—"

Normally, I'd agree with her. It was a systematic good marketing approach, but suddenly my ass was willing to veer in a different direction just to hear her opinion. "What data points are needed when you get what you want?"

"Dex, as much as most girls would love to go wave around an engagement ring from a Hardy brother..." She glanced over at the nightstand where the box still sat. "Not that it's the one I want." She giggled with her declaration and then clapped a hand over her mouth. "Sorry."

"You don't like your engagement ring?"

"I drank too much. I'm just being ridiculous. The ring is beautiful."

"But it's not you." I knew that. I'd told Penelope to go out and get the gaudiest piece of jewelry for this reason.

"I have picky taste."

She didn't. I knew what her preference would be had this been real. "You probably want purple stones around the diamond. The wedding band would be solid gold because I know you hate flashy, gaudy things. You'd probably barely wear the other even if it was your favorite."

The smile that spread across her face was lazy and genuine, relaxed. We were back to us for a second as she said, "Ah, my Dex Hardy is still in there. The guy who knows every single thing about me."

"Unfortunately," I grumbled.

She blinked once and then twice before she nodded and glanced away. I was creating the barrier between us, and I knew that. I had to, or I'd be lost to her again. She'd inevitably follow the fame. I'd be thoroughly destroyed. It wasn't a cycle I would repeat.

"Right." She took a deep breath. "The media needs a story, and they need to see we're in love, that we're engaged, and that my music has changed because we've grown and matured together—"

"That statement seems perfect," I cut her off. "Let the PR teams do with it what they will. They can release it in a week or two."

Kee frowned and then paced the living room in her high heels. "Do you just do all this"—she waved out at the city—"and not think about the blowback or the repercussions? How they'll spin it for the next few months? If something doesn't work, how we'll navigate it?"

I crossed my arms over my chest and watched her wear down the carpet. Her legs were so damn long, and the dress bunched higher and higher with every stride she took. And she'd been out with my brother, having fun, talking, letting him learn more about her when I knew nothing about who she was now. Letting him watch her in that damn dress.

"I consider what's necessary, like the security of this resort.

I don't care what they write in the papers, and the press having a field day isn't part of my job."

"Well, this isn't about security. It's about presenting a mirage to my fans and hoping they believe it."

"It's not a mirage if it's true. You've changed. You want your real sound out there."

"We're not true, though!" She threw up her hands and then placed them on her hips as she stopped to stare at me. "We aren't engaged, and no one has seen us together. We can't act in love. You barely talk to me except, well..."

"Except when?" I wanted to hear her say it.

The pink blush on her cheeks turned almost red before she lifted her chin. Then she stepped up to the plate I'd baited her to. "Except for the other night when we slept together. This is going to be a disaster. It's not like we're doing that anymore. Obviously. You don't even eat dinner with me!"

"I don't need to eat dinner with you to fuck you, heartbreaker. We both know that."

"You do if you think you have a chance of fucking me." She turned and started to walk without her stride even faltering. She was ready to fight fire with fire now.

"If that's the case, you should have asked me to come home."

She whirled to face me and continued pacing right up to me to glare into my eyes. "Why? So you can work through your emotions and muddle mine? So you can wrap up the ends of our past into a neat bow and throw it away while my career and life unravel in the process?"

Her breath came fast, and her eyes looked wild, like she was barreling toward a disaster and didn't know how to stop. Kee was scared, probably about as scared as I was.

"Your career and life aren't my problem," I blurted out as I processed everything else. It was the wrong thing to say. It was a knee-jerk reaction to how I'd compartmentalized her over the years, how I'd compartmentalized everything.

She nodded and combed a tiny hand through her hair before she stormed off to her bedroom. Well, my bedroom.

Fuck.

I went after her and found her in there untying the back of her dress with jerky movements and a blotchy face. I knew she'd wiped the tears away, and I didn't know if I should apologize right then or act as if I didn't see them. I stepped up behind her and murmured, "You and these damn strings for tops. Let me help you."

"I don't need help," she grumbled as she looked in the long mirror to the left of my closet. I'd stood there so many times on my own, straightening a tie, looking at myself, or looking at me and another woman.

Most days, I didn't feel a damn thing when I stood there. With her, that feeling of missing someone and them coming back walloped me hard enough that the tears probably should have been in my eyes too. "I'm not used to having someone else in my life, Kee."

I let my fingers thread around the string and brushed them over her back. She gasped, and I saw the goose bumps form immediately on her skin. Still, she responded, "You had a girlfriend for two years."

I loosely played with the strings rather than untying them and watched how her lips parted at my touch, watched how her nipples tightened. "I told you, my ex wasn't so much of a girlfriend as she was a plaything. Our commitment to each other never spanned a certain amount of time, and she didn't expect anything from me. I don't help people for no reason. It's not who I am."

Kee gulped and murmured, "I'm as good as your plaything now. You getting over me is essentially fucking me out of your system, correct?"

Her words grated me in the wrong way, made me out to be the monster and not the victim when she'd actually left me to rot first. "You sound so against it now when you were on board the other night, Kee. You enjoyed it."

Chewing at her cheek, I saw the ideas running through her head. "I guess we can both benefit from it. Like I said, I need more experience for—"

"I'm not helping you sell our sexual experience—"

"It's not just sex. It's just...living. I haven't lived, Dex. I do whatever they want me to. It's my experience that I'll be writing about. My heart, my soul. You're essentially teaching me how to tap into it. Plus, we'll be all over each other for the cameras anyway."

Fuck the cameras.

That's what I wanted to say but she leaned back into me then. My cock rubbed against her and I strained to find some damn control. I'd been hard for her for days now, trying to avoid the inevitable of wanting her again so soon after taking her virginity.

She turned suddenly and looked at me with those vivid violet eyes. Then, she pushed her dress down to her hips, letting her breasts spill out. "So teach me."

"Fuck me," I whispered out as I stared at her standing next to my bed. "Kee..."

"Don't make me beg."

"You've had way too much to drink tonight."

"I'm practically sober. I'll beg if you want."

She stepped closer to me, but I took a step back. "Jesus, I want to say you should beg, Kee. But it's not the time."

"I do deserve it," she murmured. Then she grabbed my wrist and brought it to her cheek. "You had me once." She took a step closer and dragged my hand down to her collarbone, to her chest, down, down, down to the peak of her breast. I indulged because I couldn't stop myself. I was lost to the feeling of her soft skin. She whimpered as I circled her nipple with my thumb and her hands went to grip my shirt. "Have me again."

I shook my head. "I'm doing too many favors and not getting any in return."

"What do you want in return?" she whispered, and my cock jumped in my trousers.

"You know, a couple nights ago, I should have been yelling at you for taking over my room and letting my brother practically undress you. Tonight, I still can't believe you went and hung out with him." I was almost hypnotized by her, admitting all I was frustrated with.

She pulled me closer, and her eyes were hooded. "Does it bother you that I was out with my friends instead of being in bed with you?"

I didn't answer her right away.

"Punish me for it. Show me what you'd do to me. I want it, Dex."

I dipped a finger into the dress that was bunched at her waist to pull her close so she could feel what she did to me. "You wear underwear with this flimsy of a dress?"

"Check and see." Her breath came faster now. She was pouring gasoline on my already brittle and dry reserves, goading me. It was like she lit and threw the match.

"Knowing you, probably not." I bunched up the fabric and saw I was right. Her pussy was bare and dripping arousal down her thigh. "Kee, you can't even be a good fiancée for our very first week together?"

Chastising her was like stoking the flames that were already burning. She whispered out, "I don't want to be good."

I already knew that about her. She wanted to be free, and being free didn't consider good or bad. Being free meant you weren't worrying about any of the moralities.

I brushed my finger over her sex and told her, "This is my bedroom."

"You sure?" She shook her head. "It's filled with all my things. It's mine."

"How do you intend to live in harmony with me if you can't take one step in the right direction away from taunting me?"

"You need a little disruption in your perfect life anyway." She whimpered and bucked her hips over my hand while I worked her slow. This wasn't a gift of pleasure to her. She'd learn that pleasure could be pain, could be frustrating, could be downright infuriating.

Her pussy coated my knuckles as I rubbed them slowly over her clit then over her entrance, not giving her what she wanted. "You being in my home is disruption enough. You being here, drunk, begging for me is pushing the limit of what I'm capable of enduring."

"It's what you wanted. You asked me to live here. Demanded it."

"I don't want you here. I *need* you here. There's a difference."

"What's the difference, then? What do you need me for?"

"So I can get you out of my system forever once and for

all." I only answered one question but not the other. Then, I pulled my hand away and said, "Take your dress off."

"But you're fully clothed still," she pouted.

"Baby, I'm making you feel good right now. I don't need my clothes off for it."

She glanced at my cock. "How is that helping you work out your need for me? Don't you want to screw until you've had enough of me?"

"I fucked the virginity out of you already, heartbreaker. Now, I want to hear you scream my name over and over. It turns me on. Take your dress off and lie on the bed."

First, she licked her lips and stared at me as she slipped the dress off. Then, she murmured, "You take your shirt off too?"

She'd tried last time to take my shirt off, but I'd avoided it. I hid what I knew she'd understand on my ribs from her now too. I'd told myself I'd get the tattoo redone over the years but never was able to bring myself to. I shook my head at her and said, "Get on the bed, first."

When she listened and scooted onto the bed slowly, I barely restrained myself from unbuckling my pants to fuck her sideways. "Hands against the headboard, babe."

"For what?"

"Brace for what it's going to feel like to have me between your legs. The man you left behind."

"Dex—"

I stepped over to the bottom of the bed and pushed her legs apart to see her pussy glistening, pink and swollen for me. "Make sure when I make you come, you yell your fiancé's name. Loud."

I didn't wait for her to tell me she would. I was confident enough to know that our bodies worked well together. She'd scream for me and only me. I tasted the salty-sweet mix of her arousal and groaned into her pussy. I loved how she shuddered, how her legs instantly clamped around my ears like she was going to hold me hostage all night.

I sucked on her clit and felt how it swelled in my mouth as she got closer and closer to coming undone. Even still, she kept her hands above her, pushing against the large wood posts of the headboard. I'd wanted a solid bed, one that could withstand the force of passion, and it had done well so far.

I had a feeling, though, these six months would put it to the test because Kee didn't just enjoy this, I could see she would crave it. I could tell in the way she leveraged against the headboard to push her sex down harder against my tongue. I loved hearing how wet she was as I lapped roughly at the most sensitive part of her. I gripped her ass cheeks and thrust my tongue in. I wanted to taste the parts of her no one else had. I wanted to live in the space no one else got to. I came up for air just to say, "This pussy is only going to want, isn't it?"

Her eyes were wild as she opened them in fury that I'd stopped. "Whatever, Dex. Just, please."

"Say it."

She whimpered, her head thrashing back and forth like she was jonesing for a release. I loved that her hair was sprawled out around her, making her look perfectly unraveled.

"Say you only want me, Kee. I need to hear it."

She practically growled as she repeated it back to me, and I dove in again to suck her clit while I thrust a finger slowly into her sex, testing if she could take anything firmer and longer than my tongue today. When I did, she moaned rather than winced. "Such a greedy pussy. Look how you want it even after being sore a couple days ago."

"Dexton Hardy, please. Just let me have this. Give me what I want."

"I should. Shouldn't I? Pretty girl like you in my bed. It's mine, you know that right? Even with your purple bedspread on it and with you inviting your friends into my bedroom, it's still mine."

"Fine. I don't care. Have the room. Just *please.*"

I slid another finger in and rolled her clit around in my mouth. "I like how you listen, Kee. It's what we need to make this relationship work."

"Faster, Dex. I need more. I need you."

Hearing her say she needed me after all these years was too much. "You don't need me. You only need something to take the edge off."

"No, I need you," she moaned.

"Do you know me, Kee? You don't even know what I like anymore."

"I know that. I want you to show me. Show me now. Show me everything."

My hand was already gripping her thigh too hard, showcasing I was losing control. We were only a week in, and I wasn't sure I could handle her, handle this.

"You want me, then you're going to see. And I don't know if you're going to like what you see at all."

She looked down at me, determination sparkling in her pretty eyes. "Show me."

CHAPTER 20: KEELANI

I'd regret this in the morning. I knew that. Yet, the alcohol had liberated me, and I wanted every inch of him right then and there. He needed to lose control like I needed to be free of being good.

He thought he could keep a lid on this. Screw me out of his system and leave, but I wanted to dig deep into our souls and find a way to exorcise each other from the hell we'd been trapped in over the years. He struggled with letting me in, but I saw the moment he surrendered to it. His shoulders relaxed, his grip on me loosened, and he stood up rather than continued to stroke my core.

"Wait," I stuttered out. This wasn't the exact plan. I still wanted to get off.

He turned toward his dresser, slowly opened it, and grabbed something from it before turning around with a smirk. "Be patient, Kee."

Then, he pulled from his drawer a silver egg with a thin chain attached. "What's that?"

"What I like." He said it simply, no embarrassment or hesitation.

"Exactly what do you like?"

"To indulge women." The words rolled slowly from his tongue as if he was giving me time to understand.

I narrowed my eyes, my stomach twisting. "Have you used that on someone else?"

He chuckled. "You're as jealous as I am. For that reason, I can honestly say with this one in particular, no. I haven't."

"Show me so I can feel it, Dex. Show me so I know." My eyes were on the small ball, my body humming with curiosity, and my pussy clenched like suddenly it needed to be filled. "I think I might like it."

There was desire and a plea in my voice. I couldn't hide it if I tried. I trusted him in a way I probably shouldn't, and I knew that this was what I wanted from him, needed from him.

"*Fuck me*," he murmured, and then he placed the ball back in the drawer and shook his head. "Kee, knowing you're so much more inexperienced is a mindfuck for me, you know that? I'd teach you everything, but I know you're going to take all that knowledge with you."

The words he didn't say echoed loud and clear in that room. *When we left each other.*

"So, let's do what we want *now*, then." I wasn't holding back. Not this time. I glanced over his body and murmured, "Why are you always dressed and I'm not?"

"You're learning. Not me." He pointed to his dresser where a large mirror hung behind it. "Get up and go put your hands on the dresser."

I scooted off the bed and walked slowly past him to do as he asked. He came to stand behind me, and I looked at how tall he was with his chest to my back. I was almost a whole head smaller than him but seemed to fit perfectly there. He wrapped his arm around my waist, and we took a step back together. Another. And another until my arms were mostly outstretched and I was bent at the waist the way he wanted me to be. My ass was on display for him. My legs flexed a bit as he pulled me up so I was on my tiptoes. He massaged my cheek and murmured,

"I like control, Keelani."

"So, control me." I breathed out once, then twice.

"I intended to before I knew you were a—"

"I'm not anymore." I knew he was going to say I was a virgin, but that didn't matter. Our past didn't matter now. I looked over my shoulder to glare at him. "You've fucked enough women, Dex. I'm sure of it. You can learn to treat me like the others you've been with."

"You're nothing like the others I've been with," he growled.

But I could be. Didn't he understand that? "Well, I want to be. I want to understand my sexuality, what I like and what I don't. I want to experience things I haven't, Dex. So, just... control me."

His jaw ticked as I looked at him through the mirror. "I'm not saying I want you like anyone else. Jesus, Kee. You're asking for a lot. A lot more than what I gave you the first time. You need to work up to—"

I didn't need any of that. I pushed my bare ass against his hard cock and rolled it. He growled at the sensation. "I need you to show me what it's like to crave something."

"You don't need that right now."

"If you won't, I'll ask someone else, Dex."

"You're my fiancée. You're not asking another man to do a thing to you."

"I'm your *fake* fiancée. I won't be seen with anyone else. But if we want to do stuff privately—"

His firm grip became bruising as he gritted his teeth to say, "You do anything privately or publicly with another man, and I'll make it my sole purpose in life to obliterate him."

I hummed and arched my back so we both saw every curve of my naked frame in that mirror. "If I can't learn from you, who will I learn from?" I wanted to push him, he had to know that.

"Open the top drawer," he growled out, and I felt the shift in his mood.

His eyes simmered with darkness as he caught mine in the mirror. I froze the second I pulled that top drawer open. I knew what would be in it. Still, my heart lodged in my throat. Lined in velvet were tools he used when he fucked women. A small whip, vibrators, anal beads, handcuffs, ropes.

He let me stare at it quietly as if he wanted me to take it in. "Now you see what I'm into?"

I was getting a better idea. I pushed him further. "This it?"

"Well, that black chair in the corner of the room is a sex chair. Made for fucking you at every angle possible," he told me, and suddenly I realized why he hadn't sat down on it with me the night I lost my virginity. "Now that you understand, you can close it, Kee." He rubbed my pussy again and slid one finger in. "I don't normally lose control in the bedroom. But I'm happy to make you lose control real quick. It's how I live my life now."

"Now?" I whimpered at how he slid another finger in and then moved them back and forth over an extremely sensitive spot. "What about before?"

"Before, I was a kid. Before, I made mistakes." He curled his fingers in me like he wanted me to stop talking about it, which I did because he was immediately easing my tension, immediately tapping into my libido instead.

"Close the drawer," he murmured against my ear. "I'll still make you feel good. But it's better if we go slow and—"

I didn't want to shy away from it. "You used these on other women?"

"Yes."

I gasped as his thumb grazed my clit. "With your ex?"

"Kee—"

I stared at that dresser drawer, too many emotions flowing through me as he pleasured me. My hands were white-knuckling the wood now, and I was panting even as I told him, "Get rid of anything you have in that drawer, Dex, if you used it with another woman." I shouldn't have been this jealous. Not this fast. Not with this much vehemence.

"Maybe you're even more jealous than I am."

"No. I'm holding myself to specific standards. I'm not sharing toys with other women. I don't want them here if I'm going to be here."

"We're not using toys," he ground out, and his nostrils flared.

"We are." I picked up the ball he told me he hadn't used on anyone. "Only ones that are mine, though."

"You know, if we even contemplate doing this, heartbreaker, you're not going to make the rules. I am."

"But you're going to listen to my requests?" I lifted a brow as I looked at him in the mirror and then rolled my pussy hard into his hand. "Because I'm going to have them."

"Jesus, you've always been a demanding little thing."

"No different than how bossy and controlling you are."

His jaw worked up and down as he stared at me in the mirror. But then he snatched the ball from my hand and ground out, "We're going to be the death of each other. I'm going to drag you to hell, Kee, and neither of us will be able to save the other from the fire."

I nodded and then whimpered as he took his time dragging that cool metal on my inner thigh. "Better with you than someone who doesn't understand."

"Understand what?" he asked as the metal met my center.

"I don't know, Dex. Understand this. Wanting and needing you and hating you for it." I was past the point of caring anymore how far we were taking things. I wanted to feel everything with him. I wanted our wounds ripped open.

He didn't respond to what I was saying. His gaze was on my pussy and how he worked it so slowly. Back and forth over my entrance again and again to the point that I bucked against him. "Patience, Kee."

One of my hands fisted against the dresser. "How do you use it on me? Just do it."

"I use it by letting you feel the metal first." He dragged it slowly to my clit then, and when he reached it, I gasped at the sensation. "Tell me how it feels."

I breathed in and out fast, unsure if I could handle something so new to me so soon after losing my innocence. My body vibrated, spiraling in a new direction.

"Tell me," he said again with a firmer tone this time.

"Like your piercing. Cold, heavy, powerful."

"Yes. Exactly." And then he took his time sliding it back toward my entrance and into me so that my walls clamped down around it. "You're so wet, heartbreaker, you're overflowing when I put it in you." The sound that vibrated through him traveled to me and rattled my bones, my heart. "Fuck, you're too perfect."

I wiggled at the new sensation of feeling something so cool and then how it warmed in my body but seemed to weigh my pussy down and cause an ache there, like I was nearing ecstasy but it was just out of reach.

"You feel how your body holds it, Kee? Like it wants to be fucked and full all the time." He pulled on the chain to reposition it, and I whimpered as I wiggled against his hand.

"I want you, Dex."

"Not now." He stepped back. "This is a good start. A good way for me to see if you're ready for more with me."

I narrowed my eyes at him. "I'm ready for anything."

"Then prove it." His eyes hardened, that green darkening like his soul was turning to stone. "Take a few days with this. See how you feel with that in. Maybe after a concert or two—"

I straightened away from the dresser then. When I did, even my breasts felt fuller, more weighted, and definitely more aroused. I was turned on to another level. "A concert? That's weeks away and..." Should I admit that my body literally wanted to beg for an orgasm now?

"If you can't handle it—"

"I'm capable of handling whatever you throw at me, Dex. People have underestimated me time and time again." The anger I felt at his words was amplified too.

And when our eyes met, the war between us was almost palpable. Hate and pain and love and brutality clashed there in that room.

"I never underestimated you, Kee. If anything, I overestimated what you could handle with me. I expected you to stay, remember?"

"I came back," I whispered out.

"It was too late." No man could peel away the layers that Dex did when he looked at me like he was at that moment. I couldn't hide from his gaze, couldn't stop the connection between us even if I wanted to. "And still, you're standing here, fucking beautiful as ever, and I might just fuck you if I don't leave. I might lose control. I need to know, when I do, that you'll be able to handle it. So, we'll see. Go to your mic checks tomorrow.

Go to rehearsals. Three hours a day. No more. See how you handle having that in you throughout. Cleaning supplies are in the drawer."

"And what? That's going to prove I can handle you?"

"It'll be a start." He rubbed at his chin and took a step back from me. He was always distancing us from each other. I knew it was self-preservation and him controlling every aspect of the situation, but I'd started to spiral.

I'd experienced things already so new and blindingly good that I couldn't understand how I'd let my record label do what they'd done for so long. "I'm going to prove myself, Dex. Prove to you that I'm exactly like I was but not at all who I used to be. I'm going to prove I can handle this venue, and I'm going to prove to everyone that I can make it singing my own songs."

"Heartbreaker, you think I'm doubting you?" He tilted his head.

"I know you are. But after we're done with this first step, you're doing what I want. And that means you're cleaning out the items you've used with other women. If you're going to be a jealous, possessive ass with me, you can expect it in return."

"*I'm* the jealous one?" he balked.

"I didn't go out with your brother tonight. I went out with Olive—and that was it. Maybe next time you should check your cameras if you want to be right." With that, I grabbed my clothes and walked into the bathroom, ball still clenched tight enough in me that I felt every stride I took. I felt his words too.

"Don't tempt me into watching your every move, Kee, because God knows I'd enjoy it." He slammed the door behind him, and I stood there thinking I was twisted in the head because I knew...

I'd enjoy it too.

CHAPTER 21: KEELANI

After my shower that night, I pulled the chain of the Ben Wa ball to get it out of me, fascinated that such a little thing that didn't move could have my body keyed up so much. The water drops from the shower were harder, the heat more intense, the way the water dripped down my body more sensual.

And because Dex had insinuated I couldn't handle the sensation, I tried to ignore it. Ignored the feeling of wanting to slide my hands between my legs, of wanting to indulge in not *his* shower, but mine.

Yet, even washing my hair felt erotic, rubbing the soap over my body had me gasping, and when I dragged my hand between my thighs, I whimpered.

The ball was powerful.

Or I was weak.

Somehow, just a small thing could shine light on all the big things wrong with me, how much I didn't know about myself, how much I avoided, how much I was letting pass me by. I immediately slipped the ball out of me, ran it under hot water at the sink, went to the stupid drawer he'd directed me to before he'd exited, and used the cleaning supplies in there.

He'd left me to look at the rest of the things, and my eyes drifted over the other gold Ben Wa balls. Vibrators. Beads. Handcuffs. Sex toys I didn't even know the names of. I didn't need to.

I slammed the drawer shut and closed my eyes as I breathed

in deep.

How many were in here? How many had he enjoyed while I thought of him? It made me want to be reckless, want to cause him pain, want to retaliate. Didn't he know we'd belonged to each other over the years, even if we hadn't? Had he hated me that much?

And did he think another woman would be as connected to him as me? That question hurt the most. He'd saved my life. He'd been in that car and told me he had me. It may have changed every part of our lives, but he'd also imprinted himself on my heart.

In the deep recesses of my mind, Dex was still mine. And if I had to be his, he'd need to know what that meant.

I ripped the drawer back open and yanked at the velvet lining until it tore from the drawer. I used it to wrap every single toy up—except for my Ben Wa ball—and then I went and threw them in the bathroom trash.

That night, I texted him.

Me: I got rid of your sex toys for you. You're welcome.

Dex: Getting bolder in that fiancée role of yours.

Me: Coming from the guy who gave me a Ben Wa ball.

Dex: You know how to spell it, huh? You must have researched it then.

Shit. I had googled it before I texted him.

Me: Whatever.

Dex: Want to come do more research in the guest bedroom with me?

Me: Nope. You can call some of the women who enjoy those sex toys instead.

Dex: Why would I do that when the only woman I hate thinking about but always do is in my suite?

Me: Our suite.

Me: Which I should reimburse you for btw. I can pay rent.

Dex: Pay me by coming to my bed.

Me: How about you just take it out of my paycheck?

Dex: Let's be real, Kee. We're engaged. I'm not keeping tabs. You're not paying me to stay here.

Me: Seems like you're practicing acting like this engagement is real already.

Dex: You being mine for six months is real whether the engagement is or not.

Me: Only thing real about it is the contract.

Dex: And the fact that I've already made you come and taken your virginity. That Ben Wa ball something you'll be using in the future?

Me: Not with you.

Dex: As long as you're thinking about me when you use it alone, that's all that matters. Wear it to a rehearsal. See how you feel.

Me: I'll do what I want with it when I want.

Dex: You get through a rehearsal with that, babe, I'll do whatever you want.

Me: Go to bed, Dex. You're dreaming of impossible things.

Even though I'd pointed the finger at him, I dreamt about it all night long.

***

The next morning, I woke up groggy and still frustrated.

I glared at the dresser more than once. "I hate you," I even mumbled as I passed it a few times. Then, I told myself not to think about it. I was actually going to actively avoid it if I could.

I had a million things to do. At the top of my list, I knew I needed to call my father. I normally tried to touch base with him much more frequently. I dialed his number and when he asked how I was, I told him, "I'm just fine, Dad. Figuring it all out here with the Hardy brothers."

"Ah. They'll take care of you. The Hardys are good boys." I heard my mother grumble the same in the background. She may not have known where she was, but her long-term memory of them was set.

When I hung up the phone, I didn't hear a sound, and I knew that meant Dex wasn't there.

I didn't expect him to be. Yet, he'd given me hell about dinner. So, I returned the favor as I walked around the dresser to get to my clothes and throw on jeans and a T-shirt.

> **Me: When I'm not at dinner, you're mad…but you're not at breakfast.**

> **Dex: I only stay for breakfast if it's you I'm eating.**

So he was sticking with bold text messages the next day, it seemed. The butterflies in my stomach proved that I wasn't so bold, though, after the alcohol I'd had last night. My fingers hesitated over the screen before I wrote:

> **Me: Ha. Ha. So funny.**

> **Dex: I'm not kidding.**

My eyes flew to the dresser, and my mind wandered around thoughts it shouldn't be having. Did he think I was using it now? Did he actually think I couldn't handle it?

Instead of worrying over it, I rushed out of my room and down the hall to the kitchen as I texted back.

> **Me: Don't be ridiculous. Most guys do not want that in the morning.**

At least not one I'd ever met. I'd only fooled around a handful of times, but I knew a man only was going to do that if I reciprocated.

> **Dex: I'm not most guys. I'm your fiancé and I want your pussy in the morning. Noon. And night. No doubt about it. Doesn't mean I'm stupid enough to indulge in it.**

My whole body shivered and then balked at his words. My fiancé knew how dirty to be through text. I shouldn't have been partaking in it, but I knew if I ignored him or showed weakness, he'd think I couldn't handle any of it.

> **Me: Well, doesn't matter because you shouldn't expect me to give you a meal if you can't join me for one.**

> **Dex: Food was catered up for you, heartbreaker. Had you been up, you could have eaten with me.**

That text was what began the muddling of my emotions. Without acting like he cared, he still somehow managed to show me he did. My breakfast was scrambled eggs and a cinnamon roll. It was what I loved so long ago for breakfast, and time hadn't changed a thing when it came to my taste buds.

I didn't know how to thank him for it, didn't know if he even wanted a thank you. So, I didn't text him back. I didn't text him that night either, even though I heard him in his office at dinnertime. I couldn't even bring myself to knock on the door.

We were strangers who'd once been lovers and were now wobbling on a tightrope of indecision as to whether or not we could be anything more.

The whole next week, though, breakfast seemed to be the one thing that unraveled me. I wanted to share a meal with him, and I knew he ate at home, so I woke up earlier and earlier. Truth be told, I wasn't an early riser, but I wanted to catch him before he left.

The first day it was 9 a.m.

Then 8:30 a.m.

Then 8 a.m.

Then, I told myself I didn't need to talk to him. I had rehearsals and other things to do.

I went the whole weekend and even Monday and Tuesday of the next week trying to ignore him.

The following Wednesday, though, I woke up at 7 a.m.

Was he avoiding me?

Every morning, my cinnamon bun and scrambled eggs were there waiting, but now he didn't text me about them. I tried not to let it get to me. I focused on how I needed my performances to be great rather than on how I felt about what was happening between Dex and me.

That was nothing.

It couldn't be.

I finally woke up at 5:45 a.m. the next day and called my dad. He gave me updates on my mom like always. Then he rushed me off the phone because she kept asking who he was talking to.

She sounded so cheery, so lucid, so normal. "Tell her I love her today, Dad."

"Will do, Kee. Ah, your mother says do well in school today. She says you shouldn't be using that cell." He sighed at the storyline I knew all too well. Then he stopped for a second as my mother instructed him. "Your mom wants me to tell you that majoring in music for college is only possible if you focus on your grades."

"Right," I whispered out. "Love you. Miss you both."

Mornings were hard when I talked to him, but they would have been lacking if I didn't call. I swiped away a lone tear before I turned.

I jumped back and grasped at my heart. "Jesus, what are you doing here?"

There Dex was, completely dressed, leaning on the doorframe on my bedroom, totally eavesdropping on me. The smile that spread across his face was so slow and so genuine that I completely forgot about everything for a second but him and how carefree he could look. His eyes twinkled as they raked over my body. "Can't I wish my fiancée a good morning?"

I crossed my arms. "We don't do that."

He hummed. "Maybe we should. Anyway, why aren't you talking to your mom?"

Immediately, I took a step back. My guard flew up, and my mind shut down. When it came to her, I was like an animal protecting a life-threatening wound. My father had always instilled in me that what was family business stayed in the family. Plus, my mother was slowly losing everything, fading away, and I wouldn't let anyone come near that pain. It was my job to protect them and I would at any cost.

So, I lashed out. "Why are you eavesdropping on me? You're not going to give me privacy now?"

His interest obviously piqued as both of his eyebrows raised. "Why would I when you're in my room?"

"This is my freaking room." I stomped my foot and pointed to all the clothes I'd yet to hang and unpack. "I live here now. Get the hell over it and stop spying on me. Don't you have work to do?"

"Sure." There was a drawl in his voice as if he wasn't at all in a hurry to do it. "I'll get to it after you answer my question."

I narrowed my eyes. Why did he care anyway? "Did Dimitri tell you?" My tone came out accusatory.

"Tell me what, heartbreaker?"

Scrambling to cover up my mother's disease was necessary. Our last time traveling together ended with my mother lost in a hotel, and when the story leaked, media outlets hadn't used discretion in showing the video of my father restraining her when she'd seen me, when I'd said I was her daughter but she didn't recognize me. There'd been no sound, but the video showed a family in distress, and I wouldn't give details.

Mitchell had begged me to use it for the media but it was one time my father had stood by me and agreed that our family's health would not be used in the media.

Her pain wasn't a tool and I wouldn't ever use it for sympathy or to make people feel bad for me. I definitely wouldn't use it to make Dex understand me.

"I don't talk with my mother anymore," I said, not offering anything else.

He ran his tongue over his teeth slowly as he nodded. "So, you'll tell my brother things but not me?"

"I just told you." I straightened up and tried to appear as put together as he was, except I was wearing an old sweatshirt and underwear. No socks. No bra. Nothing else.

He hummed and then he pushed off the doorframe before he pointed behind him. "I came to tell you breakfast is ready."

"Breakfast? But... We don't... Why did you make me breakfast when we don't eat together? You're always gone when I wake up."

There was his smile again, so big even a dimple showed. "Keeping tabs on me, huh? I heard you talking, but for your information, I normally I leave at 5:45 every morning. In case you want to eat together," he said before turning toward the hall and leaving me confused. "Move your ass, heartbreaker," I heard two seconds later. "Your eggs are getting cold."

I blinked twice at seeing him at the island counter with a plate in front of him and another nearby.

"Scrambled with a cinnamon roll still good enough for you, Ms. Keelani?" he murmured, not looking up from his laptop.

"Did you make this?" I stood there frozen.

"Yes," he said without looking up as he sipped on some coffee. "Coffee's in the pot if you want some, but I'm guessing you still don't drink it because—"

"It makes me jittery," I whispered out. "Wh-Why did you make breakfast?" I pulled at the sleeves of my sweater and tried to shrink into it. The sunlight from the living room windows was shining its bright rays on the fact that I'd just snapped at him. I was here at breakfast with my hair a mess, my teeth not brushed, and probably still had pillow-wrinkle lines on my face.

"I just..." I stumbled over my words. "You're never here in the mornings."

He slid a plate over and patted the stool next to him.

I didn't move to sit down, and finally he looked up from his plate. His gaze drifted over me. "Like I said, I'm here until 5:45. Whose sweatshirt is that?"

I crossed my arms over the Harvard insignia and felt heat rise to my cheeks. "I never ended up going to college. Olive and Dimitri thought it would be fun to buy me Ivy League sweatshirts so I'd feel included."

He hummed and his eyes traveled up and down my body again, but this time they stopped on my thighs that were bare. "You never would have felt included in college anyway."

Dex said the statement so matter-of-factly I wasn't sure whether I should take it as an insult or a compliment. "Well, still would have been nice." I rocked back on my heels. "My mom always wanted me to go to college."

He nodded. "I know. She was dead set on it. She holding on to that? Is that why you don't talk?"

He was still prying, but I couldn't make myself discuss it now. "Something like that."

He tsked at my lack of opening up, but we weren't friends. We didn't just share intimate details of our life like we once had. "Come eat." He pointed to the stool again, and when I didn't move, he murmured, "What's wrong, Kee?"

"Why did you make my favorite breakfast, Dex?" How could I not point out the obvious?

"It's a meal." He rolled his eyes. "We need to talk."

"Ah." My heart settled its rapid speed at his declaration.

The good always came before the bad. I was used to that with my father, with my record label, with my life. "That makes sense, then. You're going to tell me something horrible."

"I'm going to tell you a few things." He took a deep breath. "First, our press release is today."

My whole body coiled up at the idea. "Olive keeps reminding me, but I keep brushing it off. I'll go where we need to and—"

"You look like you want to vomit, Kee."

"Well, what can I say? It's going to be fun going to some extravagant restaurant and faking that I am so excited when you get down on one knee?"

"Where do you want to go if not some extravagant restaurant?" He turned to look at me, he in a perfectly pressed expensive suit and me in a ratty sweatshirt.

"Didn't Mitchell—"

"It's not his choice."

"They'll want a proposal of a lifetime and—"

"What do you want?" Dex cut me off again, placing his hands on the granite counter and staring at me. "You never actually told me."

"I don't need an audience. I never wanted one. There's a reason I prefer to write songs, rather than just sing them. If I could just..." How could someone be blessed with a gift but not want it? Was I so selfish to not want to sing anymore? To not want the fame that came with it?

"Say what you're thinking, heartbreaker," Dex prompted with the nickname he used on and off with me.

I didn't know why it struck such a cord with me sometimes. I wanted to hear it but hated to at the same time. "You use that nickname like a term of endearment when back in the lilac garden..."

"You broke my heart?" He smiled softly like he was willing to offer information this morning. "It is a term of endearment now, I guess. You're the only woman who's be able to do it. If anything, it's a compliment now, not a slight. I'm giving you credit for that."

"I'm not sure I want the credit, Dex." I sighed but somehow it softened my heart to the idea of the name. Being the only woman who'd impacted his life in that way meant *something*. I gave him information back. "Anyway, I'm not sure I want a lot of things, if I'm being honest. I want to live without every single step I take being scrutinized. I used to literally run through the woods with you, Dex, and not care about anything except if the lilacs were in bloom. Don't you want that again?"

"We're adults now," he murmured.

"I know. Sometimes adulting sucks though."

He nodded again and again as he searched my eyes. "Okay."

He shrugged, got up, and disappeared from the room. I frowned at his retreating figure and waited to see if he'd come back because I wasn't sure what the hell was going on. He reappeared with my engagement ring box and held it out to me. "Put it on."

I frowned at him but was willing to listen in order to see where he was going with this. I wiggled it down over my knuckle until it was snug on my ring finger and glinting in the sunlight. While I did, he unbuttoned his cufflinks, rolled them up, stepped behind me, tipped my chin up to have me meet his eyes. He rubbed his thumb back and forth over my skin there. Then he murmured, "You look pretty with my ring on your finger," before he bent down to kiss me.

He started slow, his tongue swiping softly over my lips and

then when I opened for him, his hand drifted down my neck to hold me there. He tasted of coffee and memories and dreams. He tasted so good I moaned into his mouth and his hand slid farther down over my thin sweatshirt to knead at my breast.

My nipples instantly reacted and he groaned, "So fucking tempting in the morning, Kee. You're killing me."

He sighed and pulled back to then drape his arm around my neck.

I was still looking up at him as I gripped his forearm, and murmured, "What are you doing?"

"Do you still trust me after all these years, heartbreaker?" He shook his head and brushed his lips across my ear, while his other hand grazed the soft skin of my thigh. "You must to let me be the first to touch you."

"Why are you asking?" I shivered at his words and the way the back of his other thumb brushed against my neck.

"Because I need your trust. They'll give us hell at some point, but we're safe here within the HEAT empire. You go out there, you've got to trust me." He massaged up my thigh, working my body while he worked on his idea. "We're in it together this time. I only want this if I'm getting you too. So, we're doing things the way you want. I'm not playing house with anyone but the real Kee, the one I loved and hated. You get me?" He nipped at my ear and then his hand grazed my sex where he must have felt how soaked my panties were.

I gasped at the liquid fire that ignited in my blood at his touch, and then he pulled his hand away to pick up his phone. I didn't even realize he was angling it in front of us as I stared at him. He snapped a photo quickly and then his arm fell away from me.

He turned the phone my way so I could see us together.

My dark eyes were full of emotion, my cheeks warm with my natural blush, and I wasn't sure if anyone else could see it, but the love in my eyes was still there. The trust in him. The want for him.

But I told myself it was all just lust. The man had recently taken my virginity.

"Why'd you take that?"

"Our announcement." His response was easy and not at all affected as he typed for a few seconds before turning the phone toward me again. "PR will take care of it."

"W-Wait," I stuttered out, confused as to what this was.

He was already backing away, and he didn't give me any other information. "Forget about the dinner proposal. I'm busy this week with meetings anyway, and you've got to rehearse. I'll tell them to push out something soon. In the meantime, if you don't come home for a meal, text me."

"That's... I don't report or belong to you, Dex."

"But you do. For now. Meals with me or texts to tell me why you aren't home."

"Why? Who cares where I am?" If he was going to make me do this, he was going to give me more than a command.

He rubbed his large hand over the scruff of his jaw. "I don't need the temptation of checking up on you. I like you home for meals so I don't think about where you are instead."

I shook my head. "Dex, let's be realistic. You aren't home sometimes—"

"Do you wonder where I am?"

"That's not the point."

"It is. What are we going to do? Avoid this?"

"I'm trying to survive it," I murmured. Of course he had nothing to say in response. So, I stabbed at the eggs and shoved a few pieces into my mouth in anger. "Are you going to inform me of your eating schedule too?"

"Penelope will communicate my schedule."

"Your meal schedule?" I squeaked out. "Does she just follow you around like a puppy?"

He smirked at me knowingly. Damn, I needed to get the green-eyed little monster in check. "Want to follow me around too?"

I scoffed and went back to eating the eggs. "Do whatever you want, Dex. I'm not going to wait for you to eat when I'm hungry. I'll be doing lunch at rehearsals and dinner here. Show up if you want. Or don't. Whatever."

"Are you always so grumpy in the morning? You didn't used to be—"

"We didn't wake up and live together in high school. We were kids." Maybe we both needed a reminder of that, but his face hardened at my words.

Those green eyes of his weren't vibrant anymore as he grabbed his laptop off the countertop and murmured, "See you tomorrow at breakfast then."

It was his way of saying he wouldn't be home for dinner, and my heart dropped at the words. Somehow, even if I was trying to be nonchalant with him, I couldn't.

CHAPTER 22: KEELANI

I went to rehearsals, trying to place my focus somewhere else.

Another week went by. No press release was dropped about us.

We were only weeks away now from my show, and Pink insisted she bring by some other dresses she'd found. She waltzed into the penthouse and belted out, "Dex Hardy!"

"He's not here." I shook my head at her while Olive walked in behind her.

Two men pushed a clothing rack much less colorful than the last one they'd brought up through the room, and Olive pointed them to my bedroom. "Why are you looking for him?"

"Because the man knows how to make a statement, and I need to tell him."

"Huh?" I wrinkled my nose at her, not knowing what she was talking about.

"I bet that's why your follower count is up," Olive murmured, tapping away at her phone as she stepped in after Pink. "Be happy that I silenced all your social notifications, Kee. You're blowing up online."

"What are you talking about?" I waved them in and looked up and down the resort hallway. No one was around, but my habit of worrying about it wouldn't die off so easily.

Olive wagged her phone at me the second she made it into my bedroom. "This is brilliant, Kee."

"What?"

"Dex's post with you!"

"What post?"

Not waiting for her to hand me her phone, I pulled up my social media and saw my follower count had nearly doubled. Hundreds of thousands of followers were pouring in. "What's happening?" I whispered, but I was already going to his page, where I saw he'd posted our picture.

And he'd tagged me.

She was too shocked to eat the breakfast I made for her, but doesn't my fiancée look good in the morning, even in a college sweatshirt that isn't mine? We're taking time now to enjoy each other before her performances begin at my resort. Don't expect us to be on here until then.

He'd controlled the narrative without mentioning Ethan or the label. He'd let fans know we wouldn't be posting on social media, and he'd been unapologetic about it.

"Why?" I whispered.

"Why what?"

"He said to not worry about it. That he'd have his team handle it." No one could handle it this way though. He'd known I could hardly eat breakfast. He known about the sweatshirt. *He'd* written that post. And he'd controlled the story. For me.

My friends had moved on to my wardrobe and threw some cocktail dresses at me to try on. Each was beautiful, long, tailor-made for my body and classic rather than pop star. They were sexy in a sort of timeless way.

Yet, my mind was elsewhere.

"Why do you keep looking at that dresser instead of the pictures I'm showing you?" Olive nudged me where I sat on my bed. She was going over how my dresses would be complemented by the lighting, that my Vegas show would be remembered as the time everyone truly heard my voice.

"Because your pictures are boring. We already have her wardrobe lined up," Pink answered for me as she wiggled in her schoolgirl checkered skirt. Pink's taste in clothing was punk rock mixed with rock star, and somehow she pulled it off.

She'd pulled off getting me classic dresses I wanted for the second half of my show too. "Do you think I'm going to get away with telling everyone I want to just sing in the second half?"

"Get away with what?" Pink put her hands on her hips. "It's your show. You get to do what you want. Plus, you've got a couple weeks for them to get accustomed to it during rehearsals. It'll be fine."

"Well..." Of course Olive was the voice of reason. "She has to cater to her base fans a little."

"That's what the first half is for. If they don't like the second half, they can leave."

"That's not the way it works, Pink. Sometimes you can't—" Olive started.

"You can leave whenever you want." She stared at Olive with a fierceness we all knew brewed under the surface, but she was letting it boil over. "Unless someone is holding you hostage, you should be willing to do whatever you want. It's your feeling, your body, and your choice." Her words echoed through my room as her voice grew louder.

"Right," Olive whispered, and then she reached for Pink, who jumped when Olive's hand touched hers, but my friend was always overly compassionate and didn't back away. She threaded her fingers through Pink's hand and said, "I know that, Pink. You know I know that."

Pink was a new friend of ours, but Olive had taken her in fast. She seemed to know more than I did about the situation, because she widened her eyes at me like I should say something.

"Um, yeah." I jumped off the bed. "And I am going to show everyone that." Pink squinted at me like she wasn't at all convinced. My gaze flicked toward the stupid dresser. I whispered out, "I'm really going to do it this time. With this concert, with this contract..." I hesitated but I said the next words like I was getting rid my own demons. "With Dex. With everyone."

"Huh?" Olive's face contorted now like she was confused, but I was on a roll.

"I'm going to show him I can handle every single thing he throws at me, and I'm going to do it well."

That seemed to spark life back into Pink and pulled her from whatever nightmares were weighing her down. She punched at the ceiling. "Absolutely. Fuck that man up."

"Now, wait a minute. Slow down." Olive had to put a damper on our newfound goals. "You and Dex could probably use a time out so we can think about what happened last time and—"

"What happened last time?" Pink looked between us. "Oh my God. What? Tell me right now."

And of course Olive blurted out that I'd been a virgin, that now I wasn't, and that she thought Dex still had feelings for me. She ended with: "So, they're going to fall in love all over again, and we're either going to be attending a real wedding or scraping her off the bathroom floor."

"No." I shook my head. "I'm not going to cry over him. Honestly. We haven't even done anything really since, and now I'm just stuck staring at that dresser."

"What's with the dresser?" Olive frowned.

That prompted me telling them about the Ben Wa ball too. "It's taunting me!"

Pink stomped over to the dresser and whipped open the drawer. She looked between me and it. "You're putting that thing in tonight. You got this."

"Do I, though?" I tilted my head.

"Yes, because you can do this, right?"

I nodded and gulped while Olive looked on at both of us with doubt in her eyes. "I know I shouldn't, but I'm still going to say be careful. The Hardy brothers are—"

"We can handle any man. We're *women*," Pink cut her off with a glare. "Women handle men. Not the other way around."

They left me with that thought bouncing around in my head. I ate alone and stared at the drawer. I stared at my bedroom door, too, wondering if Dex would come home.

But of course Penelope texted me his schedule and he had a dinner meeting. I liked his assistant from the little interaction I'd had with her, but I still thought her texting me was ridiculous.

Late that night, I heard him come home, and I could have gone to talk to him or ask if he wanted a snack, but after a week of no real communication, it felt too awkward. We had nothing to discuss. He obviously didn't find me capable of experiencing things with him or good enough company to talk to. He'd probably shaken the idea of me from his system already and was just following through with the contract.

Plus, my mind wasn't in the right place after I'd lain down that night and received a text that had me feeling sick anyway.

Ezekiel: I see the fake engagement is on. I'm a bit disappointed but I'll see you soon.

The problem with social media was it spread like wildfire, sometimes into the hands of people you didn't want anywhere near your life.

I deleted the text without responding. Tonight, I acted like Dex and filed away my problems in a box I would ignore.

CHAPTER 23: KEELANI

The next day, Dex wasn't even there for breakfast at 5:45 after I stupidly woke up early. Instead, I talked to my dad and then got a call from Mitchell telling me I could take my time with the engagement, that he was following Dex's lead. "He's such an asset, Keelani, and has been really accommodating. His assistant was able to work with our PR. It's been great. Just make sure he doesn't dig too deep into our contractual stuff. You know how that goes."

"I got it, Mitchell." He always reminded me but he didn't need to. Dex didn't talk to me.

"Oh, and Ezekiel and I discussed your engagement. He wants to see you."

My stomach curdled at the thought. "Discussed what?"

"That this is more for show, right?" Mitchell was prying and I guess I hesitated too long, because Mitchell laughed with relief. "Right. So, it's more of an engagement for PR purposes. Ezekiel understands, and he just wants to discuss it."

"What for?" I murmured.

"You're a large part of Trinity, Keelani. He's a major shareholder. It's just business," he soothed but then dropped it.

I hurried off the phone without agreeing or disagreeing.

Instead, I focused on my schedule. I needed to tell the team I was switching up the last half of everything. I needed to rehearse it, learn it, and be comfortable with it. Yet, by the next rehearsal, I'd done nothing.

People found comfort in routine, and my routine had been going with the flow, letting my management control it all, and operating how they wanted me to.

I stared at all my clothes still in boxes and suitcases in the closet. Unpacking wasn't something I did well, not after I'd moved away from everything I loved so long ago. Since then, the label had moved me around over and over. They kept me busy on tour. I usually hopped from show to show.

I normally just gave in without feeling a single thing. Self-preservation masked itself in disconnecting and not making a fuss. But without feeling anything, I was disgusted with the idea that I was missing so much of my life. What would happen if I started to make a fuss? What would happen if I started to feel everything freaking thing?

I went to bed unsure of myself and of what to do. My life was changing so fast and I wasn't sure I could keep up.

The very next morning, I woke up to numerous texts from Olive and even my father mentioned the engagement on the news when I called him. Of course, something new had gone viral with Dex's post and the whole world was talking about us even more now.

Yet, the resort's security and Olive blocking my notifications had kept me out of the loop. I sighed and finally searched us online to see.

"Our Sweet Keelani in Love Again." There were people commenting how happy they were for us, how he would make me better, how I would have such cute kids with him.

All of it felt like a dagger to my heart because it was all something I'd once dreamed of that I'd lost. And what if I was falling in love with him but he wasn't with me?

He'd posted that picture and as I stared at it, I wasn't sure why he'd kissed me right before he had. Was it for the post? Was it because he wanted to?

Suddenly, that feeling of disgust for not making a fuss catapulted back into me. I was furious that I didn't know and that I hadn't tried to find out. Furious that they'd written I was so in love again, as if they knew who'd I'd been in love with before. It wasn't Ethan.

It was only Dex. I had been in love, but I'd never acted on it, never done what I wanted to do.

I shoved my blankets off, yanked all my clothes out of the boxes and suitcases, and then stomped over to the dresser.

I'd agreed to getting engaged to Dex because feeling everything was what I wanted. It would either heal or ruin me. I grabbed a small black dress and changed before I opened the drawer.

I took a deep breath. I stared at it for a minute before looking up exactly how to put it in online. I was determined to master this on my own now. I grabbed the small, smooth ball of metal and slowly worked it into me. My body shivered at the sensation, my nipples tightening, my sex pulsing at the feeling.

I straightened and smoothed my dress down. I was handling it. No one else would handle me anymore. I was going to do what I wanted.

I even pulled up Dex's number and wrote:

> Me: We've gone viral for looking like we're in love in your social media post.

Dex: And?

> Me: And is that why you kissed me?

I couldn't believe I wrote that out and pounded the send button. Yet, I needed to know. It was a small step but also a colossal first one in pushing for what I wanted, in changing who I was, in becoming who I wanted to be.

> **Dex: If that was the case, I would have just posted an actual picture of me kissing you.**

> **Dex: As much as I hate to admit it, that kiss was for me. You taste good in the morning, heartbreaker.**

Seeing that text settled my nerves. It made me believe just a bit that I could push myself, that I could get answers, that I could be who I wanted to be even if I'd suppressed that person for so long.

> **Me: I'm proving myself at rehearsal today. Come see if you want.**

He didn't text back, but I didn't care. I was following through with furthering my life that day.

It'd only be a few hours of making changes, I told myself. And a few hours of the ball inside me.

After just one, I was sweating.

"Let's take it from the top again." I whirled my painted fingernail round and round in a circle because this would be the fifth time.

Something was off. Or maybe everything was. My body was more in tune, coiled and wound up tight around a tiny little smooth piece of metal that somehow seemed to magnify every emotion I had.

My vocalist, Janice, was sitting in one of the chairs and she shook her head. "Well, you have a lot to say today, Keelani. I agree, though, the drums aren't working in this theater. The echo is overpowering."

She didn't say it to me. She said it to Frankie, who was at the side of the stage. He'd been the creative director now for most of my shows, managing all aspects of them. He rubbed his bald head before scratching it and nodded. "We could just have the music play instead of doing it live and have her dancers—"

They discussed my show like I wasn't there, like I was a prop to their show. I'd been so malleable before, flowing like water in the direction they wanted that they would have never expected a shift in the current. I felt the need to be present now, the need to be heard.

"I don't want dancers," I blurted loudly. The words fueled a liberation within me. "I don't want drums either. And my music will be live."

"Keelani, do you need a break?" Janice said like she was talking to an overtired child.

"No." And I saw how Janice's gaze flicked to Frankie's. My body was on fire with irritation now, my mind going in overdrive. The Ben Wa ball intensified everything, and I was too sensitive, too emotional, too in tune to hold back.

It was all wrong. The set was wrong. The music. The heart of it. When someone came to my concert, I wanted them to feel like the songs were alive, that they were living entities, breathing and moving and rushing through all our veins. Didn't my creative team want that too?

"Let's take a small break." She waved everyone off. "Be

back in five." Immediately, she beelined toward Frankie, and I saw the dancers who had been hired start to back away from me.

"Hey!" I called out to one of them. She smiled softly at me, but her eyes flicked toward Frankie before she meandered over. "What's your name?"

"Winter," she said quietly, but I saw her fear and instantly knew this was like other times. Frankie always got me new dancers and most of them never talked with me.

"Were you told not to talk to me?"

"I just..." She cleared her throat. "No. Of course not. We don't want to bother your process and... I love my job, okay?"

"Of course you do." I patted her arm, and she nodded meekly.

"Also, congrats on the engagement if it's... Well, um, congrats."

There was speculation it wasn't real. We hadn't been seen together outside of Dex's post. Most people knew I went up to the penthouse, I was sure, but I didn't wear a ring to the rehearsals.

"Winter," Frankie bellowed, and the girl practically jumped out of her skin. "Let Keelani have a break."

I think that was the final straw. He'd spoken to me that way for years, but he never should talk to anyone else like that. Never should my dancers be scared of me. Never should my set list have gotten this far off of what I wanted it to be.

I'd let things go for too long.

"I want nothing but my voice and the instruments for the second half of the concert. The dancers flow in the background with the music, and I'll be changing my wardrobe and the songs."

"Keelani," Frankie started softly, like he was going to try to accommodate me. "Let's think about this—"

Suddenly, I didn't want to be accommodating or compromise. He was going to listen to me. "Pull the lights back. I want to perform the songs we've been working on, but only with violins and piano. I can play my guitar if—"

"We don't have time for this." He stood up and huffed, his blue eyes narrowing on me. "Are you out of your mind?"

"Why would I be?" I lifted my chin and took a deep breath because I knew I was about to really piss him off.

His bright white veneers clenched together. "We're not showcasing your voice here. We need to entertain these people."

"I'm aware." I felt the anger building, the frustration, the lack of confidence in me that propelled me to prove them wrong.

"It's not happening." He rolled his buggy eyes and pointed to the dancers. "Let's take it from the top."

I turned to my dancers and saw them all listening to him, listening to a man who never asked my opinion as the headliner, didn't bother to greet anyone when he walked in, and wasn't on stage with them ever. The energy in me was building. "No." I said it softly first and then let the words escape from my lips loudly. "No. That's not how I want to do my show."

"I'm sorry. What?" His question was full of surprise but also anger as his eyes widened to double their size.

"I don't want my show to be this way. We still have time to change it. So, that's what we need to do."

"You think you get a choice? This is Trinity's production, and we're doing it how they'd want." Frankie's voice cut through the space in agitation now. His face had turned blotchy with red spots as he stalked up to me. Frankie was a large man, large enough to tower over a woman and make her feel small. In heels, though, I could stand my ground. I didn't back up, not even one step. "Mitchell would be—"

"It's not Mitchell's or Trinity's show." I heard Dex's voice from the back of the theater before I saw him. It rolled across the space smoothly but with a rumble of power, even if it sounded effortless.

How long had Dex been standing there? Watching me? Watching us? He stood there so quietly that we'd all missed his presence. Had he seen everything?

His hands were in the pockets of his navy suit pants, and he rocked back on his heels as if we were all having a casual conversation. Even from afar, though, I saw how straight he held his shoulders, how his chin was raised, head up tall, and how his eyes were locked on Frankie.

Frankie squinted out past the velvet seating and chuckled. "Sorry. We're rehearsing here. If—"

"I'm here for the rehearsal." Dex walked down the aisle slowly, and a few whispers were heard across my crew. "I want to hear my fiancée sing the second half of her show. I'd say that's what? Six songs. Violins and piano only. In *my* resort."

"So it's true?" someone murmured, and then the dancers' eyes flew to my hand. I think most of my team thought the social media post was a PR stunt because I didn't talk about it and they didn't ask. None of us were that close. We'd all been pushed together this last month for the concert because Trinity didn't believe in flying dancers around with me.

I hadn't worn my ring to rehearsals and never mentioned the engagement.

Until now.

Frankie nodded like he knew all too well what was going on. He rubbed his large belly while he scoffed and then shook his bald head before he stumbled over his words. "Mr. Hardy, so good to meet you. Mitchell has told me great things. Congratulations, by the way. On the *engagement.*" I noted that Frankie hadn't congratulated me, even though Mitchell must have told him. He waddled over to the side stage where stairs that would be blocked off during the concert were located. He hurried to shake Dex's hand like the man was a god.

My fake fiancé didn't extend his hand though. He just stared at Frankie. "You're aware that I own this resort?"

"I am." Frankie dropped his hand and shuffled on his feet awkwardly.

"You've been informed of our engagement?"

"Well, yes. We're all very happy with—"

"Good." Dex walked over to me and extended his hand, signaling me to hop off the stage. When I did, he murmured in my ear, "Go with it." And then he said loudly, "Missed you too much not to come see you today."

He wrapped his arm around my waist, and I saw his smile before his lips descended on mine. He kissed me. Softly. Poetically. Like he loved me. And I kissed him back the same way because when Dex Hardy kissed me, my soul melted. I wanted the man who took care of me, who remembered my breakfasts, who'd saved me from that car wreck, who'd save me from anything.

He was doing it here too—saving me—even if he probably wouldn't admit it later.

All I felt was him and the cocoon he wrapped me in. His full lips slid over mine, and when he stepped back, I whimpered because I didn't want to let him go. He made a point to pull my engagement ring from his pocket and murmured, "You forgot to put this on this morning. Here."

He slid it on slowly and then rubbed my knuckles with his thumb after. It's when I saw that on his left hand, he now wore a gold band too. We hadn't discussed it, but it was there, clearly showing everyone he was taken.

Then his gaze turned hard as he spun to face Frankie. "So, you've been informed of our engagement?"

Frankie nodded as he gulped.

"Good. It means you're aware that my fiancée and I decide what happens in this theater. She has complete control if I'm unavailable, and towering over her while she's making a decision won't be tolerated ever again. She has the authority to fire you and replace you in seconds. You understand?"

"Mr. Hardy, let me explain." His tone was cajoling. "As the creative director of Trinity's artists across the globe, they have all had hit—"

"Is this a joke?"

"What?" Frankie squeaked.

"Do you think I have time for this? Because I don't. I've had a long, frustrating day. I was in and out of meetings about the security measures we're taking for all of you to stay here. I had to make a decision on investing in two more properties. Then I had to sit down with the Armanellis. Do you think I want to hear about the title of your job, Freddie?"

"Frankie."

One of the dancers murmured, "Oh hell no," to the other as Dex's gaze turned lethal. It was like the theater's lighting even dimmed with his mood as he took a step toward Frankie. He didn't have to say a word. The tension all around us crackled with his frustration.

Maybe I hadn't seen it with my best friend because he was just that to me. I didn't see Dimitri exert his power, but here in this resort, I saw what the Hardy name meant, what Dex Hardy meant.

Power.

Fear.

Dominance.

How was I going to handle all that?

"Or you can call me Freddie," my creative director corrected himself.

"Yes, Fred. Do you know my fiancée told me just days ago that she wanted a new sound for the new person she's become, and I told her she could have it. You know why?"

"Why?" Frankie asked.

"Because she can have *anything* she wants."

"Of course." The man didn't even bother arguing. "It's just... I wanted you to understand that I provide Keelani with a scope of—"

"You don't provide my fiancée with anything. She's the talent. She provided you with a job. So, she gets what she wants. You understand? For this Vegas residency, and honestly"—he looked at me pointedly—"it should be for the rest of the time you're employed by her, you do as she says. No arguments. No pushback. If my fiancée wants to sing on stilts while elephants weave through her legs, you make it happen. You say yes and find a way. You don't question her vision. I don't give a fuck what your title is. Got it?"

Frankie nodded but didn't open his mouth.

Dex smiled and rubbed a hand over his jaw like Frankie had annoyed him further. I watched how his hand slid across his face. I listened to how the scruff scraped against his skin. Everything he did for me here right now pulled me toward him as he stood up for me.

Then he said, "How clear have I made myself?"

"I... But... You—" Frankie floundered while I sat on the edge of that stage to watch them both. I was the only one to move as everyone else stood stock-still, their eyes glued on the interaction. Frankie was used to getting his way, and I think we all knew that he wouldn't be here.

Dex had put him in his place. For me.

Dex, who seemed to not want to care but who'd arrived at the rehearsal and stood up for me. Dex, who wanted me out of his system forever but came to my aid.

He leaned in and murmured, "The answer you're looking for is *crystal*, Fred. I'm making myself crystal clear."

Frankie's whole face was blotchy now as his mouth snapped shut and he glanced around.

"Say it, Fred," Dex prompted, making an even bigger fool of my creative director.

"Yes, Mr. Hardy. It's crystal clear."

Dex nodded once and then glanced around the theater. "Good. We're all on the same page. Now, I'd like to enjoy my fiancée's voice for the rest of her rehearsal. In private."

"Dex—" I started, trying to stop the inevitable.

"You can all leave."

There it was. If everyone left, I'd be alone with him, my body already in overdrive, I wasn't sure I could resist. The Ben Wa ball felt so heavy now, and my pull to him was almost like gravity. I couldn't avoid it forever.

Still, I tried to make people stay and turned to tell them, but everyone was filing out. They didn't hesitate to beeline toward the exit, not even Frankie, who punched numbers into his phone rapidly as he walked.

As the doors at the front of the theater closed, I murmured,

"You're going to hear about that later from Mitchell."

Dex sat down in the front row, parallel to where I sat on the stage. My feet dangled, and I swung them back and forth as he said, "No I won't. Your boss would be stupid to call me about something so trivial."

"Trivial?" I side-eyed him. "It's my whole life."

"What? Fred bossing you around?"

I smirked at his name calling. "You're being childish, Dex."

"Or I'm meeting him on his level." He stared at me before he continued, searching for something. "Has he talked to you like that before?"

"Like what?" I gripped my thighs, and his eyes trailed my legs, stopping on where my fingers indented my flesh, where I felt the pads of them digging in so tight I might explode with that feeling alone. "Like him bossing me around? Sure, but it's not something I haven't endured time and time again."

"You're handling it, it seems."

"I'm flying by the seat of my pants," I confessed. "That's not something you ever do."

He leaned close. "You don't need to be like me. You never were. Don't you remember? You ran my ass down to the lilacs more than a time or two in the middle of the night without even a jacket on to tell me about some random thing."

"I don't run to you about any random things anymore though."

"No. You're bottling up your whole life in there, aren't you?" He studied me then, his green eyes scanning my face like a laser looking for clues, like suddenly he could tell me all about myself. "Just be how you were before."

"How I was," I emphasized. "I'm not that way anymore. I can't be..."

He leaned back in that seat and folded his hands in his lap. "What way are you now then?"

"Honestly? I hate to admit it, but I'm a doormat," I confessed. "I can't be anything else when there are a million people walking all over me to make sure I do what needs to be done for my career. I go with their flow and let them do what they're trained to—"

"I didn't sign the contract for them. I wanted you. I agreed to this for you." He shrugged. "So change the trajectory."

"Right." I chewed on my cheek. "I am. Well, I did. For now. But for how long? You know Frankie's going to call Mitchell and this is going to blow up in our faces."

"You don't seem to realize..." He stood then, and my eyes gobbled up the sight. I'd looked him up and down too many times over the past few days, and still, I wanted to gaze at his appearance for so much longer. "I own this resort. I own your contract and you. They cannot and will not ruin their relationship with me, Kee."

"Why?" I whispered now, because Dex was unbuttoning his navy suit jacket. His hands worked so effortlessly that I had to squeeze my thighs together and try my best not to focus on what other tasks those hands would do well at.

I knew.

My body knew.

The freaking Ben Wa ball in me probably knew.

"Because I control my destiny and now *yours*."

"You're saying *now* like you didn't always."

He smiled down at me, but his eyes swam with turmoil. "How could I control you? You were sparkling bigger than my life in that small town. And I would have done just about anything to keep you there, including..."

He let his statement trail off, but I knew where he was going. "That car wreck wasn't your fault, Dex."

His hands went to my hips, and his forehead fell to mine as he whispered, "When you're with me, it's always my fault, Kee."

I gripped the lapels of his suit jacket to pull him closer so he'd feel what I felt then, so he'd understand like I understood. "I went to therapy for that night. I racked my brain on how it would have turned out had I not had another drink, had I kept you in the woods, had I not pushed Gabriella on you. None of it mattered. We can't change the past and we can't dwell on it, especially when we were all kids—"

"I was nineteen."

"And I was almost eighteen." I slid my hands to his shoulders and shook him. Did he not get that? "You weren't going to control me from getting into the car that night. We were all going with or without you. Don't you see? You didn't cause that car wreck at all. If anything, you saved us from it."

His eyes squeezed shut so hard I knew the fight inside him was barreling around in his mind, trying to find its way out. I wanted to hug him, to pull him close, to make him see that trauma shouldn't have blame. Yet, he placed all that blame on himself.

I saw it now, and I was starting to realize why he'd told me he would control this relationship.

"You can't control everything, Dex," I whispered.

His hand slid up the bare skin of my arm and then down over my dress to my thighs. He gripped me there while he kept his eyes closed. His hand shook just like my whole body shook at his touch. Did he feel me tremoring, my breath coming faster? He gave no sign of it other than how his muscles bunched.

"Everything in my life I can and do control, Kee. That's

why you're normally not in it. For these next couple of months, you'll have to learn that."

"I don't want anyone controlling me anymore, Dex."

"I know, heartbreaker. We need you wild and reckless again. But not with me. I don't think I can endure it again. It's the one thing I can't do."

His other hand went to my cheek, and he breathed in and out with me, like he could take my oxygen and I could take his. We'd gone so long without each other, yet I sat there with him between my legs on that stage like he'd never left.

Like I never wanted him to leave again.

Maybe it was what he wanted too. He kissed me then, his full lips pulling mine into his mouth and tasting me slowly and softly. He took his time relearning how I felt. We weren't rushing at all.

I had the wood floor of the stage under my thighs, but I hung my knees from the edge and swung my legs back and forth. The audience's seating was lower than the stage at just the right level that Dex could step between my knees easily. And maybe it was him being right there or the fact that I'd been holding metal inside me for over an hour, but I couldn't stop from whimpering and wrapping my legs around him. His cock grazed against my panties, and I felt his length so solid, so close, and so big against me.

"I want you," I admitted, pulling away so I could tell him, but he took the opportunity to step back.

He practically yanked himself away from me, out of my reach, while combing a hand through his thick dark hair before he shook his head and sat back down on the front-row chair to look up at me. "Sing me the song you want to sing the most on opening night, first."

Everything was too sensitive. My body was too tuned in. "I don't want to sing right now. I want—"

"Is that blush you're sporting because you're mad I'm denying you, heartbreaker? Or because you don't think you can sing right now?" He pointedly looked at me.

"Excuse me?"

He didn't miss a beat as he responded, "Is it in you today? Your pussy holding it like it should be?"

"Honestly." I knew the blush on my cheeks was deepening because the heat that traveled to my face was enough to burn through my skin. "You have no idea what you're talking about."

"Show me then."

Jesus. Was he playing with me? While I was trying to connect with him? Fury made me stand up and scramble back fast. I straightened my dress and stomped to the middle of the stage in the sneakers I'd used to dress down my outfit, my body vibrating with a newfound emotion.

I saw each seat in the theater. There were only a thousand of them, empty but waiting to be filled with a person ready to feel what I felt. Even if Dex wouldn't. Even if he was only playing games.

When I sang, I needed my audience to connect. I may not have had confidence in much else, but I knew I could do that. I'd grown up with this, felt it from when I was a freaking baby.

I tested the mic by humming a tune, and my voice traveled through the speakers, filling the theater. All I needed was that. All I needed was to be a part of the music. Closing my eyes, I let my heart take over as I let the words flow out. Each note was a memory, an escape back to where the lilacs grew and our love did too.

Did you want me then?

Didn't you love me too?

I'd have bled for you in a field of flowers

I'd have waited for you in the dark

We weren't too far from each other

How could we be when you already had my heart

I'd have bled for you in a field of flowers

And I did because you left me

Left my heart broken and torn apart.

I held the last note as I opened my eyes and caught his gaze staring back at me. I couldn't read what he felt right then. Instead of running through the forest-green of his eyes, they were solid emerald, so cold and distant I wasn't sure if they were ice.

My voice was my superpower. His superpower was closing me off to his emotions. My heart was bleeding out in front of him as I ended the note, but still my voice echoed around us both, ricocheting off the walls and into our bones.

Music was our journey, leading us down a path of thorns and obstacles to the darkest parts of our emotions. Standing there, letting him see me breathing heavily on that stage, was the most vulnerable I'd felt in years. He had to see the love I held for him in the past, the pain I felt in how we ended, how broken I was when he walked away.

Did he feel it? Was he moved too?

"You're truly breathtaking, heartbreaker," he whispered,

and those words alone coming from him almost moved me to tears.

"Thank you. I think it's coming along." I didn't know how to take his compliment about such an intimate song that shared my heart. "I'm thinking maybe if I get a few props...maybe a chair like you have in the room of my suite. Do you think it'll work for everyone?"

Yet, it must have been the wrong thing to say because he stood abruptly, and his tone came out clipped. "Yep. Of course it will for everyone. When did you write this?"

"After you left."

"You've never sung it on stage." His words were stilted, and his movements were too. Instead of walking toward me, he backed away, up the aisle toward the theater doors.

"How do you know that?"

"Because I know too fucking much about you, Kee," he bellowed and threw up his hands. "Jesus, you wrote our love into so much and fucking skyrocketed to the top, didn't you?"

"What?" The harsh accusation was the opposite of what I'd thought we'd be discussing right then. "I never used this song to—"

"It's on an album, isn't it?"

"Yes, but not like this, not just me and the—"

"Then you used it." He pulled at his neck and looked toward the crown molding of the theater, so beautiful and ornate in its architecture I was sure his brother had designed it. "It'll be good for the show. Hell, I almost cried listening to it even if I don't give a shit about it anymore."

"It's not for the show, Dex. You think I sang that for..." I couldn't even finish. "I lost you just like you lost me. Don't you see that? Your pain isn't isolated or singular. I've been broken since the moment you left."

"Do you think I wanted to leave?" His voice cut through the air, his eyes blazing with agony. "Jesus, I didn't know how to cope with losing you again, so I walked away that time. And you were leaving, Kee. Don't fucking tell me you weren't. You were going back to your career whether you begged me to stay or not."

"I..." How could I respond when he was right? "My heart has always belonged to you, Dex. But I have responsibilities to—"

"A career? Your fans?"

To my family. To my mother. To my father. To problems I didn't know how to make him understand, nor would they be problems I would use as an excuse. Plus, I knew how I allowed my father to continue doing what he was doing showed how spineless I'd become. "Something like that."

He hummed like he didn't believe me, like it wasn't good enough even if he did believe me. Then, he nodded over and over. "I don't know what's real and what's not with you, Kee. You're larger than life, and then you're still..."

"Me?" I grabbed at the end of his sentence, wanting him to understand. "I'm just me."

Wiping one of his hands over his face, I saw how he tried to wipe away his emotions too. "But I don't know you anymore. You're hiding too much."

"Okay. Fair. I don't know you either," I threw back, and suddenly I felt anger at that statement. "Because you left too. And I was broken just the same. I still am!" I gasped at the words and felt the tears sting my eyes before I blinked them away. "I can barely breathe when I think of what you went through and how I couldn't go through it with you. Kyle was—"

"Kyle was irresponsible, and he shouldn't have—"

"He was your friend, Dex. You lost your friend that night, and I know you blame yourself, but you saved me and Dimitri and you looked for Gabriella. Have you talked to anyone about—"

"There's no need." He stepped back as he blinked hard, and I saw how all the emotions drained from his face. "I'm aware of what happened that night, Keelani. We've grown up with trauma like many."

"That doesn't mean we should ignore it."

He looked up at the ceiling and then around the space, keeping his gaze anywhere but mine. "I'm not ignoring it. I'm moving on." He said it in a way where I knew he was packing it up in a box to put away. "Do you have everything for your concert?"

"That's what you want to talk about now?" I crossed my arms.

"I'll be busy over the next few weeks. Don't expect me to be available. Your show should be taken care of."

"You won't be there?" I didn't know why my voice sounded desperate. It wasn't like he'd ever attended *just* to see me. There was no reason for him to do so now either I supposed.

"Keelani Hale, you're a star. You don't need me in the crowd. You have your fans, your career, everything you wanted." With that, he spun on his heel, walked up the aisle, and shoved through the doors. They slammed shut behind him, closing me off from what I thought our relationship could become.

I stared at those closed doors for much too long and whispered out later, "Everything I wanted was you."

CHAPTER 24: DEX

My control was slipping. I'd left my meeting to see her sing. Her text that she was proving herself that day had taunted me into it. I couldn't resist her even though she was the one thing I should be resisting.

And I'd sat there so confident in myself that I could handle it. Yet, that rasp, that voice, her words... I knew she'd written them.

No one thought of a field of flowers like Kee did. No one could talk about the stars in the skies being fireflies when we'd stared at them together. And that's when I'd lost full control of my emotions.

How could I shake a love that was a part of me, my trauma, my damn soul? She'd woven herself in, and I wasn't getting her out. Of course I'd loved her back then, but I fell in love with her now, too, with her heart breaking for me on that stage.

And I wasn't even sure it was real.

She was a performer. She made millions of people feel what I was feeling. Shattered their hearts and let the tears seep out of them. I was even convinced she was feeling that same emotion on the stage because how else could she eviscerate me?

The residency at Black Diamond was going to change who she was. I could see it already, and I couldn't risk losing myself in the process. Escaping her and putting distance between us was the only way this would work. That and me disconnecting emotionally. I left her on that stage, running from the feelings that had gotten me in trouble before.

Emotions blurred logic. Love made you weak. Love made you do stupid shit. It's how I'd almost lost her once. How we'd lost friends. How I hadn't seen the signs before we got in the car that night.

"You're not paying attention." Bane elbowed me during our Zoom call with Cade. To anyone else, his low warning would probably have scared their attention back to the screen.

But Cade was my brother-in-law. And Bane was my business partner, not my boss. And a questionable partner, at that. I'd started to think he was more involved with my brother-in-law than he should have been.

Cade headed up cybersecurity within the government but was also a member of the Armanelli family, infamous for being a part of the mafia. Rumors upon rumors flew of murder, greed, and power. Most of the rumors were true, except my brother-in-law had cleaned up the family name over the course of about a decade now. He was married to my sister Izzy, who I knew he'd kill for, and I'd come to terms with it.

I'd practically let others die to save my little heartbreaker's life too. And I'd do it again.

Even still, Cade was pissing me off, and I wasn't in the mood to deal with him or Bane. My fake fiancée was most likely in my hotel suite removing a sex toy I'd instructed her to endure for hours.

I knew she'd done it too. There was no mistaking the blush on her cheeks during the songs she sang.

"I already know all this, Cade," I ground out as I stared at him on the screen.

The fucker bounced one of his kids on his knee as he threw back, "Then what am I on this call for?"

Bane raised an eyebrow, glancing over at me with blue eyes that were so clear, they almost looked translucent.

"You're summarizing the problem when I simply need an answer to it."

"Do I look like your employee?" Cade's face showed disgust.

Bane's eyes jumped back to me.

"You look like the guy who has saved the country once or twice from cyber attacks." And he was. He had a direct line to the president.

"More than once or twice. But I have the next generation here now. That's what I'm worried about now. Anyway, your casino's security is fine. No one is trying to screw with the HEAT empire...or the Armanelli empire for that matter."

"Right. But something's off," I explained. "That small glitch in the system could be—"

"We're talking about seconds of the day, Dex. If someone wanted to rob the casino, they'd have to literally plan a heist better than—"

"It shouldn't be plannable. It should be impossible."

"What he said," Bane interjected. "It's not just the HEAT empire, Cade. It's my name too. The Blacks will not be open to weakness."

"Don't you have a team to work on this?"

"Not when I have a sister and brother-in-law who are better than everyone in the fucking world."

"Hey." Bane turned to me. Suddenly, his eyes held fury and something maniacal. "Careful how you talk in front of the little one."

Cade busted out laughing. "Yeah, Dex. Careful. The next generation of the Armanellis are most important." He looked at

Bane Black. "And the Blacks' generation will be quite important too." With that, he was gone.

Bane stood immediately from the conference room chair and frowned at me. "You sure you're good?" he said and narrowed his eyes like he was trying to pry open my damn mind.

"You think I'm not?"

"You need to figure out your love life. It'll hinder our casino if you can't. I know you normally never miss anything. I've assessed your security measures for years. I wasn't about to go into business with someone I didn't research. And I don't want that changing because your mind is elsewhere."

I hummed. "Maybe you should have gone into business with Cade then. Has he missed anything?"

"Cade's technically not in business with anyone but his family now. You heard him." He smiled slow. "You know this. You also know what he missed." We all did. He'd almost lost my sister because of it. "Don't make the same mistake as him." His words held a sense of foreboding.

"What the hell is that supposed to mean?"

"It means you're not focused. And when you're not focused, people take advantage. You own a place that now makes billions of dollars a year. I funnel even more through this casino. People who have power don't like that. They don't like that I'm intercepting their business or potentially hindering other businesses."

"If you're talking about laundering, we've had a handle on—"

"Platinum Casino took a huge hit when we invested and opened our doors here. They're not happy, Dex. You think they're so squeaky clean they wouldn't somehow try to hurt our business?"

"They would be stupid to do so."

"I didn't claim that they were smart. All I said was you'd better focus. Protect what's most important." He leaned in. "And I don't mean that girl."

He left me reeling. *That girl*...like she was only that and not *my* girl. My fiancée. The woman who broke my heart but still had the pieces in her grasp. Control of emotions slipped faster and faster, gaining momentum down a slope that wasn't stoppable. I wouldn't allow it. I wouldn't fall off the cliff again.

I pounded a number into the phone. "Mitchell, I want that fucking contract in my email by the end of this week."

"Oh, Keelani has it. She said she'd discuss it with you." His voice shook over the phone. It's how I knew the fucker was lying.

"She'd better." I hung up, not willing to deal with that now.

I went to work instead. I had Penelope cater in some food to the conference room for me, not willing to go back to my place, where I could smell Kee everywhere, hear her tiptoeing around that room, feel her presence but never see her step over the threshold to talk to me.

Penelope set the food down on my desk once it arrived. "Dex, I'm putting your first few events with Ms. Hale on the calendar. How would you like the next event handled regarding your engagement? I've got a few options for—"

"Keelani and I will handle it." I wasn't sure how, but I knew we would even if we'd been avoiding each other now for damn days and still her words about wanting experience were clamoring around in my head. Could she handle that type of experience with me? Could she want who I was now instead of who I'd been?

"Like you handled your engagement post too?" She glanced up from her phone with pursed lips. "That was surprising, Dex. I can at least help you with the next location of—"

I frowned. "That's not going to be public."

"Why not?"

"Because I'm not... We're not..." I narrowed my eyes at her.

Penelope was quick to figure things out, and her blue eyes searched mine so hard I felt like she was using a jackhammer to break through my thoughts. "You're not what, exactly?"

"We don't need attention."

She lifted a brow and leaned back. "Interesting, Dex. Isn't this all for attention?" she murmured.

"It's for something. I'm not sure what yet."

She smiled and went back to her phone. "Don't expect to avoid the paps if you go outside of HEAT territory. They'll be circling, and you're both well-known."

"I'm aware," I grumbled, stabbing the fork into my salad.

"Also, make it believable, please. PR stunts never go over well publicly if you're found out."

Was she my mother? "Why would you think this is a PR—"

"It's only obvious to me because I'm in and out of your home. The bedroom separation is a pretty good indicator—"

"Penelope, can you please let me eat in peace?"

"You're such a drama queen." She patted my hand before standing and straightening her skirt. "Ask her what she wants, Dex. Controlling the narrative with the one you love never works."

"Penelope, *you're* giving *me* relationship advice? Are you married all of a sudden?"

"No." She tapped the desk. "But I'm a woman. I know. Also, make it clear when you open car doors, escort her into dinner, and—"

"I know how to woo a woman."

"Is it all about wooing her? Are we not concerned about the media now?"

I threw my fork down and leaned back in my chair to glare at her. "Jesus fucking—"

Yet, she was walking out as she held the door open for Dimitri.

He poked his head in. "What the fuck are you still doing in the conference room? Go home."

I nodded, not about to tell him the real reason I wouldn't be doing that anytime soon. "I'm finishing up a few security checks."

He stepped in and glanced at the food on the desk. "We good for next month?"

"When have we ever not been?" My tone was defensive after dealing with Bane.

"It'll be a big month with Keelani's concert opening. And with the fact that you dropped the news about this engagement—"

"Dimitri." His name came out a warning rather than a sigh. He sat down across the table from me, and I tried not to grumble. "I'm not in the mood."

"Of course you're not. You're never in the mood to talk about her. But I still need to say a few things."

My stomach churned, and my mind ran away with thoughts of my brother and Kee betraying me somehow. They were illogical and near deranged but that didn't stop them. "Whatever you need to say probably isn't relevant to—"

"She's had stalkers before," Dimitri said as if it were a revelation to me.

"She mentioned it." I shrugged because she had when her eyes had skirted around my resort halls.

"No. Not like she says. These people aren't just obsessed. They're out of their minds and dangerous." He dropped the bomb like it was nothing. "I'm not talking about someone peeping in her room here and there, Dex—though she'll describe it that way. They've come to every one of her concerts, followed her home, filmed her, tried to..."

His voice drifted off while my whole body leaned forward to get the rest of that sentence. "To what, Dimitri?"

He shook his head. "She goes with the flow when asked about it, like it's no big deal and part of the job. I'm ninety percent sure she hasn't even told me everything."

My brother stopped to rub his knuckles together. I did the same thing when I was trying my best to keep a lid on my emotions, to come to terms with something. I let the silence fill the air while I took one deep breath before asking quietly, "Why didn't you tell me?" The question was a selfish one, and immediately, I wanted to snatch it back because I knew the answer.

He leaned forward and pounded a fist on the table. "I don't tell you shit about her because you don't deserve to know. You left and wanted nothing to do with her. Remember?"

I winced at his words.

"Look, damn it. It's no one's fault. We got dealt a shit card."

Dimitri was the baby boy of the family. He would never understand that the car accident was on me, not him. I was supposed to keep his ass safe, not the other way around. I should have kept them all safe, and instead we lost a life and nearly ruined all of ours. "Sure, D. It's a shit card."

"But we don't talk about it, and we don't discuss Keelani or her family, which is a whole other issue in and of itself."

"What's wrong with her—"

"I'm not here to give you a damn summary of her life, Dex. She can do that when she's ready. Maybe try asking her."

"Maybe I should hack her records," I grumbled, irritated that he wanted to protect her privacy over helping me.

"I'm actually surprised you haven't," he threw back, but the fear of falling into an obsession over her was real, and I didn't want to go down into that black hole, unsure of if I'd be able to get out.

"Whatever. What else do you want?" I asked.

He took a deep breath, as if he was trying to cool down. "Look, she needs security all around that fucking concert, okay? Not just normal security. I want them crawling up the damn walls. Cameras everywhere. The last guy wrote her letters, enclosed her own panties in the envelope, and he was found in her hotel room."

"What do you mean he was in her goddamn hotel room?"

"Police got there before she did. She was fine, but we need to be vigilant."

"Now wait. What the fuck? How had he sent her her own panties?" I bellowed.

Dimitri stared at me like I was born yesterday. "If you got a girl's panties, you either were given them or—"

"He was in her home before that and was searching for them?"

"Bingo."

"Fuck me." This is why I couldn't have her blurring lines. It fucked with how I managed my resort and infected my mind with something I thought might be love. If I wasn't focused, I'd lose her in a much more permanent way. I grumbled and then I grabbed my laptop. "She's got a security team, right?"

"One Mitchell assigns every tour. She doesn't trust them, and I don't either. Your eyes had better be on her at all times during performance nights. Mine will be."

I opened my laptop and typed away, pulling up camera after camera until I saw her in our apartment. I breathed a sigh of relief. My system's technology was state of the art and innovative. We tracked the rate of a heartbeat, could decipher the difference in fear and pain and pleasure just from the room-monitoring capabilities.

Our watches also alerted us to information on each of our clients. They'd all signed off on us tracking their every single movement. Being a HEAT member meant safety, security, and protection. Not intrusion.

At least not in the past. But fuck if I wasn't going to cross that line with her. "I can take care of her."

"I don't give a shit what you think you can do. That's my girl out there."

I couldn't help that my eyes cut to his fast. "Your girl?"

"She's been mine all the years you were too much of a coward to get over your feelings and do what you should have done long ago."

"What the fuck did you just say?" I stood up.

Dimitri knew not to go down this road with me. He never did. It was a line he wasn't supposed to cross. Still, he stood up too. "You heard me."

"What is it, exactly, that you think I should have done?"

"You should have wifed her up years ago. She should be my sister-in-law." He said it so matter-of-factly. Like I had a choice.

"She left me," I clarified, even though it sounded like a weak excuse at this point.

"Oh, grow the fuck up. She never actually left. She would have done long-distance had you given her the chance, and we all know it. She even came back and nearly begged for you to get back together. *You* left her."

"You don't know," I whispered, but my voice almost cracked. I almost gave into the pain I felt as I crumbled back into my chair, not willing to fight my brother over a girl we both loved but in different ways.

"Fine. Maybe I don't. But I know she's been through enough hell. You get me? So, don't fuck it up this time."

"Or what?"

"Or one of us will have to call Mom and Dad to say we fought to the fucking death. I don't know if I can take you, but I'm starting to think Dec and Dom would be on my side. All three of us can definitely take you. Cade and Dante will hide your body after Mom and Dad cry over you."

"You're a dumbass, you know that?" I shook my head as I rolled my eyes, pinching the bridge of my nose. "I'm not going to hurt her. And I'm sure as hell going to protect her."

"How can you be so sure?"

"Because, Dimitri, she sang to me today." I slumped with the confession because we all knew what it meant.

"Just to you?" He lifted a brow.

"Yes, and it felt like she literally peeled back my skin and pulled my spirit from my body."

"That's dramatic."

"Probably, but there's no use lying to you. It's about as dramatic as I feel about her." I waved him toward the door. "Go home and leave me the hell alone. I'm going to take care of my girl. And let's be clear, she is mine. You may be her best friend, but she's my fiancée."

"That's a PR stunt."

"Is it?" I held his gaze now, daring him to answer that question wrong.

"I'm beginning to think you've lost it, brother."

"Maybe." I sighed. "Maybe I have. Just know, if I can't have her, I'm not going to let a stalker or someone unworthy have her instead, that's for sure. No one gets my girl but me. And I'm not even sure she'll let me have her anyway."

"Not sure you deserve her," Dimitri mumbled.

"I'm not sure I do either."

"Better figure it out before you commit, brother. I won't forgive you if you don't."

He didn't break eye contact. He didn't smile. He didn't even freaking blink. It's how I knew he'd choose Keelani over me.

It's how I knew I needed to figure out how I really felt before I went further.

CHAPTER 25: KEELANI

I knocked on Dex's office door days after that fateful rehearsal. It was early in the morning, but I still tried because I couldn't stand that we were back to formalities. He'd walked by me in the hallway these past few days with just short hellos and head nods.

How could we be back to that after everything we shared?

And my opening show was tonight. The show he'd single-handedly gotten changed for me. Could I perform it after how he'd kissed me on that stage and then been practically radio silent after?

There was no talk of breakfast or meals, even if I texted him. Instead, Penelope would respond minutes later, like she was intercepting the messages, and proceed to tell me he was busy. I knew something between us had bonded and then broken after my song in rehearsal. But the show opener was important to me, and for some reason, I wanted him to say something.

Anything.

Yet, his silence on the other side of that door spoke volumes, and it set the tone of my mood that day. Especially when I saw the flowers throughout the kitchen. Lilies and roses and peonies, all from different people. Other celebrities. Other singers. From Dimitri. From Bane. From people at the record label.

From Ezekiel.

I'll see you soon.

I should have been excited, should have had adrenaline pumping through my veins and revving my insides up for the show. Nerves had me rattled instead, and that note had my stomach revolting. I crinkled up the little paper card and threw it in the trash.

Mitchell called to say the sponsorships were rolling in, that talk shows wanted us to be on them, that I was sold out, and that the PR stunt was working, that I'd better not fuck it up.

"Frankie said you and Dex had changes. I told him to do what Dex said, but you better not be doing something crazy. We've got people there tonight." He said it pointedly, and I knew exactly the type of people he meant.

"Probably best for him to keep his distance with Dex around, Mitchell," I reminded him.

"Just be discreet, Keelani. Ezekiel is a major shareholder. It's not like it's Ethan coming to your dressing room. I don't have to tell you this." His lecture had my stomach curdling. He went on and on, and I lost more and more of my excitement for the night.

Should I have told Mitchell I was sick of being bossed around by him? That I didn't even intend to listen to Frankie about my show? Should I have told him I was done listening? That if that man came into my fitting room, I was most likely going to rebel in a way I never had?

I took deep breaths as Olive continued to work on my hair. Meanwhile, I hollowly agreed to everything my manager voiced to me on the phone.

When I hung up, she leaned in. "You got this, Kee?"

Pink answered for me. "Of course she's got this. Remember,

you do you out there. Oh, and we got in the chair you requested."

"It's lined in velvet?" I asked just to be sure it was the right one. I wanted that chair to be sexy but classy as I sang a few of the songs at the end of my concert. The tantric chair would help to represent that.

"Of course." Pink winked at me and then turned to D. "Dimitri, where's your insufferable brother?"

Dimitri sat in my dressing room on the couch, staring at the door. "I'm wondering the same damn thing."

"He's probably working," I muttered. Even if this was a PR stunt, it still hurt that he hadn't come to wish me good luck, that he hadn't opened his door, that he didn't want to.

He was protecting his heart from me while I swam out to him with mine in my hand, ready to throw it to him without a lifeline. And as if on cue, the door opened, but standing behind it wasn't Dex.

It was Bane.

"What are you doing here?" Pink's eyes narrowed first on me and then on the overpowering presence that the man had. Every time he was in a room, it shifted to a darker place, like his all-black suit radiated foreboding along with his stone-cold stare. And it cooled even further as he looked at Pink.

"Here to wish Keelani a good night, Bianca. That okay with you?"

"Bianca?" I blurted out. "Is that your name?"

Pink waved the blush brush at me. "Oh, like *Keelani* is really your name?"

"It is."

"Makes sense if it's true." She squinted at me, ready to call my bluff.

"It is," Olive confirmed and then pried into our new

friend's life. "Why Pink instead of Bianca?"

"The hair of course." She said it so fast, we both looked at her.

My eyes drifted to Bane. I saw a small smile, one that didn't even seem to belong on his serious face, playing on his lips as he watched Pink squirm. Then he said, "That's not what I recall—"

"Quiet," she hissed at him. "Bane thinks he can use *Bianca* even though it's from my past, but"—she looked at him then— "he can't."

He hummed but didn't fight her on it. His piercing gaze was back on me instead. "Keelani, it's been a pleasure for my crew within the resort to work with you so far. I'm sorry I haven't been around more, but I wanted to stop by and let you know that if you need anything, make sure to alert Dex or me. Your time here is important to all of us. We've done lighting and sound checks. The theater is filled. And extra security measures have been implemented at Dex's request."

The man rattled off things that normally would have been managed by my security team and creative director. "Frankie and the security team—"

"We're very thorough here, Ms. Hale. It's the Black and HEAT names, after all. Your new security team is being briefed, but at this time, we will have our security crew handling your stay."

Dimitri hadn't said a thing from the couch he sat on, but he muttered, "About time." And then his eyes met mine. "Our team's the best, Keelani. You're taken care of. I would have done it myself, but Dex had already put the wheels in motion."

"Oh." I frowned. Dex hadn't told me anything about it, but telling the whole room that my fiancé and I weren't really talking felt a little ridiculous. "Okay. Well, thank you."

Dimitri sighed as he closed the laptop that rested on his legs and stood. He waved away Olive who was behind me, and Pink scoffed as he came to stand behind me in the mirror. "Don't thank me when you're the one getting on stage here, Kee. I know what it means. You sold out."

Bane looked between us before he nodded. "We appreciate you." He didn't say anything else, yet most everyone in that room murmured words of encouragement and affirmation after him.

They told me I was the star. I was the show. I was giving them all a gift with my voice.

When I asked for a minute alone, I only shed one tear staring at myself in the lighted mirror. I had a full face of makeup, smoky eyes, my dark hair curled in soft waves down over my shoulders. My dress was short, shimmery, and swayed if I sashayed just a little.

Beauty could wrap up emotions and package them as perfection.

I took deep breaths before walking out there, deep and measured and shaky. I reminded myself it was only a few months of doing this for my family, and then I'd be done.

I called my dad, trying my best to breathe. "How's Mom?"

"Isn't your concert in a few minutes?"

"I think... I'm tired, Dad. I feel like I might need to..." My voice cracked.

"Oh, Keelani. Honey, get a drink of water. You're going to be all right. You've done shows like this over and over and over again, huh?"

I closed my eyes tight. "Sometimes I just want to be singing in my room with her one more time, Dad. One more time."

He sighed. "Want me to try to get her to sing?"

"No." I fisted my hand tight at my side. What was I doing? They didn't need this now. "I'm sorry. I just needed a second. I'm fine."

"Of course you are, honey." My father always reassured me of that. "If you want, I can come there for a few days."

I didn't know if it was his attempt to get into a casino or to be a father. The question gutted me either way, along with the fact that I couldn't know and the fact that I couldn't ask. "No, Dad. I'm fine. I gotta go, but I'm fine. Tell her I love her."

"We love you too, Keelani. Don't forget that. We love you very much and are very proud of you."

When I hung up, I took a deep breath, but it was different now. I was stronger after I reminded myself this was for them. My focus was there, and I stepped out on stage with a brilliant smile on my face. I didn't drop the mask. And the music took me away to a world where I could escape the burdens I carried.

I looked out at the crowd and saw they were on that journey with me. I sang of love and home and heartbreak, but the music soothed me...until the end. I only had four songs left to sing. All of them were different. I'd done a costume change into a classic cocktail dress and slid silk gloves on over my engagement ring.

On the stage, the lights were lowered. The dancers were gone. The projectors and glitter and the distractions were all gone.

All that was in the middle of that stage now was the velvet chair I'd requested, my mic, and me.

I stood there, emotionally vulnerable in front of everyone. I glanced one last time at the side stage as I told the crowd I was giving them something a bit new but something old and dear to my heart.

And that's when I saw him.

The lights were on me, but my soul gravitated to where he stood with Dimitri. They were both watching me. Each had their arms crossed, looking so much like one another. Yet, Dexton Hardy stole my heart with his sad smile. His eyes were locked on mine as he mouthed, *You can do anything.*

And I felt, right then and there, that I could. As the fans clapped for me, as a girl cried out she loved me, that I'd saved her, I knew I could. No one had ever told me I could do anything on the stage, but suddenly I wanted to.

"Words and writing music saved me, you know that? It brought me back from the depths of hell, and I think it will again. I'm working on writing some more songs that I hope others, not just me, will sing one day. Tonight, you'll have to hear it from me though."

I spoke what I wanted out into the universe for my most dedicated fans, and they screamed like they believed in me. As their camera lights swayed to the beat of my first two songs, I glanced back at the Hardy brothers. Dex clapped my best friend on his shoulder and nodded at me before he stepped back into the darkness. He was determined to let the spotlight be only on me and not on us. We didn't need it in that moment. He was giving me this, and I'd be forever grateful.

I turned back to the crowd and swayed to the violins lifting us all up into a different space. We were on clouds, flying high in the notes, and I was suddenly free of every worry.

Until I saw him in the crowd.

Ezekiel.

He'd probably gotten a ticket from Mitchell, and I hated that his presence affected me. I cut the show short, looking to my band and signaling it was over.

I accommodated his presence, let him shrink me and

protected the one song I should have sung. But it was one I held too dear to expose to him. I didn't want my creativity and my heart tarnished with the memory of him being there. When we've dealt with trauma before, we protect what we love— especially when so many memories are already marred with pain.

So I ended the set early and was met by the head of security, Jimmy, as I walked off stage. He spoke into his comms, listening through the earpiece, and then he offered me his arm. "Only if you feel comfortable, Ms. Keelani, but I'll be walking you to your dressing room after every show. And it's easier for me to protect you if you're by my side."

His large smile and the way he actually asked made me immediately slide my hand through the crook of his arm. "Thank you," I murmured.

We turned the corner toward the dressing room, and there stood Ezekiel. He was tall, with a dusting of gray at the temples of his dark-blond hair. His sunken eyes always made me wonder if he ever slept or just indulged in drug after drug to keep up his lifestyle. "Keelani!" He almost purred my name.

"Ezekiel, it's my understanding you're with Trinity Enterprises and were approved as a backstage guest." Jimmy looked at a sheet he'd been given. "My team is going to clear her room before your meeting."

With that, two men passed us, and Ezekiel raised an eyebrow. "Fancy, Keelani. You're getting the superstar treatment now, I see."

I smiled without letting my mask slip. The deep breaths I took were for my family.

"I think anyone at HEAT gets this type of treatment." I waved away his comment and turned to Jimmy as his two guys exited my room. "We good?"

Jimmy nodded, but he searched my eyes for a beat longer than I wanted him to before he said, "We'll be outside your door if you need us."

Ezekiel chuckled but stepped back for me to walk in before he closed the door behind him. He lifted a brow as if he wanted an explanation. "You telling people I'm dangerous or something, Keelani?"

His tone was joking but I knew that look. "Of course not. It's just protocol here."

He hummed and stepped over to my vanity where he looked at more flowers that had been delivered. Dimitri always sent some to my residence before the show and had some sent after to my dressing room.

"Dimitri's still sniffing around as always, I see."

"He's a great friend."

Ezekiel turned his eyes on me, and they looked more wild than normal. "Is his brother a great fiancé?" He glanced down at my ring.

I cleared my throat and tried my best to stand my ground. "Ezekiel, I appreciate you coming, but I have a lot to do before I go home."

He curled his lip. The thing about a man in power was that he thought he always had power. Ezekiel exercised it in the worst way. "It's a PR stunt, isn't it? Just for the label, though?" He dragged his thin finger along my arm down to my ring where he tapped it.

"Dex and I have a long history." I wanted to explain without explaining because I needed him to leave. My eyes flicked toward the door. My heart rate picked up at the thought of making a run for it. Would I be able to outrun him? So quick did a woman's mind have to weigh her options around sleazy men. He shouldn't have had that power over me but he did when I knew the record label wanted me to appease him.

All the more reason to get out from under the record label as soon as possible. Then, his influence wouldn't matter.

"Not as long or as good of a history as we have, I hope." Ezekiel had been around since I was young. His stares were always lingering, his hands always grabby, and his intentions always murky. In the last few years, though, he'd started coming to my shows. A lot of them. And I'd get flowers and lingering kisses on the cheek. He'd send me pictures of myself from afar, like he'd been stalking me.

I never felt alone...until I got here. Here in this casino, I felt like maybe I'd be safe. Yet, I'd miscalculated. "Our history is great. I appreciate all you've done for me as an artist with the record label, Ezekiel."

A woman can feel a man caging them in like an animal. The instinct is there to run, but the social norms hold us back. We question our sanity, our gut reaction, our rationality. Even still, I measured the length of the room and estimated how fast I could get to the door.

I considered, too, how Ezekiel would make it sound. If I didn't endure an advance, if he wasn't caught in one, then it would be my word against his. He'd win, and the thought had my throat almost closing in disgust and resignation.

When he shuffled forward and wrapped an arm around my waist, I whispered, "I think you should go." But the sound was meek, soft, and too nice.

I'd been so freaking nice to him over the years, even smiling when his hands grazed over me in a way they shouldn't. "Why would I go, Keelani?" he said in my ear, and I smelled the rancid stench of alcohol on his breath as he pushed his length against my stomach. "I've been excited to see you all night."

"I'll scream, Ezekiel," I warned, but it was hollow and empty. My bravery was shrinking.

The laugh that rumbled out of him showed he didn't believe me. "You won't, Keelani. Can you imagine the scandal? I'd ruin you, this resort, and your family. You're my little sweetheart. You would never."

His mouth dragged across my neck, and I felt the tears as I stood without moving. I was frozen in shame and fear immediately. How could I let this be happening?

Yet, how was I supposed to know how to confront a man taking advantage of me? I'd be practically trained by the record label to allow it, to just endure. I'd known this day would come, where he'd take advantage of me like he had so many others. I knew so many women before me had been told to keep quiet about him, to not cause a scene, He was too influential. He'd ruin me and everyone close to me.

And I was in Dimitri and Dex's resort. I couldn't bring that publicity onto them. I stayed quiet so as not to cause a scene everyone would have to navigate later. I didn't need this spreading in the news I didn't need Ezekiel going to the label about me.

I told myself to take a deep breath, but instead a gasp flew out of me as the door swung open and Dex Hardy stood on the other side of it. His eyes were full of rage, his hands balled into fists, his suit almost too tight around his body as it strained against his muscles. "Ezekiel Ballister, get your hands off my fiancée."

"Oh, I wasn't— Of course. It's...uh...great to meet you. Keelani was just telling me how this arrangement is fake between you two." Ezekiel chuckled and pulled at the collar of his shirt before he glared at me like I was supposed to come to his rescue.

"Kee." Dex rasped out my name and his eyebrows dipped as he looked at me with such emotion that I almost broke down as he breathed out, "Heartbreaker, tell me you'll leave the room while Ezekiel and I chat."

He was warning me. Giving me an out. It was an invitation to excuse me from what he was about to unleash, something he thought I didn't want to see.

It was a turning point for me. I wasn't the sweetheart Ezekiel thought I was. I wouldn't be ever again.

"I want to stay, Dex."

CHAPTER 26: DEX

I knew the moment I saw him step close to Keelani on the cameras that I was going to kill him. I'd avoided her for days trying to work out if I could figure out where she belonged. Next to me. Or away from me. With me or without me.

Real or fake.

My wife or my heartbreak.

It only took one second of seeing her in danger, of her heart rate picking up to decide it all for me. Monitoring her heart rate and other stats from her ring showed me there was fear there too. I'd made sure the high tech tracking we'd made for HEAT watches was implanted on that ring before she ever slid it on. I wasn't sure if I was going to use it but after hearing from Dimitri about his concerns, I couldn't stop myself at least for the night of her concert.

Now, I knew I wouldn't be able to stop at all. It was a complete invasion of her privacy and still, I stood there, ready to commit every crime with no remorse for her.

And she wanted to witness it. I could see it in her eyes.

"Jimmy, close the door," I said quietly. Jimmy knew. He swung it shut fast, and I heard in my earpiece that no one was to enter the room. Right after, a notification sounded that the cameras in Kee's dressing room went down.

Good.

He got the message.

"No need to keep you both, actually." Ezekiel chuckled like

we might all move past what he'd just done, but I saw how his eyes jumped to the door. "If you two need some time, I can come see Keelani later and—"

"Kee, did you ask this man to leave your dressing room before he put his hands on you?" I didn't even feel the need to apologize that I'd had security cameras installed in here. Only I could access them and I would if it meant keeping her safe.

She hesitated. I saw it, and I fucking hated that she felt she needed to. Yet, her strength was there when she nodded and murmured, "Yes."

"You're acting a little off, honey. You need some water? She had a great show, but you know how the lights and the adrenaline can get to an artist, right? I've dealt with many over the—"

"I'm talking to my fiancée." My tone made his mouth snap shut.

I cracked my neck, trying my best to hold on to the monster that rattled to get out now. I grew up with three brothers who could all fight. We beat each other up for sport until I went to college. Then, I graduated to dispelling my anger pointedly in my work or via a boxing match. Hitting this man would feel good. It'd feel even better to ruin him and kill him, but I wanted the lesson to be delivered first.

Restraint and patience were key.

"Heartbreaker, is there anything you want to say to him?"

Her eyes widened, and I saw how they shimmered, how the tears still hung there as evidence this man should have never been in her presence. "I... He shouldn't visit me anymore. Not while we're together."

"Not ever," I corrected her and nodded as she looked at me in fear. "You can say it, Kee. I got you. You know that, right?

Even when you think I don't, I'll always have you. Forever."

She bit her full bottom lip before murmuring, "Dex, this won't end well. You and Dimitri have done a lot for me, but Ezekiel has been involved in the music business for a long time and he knows so many people in so many circles..."

She shook her head, and that's when I realized she truly feared for not herself, but us. She was honestly protecting me over her own well-being.

I took a breath and looked at Ezekiel. "Did you know she was engaged to me when you sent flowers to her suite this morning?"

"Oh, I... Well, we're friends, Dex. I always send Keelani roses. She loves them. Tell him, Keelani."

She didn't respond this time. Her face actually looked pained. But she didn't answer, which meant I wasn't doing a good enough job of showing her she'd always be safe with me. I hadn't shown her that at all yet really.

"She doesn't love anything from you. And if you send her flowers again, I'll personally deliver every one of them to your door and shove them down your throat. Thorns and all." I cracked my knuckles before I commanded the man in front of me, "Now, move two steps to the left."

"Huh?" He narrowed his eyes at me like he didn't get the command, but his body was already moving. "What for?" He glanced around like maybe he was on camera.

"When I hit you, Ezekiel, I don't want the blood from your fucking mouth to get on my fiancée." I moved slow enough. If he'd have read the room even just a little, he would have seen it coming.

My first and only punch to the right side of his jaw was measured. He tried to duck at the last millisecond, but he was much too slow. He crumpled to the floor, his face completely calm, even as blood and teeth flew from him. He looked asleep, knocked out from just the right amount of force I'd inflicted.

"Jesus, Dex," Kee whispered while I stared down at him, not sure if I should keep hitting him. I wanted to, but it wouldn't be a fair fight.

"How many times has he dragged his lips across your neck the way he did tonight?" I wanted the question to be pointed. I'd been watching them both, and I wasn't just a bit unhinged. I'd gone all the way down the rabbit hole. Her eyes narrowed on me before she glanced to the corner of the room. "You won't see the cameras, heartbreaker. Our technology is better than that. But your ring will alert me anytime you're scared. The temperature your body gives off showcases your fear too."

"You were watching?" she whispered out in disbelief. "Have you been watching me since I've been here?"

"What if I was?"

She didn't answer at first, just chewed her lip. "Like I said before, I'd rather it be you than someone else."

"Jesus fucking Christ, Kee. You know when you say that, I actually consider doing it?"

"I don't care." Her eyes blazed with defiance now. "I mean it."

"Well, it was only tonight that I watched for your security. And even if you wanted me to, I wouldn't apologize for it."

She pulled the gloves she'd been wearing off one finger at a time. Underneath them was the ring that helped alert me to her distress. "I don't expect you to. The fact that you considered it when the rest of the world doesn't is nice of you." She smiled as if it was okay to make a joke about this.

"Kee, people have been watching you," I said quietly even

though I wanted to shake her. "What the fuck have you been allowing to happen?"

"It's not just black and white, Dex. Plus, it's easier not to make a fuss and—"

"Go with the flow?" I knew this wasn't the time to argue. She'd been practically assaulted. Yet, she was acting as if it weren't a problem, and I knew my ass would argue that it was until my dying day.

"Just... I have to consider all angles, okay? It's not as bad as it seems, and I've learned to get through it."

Even now, her mind worked fast. I saw how she had a far-off look for a second, like she needed to contemplate her next move. She'd looked that same way on the stage at the end of the show. The crowd had leaned in, wanting more of her, and she'd suddenly closed them off to everything. Now I knew why. "Learned to get through it? That's fucked-up and you know it. You changed the end of your concert for him, didn't you? You didn't sing our song."

"I... It wasn't the right time."

"No. But it would have been." And suddenly I was fucking pissed that she hadn't sung it. "He stole that from you. From *us*."

"You don't care if I sing that song anyway, Dex." She turned away from me, but I saw the hurt in her eyes. So I softly grabbed her chin and brought her gaze back to mine.

"I do care," I ground out. "I'd rather you be up there as yourself than up there as a caricature of yourself."

"Okay," she scoffed. "Well, I'm working on it."

That wasn't good enough. "If you can't be yourself here because you don't feel safe, I've fucking failed at making this resort—"

"If you're concerned about the resort, you can rest assured, the security here is—"

"It's not about the fucking resort." The words flew out before I could stop them. Jesus, it wasn't about anything but her. I'd avoided her for days trying to figure it out and classify what I was feeling so I could handle it correctly, but there was no way to do so other than to say it was love.

I still fucking loved this girl, and I wasn't going to let her go. I knew that now. I had to come to terms with it too because my brother would have killed me otherwise.

"What's it about then?" she asked. It came out delicately, and I finally saw a crack in her armor as she gulped, waiting for the answer.

Kee was strong. She was strong because she had to be, and I knew that was why she didn't want to let me in. We'd broken each other down too many times. I was the same way with her. Yet, here, I had to be honest. She deserved that.

"It's about you showing them who you really are without holding back. You were fucking magical tonight, heartbreaker. People cried for you."

"People cried for us, because every song is about you."

My emotions were all mixed up, and I didn't know which would win—the love I had for her or the heartbreak I was scared to endure from her again. "That may be—"

"May be? Who else would they be for? Ethan loves someone else, Dex. I'm not talented enough to just write—"

"That's the thing, heartbreaker. You are that talented. I don't know what to believe and what to write off as fantasy when it comes to you on that stage."

"Well, I guess I should take that as a compliment even if it feels like a freaking bullet to my heart. The record label will love knowing that I'm believable enough for my amazing fiancé, and maybe Ezekiel will let me stay for—""

"Are you seriously contemplating what the fuck that man is going to do?"

"He's a major shareholder, Dex, and—"

"There's no justification for what he was doing. He was forcing himself on you." I said the words with emphasis so they would sink in. They sank into my bones too, rattled me much more than I wanted them to. "Has this been happening since—"

"Dex." She shook her head at me and then set her gloves down before she walked over and nudged my shoulder with hers. "It hasn't been that bad, okay? But you realize this is the way the industry works sometimes? Do you have any idea what the corporate world looks like for a woman? How many loose hands we have to avoid? How easy it is for a man to grab at something he shouldn't and then laugh it off because he's in a position of power?"

I watched our reflections in the mirror, her face completely relaxed while mine turned green. "It shouldn't be that way."

"And yet you have two sisters. You know it is."

"No. They were never celebrities that—"

"All women go through something. But, sure, Cade and Dante Armanelli are married to them. People might not respect those men, but they fear them enough to keep their distance."

I suddenly had more respect for those men protecting my sisters right then and there. "Yeah, well, tonight marks the night people will start to keep their distance from you." I vowed it, etched it in my brain, and could see it as my only goal now. "I'm going to make sure of it, Kee."

I saw the way her eyebrows dipped low, and she chewed her cheek before leaving my side and sitting down at her vanity mirror to start wiping away the makeup over her lips. She sighed. "Do you know I used to want to make waves? Approach the issue of Ezekiel just based on principle. I did one time with Mitchell, and you know what he said to me?"

"I don't know if I want to know."

She smiled sadly. "He said it could be worse, that Ezekiel thinks I'm such a sweet girl he doesn't even want to take me to bed like he does the other women."

Was there a way I could slowly kill him and get away with it? I was already racking my brain for ideas.

She continued, "You look sick, and the first time I heard that, I was too. I vomited in the bathroom before I went out on stage that night."

"You should have left."

"Exactly. It's never easy to leave." She said it with such conviction. "Not when they've threaded their life into yours. I don't even know how to operate without them. Like, what would I have gone on and done?" She threw the makeup in the small tin can at the wall. "I'm under contract and—"

"No contract should hold you to that." The words rumbled out of me, mean and full of frustration.

"Your contract allows you to pretty much own me, Dex." She smiled softly and her words filled my stomach with bile.

"I'd never—"

"I know." She cut me off. "It's just easy to exert power. They're, unfortunately, exerting it for their own benefit in a way you never would. Although, I'm sure you wanted to hurt me in some sense."

"I wanted to get over you," I threw back.

"Wanted or want?"

"I'm not sure." Fuck if I knew what I wanted anymore. "I want closure one way or another."

"And we both deserve that." She shrugged. "Look. We've handled it for now and maybe he won't come—"

"He's being banned from every HEAT property as we speak, heartbreaker."

"Dex, you can't—"

"I can do anything I want when it comes to my business, Kee. Don't you get that? I have him on camera *assaulting* you." Did she not understand the gravity of the situation?

"He didn't agree to being recorded, and he'd probably sue you and Dimitri for—"

"Everyone that steps into a HEAT property or Black-owned building gives us that right," I informed her. "You signed that when you looked over our handbook."

"That handbook is a million pages long." She curled her lip at me.

"Exactly." I shrugged. Our lawyers knew what they were doing. "Plus, people pay hundreds of thousands of dollars for the protection of our resorts. I came to your aid tonight, didn't I?"

"Because you were monitoring my heart rate via a ring. Do you know how crazy that sounds?"

"Want me to apologize for it?" I asked her without an ounce of remorse in my tone. "I'm going to watch your every fucking move, Kee, and I'm not going to feel guilty at all. I'm here to protect you. Fake fiancée or not, you're mine and everything that's mine stays safe, heartbreaker. Even if I can't decide whether watching you will break me or put me back together."

"That's borderline obsessive, Dex."

"I didn't claim to be sane, Kee." I took a deep breath and leaned against the doorframe to try to quell the need running through me now. I wanted to bottle her up or wrap her in bubble wrap and lock her in a damn room so no one could hurt her after this.

"I guess I'm not exactly sane, either, because I want you watching me. Just you. Only you."

CHAPTER 27: KEELANI

On the way back to our suite, Dex called Jimmy. "Take care of Ezekiel discreetly. Inform him that he's banned from HEAT and Black Diamond resorts. His lawyers can contact mine."

"Dex, I can take care of him," I said, even though the idea made my stomach curl.

"Yes, but I will instead," he replied and then he ushered me into our suite where I had him show me every camera throughout it.

He didn't apologize for any of them. He pulled me through each room, even the bathrooms, to show how his technology worked. It was extensive in that it could track even the body temperature of skin, alert him to fluctuations, and pretty much monitor all my activities.

"So you basically know when I've..." I couldn't even say it.

"I haven't monitored you yet, Kee." Still, I saw the hunger in his eyes. He wanted to monitor me. It was in him to control every single thing.

"But you're going to." My body heated at the thought, and I couldn't hide the blush as we walked back down the hall to the kitchen where all my flowers sat in vases. I moved one so the petals of the peonies shone in the city lights just right, and my ring glinted as I did it. I remembered his statement about my ring earlier that night. "Is that why my ring is so big? So you could get the tracking in it?"

"The wiring is in the metal, heartbreaker, and the computer

chip that transmits me the data is smaller than a grain of salt. I can fit my technology in just about anything, Kee. Your ring is big for other reasons."

"Like what?"

He stared at me in the cocktail dress I still hadn't taken off from the concert. The dark-purple sequins flowed around my hips and tapered off as the mermaid shape of it flared out. It was my favorite one that Pink had found for me because it stretched over every curve of my body but I could still move fluidly if needed.

A low rumble came from Dex's chest as his eyes drank me in. "To show you're mine even if you are the star that you are. You're mine first, and I want a blinding display of that everywhere you go."

"That's ridiculously territorial of you especially considering you haven't talked to me in nearly a week," I chided. "Or especially when this is only for a few more months and you don't even care to be seen with me."

"I don't care to be seen with you?"

"We don't go out in public. Your social media post made sure of that and you haven't asked me to—"

"I don't care to be seen out in public when it's only serving that crooked label of yours."

"They aren't that crooked." I tried to keep some semblance of respect intact for them.

Dex scoffed at the absurdity of it. Then he said, "You want to go on a date, heartbreaker, just ask."

"Over the past week when you were practically ignoring me?"

"I needed to figure a few things out first." He smirked like it was all done now, like it was that easy.

"You know you can't just go dark when you're trying to work through something. You're supposed to share it with the people you're in a relationship..." My voice faded as I realized what I was saying.

Dex didn't back away from my statement though. Instead, he smiled at me. "Is that what we're in now, Kee?"

"Whatever. You know what I mean." I sighed and crossed my arms as I leaned on the counter to stare up at him. "And we don't need to go on dates, but it helps our brand to—"

"You think I need to drive my brand up?" Now he chuckled.

"What?" I knew he thought my reasoning was silly and so I turned to rearrange the flowers again. "It always helps."

"My brand drives itself at this point." I heard him approach me from behind. Then he moved his mouth near my ear as his hands went to the sides of the counter to cage me in. I felt his length against me as he growled, "The only reason I need to take you on a date is so I can make up for the years I haven't."

"Wooing me all of a sudden, Dex?" I couldn't help but antagonize him now that I had him there.

"Or I'm showing you what you've missed." His mouth skimmed along my neck, and his teeth grazed my skin. "I've missed you too. I've been warring with myself over how to stop what I'm feeling, but I'm finding I can't. I can't have another man touch you. I can't have his lips on you. I can't even think about it. I want to kill Ezekiel, Kee. I just might."

I glanced at the roses. "Enough men have tried to touch me over the years, Dex. It comes with the t—"

"They won't again," he ground out.

I shrugged. "For now. But we'll be apart soon enough, and then someone else will try to woo me again or—"

He hummed. "Should I take you on a date to show all the

men who've sent you flowers that I should be the only one doing so from now on?"

I turned to see his eyes locked on one of the notes that Ethan had left.

For my girl who's shined bright with me for years. I know you'll shine even brighter now.

"None of them wooed me, Dex."

His hand left the counter to touch one of the flowers. "Do you like peonies, Kee?"

"I like all flowers...except roses."

"Why?"

"Because Mitchell, Frankie, and Ezekiel send me roses every time. It also seems to be the one flower random men find perfect for—"

He didn't let me finish. He pushed away from me and rounded the counter as he started grabbing bouquets of roses from their vases. He threw some in the trash. Piles of them. And then he moved to the garbage disposal. He flicked on the switch, and then bouquet after bouquet went down it. When he was done, his phone rang, and he stared at his HEAT watch before silencing it. Then mine went off.

"It's your record label," he announced before I could look.

"I should answer," I said quietly, but before I even took a step in the direction of my phone, he was around the counter and grabbed my hand.

"They'll wait." He pulled me toward the door.

"They won't, Dex." I wiggled my fingers in his. "Where are we going?"

"You didn't finish the concert. You didn't sing me my song. I get that before anything else."

"Your song?"

"I've been alerted that the theater is cleared out." He held up his wrist to show that his watch obviously gave him security updates. And then his hand grazed over my jaw. "You know, the song you rehearsed for me. I expected it."

"It has to be perfect, Dex."

"You're going on that stage to sing to me tonight." His hand fell to the strap of my dress. "In this dress."

"Why?" I whispered, and then I couldn't stop myself from licking my lips as his hand came up to my jaw and his finger rubbed against my bottom lip. The tip of my tongue brushed against his thumb, and I saw how his jaw worked up and down.

"Because I saw you changing up there on that stage tonight. I saw you changing into who you want to be, Kee. But I want the whole transformation. I want the woman from the girl. I want your whole fucking heart given to me on that stage tonight."

He didn't wait for confirmation. He pulled me through the doors and walked me through the resort, pointing out where more security measures were enforced. Every camera, every pathway, every nook and cranny of his resort was packed with security features that I couldn't even begin to list off.

No one was stealing from a Black Casino and no one was taking advantage of the HEAT resort's guests. It was clear to me then: Dex didn't leave any stone unturned. He had complete and utter omniscient and omnipotent control when it came to his buildings.

When we got to the theater, he murmured, "Go to the stage, heartbreaker. I'll set up the sound and lighting."

He moved with purpose then to adjust the lighting so a soft glow dimly lit the expanse of the theater. He strode around the stage, still dressed in his suit, looking so in control. He had such quiet confidence as he meticulously checked positions of the lights so that they caressed the stage at just the right angle to accentuate my shadow.

Then, his fingers flew over the buttons I knew controlled the audio. He understood how to control every part of this theater. The man was a perfectionist when it came to managing what he owned, and I wondered if he would be the same with me.

He walked over after all the adjustments with the small mic that he himself slid over my ear and adjusted so the mouthpiece was just the right distance from my lips. "Breathe, Kee. And then say something."

I didn't know why I was holding my breath as he stood there in front of me. "This song is supposed to go to a violin."

He shrugged. "You can sing to anything, heartbreaker. You and I both know that."

Then he walked to the side stage where the tantric chair had been stored and lifted it to bring back to the center of the stage. I saw how his arms flexed, the muscles rippling under his suit. Yet, he didn't sit there just yet. He circled me and murmured, "I want you to sing the whole song, Kee."

And before I could answer, he knelt before me and slid a small case from his pocket. When he opened it up, he murmured, "You didn't have one in tonight. You will now. Just for me."

The metal he held was a vibrant red and I saw as he pressed a small button that this Ben Wa ball wasn't like the last one. "Ready to teach me again? You think I'm worthy now?" I stared at the device, knowing it must be new because I'd thrown all the others away.

"You had to be ready, and I did too," he said in a grave tone.

"Ready for what? It's not like you haven't done this with

others," I said to try and keep the conversation light, but Dex never seemed to allow that with us. He slid the device over my thigh roughly, making me gasp.

"Everything I do with you can't be compared to others, Kee. You realize that, right? Even in your jealousy, you must know that you affect me like no woman can. I'm fucking addicted to even the sound you make when I touch you."

"Don't be ridiculou—" I gasped again as his hand traveled under my skirt and directly up to my clit where he held the device. I felt the vibration of it all the way down to my toes. The man didn't even ask if he could go under my skirt. Yet, he knew he didn't need to. I wanted him there and even stepped to the side a little to widen my stance as he rubbed the device back and forth, back and forth.

He didn't look up at me, but I saw the smile playing on his lips. "Of course you didn't wear anything underneath this dress."

"I couldn't have lines when I was on stage and—" He rolled it over my center and let it hover there. Immediately, I covered the mouthpiece and hissed, "Dex, I can't sing with this in."

"You can always sing, heartbreaker." He slid it in me then, and I felt the shake of it through my whole body. "Don't cover the mic. The theater is soundproof. You know that."

He had my dress bunched to the side in his hand, and he yanked me forward before he pressed a few buttons on his phone. It was the time I was supposed to breathe out the words. It was the time for him to feel what I felt.

The theater filled with the notes of that last song. We had the instrumental audio for it, and Dex obviously knew exactly where to find it.

"Sing for me, Keelani." His voice was just above a whisper,

the command almost wrapped in a plea as he leaned back in that velvet chair, pulling my body closer to him. He used my full name—what I now thought of as a stage name—and I wondered in that moment if I was a prop to him too. Did he want the entertainment of me just for tonight?

"You don't call me Keelani, Dex," I reminded him. I wanted the distinction.

He stared up at me, his eyes a vivid green as he tore through all the layers of me right there on that stage. "No. I don't." He didn't drop the side of my dress but rather left me exposed as he draped the fabric over his forearm while his hand started to massage my thigh. He stared up at me as I missed the first few lines of the song. "Sing. For. Me. Kee."

I shifted closer to him and saw the soft shadows of my body dance over his features. There was an intimacy to having him sit in that chair with me on the stage, even if it was in an empty theater. I felt the weight of who we were as I sang the song and the weight of who we would become.

Together.

We were bound together whether we wanted to be or not. Forever. The air shifted as I sang about our flowers in a field and how he'd broken my heart, but this time, he pulled me closer, his fingers drifting higher and higher toward my center, like he wanted to be a part of me.

The air shifted as I hit the bridge, and I gasped as he slid a finger softly into my pussy. He pushed against the ball, and it rolled farther into me, against walls I never knew could be touched. They were so sensitive, I whimpered instead of sang, my hands falling to his shoulders as his eyes stayed glued to his hand between my legs.

"Fuck, your pussy is so ready for me, Kee. Look how you

drip for me when you sing. So wet. So pretty in your glittering heels."

I moaned out a *please* rather than sang the next line.

"Sing. Or you don't come, Kee. I want this song."

The lyrics came out breathless and raw, the air around us now full of my sexual frustration. Every second there was a moment of silence in the song, I breathed out pleas.

He leaned forward and dragged his tongue up my thigh. The warmth of it against my cool skin had me gripping his hair, pulling his head as close as I could. I wanted him to taste me, wanted him to lap at me like he needed me the way I needed him. "You taste better every fucking time, heartbreaker. Is it that you feel the words you're singing to me so deeply that your pussy feels it too?"

"I don't know," I whispered. "I don't know." I was shaking, my hands wringing the shoulders of his suit, my skin pebbled everywhere with goose bumps.

His tongue was on my clit, and he sucked it hard before he said, "Fucking sing. Show me you can handle it, Kee. I want to see you be what you want. Not a sweet girl but the damn firework you always were to me."

He wanted me completely vulnerable, completely me, completely unhinged.

I growled as I lifted my leg and wrapped it around his shoulder. His hands went to my backside and pulled my pussy so close that the scruff from his five-o'clock shadow would leave marks the next day. I rode his face as he growled a muffled, "Yes," and pulled me onto his shoulders, yanking my other leg up around him too. He balanced me on him as he leaned back in the chair. The tantric chair had two large curves to it. One side he leaned against as his tongue tasted me but then he growled and slammed me down onto the other side of the chair. My body arched against the curved seat, the supple velvet fabric against my back.

Somehow, being close to him, feeling his hard chest against me while the soft fabric caressed me, grounded me. This was me with him, me in my element, me coming into my own. I was able to sing one more line before his hand slipped between us to reach inside me again. This time, though, he maneuvered the ball in me so he could touch the button again.

I cried out the lyrics as his tongue swirled around and around my swollen center. He slid another finger inside me and worked the Ben Wa ball back and forth, round and round. Everything faded away in that theater except him between my legs. Everything I knew or thought I knew transcended into something more.

It all surrounded him. My pain, my pleasure, my love, my every emotion flew through me as I cried out the words until I couldn't anymore. Until all that could be heard on the mic was my breathing, my gasping. "Oh God, please, Dex. Please."

"Say what you want, Kee. Tell me."

His thumb pushed on my clit, and I shook my head as I buried it in his neck. "It's too much, Dex."

"Say it. Into the microphone. Say what you need, Keelani."

I was on stage, riding his face, my legs spread wide on a chair I performed for the public on. Gone was the good girl. Gone was the persona. I lay there, bare for him. "I want to orgasm. Please. Make me come, Dex. Make me—"

I didn't finish what I wanted. He finally took pity on me and curled his fingers into just the right spot before he finger-fucked my pussy so hard it almost felt like his cock in me. So good. So fast. So rough. I found my body liked it that way, like he was so hungry for me he couldn't go slow.

The song had ended, the final notes faded into the ether, mingling with my rapid breathing. Other than that, there was silence mixed with a slew of emotions as I came down from my high. Tears were in my eyes as I gazed at him, his tongue still lapping at me like he wanted every last drop around my pussy. He didn't pull his fingers from me either, just slowed his rhythm, like he still wanted me to ride out my aftershocks.

My body started to relax, but my heart didn't. I wasn't singing anymore, but a new song, an ode to him, now flowed through my veins. My breathing synchronized with his, a rapid rhythm that tied me to his presence, tied me to who I was with him, who we wanted to be.

The theater behind him was soft reds with the chandeliers shining and sparkling, reminding me this stage was mine for months. He was mine. But that was only for months too. And the thought had me pulling back. "Thank you. That was—"

"Just the beginning, Kee." He didn't let me move away. Instead, I felt him maneuver the ball inside me and the vibration started to pulse.

"Dex." My voice rose, trembling with an urgency to stop or keep going. I couldn't decide which. "We shouldn't, and I can't—"

"You wanted me to teach you, right, heartbreaker?" His hand moved in me while his other slid the strap of my dress down.

We both watched as the fabric fell over my breast and then I glanced up at him. "You all of a sudden think I'm ready? After so many days of thinking I wasn't?"

He swiftly drew me against him then, away from the chair and resettled my legs over his to straddle him. I felt how hard his cock was against his trousers. My body rocked immediately over him like my pussy was already trained to want him in me always. "You think it's only been about me wondering if you're ready? What about me? You think I can so easily control what I feel for you?"

"Haven't you always?"

He leaned close and licked my ear. "You want me to fuck you with that ball inside you on this stage, Kee? See how much I control what I feel then? And maybe we'll see what you can really take too."

My hips had a mind of their own and had completely fallen victim to being a slut for him, because they rocked back and forth, grinding hard into him at his words. My mind was smarter though. "You're too big for me already. I can't fit both."

"You fit what I say you fit, heartbreaker. I'm the one who knows this pussy. I'm the one who took its innocence and made it mine. Remember that when I ask you again. You want me to fuck you now, Kee? Stretch you to fit?"

His hand was at my clit now, massaging it back and forth while his other hand was on my nipple, rolling it at the same pace, pebbling it just right so I felt the pleasure and the pain. My adrenaline didn't know which way to go as I begged him, "Just do it all to me, Dex. I want it all. I want it, please."

"Show me you're ready, heartbreaker. I'll fuck that pretty pussy if you show me how much you want it."

HEAT

CHAPTER 28: DEX

"How?" she breathed out. Kee was ready to do anything on this stage for me, and I wanted her to do everything.

Years of missing her, my jealousy at her singing for other men, her shaking her hips for the world instead of me. Years of not having her had me wanting to fulfill all my twisted fantasies right then and there.

"Let me see how wet I make you." I looked down at her pussy, seeing her cum against my trousers, and her eyes followed mine. "Do you know how long I've thought about fucking you while you sing, Kee?" I shifted in the chair so she could slide that pussy up and down more easily.

"Oh my God. I'm ruining your pants." She tried to move away, but I gripped her hips.

"That's right. You're a mess. Totally and completely. Does it feel good? Unraveling here on this stage just for me? How long have you tried to keep this all bottled up, Kee?"

"I don't know." She shook her head, her hair flaring out around her as she rocked faster and faster.

"Does it feel good to be a slut for me instead?"

Her eyes locked on mine, and she didn't even hesitate. "It feels real. It feels freaking right, Dex."

I hummed. "Take your hand, Kee, and touch yourself. Show me."

I loved that I'd put a mic on her for this, that I could hear even the smallest gasp as she slid her hand down herself. I held her gaze as she slipped that finger against her sex. I knew the second she did because she moaned then and rocked on me without shame.

"That's it, heartbreaker. Nice and slow, ride your hand. Feels good to be who you want on this stage, huh?"

She whimpered and murmured my name, like she couldn't take much more. She didn't get to decide though. I was the teacher here—and I had to remind myself of that as my cock throbbed under her. "Slide another finger into your pussy, move the ball around, Kee. See how you like it. How it moves with you."

Her other hand drifted to her tits, and I knew she wanted every sensation. I got a sick satisfaction in knowing she was at my mercy. When she grabbed her exposed breast, her eyes started to drift shut. "You're flawless when you're a mess like this, Kee. Fucking your own hand like you couldn't be good if you tried."

"Dex, I need to come." She said it softly, but her words echoed loudly around us on the speakers.

"Of course you do." I removed the headset from her ear and brushed it over her skin now. We both listened to it drag down farther until I reached her hand.

The slip of her fingers against her arousal was amplified. "You hear that? Keelani," I hissed out her name. "Such a good fucking girl. But her pussy is bad, isn't it? This pussy sounds fucking deviant, all wet against your fingers while you think of getting fucked. Do you think about it a lot, heartbreaker?"

I loved seeing the heat rise on her cheeks as her lips parted at my words. She didn't stop moving her fingers down below either, and I loved the sound of it. My own fucking personal ASMR. It was almost as good as her voice.

"I love the sound of your wet cunt, baby. It sounds like your pussy is begging for me. Will you beg too?"

She didn't even wait a second to respond, her dark eyes heavy with hunger. "Please. Fuck me if you're going to. I need you."

"I want to see how desperate you are," I told her before throwing the mic to the ground and gripping her wrist to pull her hand from her sex. Her cum dripped down her fingers, and I saw how her cheeks flushed immediately. "You embarrassed?" I lifted a brow. Then I took my time bringing her fingers to my mouth and sucking them clean.

"This is torture." She stared at my lips around her fingers, swirling through them. "I'm done with it."

I smirked at her, but suddenly, her hand went to my trousers rather than her breast. She unbuckled my pants and pulled me from my boxers like she was a pro at undressing me. Her hand wrapped around my cock, and I couldn't stop from swearing. "Fuck. You're not ready for me."

"I am." She shifted closer. "I showed you I was. Now, show me." She pushed off me and knelt before me in front of the tantric chair. She pumped my cock, and I felt the pre-cum already forming. Her mouth was too close to my dick for me to even think straight.

"What are you doing?" I frowned down at her.

She looked up at me with those big chocolate eyes, violet hues reflected in them from the color that shimmered on her dress. "I want to taste your cock, Dex. I want to see you as desperate as me on this stage. I need it."

"Keelani..."

"I'm just Kee when I'm on my knees for you, whether it's on a stage or not."

"Tonight isn't the night for me to fuck your mouth."

She licked her lips and shifted closer. There was no way I could move away from her, not when I saw that little pink tongue preparing for it.

"I'm just going to taste you, Dex." The smallest smile played on her lips, and then she leaned forward so I could feel the pillowy softness of them as she kissed the tip of my pierced cock.

Her tongue flicked over it, then she wrapped her lips around me and moaned. The vibration alone would have had me coming had I not gripped her hair and yanked her back. "Jesus Christ—"

"No. Kee Hale, the girl who broke your heart but also the one who's going to put it back together."

"Fuck me," I murmured as she dipped her head back down to lick me from base to the tip. She somehow knew how to get me harder than a damn rock. Her small hand twisted on the base of me, and when she hollowed her cheeks, I knew I had to stop her.

"Enough." I gripped her arms and brought her up again to stand in front of me. "Do I want to know where you learned to suck cock like that?"

"Probably not, considering I don't want to know where you learned to use the ball that's in my pussy."

Touché, but my eyes were already glued to her sex. "Take the dress off."

"Leave the heels on again, I assume?" She eyed me with more confidence now. She had to know here on this stage that she owned every part of it, even me.

"She learns fast."

The fabric slid slowly down her as she pushed the straps

of her dress off, letting it fall and then she stood there naked before me. "If someone comes in here—"

"I'll kill them," I growled out and I meant it. "Come here, heartbreaker."

She sauntered over and said, "If you don't fuck me, Dex, I swear I'm going to—"

I grabbed her ass and yanked it close. "I'm going to. You've been rubbing against my dick for the past half hour, and my cock has been rock solid for you for days. I'm not going to do it with this in though." I was fast with entering her this time because I knew she'd object.

"But I want it. I want to try every—"

"You will, Kee. You will." I slid the ball back, letting the chain dangle from it instead of putting it away. I let her feel the metal in another place. The tight hole of her ass puckered as she gasped, and my cock jumped just thinking about how I was corrupting her and how she enjoyed it. "Want to try something new even though I shouldn't let you right now?"

She whimpered as she stood there trembling, but I saw her nod softly.

"Come up on this chair and look out at the theater that's yours now." I held her hand and pulled her forward so she could step over the middle of the chaise and straddle the curve of it. She faced away from me, and I pushed her forward, leaning her over the taller back so her ass was on display, her puckered hole exposed for me to slide the device covered in her cum in slowly. "You'll sing to them all knowing I did this to you up here on this stage. Will you think about this, Kee, when you sing to all of them?"

She turned slowly, and I saw how her silky hair fell smoothly over her shoulder. "I always think of you." Her eyes held all the truth I needed to see in order to believe she meant it, that she wanted all of me and wanted me to hold nothing back. "I can't stop thinking of you even when I try."

I pushed the device a little farther and felt her hole resist and tighten. The fight to give up control was in her body. It wanted to war with me, but it wouldn't win. My cock throbbed at the thought. Still, I didn't go farther with her. Not yet. "You have to trust me and relax, heartbreaker. I won't push you further until you do."

"Don't you get it, Dex? I've always trusted you. I never stopped." With that, she arched and pressed herself back with enough pressure that the device disappeared inside her. Her breath came faster and faster as she moaned out, "I want you to take me past all my limits, Dex."

I was lost to her now. She was the center of attention on that stage, in that theater, in my world. "You realize, if I do, you'll think of me, Kee, even as you're singing to everyone. You'll think of me everywhere. I won't let you forget. I'll ruin you for everyone else."

My palm massaged her ass cheek as my thumb probed her ass and rolled it back and forth. My fingers worked her clit and pussy, and she didn't respond. Her back now shimmered under the lights, and I knew she was approaching another orgasm. "Do you want to be ruined, Kee?"

She whimpered out that she didn't know, but then she begged and begged.

"What are you begging for? You want to come again now? After saying you couldn't take it? From good to bad again? Can't make up your mind. Seems reminiscent of us years ago."

I heard her whimper, her sexual frustration building now.

"I made up my mind. I want you and only you to fuck me,

Dex. I want that now. I want your cock in my pussy right this second. Fill me up everywhere."

The woman knew how to take me over the edge. She even reached her hand back to grab my length and nudge it between her legs as she bent forward, pressing her other hand against the curve of the chair for balance. "Don't you want to fuck me, Dex?"

The sound of her throughout the theater was my weakness. She was my weakness, but at least for now she was mine. All that could be heard was her gasps as she writhed against my cock now. She begged me to fuck her over and over, and I knew I was going to. I also knew I shouldn't.

Yet when she turned to catch my gaze and whispered, "You'd better do it," her stare was aglow with a mix of vulnerability and love and fucking pain. I knew that stare. It mirrored my own when I thought of her time and time again.

She deserved for someone to make love to her and to make her feel protected tonight. Instead, I knew my body wanted to ravage her and fuck her so rough that I'd convince myself I was the only one who could do so forever and ever.

When she lined my cock up to her sex this time, I thrust in. I could lie and say I did it softly, but nothing about us was gentle now. She bared down on my cock, but I filled her up with so much enthusiasm, her hands dug into the curve of the chair and it scraped against the wooden stage floor.

She screamed as I pulled back and thrust into her again.

"Fuck, heartbreaker. You wrapped around me so perfectly, so tight, like you need it. You do need me, don't you? Need me here to show you what it's like to feel it all, huh?"

She cried out on the third thrust as I pushed the device a bit farther. "I'm going to come. Oh God."

"No one, not even a god, can fuck you like me, heartbreaker. I own this ass and this pussy. I'm going to take them over and over again until you learn. Until you're ruined. Until all you want is me."

"I know, I know," she whimpered as her breaths panted out to the rhythm our hips set. "It's all I want now."

"What do you want?" I grabbed her hair, fucking her even harder, needing her to say it.

"I want you everywhere."

"Yeah? How?"

"I want your eyes on me, your cock in me, your hands over me. I want you everywhere all the time."

"That's fucking right." I grunted hard with each thrust. "You're. Mine. My future wife. Fucking mine. You might perform for the world, Kee, but they'll only ever get a sliver of a version of you. I'm going to take all of you from now on."

And the idea cemented into me as she screamed out, her pussy tightening around me like a vise, like it was dying of thirst and my cum was its only hydration. I emptied myself into her as she convulsed around me.

She crumpled into the chair, but I pulled her close, her back to my front, and leaned back so I could take her weight on me. I let her milk the aftershocks from both of us as I rubbed over her clit, feeling her arousal and my cum still there. Then I swirled it up over her stomach onto her tits.

She shivered. "Dex, I'm too sensitive."

I hummed into her neck. "You're fucking irresistible on this stage is what you are."

She chuckled. "We're going to need a new chair for my performances and probably a new mic too."

She mentioned just those things, but with her in my arms,

I knew there was so much more that was needed. She'd been taken advantage of too many times to count, and now I had her under my roof, under my care, under my protection, and she'd allowed it. She'd begged for it. Said she wanted it. Wanted me to watch her every move.

She shifted and started to get up when I didn't respond to her. "Sorry. We probably should get back so you can—"

I held her down. "Give me a second, heartbreaker. I'm still processing how much I like fucking you."

She turned to look at me, and then she fucking did me in by rotating on my cock. Lifting her leg over my chest, she turned so she could be face-to-face with me. It wasn't just the maneuver though. Instead of continuing to make light of what we'd done, with a trembling hand, she reached out and pulled me close.

She kissed me softly and wrapped her arms around me, a wordless embrace that spoke volumes of what was to come. The echoes of her song still bounced around my head, her gasps and pleadings, too, amid the silence of that empty theater. The sound of them spoke loudly to me while I was in her arms.

"I'm happy I'll be with you for now Dex," she whispered against my ear.

I knew then I was bonded to her forever in the purest and most obsessive way. I could feel how I gravitated toward her, how everything I shouldn't be doing with her still felt completely right. Through trauma, through hell and back, through warring with my own emotions and coming out bloody and bruised, I knew there was no way I would ever let her go again.

I just had to convince her of that. It wouldn't be only for now, like she said. It would be forever.

After I put her to bed that night, I got up, even though it

was well past midnight and made a call.

"Mitchell, I'm calling about the show."

"Oh yes. I heard from Ezekiel. I'm— *We're* going to have to talk about—"

"Make sure to send me his number. He and I will have a chat. In the meantime, can I ask why you and he sent my fiancée flowers?"

"Oh, it's just a courtesy—"

"You send another rose to her, I'll personally shove every one of the thorns down your throat."

CHAPTER 29: KEELANI

I woke up the next morning to the smell of lilacs. They were everywhere. On the dresser in my bedroom, overflowing. Down the hallway on the side tables. In the freaking chandeliers. He'd put them everywhere. On the counters in the kitchen. Even in my bathroom next to the tub.

And he'd left Olive's, Pink's, Dimitri's, and Ethan's flowers, like they were allowed.

The note on the counter was telling.

Their flowers can stay only because they don't pose a risk, Kee.

I stared up at the security cameras and then a text from him came through.

Dex: Don't cry. They're just flowers, Kee. Get ready. We're going to breakfast.

Me: You're watching me.

Dex: You said I could.

Me: In the heat of the moment.

Dex: I can't really look away. You'll have to get used to it.

Dex: Anyway, come down to the Sapphire. I ordered you scrambled eggs and a cinnamon roll.

Me: What if that isn't what I wanted?

Dex: You always want it. Get your ass down here. We need to talk before we start going out in public.

I narrowed my eyes, and now that I knew exactly where cameras were planted, I flicked each of them off as I got dressed and got a tiny thrill from every one of them. Instead of worrying if someone was spying on me, the concern was replaced with exhilaration.

It might have been twisted. It might have been unhealthy. Yet, I couldn't stop smiling even as I threw on some cutoff jean shorts and a college shirt that read *Wisconsin* across the chest.

I now only worried a bit about what I said to my father on the phone, but Dex already knew I wasn't talking to my mom. So, the conversation made sense still.

"Mom doing okay?"

"Good, baby. I think she's just a bit tired."

"Tell her I love her." I wanted to tell her how much I missed her. She might have smiled when I told her about the flowers Dex got me. About the lilacs everywhere. She had always loved them as much as me.

When I walked into the restaurant, no one seemed to bat an eye at my attire. I was getting used to feeling at home in the hotel where most everyone was trying to avoid being approached and noticed for their celebrity status. So far, no reports of me that I knew of had gone out. Olive was very good at scanning all the pages for me.

I only got one comment about my outfit, and it was from him as soon as he saw me and stood from the table to pull my chair out for me. "You're giving me a complex wearing other college shirts," he murmured before he kissed my neck from behind and scooted my chair in.

"You don't need to get up and pull my seat out for me, Dex. No one cares here and—"

"I'll always stand when you enter a room, heartbreaker. You were the woman of my dreams for years and then the woman of my nightmares. Either way, you deserve respect for that."

How could I argue?

He rounded the table and sat down to open the laptop he'd placed on the table as I took him in. His suit was gray today, which somehow made his hair a darker brown. And he'd combed the waves back so they were tame enough that I wanted to run my hands through them and mess them up.

"Do you always wear suits to work?"

He pulled at his gold cufflinks as he looked me up and down. "As opposed to college shirts?"

We were still on this? "I told you why I had them. You want me to wear your college that bad? Get me a sweatshirt then." It was ridiculous how jealous the man could be about nothing.

He huffed in his three-piece suit but then smirked. "If I wore another singer across my chest—"

"You would never," I cut him off immediately, but he'd made his point as I glared at the idea. "Whatever. Get me a shirt and I'll consider adding you into the rotation."

Our food was delivered right then, and he chuckled as I stabbed my fork into it without thanking him at all for ordering it.

"I just might do that, but it'll have to be after we discuss this."

And in the middle of the restaurant, Dex turned that laptop around and I stared at the email from Mitchell.

From: Mitchell Hendrickson <m.hendricks@trinityenterprises.com>

To: Dex Hardy <Dexton.Hardy@heat.com>

Attached you will find the last fifteen years of contracts for Keelani Hale. We are so excited to welcome you into the family and as soon as you are married, I know we will consider even bigger and greater contracts with Keelani in the future. Cheers to more endeavors.

The room felt like it was spinning as the fork I dropped clattered onto the plate. He knew then. He knew how I'd signed off on everything, how I'd let them control me, how I'd sold away my rights over and over again for money and for medical services. Nothing was written specifically about my mother, but he'd put two and two together. Money and medical bills. It was clear as day once someone started reading.

And what I'd sold. I gave them the right to print whatever they wanted all those years ago. I specified that I'd never go against their word in the media. I'd basically agreed to let them rip Dex apart.

"I haven't read them yet, Kee," he said softly, but I saw how his face had hardened. How his jaw was working. "At first, I thought we'd sit here and read them together. In public. Where I wouldn't feel inclined to go insane because I'm guessing I'm going to feel the need to."

I grabbed for the orange juice and took a big gulp before answering. I kept drinking and drinking, and he stared at me like he had all the time in the world. Fuck, the man was going to wait me out.

"We don't have to look," I tried.

"I'm going over your contracts, heartbreaker. It's not a choice. I guess before I do though, I need to ask you if you want to share anything with me. Or should we just dive in? From the look of sheer panic on your face and the fact that it looks like you've seen a ghost, I'm guessing you'll want to disclose something?"

He'd never forgive me. And I finally realized in all this, I wanted him to. I was an idiot to believe I would be able to avoid my feelings. Dimitri was going to say he was right. That I should have been careful. I could already hear him. Because Dex would tell Dimitri. No doubt.

"Can we..." My voice was shaky. "Can we not look today?"

"When?" His tone was hard. That he was even considering giving me time was probably more than I should have asked for.

I closed my eyes. "Never?"

"Not an option."

When I opened my eyes and reached across the table for his hand, for some reassurance or sign we would make it through this, he pulled it back to check his watch. "You have sound check for the show tonight, and I have to get to work." He closed the laptop and stood in front of me. His height alone was intimidating, but when he looked down at me like that, I felt so small.

I couldn't ask him not to be hurt, couldn't really beg him for all this extra time when he'd waited years in silence.

Then he leaned in so I was the only one who could hear him say, "I fucked you on the stage you're going to perform on tonight. I lost complete control of my emotions there. You're mine now and you know what that means?"

"What?"

"I will fucking destroy every single person who came between us in those contracts, you understand?"

I bit my lip and looked at those green eyes that had hardened into stone. I remembered him this way—passionate and determined. Dex had always felt everything just as much as I did. He simply executed it differently. I sang. He drove his goals forward. Fast. With effectiveness. And determination. He would ruin someone if he wanted to. I had no doubt.

"Every single person, Kee. So, tell me the day I get to start. It's going to happen one way or another. But I'll let you decide when."

He walked away from me, left me with the perfect breakfast and every worst thought flying through my head. He'd destroy everyone, and that included me too.

CHAPTER 30: KEELANI

I knew that statement was truer than ever when I went to my dressing room that night and it was filled with lilacs. Like he thought we'd still make it through, like he wanted to make it through. If I broke his heart again with those contracts, I'd never forgive myself, especially when I read his note.

For my dream and my nightmare. I'll be watching.

"This is fucking obsessive," Dimitri grumbled as he shoved one of the vases out of the way to place his flowers down and give me a hug. "My brother is fucking obsessed with you."

Just then his phone beeped, and he looked down at it before his head whipped up and I saw him glare at the small red light in the corner of the room.

"What?" I asked and then my best friend turned his phone to me.

Dex: Get the fuck out of my fiancée's dressing room and stop talking shit.

I couldn't hide the small smile.

"That's deranged, Keelani." Dimitri tried to look super pissed, but then he saw me smiling. "You're just as bad as him. You two have problems, you know that?"

"I'm starting to realize that." I shrugged, and he pulled me in for a hug.

"I only love you. My brother can get fucked." He said it to the camera, and I heard his phone ping again, but this time he didn't answer it. "Olive and Pink coming by soon?"

"Yeah. On their way now."

Dimitri nodded and then he sat back down. "I'll wait until they're here so fucking Frankie doesn't come bother you."

I chuckled as I brushed through my hair. "He hasn't bothered me since..."

"What?"

"Your brother may or may not have said something to him."

"Finally doing his job, I see." Dimitri leaned back in his seat and stared at me with eyes a lot like his brother's.

"What job is that?"

"Taking care of my future sister-in-law."

"Don't be ridiculous," I scoffed at him, but I couldn't meet his eyes.

And like the best friend he was, he caught it. "Just so we're clear, I'm your man of honor, not that fucker's best man. And I get to make a long-ass speech if I want to. You guys have put me through hell."

"Okay, are you seriously calling dibs on your place in a wedding that's not actually happening?"

Olive and Pink walked in right then, and he stood. "It's happening. So, yeah. I'm calling it. I'm the baby brother. I know how it works. If I don't call dibs, my ass gets left out."

"You're the baby, which means by definition you were spoiled and got included in everything," Olive said.

Dimitri narrowed his eyes at her like he wanted to argue, but then he was hurrying out of the room as another call came in on his phone. He kissed my cheek and said, "Call if you need me."

Olive and Pink said it with me—"Never if, always when"—like they were a part of our little goodbye phrase to one another now.

Maybe they were. We'd all been getting together so much lately, it had started to feel like something close to a routine, or comfort, or a team. A family I could count on.

And then Jimmy tapped on my door as Olive and Pink started to get me ready for the night. "Ms. Keelani, let me know when you'd like to be escorted to the stage."

"I will. Oh, and Jimmy"—I needed him to know I appreciated him handling what Dex and I had left in that room—"thank you, and also sorry, for last night. Ezekiel is—"

"Not allowed on the premises. Had I known—"

"You couldn't have. I was adamant that you let him through. So thank you for listening to me and then cleaning up the aftermath."

He nodded and backed out of the room quietly.

"Ezekiel Ballister came to your room after the concert?" Olive stopped curling my hair to point the iron at me. Her face turned green.

I shook my head fast to reassure her. "Nothing happened, Olive."

"What's Jimmy talking about then? Are you okay?" Then, it was like some realization dawned on her. "Oh, God. Has he come to your room before?"

"Stop," I told her because I could see her thoughts going fast. "I'm fine. He'd come by, but it's never been more than that. He never tried anything like this before."

"But he tried last night, didn't he?"

Pink set down her makeup bag and asked, "What the hell are you guys talking about?"

I sighed. "Dex walked in on him in my dressing room getting handsy."

"Oh shit," Olive grumbled. "Are you okay?"

"Yeah, I'm not so sure about him."

"Damn." Pink whistled, but then she started laughing. "Did he try to kill him? I hope so because honestly I know of him. I used to do makeup for another girl. He's... There's something wrong with him, and he has enough money that he gets away with being a creep. Serves him right if Dex threw him around a bit. Someone should write a story on his gross ass. I bet they'd find a lot of terrible shit. He's from old money."

"How do you know?" Olive had always been a gossip, and I knew she was majoring in journalism. It's why she was always so good at finding the news about me.

"Because I'm from old money too." Pink shrugged. "And we're a fucked-up bunch."

I studied her after her confession, and it seemed she'd accepted it. "I'm from no money, and I'm trying to come to terms with what I've done for the money. I was always nice to Ezekiel, probably too nice."

"You haven't done anything wrong." Olive jumped to my defense only because she knew I signed deals with the label for my mother time and time again.

"Most people make hard decisions because they're faced with hard problems," Pink grumbled. "What are you doing now that you've made the mess of your decision? Are you cleaning it up? Are you stopping the cycle? Because that's what is most important."

"I don't know if he'll forgive me even if I do."

We got ready in silence after that because I think both Olive and Pink knew I was too deep in my thoughts to talk about it further. When I went on stage that night, he sat in the same seat in the back. He didn't take his eyes off me, and it was apparent that I sang to that back row most of the night too.

Ezekiel wasn't there, and Frankie didn't bother me at all.

It was Dex and what he'd created for me. A safe place to be myself, to feel him, to realize we'd shared something intimate the night before on that stage and I could sing about it now. I sang every song that night to him; the crowd was merely a witness to it. I stared at him in the very back row, and every song was threaded with sorrow, love, and apology. He'd deserved more from me early on. Yet, he'd shown up in a way no one else in my life really had.

I'd become myself on that stage with him the night before, and I sang about it now. I was angry for what I'd lost, sad for what I could have had, but thankful for what I was getting now. Life was full of hard decisions, but it was how we cleaned up the messy ones we made—just like Pink had said.

There was a moment of silence after I finished the last note before the roar through the audience sounded and everyone stood to clap. The standing ovation went on and on as they chanted my name, a sea of love crashing like a wave onto the stage and into me as if I'd earned it.

I hadn't yet. But I was going to.

When I went back to my dressing room, Dex stood from the couch he was sitting on, and the lilacs I loved surrounded him. "You did it, heartbreaker. Tonight just changed your career."

"Did I? Or did you?"

That man's ego loved a boost because a smile so big whipped across his face, and the dimples I rarely got to see were there before he said, "Want to tell me how you think I accomplished all this?"

"You know." I shook my head and then touched a small petal of the lilacs sitting on my vanity. "Thank you for the flowers...and for everything."

"You're my fiancée. Couldn't really do less."

"I'm your fiancée under a contract. It's a bit different."

He hummed and stepped close to look at us both in the mirror. "Nope. Same thing. It's why I'd still fuck you like you were going to be my real wife any day."

I bit my lip but stepped away from him quickly, because if I didn't, I'd end up letting him fuck me in my dressing room. "Dex, we should talk about the Trinity—"

"We did. I told you to tell me when."

I took a deep breath. "I guess sooner is better than later at this point. So, we can go back to the penthouse tonight and—"

"You have off on Sunday. We'll do it then."

"Why not now?"

"Because you need sleep, and I still want to fuck you like I like you tonight."

"As opposed to Sunday?" I lifted a brow.

"I don't know, Kee. You tell me." He folded his arms over his chest.

"You probably won't want to have sex with me at all after," I whispered out.

"Not possible. Even when I thought I hated you, I still wanted to be with you."

"Why?"

"Because you don't forget a love like ours and move on. You just survive without it, right?"

So easily he said it, like we had nothing to be ashamed of.

He didn't, but I did. "Right." I nodded, and my eyes filled with tears as I stepped into his outstretched arms and then let him guide me back up to the suite.

When we walked in, candles were lit around the lilacs now and I turned to him, confused.

"I'm showing you what it is to be with someone who likes you tonight." With that, he pulled me past the kitchen and to my room.

I stopped before I even walked in. He'd had it transformed into a literal cloud of lilacs blooming everywhere and tiny little petals were spread over my comforter. "Dex, this is breathtaking."

Those dimples made their appearance again, and he murmured against my neck, "How about I show you how I can really take your breath away?"

I nodded and understood why he wanted to wait on the contracts. We'd have this memory, this moment, a perfect night after a perfect show. "Unzip my dress, please."

His fingers danced over my spine before he slowly pushed the metal down and let my dress drop. This time, though, I wanted him as naked as me, so I turned to take off his suit jacket, pull his tie from his collar, and unbutton his shirt.

He stared at me the whole time as my hands shook with nerves. For some reason, this felt like the first time all over again, more intimate, more intense, and maybe more vulnerable. So, I let the words slip from my lips. "You won't like me after tonight, Dex. I'm sure of it." He bit the side of his mouth, not responding one way or the other as I pushed his suit jacket and then his shirt over his shoulders. "What will we do, then? Avoid each other until the end of this?"

He leaned close, not answering my question, and murmured

in my ear instead, "Go lie in my bed of lilacs, heartbreaker."

I took a shaky breath and stepped out of my heels this time. Tonight, it would just be me and him. "This is like a fantasy, Dex."

"Is that so?" He unbuckled his belt as he watched me. I sat down on the bed and stared right back at him. "You have fantasies? Like what? Describe them to me."

My eyes flicked to his drawer. I knew what I'd seen in there the first night we were together. I also knew I'd thrown them all away.

"Regretting your initial decision?" He pulled the belt from his pants and walked forward.

"No." I lifted my chin. "If you want to use a toy with me, you can get a new one."

He dragged a finger over the bare skin at my neck and watched how I shivered. "I don't need a toy with you tonight. Tell me about this fantasy of yours."

"I didn't mean anything by it. It's just, you know, you read a book where he sleeps with her on a bed of roses or something?"

"A book?" He caught my eye. "What books are you reading?"

I glanced away, not sure how to describe them. "You know what books. Romance books and—"

"Why read them when you have me?" he asked as he unbuttoned his pants and stepped out of them. He stood naked in front of me, and I drank in how perfect the man was. His skin was tan, his toned muscles so large the veins danced over them as he walked forward to lean over me as I bit my lip. "I'm romantic enough for you."

"You think you're romantic?" That had me chuckling. I rolled my eyes and shoved him. He laughed at my question and fell on top of me, caging me under him. "You're nowhere near as romantic as any of them."

"Really?" He leaned over the side of the bed to grab his phone from his trousers and then handed it to me. "Show me."

"Show you?"

"Yeah, I have a reading app. Pull up one of your favorite scenes in these romance books."

He was so confident that I suddenly had something to prove. "You know every man could be better if they learned a bit of something from my book boyfriends."

"He's your boyfriend now?" Dex raised himself up on his forearm to glower over me, but he maneuvered his hips in a way that encouraged me to spread my thighs to let him settle where he wanted to be. His length, hard and big, rested against my sex. "You know you have a fiancé right here between your legs? A book boyfriend can't do that."

"A vibrator and a scene from this book can." I waved the book on the app in front of his face.

"Okay, read me your favorite part."

"What?" I asked.

Dex rolled to lie beside me and let one of his hands slide over my breast to knead it as he prompted me again. "Read me your favorite part, Kee. Let's learn what you like. I'm not the teacher tonight. Read me my instructions."

"Dex, come on."

"Does he start by sliding his hand up her thigh?" His voice was full of gravel as his eyes focused with hunger on my body, like he was ready to ravage me and give me anything I asked for.

Dex had given me too much already, and I knew tomorrow everything would change. So, I scrolled fast through the book, suddenly wanting to read to him the part where the hero slept with the heroine on roses one night and then they sixty-nined. When I started skimming the section, though, I forgot how graphic the words were, how they pulled a reader in and made them escape so quickly.

"You're blushing, heartbreaker."

I gulped as my eyes flew to his, and I turned his phone off. "I'm not doing this tonight. Tonight, you get me in lilacs. You want it or not?"

He snatched the phone from my hands and threw it over his shoulder. Then he took a handful of the lilacs and sprinkled them over my chest and stomach. "I've been waiting for this for years."

"You have not." I laughed sadly. "I hurt you and you moved on with your ex and other women. Rightfully so."

He stared at me for a second before he took my hand and dragged it over his ribs. It took me a second to see what he was doing, letting my fingers feather over his tattoo there. It was lilacs and a key, but on the key, etched in the side of it was Kee.

"Dex?" I whispered out his name. "What is this?"

"You were always a part of me, even when I didn't want you to be."

"But you... We... You left and moved on."

"I left, but I didn't move on. I got you tattooed on me because you were already permanently with me. Might as well have had the tattoo of your memory there too."

He said it simply, but it impacted me catastrophically. He'd been broken without me too. I wrote songs because I couldn't forget him. He tattooed me on himself because he couldn't forget me.

It solidified something in my heart right then: our love was real, even if we'd tried to avoid it, even if we were kids, even if it was surrounded by trauma and wreckage. Our love was there and it survived. Love always somehow survived.

I leaned down to kiss his ribs and then looked up at him to kiss him tenderly. He took my lips in his gently, so gently that it felt just as soft as the petals over my skin. He leaned back after he'd tasted me to take more of the lilacs and sprinkle them one by one on top of me.

"Fuck, you're beautiful like this." I saw how he took his cock in his hand and squeezed as he stared at me. My mouth watered at how the head of his dick swelled just for me.

"Let me try," I blurted out, and before I could stop myself, my hand drifted down to wrap around his hand and cock.

"Heartbreaker, not tonight." He grunted but he didn't completely stop me. "I won't be able to last."

"So what?" I shrugged and felt some of the petals fall from my body, all of me so sensitive to any touch. "Maybe we could—"

"We could what?"

"I could taste you while you taste me?" I said quietly, so embarrassed that I was actually bringing up sixty-nining after just reading it.

"That's your fantasy?" He lifted my chin so I had to make eye contact with him.

"Yes," I answered, because there wasn't much to lose at this point. He already had the book on his phone if he wanted to look.

"You can sit on my face while you swallow my cock anytime you want, heartbreaker." He gripped my hips to pull me over him and then maneuvered me around so I was hovering above his face. "You realize that, right? All you had to do was tell me. Any fantasy of yours, you get with me."

I kneeled over him, staring at his pierced, throbbing

cock already dripping with pre-cum from the tip. I wrapped my fingers around him and pumped him once. "I read a lot of books, Dex."

"Then you know what to do next." He murmured, "Sit that pretty pussy on my face, heartbreaker. Let me taste how much you want me to lick you."

I shivered at his command, my body immediately listening as I lowered myself down on him and took his cock in my mouth at the same time. The feeling of him tensing at my touch while I quivered from his was electrifying. My mouth watered around him, as I tasted the salt of his arousal and almost gagged with how fast I took him to the back of my throat.

His tongue lapped at me as his hands kneaded my ass. He pressed me further into his face, devoured me with such relish that I heard how his spit mixed with my slickness, faster and faster.

I couldn't control how I bucked on him or how I squeezed the base of his cock, because I was as ravenous for his orgasm as I was for mine. I wanted him to lose his mind with me. I explored grabbing his balls like I'd read in my novel and hummed low on his cock. He thrust his tongue into me as he pinched my clit, his muscles tensing.

His thighs shook like mine, his cock swelled just as my clit did from his attention. Then, he let his other hand's thumb drift to my ass, and he pressed down just as I deep throated him as best I could.

I lost control right as he came in my mouth, his release filling it. I swallowed every drop as I rocked my pussy on his face, orgasming harder than I thought I ever had. I tried to roll away to take on the sensitive aftershocks on my own but Dex rolled with me, lapping at my sex over and over. "You taste like mine, Kee. Like you were always mine and like you'll be mine forever."

I couldn't even comprehend what he was saying. I writhed against him and said okay over and over. I think I fell asleep to it, but when I woke the next morning, I was cleaned up, and he whispered he was going to work but would be back for breakfast.

Going back to sleep felt irresponsible, so I got up to shower. When I got out, there was a text from Penelope letting me know that she'd set up an itinerary for Dex and me to be seen out in public later in the day.

So, we were continuing with his schedule.

At dinnertime, he'd had her write *Contract discussion*. So to the point and so full of foreboding, I clicked it off and tried not to focus on it.

Thankfully, the doorbell rang, and when I opened it, men rolled in racks of shirts in all shades of purples and one for every other color of the rainbow in worn cotton. Each one had a different text on it. *Property of the HEAT; University of HEAT; Hardy University EST. 1995. Property of Dex Hardy* had me rolling my eyes, but I also giggled the whole time.

Maybe we could make it through this. Maybe he wanted this just as much as I did.

CHAPTER 31: DEX

She smiled at the attire I'd had made for her, and she'd accepted my regimented schedule as if it was completely normal. She'd even accepted my obsession with watching her. I think that about solidified for me that Kee was never going to be a woman I would completely be able to figure out.

She was reckless and then reserved, sultry even though she had been innocent, sweet, and then insanely sexy. And even if I couldn't compartmentalize her, it gave me peace that she would keep me guessing. I wouldn't be bored like I had been without her for so long.

Of course, the woman continued to test me when I got a text that day in a meeting.

> **Kee: Olive thinks red top is better. Pink thinks orange. Help us decide.**

A picture of her in a crop top with a ton of cleavage came through.

> **Kee: Oops. Ignore that last text. You can delete it.**

> **Me: No chance in hell. Who are you sending this to?**

Kee: None of your business.

Me: You're engaged to me, Kee. Even your phone knows it. Stop sending selfies to another man and tell me who it is before I confiscate your phone when I get home to find out.

Kee: Your brother.

Me: What? Why on earth would you think he'd be good at answering that question.

Kee: He is good at helping me pick my outfits for the shows.

Me: My brother? Dimitri?

Kee: He really is, Dex. Just forget it.

I glared up at my brother, and he smirked at me like he'd won the fucking lottery in the meeting. I was going to kill him.

Me: He's not picking shit. He's acting like it while he stares at your damn body.

Kee: Not true.

So, I started a new text thread between all of us.

Me: You and I both know you're fucking color-blind and can't even tell the difference between her orange and red top.

Dimitri: I can.

Me: Which is orange then?

Dimitri: Fuck off.

Kee: Dimitri, you never told me you were color-blind. I'm supposed to be your best friend.

Dimitri: In my defense, all your shit looks good and you don't like making the decision so if I just pick it's a win-win.

Me: You better delete all her fucking pictures right now.

I stared at him across the room, and he finally rolled his eyes.

Dimitri: Yeah. Yeah. You're a big baby, you know that? I hang with her for ten years while you grow some balls, and now I gotta shape up?

> **Me: Want me to end this meeting so you can repeat that and I can punch you in the nose?**

> **Dimitri: I would, but I'm investing your money because you can't do math.**

"Meeting's over," I said, loudly enough that everyone on the Zoom and in the room knew not to argue. "My brother and I need to talk."

Everyone hurried out, and I stared at him.

"Do I need to kick your ass today?"

"Jesus Christ. Take a damn joke."

"I'm not in the mood to joke when you're playing games with my girl and the media is going to play games too. I'm about to have millions of people looking at her again after I take her out on a date today."

"She's not even your girl, and she's got enough people watching her every move already."

I lifted a brow.

"Fine." He threw up his hands. "But she's still my best friend. You're welcome for the heads-up on Ezekiel by the way. You handling his ass?"

"In more ways than one." My brother didn't need to know the details, but I'd threatened his life, had a team break into his home, and was building a case against him.

"He's got a hell of a legal team, to be honest."

"I'm not worried. I've got cameras and eyes everywhere, Dimitri." I stood and started to leave the office.

"I'm going out with you two."

"You're not," I said as I walked past him, out the doors of the office and to the elevator, but my little brother kept following.

"You aren't going to box me out of a friendship with her now that you're fucking."

"Watch your mouth. And you're not coming on our date," I growled out as Dimitri got in the elevator with me.

"Why not? The paps know me as the best friend anyway. Half of them think we dated."

"All the more reason for you to fuck off." I punched the top floor button.

"Let me guess. You told security you had it handled for going out with Kee. Do you honestly think you won't need me?"

"It won't be that bad," I grumbled.

"You have no fucking idea how bad her fans want to see you two together."

I ignored him because I figured I'd be able to control the environment. Jimmy and I had already discussed the safest roads to take to get to the large ride I wanted to take her on. Then, I could take her to eat for everyone to catch a glimpse but still be private.

When the door of the elevator opened, I turned to him. "Stay in the elevator, Dimitri."

My brother realized his place and sighed as he leaned against the railing. "Take security with you."

He knew I wouldn't listen. I had it under control.

But I didn't.

***

Kee was dressed in one of the silly shirts I'd had made for her, and we threaded our hands together as we went out on the

Vegas Strip. The first couple of blocks were fun. She squealed at a person in costume and stopped to admire the Bellagio's water show before we got to the High Roller, one of the world's largest Ferris wheels.

"Oh, Dex. We can't ride this thing. The line will get crazy with us in it." She glanced around nervously, but I kissed her cheek.

"It's fine. I bought the ride for an hour."

"What do you mean? There's got to be thirty cabins."

"Twenty-eight. And I bought them all."

"For an hour?" she squeaked.

"Just go with it."

When we got on the wheel, I saw a crowd forming behind us. Pictures were being taken, people were yelling a few things, but we were about to leave them all behind to ride up to the top of the city. I had her to myself, looking down at everyone and everything we'd built, for thirty minutes.

Her hair whipped around in the wind as she smiled big at me, her eyes full of happiness. "This is so freaking ridiculous, and I love it. I love being here with you. It's like we're young again. I feel—"

"Alive?"

"Free," she said, and then she pulled me close and kissed me hard.

And fuck, I kissed her back just as hard for the whole world to see. I knew there would be pictures of us everywhere tomorrow, but I didn't care. She was mine anyway, wearing my ring, my shirt, so my fucking lips were on hers.

When her hand went down to my trousers, though, I stopped her. "Kee, Jesus. No. There are too many people down there."

Her eyes sparkled with mischief. "But there's no one up here. Plus, I'm guessing you didn't allow the cameras to be filming...?" She glanced at the cameras above us. She was learning.

"No shit." But my eyes weren't on her anymore. They were on the crowd gathering below. It was getting bigger and bigger. "Shit, I have to call Jimmy."

"What for?"

"There're too many people, and my watch keeps sending alerts on sightings of us. It means people are going to keep coming."

She sighed and leaned back to stare up at the sky. "Sometimes I just want to be us. Us before what we are now."

"And instead, you're becoming something even bigger."

"Or maybe I'm paving a way out." She turned to stare at me. "What if I only wrote songs? Had other singers come in to sing them for my show?"

"Is that what you want?"

She breathed in and out and then she said her next words with finality. "It's what I've always wanted. And I know you won't believe that later. But believe me now. It's all I ever wanted."

I threaded my hand in hers and kissed her over and over. We lost ourselves up in the sky, and when we came back to reality, I pulled her close. "Smile for the cameras."

Our security pushed through the crowd but coming off the wheel proved to be difficult. They were too close to me and definitely too close to her.

"Keelani, can I get your autograph?"

"Keelani, you traded up from Ethan Phillipe to a Hardy. What's it like?"

"Keelani—"

Her name was being screamed from every direction, but she kept her head down, like she knew the drill. Like she'd done this a million times before. She looked up at me in resignation. "If we don't talk, they'll get worse."

"You're not going to talk to them when they're like this. It's out of control." I'd miscalculated. I'd thought I would be able to handle them all.

I'd put her in danger.

They screamed at us as we hurried down the road, not giving them an answer to anything. My fear of her being hurt grew and grew. Security pushed us through, but it wasn't happening fast enough, especially when the questions were getting meaner and meaner because we wouldn't look at them. "Why are you with him? Why aren't you coming out of the Black Diamond?"

"Did Ethan do something wrong?" another screamed.

"Were you together years ago?" one guy shouted.

The questions came so fast from everywhere. "He saved you from a car crash, didn't he? You were drinking that night together."

I saw her visibly flinch with that statement and tried to pull her close.

"Why are you with him when he caused an accident that killed your friend?"

That was the one, the question that snapped something inside of her.

She turned with a fury I hadn't seen in her until now. Gone was the Keelani they knew, and in her place was the woman they'd hurt. Kee always felt everything too much, a lot like me, but I'd built up walls in the media on this topic. And she'd been able to get on a stage and sing away her pain. Here, she couldn't. Here, she took the assault on her character until it was too much.

"What did you just say?" I let her respond to them because everyone needed an outlet, but I didn't expect her to grab the camera and shove it in their face. "I was with him then and he saved us. He saved us when it was my fault. You can write that everywhere. And now you can get the hell away from me."

The cameraman stumbled but he got right back in her space, and his face was bright red with anger. "You little bitch."

When he lunged for her, there was no question about what was going to happen. The man's eyes widened as he saw me step forward. I heard Kee yell, "Don't, Dex."

I punched him hard in the nose anyway.

I never acted out with the press; they didn't bother me anymore. Yet, I'd seen how they bothered her, saw her starting to panic, and I was being fucking alerted that her heart rate was up even while she was with me.

She was mine, and I protected what was mine. Always. To every and any extent.

I probably shouldn't have taken the camera strap around his neck to then constrict his airway and tell him to back the fuck up the next time he came near my fiancée, but I did that too before my security escorted us away and held the crowd back. They kept their distance now anyway.

They would learn. Whether we were inside a HEAT property or not, we would not be fucked with. I would not allow it.

"Sir, we intercepted this being delivered to your suite today. Without an address, we would like permission to open it and assess any threats." Jimmy held out a red envelope and immediately Kee's heart rate spiked as she recoiled from it.

Jesus, I needed to turn off my alerts from her engagement ring when I was with her. Still, it signaled that she knew what the envelope was before I did.

"No," Kee blurted out.

I narrowed my eyes. "You know this envelope."

"I do. It's..."

Right then, Dimitri jogged up. "Dex, you meant it when you said you were going to handle your shit out there today, huh?" He glanced down at what we were all looking at. "What the fuck, Kee? Another letter?"

"Dimitri, don't—"

"What the fuck do you mean *another* letter?" I snatched it out of my security's hand even as she tried to grab it from me.

"He's going to find out anyway, Kee. Dex doesn't leave any stone unturned. It's actually compulsive behavior at this point."

"Shut the fuck up," I gritted out because I was reading.

"It's not a big deal," I heard her whisper.

But the words were a very big deal. So was the picture. Of her in our damn suite. Without clothes on.

You go to sleep with him sometimes, Keelani. This was only supposed to be a fake engagement. You're only supposed to be in my bed. Your virginity was supposed to be mine to take.

Don't you know that?

And you didn't respond to my texts. When can I see you? I'll bring down that whole hotel if you don't respond soon. I'll ruin that man. And you. The punishment for sleeping with him is going to be brutal.

I'll make you feel better though.

I promise.

Just text me back. Tell me where I can see you. I need to see you.

You know better than to ignore me.

The chaos was starting to spin out. The top that I'd had twirling round and round perfectly all this time was wobbling, ready to fall down and destroy everything. "You got texts, Kee?"

Her eyes flicked to the windows where a crowd was still outside and then to me. "Not from him."

I looked down at the letter again, and she peered over to see it, but I folded it up, my heart pounding faster by the second. He'd tapped into something well enough that he knew her secrets and mine. He'd been better at snaking through my security measures than I had been at setting them up. There was a chink somewhere in the system that I was missing.

"I want the fingerprints off this letter, Jimmy. Immediately." I looked him square in the eye so he knew the gravity of the situation.

"Is it bad?" she asked.

"Of course it's fucking bad. The last one he had your damn panties in the envelope, Kee." Dimitri looked about as worried as I felt.

"I want the other letter sent to our security team."

"They're just empty threats. And there's only been a few in a whole year." She shook her head at both of us.

"Even so, they need to be informed." I looked to my brother for confirmation.

"He's right, Keelani."

She sighed, like handling it all herself was the only way she wanted to do things. "Fine. Anyway, we need to worry about the media. Dex, punching someone is a problem. And what I said is a problem too."

I pinched the bridge of my nose. "Can't it wait?"

"I don't think so." She shook her head. "You need to see the contract I signed. Now."

CHAPTER 32: KEELANI

We stood in his office after I'd finally realized it was time to protect him rather than me. He needed to see the contracts I'd signed so that he would understand and I told him so.

"Why? What's changed your mind?" He leaned on the doorframe casually, like he hadn't just punched a man, like his whole reputation wasn't on the line. Yet, I saw how he stretched his hand and how the blood dripped from his knuckle. I knew the repercussions of that punch.

"Dex, you just assaulted a pap. Aren't you the least bit concerned?"

"No. He'll sue me for a million, and I'll settle for a quarter-mil."

"So you're willing to pay $250,000 for that temper of yours?"

He crossed his arms. "I'm willing to pay a lot more than that. I'd have done it even if it cost me a million. People need to watch their mouths when they talk to you. How about that?"

I shook my head, tears in my eyes. "You don't even know who I really am, Dex," I whispered. I knew he was about to find out, that this contract would change the way he saw me. I sniffed and wiped at my nose. "You know this contract is going to change everything once you read it, right?"

"I'll be the judge of that."

I sighed and sat down at his desk to pull up my email on one of his laptops. "The record label will be calling me soon to sue. You'll be involved unless we break off the engagement now, which is probably in your best interest."

I shoved the laptop over to him, and he sat down to read. I got up and paced back and forth. Then I turned to him, but he was still scrolling, still reading silently.

I swore I waited an hour for him to finish. Maybe a whole day. I thought I held my breath the entire time too.

He finally looked up after what felt like forever and asked pointedly, "Was half a million enough to keep quiet about that car accident?"

He'd found my Achilles heel, discovered exactly why I'd stayed quiet, and understood why I had to show him today. "No." I said it quietly.

He hummed as he sat there, leaned back in that chair, and watched me as I paced up and down his beautiful carpet. "So, are you on drugs?" he asked.

"No."

"Then do you have a terrible financial advisor? Why are you concerned if they sue you? You'll be able to pay them back just fine." I saw his eyes scan the documents again. "You have the money...or don't you?"

"Does it really matter?" What was the point in telling him I didn't? I already felt him shutting down, pulling away, coming to the conclusions he had of me prior to us ever being together.

"Fuck." He pulled at his hair, and I saw how his neck tightened in frustration. "I don't know what matters. I don't know which way is up or down with you. I think I'm falling for you, and then I think I hate you and don't know a damn thing about you, Kee. I'll punch a guy in the face for you, but I don't know if you'll even tell me the damn truth."

"I am telling you the truth," I murmured.

"Half of it," he corrected, and his eyes drilled into my soul, searching for the other half. "If we pull up your bank statements, are we going to find at least five million laying around? Because I can do math, Kee, and you should have it—even if it's much less than what you should have. They have your royalty rates set excruciatingly low."

"I... Well..."

He shoved the computer my way. "Go ahead. Show me if you're telling the whole truth."

"I can't," I whispered out.

His tone hardened. "Show me."

I knew from just those words he wouldn't bend here. Why should he? I wasn't being honest; I hadn't been for years.

And out on that street, with those paparazzi, I'd finally done the right thing. And the right thing with him now was to be honest. I typed in my bank account and the password and turned the screen toward him.

He frowned at the number. "What other banks do you—"

"That's it, Dex."

His jaw worked up and down, up and down for long seconds before he pulled his cell out and dialed a number.

"What are you doing?" I squeaked. "You're making a call right now?"

"I'm calling your dad," he said it so matter-of-factly that I almost agreed it was a good idea.

That is, until my mind caught up to what was happening. I screeched out, "What? No."

I rounded the desk and tried to grab the phone, but he stood a whole foot taller than me. He simply was able to walk away as I literally tried to climb the man like a tree to get that phone before my father answered. When he did, I knew my shit was all going to collide.

"Mr. Hale? It's Dex Hardy." There was silence as he stared at me. "Good to talk with you too. I'm calling because your daughter and I are engaged. You know that, right?" Silence. "Yes, but PR stunts turn into reality half the time. And I've always enjoyed her company. I'm just wondering, over the years, it seems she's lost a lot of money, and I'm trying to figure out where it's going. Is there anything I need to be worried about?"

I stared at his audacity. My father would never tell him. There was no way.

But of course, Dex controlled the situation.

Dex got what he wanted.

My father told him.

CHAPTER 33: DEX

"You know how..." Mr. Hale cleared his throat. He sounded older, worn out, and afraid. He'd always been a great neighbor and friend to my parents. I think he'd probably also been a good pushover too. "Well, I think being a celebrity is pretty expensive."

"Yes, but you haven't raised a frivolous woman. We both know that." My tone was firm as Keelani shook her head at me now, giving up the fight of trying to grab the phone.

"Right. No." He sighed. The man loved his daughter, I knew that. He also loved his wife. "Keelani is a good girl. She's always been great. We're working on being better with money as a family."

The words sounded like they hurt coming out of his mouth. I knew they must. No man wanted to admit they'd let their family down with a money problem. I just didn't exactly know what the problem was yet.

Their family had enough pride to hide it though. I remember so long ago when my family offered to help with even taking Mrs. Hale in for tests after her stroke so that Mr. Hale could get back to work, he'd balked.

"You know I intend to take care of Kee, right?" I said the words seriously as I stared at my heartbreaker. Nothing would stop me now from helping her, from fixing what we'd broken so long ago. She sat down on the couch in defeat, her eyes glassy now.

"Right. Well, yeah. My wife always says you have a soft spot for Kee."

"She's always been smart that way." I pushed him further now. "You have a soft spot for your daughter too, huh? So, tell me. What's been going on?"

"Ah." There was hesitation over the line. "Well, you know about my wife."

"I know Kee doesn't talk to her. That's all I'm aware of."

"Well, Keelani *wants* to talk to her mom. Who wouldn't want to talk to the woman?" He chuckled. "But with her condition, it upsets her. Kee should sound younger, you know? Her brain remembers Keelani from when she was sixteen, not now. Sometimes she even has a hard time with me. The Alzheimer's is pretty severe. And we don't have medical insurance. So, Keelani helps."

"Alzheimer's?" I only repeated it because I couldn't comprehend it. Her mother had been so full of life. To lose your mind was devastating but she'd had a stroke. It made sense that her health potentially could have declined.

"Yeah, that fucking disease doesn't discriminate. We've been fortunate to have found great care right when Keelani left...I, ah, Keelani and I have figured out things over the years."

"You and Keelani?"

He cleared his throat. "Sure, you know. I help where I can. I've been in contact with great guys who've given me some loans and what not. Trinity and I have worked on some deals together for Kee too. And, well, Kee has always tried to support as much as she could."

I tried not to lash out and extract the information in anger, but I'd dealt with enough men to know that a private loan with "great guys" wasn't a good situation at all. "Tell me a bit more about these loans."

I listened to more of the story from him. He went round and round in circles, not ever taking blame for what I could tell must be gambling. He was taking her money. And then he went on to explain how family helped family, how Kee didn't want people to know because it would hurt her mother. They weren't going to exploit her disease. They made the decision as a family.

He explained it all as I stared at the woman who I'd thought had broken up with me for fame. Instead, I saw how she'd been strong enough to do it for family, had sacrificed her life for them, not willing to put them through pain when she must have endured so much of it.

She was strong. Brilliant. And broken from her family.

She had resigned herself to a chair in the corner and chewed on the side of a nail as she stared off at nothing. When I said my goodbyes, her dark eyes shimmered as they turned to me.

"Heartbreaker," I whispered. The guilt of knowing she'd suffered for years alone with it sliced through me, almost causing me to choke on my words. "Why didn't you tell me?"

She waited a second before she looked away to say, "She's not an excuse, and I won't use her as one. Ever."

"But she's a reason. So is your father."

"She didn't have Alzheimer's back when I signed that addendum, Dex."

"I can put two and two together. Your father has been—"

"I love my dad. He's a good man." She cut me off, not willing to hear a single bad thing about him. "And we've always been taught take care of family, right? You work with your family. You take care of them."

"Of course we take care of family," I answered immediately.

"But—"

"Then I took care of my dad and mom." She shrugged, finishing the sentence with finality. She held my gaze, hers unwavering in that moment. "I would do it again."

And I realized right then, I didn't blame her for it. I would have done the same. It was the missing piece of the puzzle I needed to solidify what I already knew.

I'd never stopped loving her. Not even for a second. I might have hated her at the same time because I didn't know, but the love was still there.

"I get it all now," I said quietly. Then, I strode over to her and knelt down so I could take her face in my hands. I leaned in and kissed her. I kissed her like I should have fifteen years ago. I kissed her with no reservations but with love and softness. I kissed her like I should have every damn day since I met her. I kissed her like I loved her, because I did.

I loved that she didn't fit in any damn box I tried to put her in, that she kept me on my toes, that she sacrificed herself for others, and that she'd sacrificed our love at one point. She was selfless and good and bad in all the best ways possible.

I pulled back to tell her again, "I get it all, Kee, but I wished you'd trusted me."

"I trusted that I could handle it myself without burdening you or anyone else with it. I needed to do right by them. You don't air family drama to the world—"

"I'm not the world, though. I never was."

"I know that." She squeezed her eyes shut. "But you were my world in some weird way, and I didn't want you taking on something you couldn't handle. You didn't deserve that."

"You didn't deserve having that burden on you either."

"Yet, he's family, you know? He's just—"

"Terrible with money?"

"Right." She stood and straightened her shirt like the conversation was over. "So, we can do a press release tomorrow. We're breaking off the engagement."

I shook my head slowly. "I'm not doing that."

"Of course you are. I have to figure this out, but you need to disentangle yourself from me immediately and—"

There was no way. Didn't she see that now? "Actually, we're getting married."

"What?"

"You're marrying me." I wasn't letting her go.

"Do you hear yourself?"

"I do. You said you had to take care of family. That's what families do. Dimitri has been calling you his future sister-in-law for ages now. Are you not my family, Kee?"

"Dex—"

"You grew up next to me. You ran through our freaking fields, you went to school with us, you cried on the side of that lake with us, shivering, cold, in shock after we lost our friend. You're my family." It all made sense now. The reason I never committed before and couldn't see a clear road ahead was because she wasn't on that road. "You're going to be my wife."

Her mouth opened and closed twice before she blurted out, "I'm not marrying you."

"You are. In our hometown. Where your father and I can have a chat."

"Did you hear anything I said?"

"I heard you trying to leave me again, but it's not happening. I'm too obsessed with you to let you go."

"And what if I'm too obsessed with you to let you go through with it?" Her eyes widened like she wasn't planning for that to come out of her mouth. "What if I say no?"

I sighed at the inconvenience. "The HEAT empire will go toe-to-toe with Trinity Enterprises. It'll be a big scandal for everyone, including your best friend."

I knew exactly who Keelani Hale was now. She was someone who wouldn't burden anyone she cared about if she could avoid it.

"You wouldn't," she whispered. Dragging Dimitri into this was necessary because I knew Kee wouldn't do anything that would hurt him. "You can't."

"I would do just about anything for you at this point, Kee. I'm not letting you go. And you're not letting me go either. You need to come to terms with those feelings. Now, want to talk about the text you got last night?"

"Are you— What the hell, Dex? Are you fucking stalking me?"

"Yes, but you like when I do. So, you have one stalker threatening your life and the other saving it. Who do you want to pick to fight with?"

"I'm mad at you, Dex."

"I know, heartbreaker. That's fine. You can be mad all you want, but you also need to stay within the HEAT empire while we figure this out."

"I'm making an official statement about—"

"You aren't leaving." Didn't she fucking get that her life was in danger? "I can't protect you if you do. If you leave the room, Jimmy will be there to escort you."

She stood from the chair and combed a hand through her hair. "Dex, I am not hiding anymore or keeping my mouth shut. I've listened to everyone for a decade and a half, and I just want to be free of it and—"

"You will once we find out who's sending those texts and red fucking envelopes."

"It's probably just Ezekiel or—"

"It can't be him." I sighed. "I tracked his whereabouts. He's been seen with other women. I've also..." I tapered off, not wanting to admit the rest. Yet, I was being diligent. I wouldn't miss a single damn thing.

"You also what, Dex?"

"Let's put it this way. He knows better."

"What exactly does that mean?" She wasn't going to let it go.

"I told him no one would find his body if he tried what he did with you on another woman again. He knows better." I was very clear with him. I'd gone to extreme lengths by having someone search his home. We'd collected fucked-up evidence on him already. The man was going to have to be put behind bars either way, but my first priority was her.

I was going through building a case on him quietly with a team in the meantime. Yet, my first priority was Kee.

She wrung her hands in front of me before she confessed, "Is it bad that I want to cry over admission? That I instantly feel like you've protected so many women in the industry by just threatening him? I shouldn't feel good about that, but I appreciate you."

"Show your appreciation by not leaving the building until we find out who's sending you things." I paused. "And marry me."

"You can't fix everything, Dex."

When it came to her, I would. "I can and I will, heartbreaker. Want me to call Mitchell and see if he wants to sue you when you're about to marry Dex Hardy? Or can you make that call yourself?"

"Let's just slow down—"

"You have a weekend off in two more weeks. We'll go then." I started tapping away on my phone.

"You can't seriously think we're going back to Illinois where everyone hates—"

"Me?" I smiled. "All the more reason to marry my sweetheart. Give them something to really gossip about. Till then, you stay here, Kee. No going out where it's unsafe."

"So you just want me to wait around and twiddle my thumbs?"

"You're performing. Go to the casino. Spend some money." There was plenty to do. "Eat at the restaurants. Just stay within the Black Diamond. Your friends are here. We can invite people in."

"You're being ridiculous."

"And you're being impatient and reckless. What's new?"

"That is new. I'm never reckless." Her face brightened in anger now.

"Yes, but I have a feeling that's all you want to be lately."

She stomped off to her bedroom, and I let her go. She needed to mull over everything while I did too. I even told her I was going down to one of my offices to work because I needed to move, needed to get my head straight, needed to think beyond her in the room next to me.

I wouldn't leave her without a security detail sitting outside our room though. Someone had targeted her, and it was very, very real. HEAT security for the resort was world class. No one should have known our room number. HEAT employees signed NDAs, we had intel on everyone in the upper levels, and my staff was briefed over and over again.

I called Dimitri to the office to sift through things. He was more of a workaholic than me, and we went through staff member after staff member, firewalls, any breaches, everything. We couldn't find anything. A storm was brewing outside, and I stared at the lightning in the desert sky. "I'm missing shit."

"And you hate missing anything," Dimitri grumbled. "I get it. But we won't figure it out tonight."

A crack of thunder sounded, and my watch alerted me of Kee's heart rate picking up. Storms always made me jumpy too. Las Vegas weather normally allowed me to avoid them though. I knew it was a product of what we'd been through so long ago. I hated that I even saw the fear in Dimitri's eyes.

I pulled up my camera of her bedroom and saw her lighting candles as Dimitri grumbled about something. She was struggling to get back to her resting heart rate. Once in bed, she tossed and turned until finally her body succumbed to sleep.

Dimitri talked me into calling Declan and Dom about the stalker, and then they decided they wanted Izzy and Delilah on the call.

"We're not figuring this out tonight," I grumbled when they all started talking about family stuff.

"No. Let me get Dante. He'll know what to do." Lilah disappeared from the screen.

Then Izzy said, "I think Cade and I should just come there."

"You want to bring the kids to Vegas?" Her husband frowned at her.

"Could be fun... Plus, you'll watch them while I gamble."

"Gamble for what? All that money is *ours* anyway."

"Exactly." Dimitri rolled his eyes because we all knew he

considered gambling to be a bad investment.

"You guys are no fun," Izzy said just as Delilah came back on the screen with Dante.

"I want to go there too to see Keelani in concert." Lilah smirked at Dante. "Can we go? She mentioned in her last show she might not be performing all her songs. I want to see her before that happens."

"Yeah, let's go!" Izzy bounced in her chair.

"You two realize we're talking about her stalker right now?"

"She probably has like a hundred stalkers, Dex."

"What the—" I took a deep breath. "You're all here. So, may as well tell you. I'm going to marry her."

"What the fuck?" Dimitri spit out while Dom rolled his eyes.

Declan said, "We knew that was coming."

"Oh my God. Congratulations," Lilah squealed.

I turned to Dimitri first. "She's your best friend. She's going to be your sister-in-law. You knew it was coming."

"But like this? Did you even fucking propose?" He glared at me, and I rubbed my chin.

"I gotta work some things out." My jaw flexed up and down as I stared at him. "You knew about her mom?"

"Her business to tell you, man. Not mine." He didn't apologize, and I knew he wouldn't. That shit was on me for ghosting her all these years.

"You all know about her mom?" I asked as I turned toward the screen. None of them were dumb enough to respond but that gave me the answer I needed. "Fuck. I wish I'd been there sooner."

"You're there now," Dom said. "We made sure of it with your stupid contract."

"Fuck you guys," I grumbled, but Dimitri's hand clamped on my shoulder to provide the support I guess I needed.

"Anyway, your girl is popular." Dante cleared his throat, and I narrowed my eyes at him. "She's going to have stalkers. If we're not too concerned—"

"She's got one who took pictures of her. You understand? They're of her in our suite. And then the pictures were sent to our fucking room," I informed him, my tone grave.

Cade tsked while Dante sat down as if he was suddenly concerned. "You up security?"

"Of course I upped security." I wasn't a dumbass.

"I'm sure Keelani has her own team—"

"They were never her team," Dimitri grumbled.

I confirmed, "They were fired the second we took over."

The whole family stared at us and then they all started commenting at the same time.

"What time should we come in?"

"We'll be there next week."

"I want to go by then too. I need a vacation."

"Should we just take the jet?"

"You fuckers aren't coming here. This isn't a vacation," I tried to explain, but no one was listening.

Dimitri finally said, "Everyone stop. Just chill for a second. Give us a week or two. It's too chaotic when you all are here."

"What's that supposed to mean?" Lilah pouted.

"Yeah, you don't want your baby sisters there? We've been cooped up for months." Izzy was smiling big.

"Go to the Bahamas or something then. You guys start shit, and we don't need—"

"Kee will say yes to us being there in a week. I just texted her." I knew my sisters knew her from back in the day, but they weren't that close.

"How do you even have her number? Don't dig for information on her, Izzy."

"I'm offended you would even accuse me of that." She rolled her eyes, but I knew her to be one of the best hackers in the country, right alongside her husband. "Anyway, Lilah and I have to go. We need to get on another call so we can talk about what we'll be doing there."

Before I could say anything else, they both disappeared and left Cade and Dante to talk business with us.

"Fuck me," I grumbled.

Cade said, "We're coming next week, I guess, because I'm not fighting with her today."

"Whatever." I was only half paying attention now as I stared at my watch. I got updates on the resort and one notification came through about Kee. Her body temperature started to climb, along with her heart rate. I pressed a button to pull up her camera on my phone. Her muscles started to tense as she whimpered, and her heart rate spiked. I jumped up. She was experiencing fear on another level in her sleep. "I have to go."

"Go where?"

"Home to my fiancée," I said.

"Oh, now *he's* whipped after acting like we were ridiculous in our relationships," Dante grumbled while Cade chuckled.

I flipped him off. "You almost got my sister killed." Then I looked at Cade's face on the screen. "You too. If you're coming, your asses are working."

"Oh, like I don't have kids to take care of?" Cade acted like I couldn't figure a damn thing out.

"I know you have a nanny too. You'll be fine."

I hurried out of the conference room. I wasn't going

to admit it to any of them, but they were all right. I saw her hurting, so I was going to drop everything.

I rushed through the casino floor, around slot machines and poker tables. My fast pace turned from a jog to a damn run as I tried to catch the elevator doors closing. I swiped my watch to signal I was going to the top floor and waited.

Two seconds felt like two hours, and I found myself turning to say to a couple HEAT members, "Don't even think about coming on this elevator with me."

They got the point.

When I reached her bedside, I sat down fast to pull her into my arms and wake her. "I got you, Kee. I got you."

Her dark eyes opened with tears in them. "Dex?"

"Just a nightmare, heartbreaker. The car wreck... It's over," I whispered in her ear, because I felt her shaking against me, knew the fear she was feeling.

"How do you know it's about the car wreck?"

"The rain always triggers my nightmares too."

"You get them?"

"I do."

She snuggled into my chest and murmured, "You said I was your nightmare once."

I nodded but she didn't understand. "I get nightmares about losing you. One way or the other." I rocked her back and forth for what felt like only moments, but we might have sat there for hours. The world melted away when I was with her. The fear of losing her, the fear of losing control.

She rubbed at my heart before she looked up at me and said, "Stay with me?"

Didn't she know I wasn't going to leave again? I was done denying our connection. I was about to marry her. I was about to make sure she was forever in my life.

I stood up and stripped off my jeans and T-shirt. She watched me the whole time. Once I was beside her, she cuddled close. "Do you think they'll ever stop?"

"I think the body has to remind us of what we've lived through."

"I wish it would remind me of something else."

"Reminders are there so we can learn and prepare for the future. They mark us and tattoo a memory into our soul for reference."

"What's this memory trying to tell us then?"

"For me? It's reminding me not to fuck up protecting you again."

"That's not your job. We're not really together." She was still coming to terms with the fact that we were, it seemed. "And even if we were, Dex, you don't have to protect me."

"We've always been together. Even when we weren't. And we always will be too, Kee. I'm always going to protect you."

CHAPTER 34: KEELANI

He kept me close through the night, his arm tight around my waist as he spooned me. He didn't jump with the thunder, but I felt his muscles tightening with each crack.

I rubbed his arm as his fingers drew circles on my stomach. I drifted off to sleep wondering how I could ever again be without the man who understood me more than others.

When this contract was up, would I really be able to leave him?

And did he want me to? Would he be able to let me go? The truth was, I think Dex believed it was his calling to protect those he could. I didn't know if I could burden him with that even though he wanted it. He wanted to marry me to help, to fix the problem.

That's what he did. The man had created security systems for a luxury Las Vegas resort and casino and the whole HEAT empire. He'd worked with the best in the world to make sure his systems were state of the art too. He protected people and fixed problems.

I didn't want to be his problem though. And that's exactly what I was with my family and now with someone stalking me.

***

I woke up the next morning to find him in his home office, staring at more screens than he'd had there yesterday that he must have had set up. And he hadn't left for the day even though it was past six o'clock. He was in our hotel suite acting as though it was completely normal.

"Why are you here?" I said, my voice groggy with sleep.

"In my own place?"

"No." I shook my head and rubbed my eyes. "You leave in the mornings for work. Why are you here?"

"Because you're here." His tone was so light, almost carefree, like he'd figured it all out.

I sighed. "You can't work from home now because of a letter."

"What about working from home because my fiancée was nervous about a storm the night before?" He lifted a brow.

"You can't stay home for that either," I said.

"I can do whatever I want, Kee."

I narrowed my eyes at him and then worried over a wrinkle in my shirt. The man was stubborn, but I could be too. "You know, Mitchell hasn't called me about my contract. I'm going to call today and get it all ironed—"

"It's fine." He stopped me. "I've already talked with him. I told him we're getting married in our hometown, we'd squash the rumors, and our PR will work together to come up with a good spin. He's for it."

"Dex, you're not going back to that town you hate. They were assholes to you. And for what? To marry me when this isn't your problem? It's ridiculous."

"It's perfect. Every problem you have is now my problem."

"You're taking this agreement with me to a whole other level, you know that, right? It was an engagement so you wouldn't be jealous and to get me out of your system," I tried to remind him.

He nodded slowly. "And you know that's not what I want anymore right? Is that still what you want from me?"

My heart beat too fast with hope. I'd already tried to forget how he'd talked with my father and called me his family. It felt too perfect, too easy. It felt like something bad was bound to happen. So, I admitted, "I'm not sure."

"Well, let's keep moving forward until you are sure. It's just a little marriage after a little engagement. What could go wrong?" He gave me those dimples and my heart practically tried to gallop toward him.

"Literally everything."

"Nothing." He went back to typing on his laptop. "Your breakfast is on the counter. Penelope will text you about wedding planning today. Please answer her so I don't have to."

"You just went ahead and told them all we're getting married?"

"Yep."

"Do you ever listen?" I focused on my irritation rather than my fear of this all crumbling.

He was smiling so big now. "Sure, I'll listen. Get one of those romance books out and read it to me."

He leaned back in his chair in his sweats and a T-shirt. It was rare I saw him that way, so laid-back.

"You realize it's barely daylight? You're too much of a morning person. Should have disclosed that to me before we got engaged."

He chuckled. "And you should have disclosed how fucking pretty you are in my sweatshirt in the morning, heartbreaker."

He looked down at his lap, which drew my gaze there too. I saw the tent of his sweatpants, saw how his cock stood at attention for me. My tongue slid across my lips at the sight.

"I'll let you get back to work," I murmured as I took a step back, because I knew I had to leave before I jumped him.

"No." He held his hand out and waved me over. "Come here and see what I'm working on."

"Why?" I whispered.

"Because I want you to see what I mean when I say I'm going to take care of this, of you, that I'm going to marry you. I don't think you quite understand."

My gaze narrowed, but I walked over to him, and he rolled his leather chair back so I could walk between him and the screens. There were about ten now. All of them smaller windows of my life within the resort. My room. My bathroom. My vitals were somehow being monitored. I saw myself standing there with him and that camera was zooming in on my face.

It was a complete invasion of my privacy in every way.

"If you don't like what's on these screens, heartbreaker"—I felt his breath at my back as he rolled close to me—"you need to leave now."

"And if I do like it?"

"Then slide your panties off so I can fuck you and watch you orgasm on every one of my screens."

My hands were already wiggling my panties down as I watched one of the screens zoom in on that. And then behind me, Dex pulled out his cock so it protruded just above the waistband of his sweatpants. I murmured, "Jesus," as I watched him stroke it. "It automatically zooms on—"

"Motion." He stared at the screen when he murmured out his next command. "Take your top off."

I complied immediately.

"Now, show me how you play with your pussy."

"Dex," I whimpered. "I just want you."

"I want it to zoom in on your cum running down your legs before I let you sit on my cock, Kee." He growled out, "Play. With. That. Pussy."

My fingers danced over my sex, and I gasped at the feeling. At the same time, his hand went to my hip and pulled me back so my ass could feel his cock right away. I rolled my pelvis to feel him more and whimpered as I felt his piercings just as I slid a finger into myself.

"You're made for me, heartbreaker," he told me as he watched the screen with hungry eyes. "Look how your body loves me watching you."

My breathing had picked up. I felt the orgasm nearing while I rode my hand and watched how the cameras shifted their angles on me.

"Just a little more time now. Pinch your clit, baby. Roll it between your fingers."

I did as I was told and felt the zing through my body like it was warming up to explode.

"There she is. Look at that cum dripping down that pretty thigh," he whispered.

One screen followed it until Dex's finger wiped it, and then he swirled it around in his mouth before he grabbed my hips and said, "Sit, Kee. Sit on my cock. Ride your fiancé like you want to come."

I was lost to wanting him so badly at that point that I didn't even hesitate or try to take him slowly. I gripped his cock and dropped myself hard on him, moaning out his name.

"Fuck me," he groaned, and his head dropped forward onto my shoulder as he slid inside. We stayed there for seconds, breathing in sync, hearts beating in time together, both watching ourselves on those screens.

We were one, and the whole world around us was gone. My hand threaded through his hair, and he kissed my shoulders, nipped at them, bit them and marked them as I rolled into him. He lifted my hips so I could feel every inch of him, and then he shifted me up and down, up and down.

"Don't you see that I'm not marrying you for the contract, Kee? I'm marrying you because you're mine. This pussy is mine. Your heart, your soul, this is all mine." He stared at the cameras as he said it. "And no one fucks with what is mine."

I couldn't accept his confession now. I couldn't hope for something so perfect from him while still tied to Trinity. I had to fix my own problems first. So, I reminded him, "You only signed that contract to fuck with me yourself, Dex."

"And I did, didn't I? I fucked you in the kitchen, in the bedroom, on my stage, and now I'll have you in this office. You're about to be my wife. And I'm not marrying you to save you. I'm marrying you so I can save the world. I'll go crazy and cause too much damn destruction protecting you without you being by my side. You get that?"

"Dex." I stared at the screens, stared at my heart rate going a mile a minute. I witnessed my body temp rising when he twisted my nipple. I saw it on a screen, how the technology was so good that it could zoom in on the motion. I rode his cock faster, watched how his neck tightened.

I met his thrust with my ass, collided into him just as hard. The cameras caught every angle. I hit the sound button so we could hear ourselves—the panting, the slapping of our skin, the slickness of my pussy.

"You love it, don't you?" he murmured in my ear, and I tried not to shudder, but I knew my sex was tightening around him. He could see my reaction anyway. I bit my lip and moaned at the sight of him owning me, pleasuring me, letting me be free.

"I love it, Dex. I love it. Watch me," I whimpered. "Watch us."

And we both stared at the screens as he fucked me so hard, he'd leave marks on my hips for the next day. Yet, he'd rub and massage them the next morning when he woke up with me again.

It's how we operated for days after.

CHAPTER 35: KEELANI

He wouldn't let me out of his sight.

Every morning.

And every night. We slept together.

That was it.

The first day, Dex pulled me close as I called my father. "I should yell at my dad for telling you everything," I told him as I dialed the number.

"Or you should thank him for finally giving me closure."

And then he lay there and listened to me talk to my dad, like it was completely normal to hold me close while I teared up asking about my mother.

"What do you mean, it wasn't a good day, Dad?"

"Ah, you know how she is, Keelani. Good days and bad. She got confused with a nurse."

"Right." I took a deep breath, trying not to ask what I wanted to. Still, I blurted it out. "Should I come home?"

"Ach." He made the same noise he always did when I asked. It was a mixture of disappointment and sadness with me. He knew I had to ask, but it hurt him every time when I did. "She doesn't remember you like you are now. You know it will frustrate and confuse her."

"Right. Right. I know." I wanted to tell him this was feeding into her wrong perception of time. But I wanted to respect his wishes too. Even if doctors had explained we could help her memory by reintroducing me slowly over and over, my father didn't feel good about it.

I didn't either. Not after what happened at the hotel with her not remembering any of us. "It's just so hard sometimes, Dad."

"This is harder for her than anyone else. We need to work together to give her what's best for her."

But how could we know that this was best?

"I know, Dad. I know. Tell her I love her."

"I always do."

When I hung up, Dex kissed me softly and told me I was strong, that she'd be proud of me.

Maybe it was the fact that Dex knew her that made it so his words held enough weight that they crushed my soul and squeezed out my next words. "Would she honestly be proud of me though?"

"How could she not?" he said.

I didn't answer him. I just let the question dance around in my head that day. And the next morning, Dex woke up with me again. He listened to me talk with my father again.

"Maybe if I acted like I was on tour but came home to see her—"

"We've tried that enough times." Dad sighed. "She won't recognize you, sweetie."

"But you'll tell me if things get worse?"

"Yes. Things are okay today. The private nurse you hired is great, I promise. She's real good with your mom."

"Okay," I whispered.

And when I hung up, Dex said *okay* to me too. Over and over. He held me close like he would do it every day if he had to, like it was already a part of his routine.

I felt my heart and mind giving into the idea too. I wanted

to be part of his routine every single day.

For the next week, he was there with me through everything, like my own personal shadow. The man followed me to rehearsals. To the restaurants. To my bed.

My tall, beautiful, mouth-watering shadow. And I couldn't complain because I enjoyed being with him every minute. I enjoyed how his eyes were always on me, how his hands were always wandering, how his mouth found mine more than once a day.

He made me breakfast, went to lunch with me, and cooked me dinner before eating me for dessert. And he filled that top drawer with lessons to teach me. I was wrapped in a bubble he'd created for me, and I avoided all other responsibilities.

I sang. I enjoyed Dimitri coming by with Olive and Pink. I fell into a routine that I shouldn't have because I didn't know if it would last past our contract.

There was no way it could.

And I saw the cracks in it before it all crumbled. His job wasn't just finding my stalker. It was attending meetings about other resorts, other investment properties. It was running systems much bigger than a small show in Vegas.

Yet, he still wanted me within sight and protected, to stay put even when he had to leave. He didn't want paps bothering me. He didn't want media covering us after the date we'd had that had gone wrong.

"My PR team and yours are working together. Just stay here until I get back, and we can go out to dinner if you want," he said for the fifth time that week. His sisters, Izzy and Lilah, had come to town to see me perform. We hadn't been super close in high school, but they wanted to catch up over drinks and bum around Vegas.

"Dex, the girls and I are going out. They're coming over now."

Instead of leaving and agreeing to me going out, he stayed and gave us all a lecture when they got there. "Izzy, Lilah. Clara, Evie." He gave his sisters and sisters-in-laws a look. "You all know the concerns. Don't leave the building."

"You're acting like Dom," Izzy grumbled at her older brother as Lilah looked away from them innocently. Both Izzy and Lilah had dark hair and were smaller female versions of their brothers. As twins who were a few years younger than me, I hadn't seen them much in school growing up, but I knew of them now. Both had married men who most people believed were in the mafia, but I could tell they were extremely happy.

Lilah acted like she was much better behaved toward Dex now. "We won't go anywhere. We understand."

Evie, Declan's wife, smiled big and nodded, her wavy brown hair swaying. "We got this under control."

As soon as the door closed behind him, though, Izzy said, "We're going to the pool on the rooftop and having drinks. They can't stop us."

Pink whooped like it was a great idea, and Lilah smiled like we'd found a loophole.

I was all for it. "It's in the Black Diamond. They won't be mad."

But Jimmy was outside our hotel suite door when we left. He let us go but I was sure he reported our whereabouts. It didn't matter because we were going to enjoy ourselves and let loose.

When we got up there, I told them about how cooped up I'd been, how the fame felt stifling half the time, and I divulged that Dex made me feel safer, calmer, maybe like I could be a little more reckless and a little more myself.

"Yeah, and you should be yourself. Even if you're under contract right now," Clara, Dom's wife, added as she pushed back her reddish hair. When I eyed her suspiciously, she admitted, "We all talk in the family. We know the engagement was fake, but he's not faking now."

I opened my mouth to try to evade the topic but Pink jumped right in to tell them, "So, here's the story..."

And off she and Olive went. There wasn't really a way to stop them either. Not when I was drinking and enjoying the sun that day. When Pink explained the extreme lengths Bane, Dex, and Dimitri were going to in order to track down my stalker, I sighed. "I really think it's nothing. This happens sometimes."

"Yeah," Clara agreed. "Have you seen the news?"

"I try not to look." I shrugged as we sat around a table in loungers while a few guys ogled us from the pool. "The news is normally bad for me."

"Right. I sift through it for her," Olive added.

"It's all good right now. People are in love with you. It means more stalkers, I'm sure. But plus side is people love your new sound," Clara explained and they all nodded.

Pink jumped in to add, "And they love your outfits." She winked at me.

"Honestly, I *had* to come see you in concert." Lilah smiled at me. "I know we didn't hang out much in school, but I'm so proud to see you being a badass woman in the industry."

"I'm proud of the fact that you've lived with Dex for so long *and* put up with Dimitri," Izzy added in. "Both my brothers are annoying as hell when they want to be."

I laughed and thought about everyone saying that to me. That they were *so proud*...but would my mother be? She'd always wanted my real sound to be out there, the real me. Had I given the world that? I'd held back for so long, let the label shift my career to and fro, and obeyed when I shouldn't have.

It wasn't pride I felt when I looked back. I took another sip of the Flirtini we'd had delivered. "Yeah, I was a much different person back then."

"That's putting it lightly," Lilah recalled. "I heard the stories."

We all chuckled.

Pink squinted at me in disbelief, wanting the full story. "Wait. You were the bad one?"

Izzy hummed. "You streaked the football field when you were a freshman, didn't you?"

"Yep." I winced at that memory. "My dad was so mad. My mom said to let me live."

"When you were fifteen?" Olive squeaked out.

"I was trouble, but my mom didn't really believe in disciplining me for acting out. She wanted me to be me." I shrugged. "Then I got my record deal and shaped up quick."

"But Dex was already in love with you back then. He couldn't hide that shit from anyone," Izzy blurted out, and I bit my cheek. It didn't feel right disclosing our secret relationship.

"We all knew they were dating," Lilah told Olive, Pink, Clara, and Evie. Izzy confirmed.

"Oh, whatever." I stood up and stretched. "Who's going in the pool?"

"Me." Izzy stood too and then her smile turned devilish. "Who's skinny dipping in the pool?"

"How much have you had to drink?" Lilah chuckled.

"More than you, obviously," Izzy retorted.

"Oh no." Lilah shook her head. "I've had just as much."

"You guys." Olive's voice was just above a whisper as they started to peel off their tops. "We're on a rooftop, and Dex is concerned about the stalker—"

The alcohol had been flowing, and suddenly, I wondered what the hell was I so afraid of. Why weren't we able to just be ourselves like my mother had always wanted? Fitting into a box wasn't supposed to be a calling. We were supposed to be different. Each and every one of us. If we all fit perfectly into tidy boxes, it would make us all the same in the end. I felt liberated by the idea suddenly and frustrated with her comment. "So what? A stalker is going to keep us from having fun? One guy?"

"He could have drones!" She pointed toward the sky.

I wanted to spiral out of control and do whatever the hell I wanted. Like I had before. Like I had when I was fifteen and not tied to this damn career.

For once.

For me.

For my friends.

We all jumped in, tops off, like ridiculous teenagers. Some guys in the pool whistled and threw a beach ball at us. Olive and Pink were probably the only ones to really engage with them, but they kept swimming around us like they were happy for the show.

It was a short show, though, because first Izzy's phone rang and then Lilah's. They were out and getting their tops back on fast.

"Let me guess." I chuckled. "We're in trouble."

"Oh shit," Evie said at the same time, and her eyes were wide enough for me to know that when I turned, I was going to see him.

I saw all of them.

Declan, Dom, Dex, Dimitri, Cade, Dante, and Bane walked from the revolving doors of the resort's rooftop entrance, headed our way. They didn't even bounce as they went down the steps. It was like they glided in those suits, their watches flashing, their leather loafers eating up the cement as they strode our way.

It was a moment that should have been frozen in time. They were beautiful up on that rooftop, looking like they ruled the world, all their faces much madder than they should have been.

Only one was smiling, and that was Dimitri.

"Oh, we're fucking done." Pink was already hopping out of the pool and beelining for a towel. She was normally the most daring out of all of us.

"Throw me a towel," Evie yelled before she hopped out.

As she got to the edge though, Declan was there. "You get out and show what's mine to anyone here, and I will personally have to rip all their eyes out." He proceeded to grab her top, and then he knelt down to drape it softly around her neck.

Bane was by Pink's side by then and murmured, "Have anything to say for yourself?"

She pursed her lips, not looking at him at all and shook her head.

Clara might have been the boldest of all when she said, "Dom, want to swim?"

He glared at her. "Cupcake, you don't want me in that pool right now."

She smirked and swam up to the side. "You sure?"

He hauled her up by her arm so close to him that no one caught sight of anything because he wrapped his suit jacket around her as he murmured, "You're going to kill me, little fighter."

Dimitri was holding out a towel for Olive, and they were whisper fighting about something I couldn't hear.

I wasn't ready to get out though. This was me, here in this pool, having fun with friends and doing something I absolutely wouldn't have done for the last fifteen years.

"Ready to go, Kee?" Dex asked, but it wasn't really a question. He wanted me to hop out like everyone else and tuck my tail between my legs.

"Hmm. Not yet. I'm having fun with everyone in here."

Clara, Evie, and Pink all wide-eyed me.

Pink mumbled, "You're on your own, girl." And started to make her way back to the entrance. All my friends and their men followed.

Dex smiled at me and nodded slowly. "Well then," he murmured. "Go ahead and have fun with your friends."

He crossed one ankle over the other and sat back in the lounge chair as he scanned over the pool.

Every single guy in there immediately hopped out.

Irritated that he'd ruined my fun, I got out but didn't take the towel he offered me. Instead, I made sure to squeeze my hair out on the pool deck before I took my time sliding my cover-up on. Then I proceeded to walk to the elevators with him following me in silence.

When we got back to the penthouse, the others were already there so that the girls could grab their clothes. It only took the door closing behind Dex for him to start in. "You all realize that you have a private body of water *right there!*" Dex waved his arm toward the back patio at the hot tub while he bellowed at all of us.

Okay, he was mad. Madder than I had expected. But I

think he forgot that I didn't care anymore. These men couldn't keep us cooped up here all week.

"I told her it was a bad idea," Pink said as she rearranged her top. Bane muttered for her to get her ass moving toward the door.

"Don't get all territorial, Bane. I'm just your silly makeup artist anyway. And nothing happened."

"There's a literal threat on her life," Bane pointed out.

"Okay, but I've had threats on my life before," I explained.

"Yeah." Pink was quick to jump to my defense. "All that happened was a few guys saw a little bit of skin."

Bane growled, his muscles bunching.

"Oh stop." She rolled her eyes. "Plus, I have way less of a rack than Keelani. Most everyone was looking at her."

Evie had the audacity to agree with her. "It's true."

"Mine? Are you kidding?" I blurted out. "Evie yours are way bigger."

"Only because I just quit breastfeeding, but my one-piece is covering them up."

Dimitri chose that moment to add, "Why cover them up, Evie? You can feed me anytime."

"I'm going to fucking kill you." Declan lunged for him while Dimitri laughed hysterically just as Dom hooked his arm around Declan's neck.

Most everyone was fighting with everyone, but Dex's eyes were on me as I pushed my wet hair out of my face. There we both were, looking at each other, him trying to control everything and me spiraling so fast out of control he'd never be able to catch me.

His eyes hardened, like he knew I was pushing him the wrong direction, like he sensed I was testing how far I could go. Then he barked out, "Everyone. Time to go. I'll talk to you all later."

And although they all kept arguing and Evie gave me a hug before heading to the door, they all filed out of the penthouse to give us some space.

"I'm supposed to be having a meeting with my brothers in five minutes. How should I go about doing that when you can't seem to keep your ass in line for an hour while I'm gone?"

"You deserved that after telling me I shouldn't leave the hotel room...for days."

"The paps came at you, Kee. You had Ezekiel... And you had a damn letter sent with pictures in it. I need to—"

"You don't need to do anything. It's part of the job."

"It's not normal! And it's not going to be a part of my wife's job!"

"Well, it's a good thing I'm not your wife then." I threw the words at him, and his eyes widened before he walked up to me and tossed me over his shoulder to walk me down the hallway. "Are you joking me? Manhandling me isn't going to get you what you want. Where are we going?"

He set me on the bed without a word then opened the nightstand drawer. Before I knew what he was doing, he'd thrown a handcuff on my wrist and clamped the other to the headboard. My eyes widened. I'd thrown the handcuffs away along with his other toys. "Where did those come from? You have backup handcuffs?"

"Just this one. And good thing. It's all I need for you."

"Are you—" I glanced down at myself. "I'm in a bikini and cold and..."

He ripped the comforter down the bed and then wrapped it around me before he handed me the remote. "I'll be back in an hour. Watch a show while I meet with my brothers to confirm there weren't damn drones out filming you guys. Jesus Christ."

"Okay, honestly, though, who cares?" I giggled and then hiccupped. "So, what? I'm just supposed to sit here like I'm in a time-out?"

He wiggled my ring on my finger as if to make sure it was clearly on there before he kissed me hard. "You will and you are because you're acting like a child so I'm going to treat you like one."

With that, he threw my phone next to me on the bed. "Call if you need me," he murmured, and then he marched out of the room. I heard the door to the hotel room open and close.

"Dex?" I called out, sure he was about to walk back in.

A whole minute passed.

Dex left me unattended in that bedroom, and I jangled my wrist for another few minutes in fury. That's when I realized I'd done something completely ridiculous and hadn't been the least bit worried about the repercussions. And now, I wasn't at all concerned for my safety or that I'd been locked up by him.

I was just mad. And I was going to do something about it.

CHAPTER 36: DEX

The thing about Keelani was that she had been listening to men tell her what to do for all of her adult life while under contract. Yet, now she was acting out, reckless and free. How could I blame her for it? It's how I remembered her, how I wanted her, how she should have always been.

Sure, I was pissed about her showing her rack to some guys on my rooftop, but more than that, my cock jumped to attention at seeing her rebel. Seeing her light up, stand up, and push boundaries she knew she shouldn't. Living life without boundaries meant living a life worth living. She was coming back to life. Containing her was now going to be the problem, and I knew I couldn't.

"Are you listening at all?" Dante growled from across the conference room table. He pointed to the large screen up at the front and said, "We're about to call the president to discuss your girlfriend."

My gaze shot up, and I nodded.

"What the fuck are we calling him for? We need permission now?" Cade ground out.

Dante rolled his eyes. "Cade, just do it legally. We'll get a warrant and—"

"I could just take a quick peek at their shit—"

"Illegally. This casino is clean right now," Bane cut him off, and they stared each other down.

"You said the picture looks like it was taken in the airspace above Platinum Casino's property. That means they're utilizing their drones to spy on us." Cade held up a hand when Dante tried to say it wasn't really spying. "They did something bold, and now we are. Are we in agreement?"

Cade looked at both Dimitri and me. This was mostly our call because the resort and casino was mostly ours. We both nodded. I didn't give a fuck about the casino, just about getting the name of whoever was operating the drone. But Bane cared.

They dialed the number while Cade grumbled about not being able to just hack their systems himself. "I'm head of cybersecurity, and we have to call this dumbass about getting a paper that says I can do what I want. It's a waste of time."

"Do you have something else you need to be doing right now?" I asked him with irritation.

"Other than my wife, who needs to be punished after going topless at your resort?" Cade smirked at me.

"Fuck, man. That's so uncalled for when she's our baby sister," Dom groaned.

"She also gave me children. How the hell you think—"

"Hello?" The president showed up in the Oval Office on the Zoom call.

Bane cleared his throat, launching into the logistics.

I checked my phone to see what Kee was doing handcuffed to the bed. None of us gave a shit about what the man on the screen had to say because at the end of the day, our money funded him sitting there. It's why Cade was adamant that we didn't even need permission. Yet, we followed the laws for the time being, and I let the president drone on about what he could and couldn't do while I watched Kee in the camera.

On my phone, she wasn't under the comforter at all anymore. She'd kicked it off and was staring up straight at the cameras with a damn smirk on her face. The sparkle in her eye was there too, one of mischief and mayhem. Reckless, wild little thing. My Kee was back. And I knew that meant she was about to be reckless and wild with my heart too.

I'd only cuffed one hand, so she put the other to good use as she slid it first down to her chest to touch her nipples. She moved the fabric to the side so I could catch every part of her. I watched as she rolled it back and forth, making it peak. I leaned back to adjust myself as everyone else talked. Fuck, I needed this meeting to be over.

She stopped for a moment to pick up her phone.

Kee: You ready to come back and uncuff me?

Me: I'm on a call in my office.

Kee: I bet none of the other guys left their wives for a call.

Me: Are you admitting that you're about to be my wife?

I saw her roll her eyes.

I looked around the room at my brothers and brothers-in-law. We all looked irritated, but we were all here. It was a matter of us getting to the bottom of the situation. Keelani had already been accepted into the family as one of our own.

Me: You think you deserve me home after the way you behaved today? That'd be like a damn reward for your bad behavior.

Kee: Maybe it's a lesson for it.

I should have put the phone away, but I couldn't stop watching her. I was watching her every movement now.

Me: What exactly would the lesson be, heartbreaker?

Me: Show me.

She threw the phone to the side and glared up at me as she took her time sliding her bikini bottoms off. She slid her hand to her sex, rolling her clit first and then worked her pussy faster and faster.

Me: I think I've finally broken you of being that all-American good girl.

Me: Keys for the cuffs are in the nightstand, heartbreaker.

Me: Don't leave our hotel room.

I saw how her body tensed and how she cried out for me. Then, she stared at the camera and licked the arousal from her hand before grabbing the phone and texting me back.

> **Kee: If you're not here in five minutes, Dex, I'm coming to your office.**

Kee was getting bolder, shining brighter, and throwing away the bottle that had kept her contained for so long. I smirked thinking that she might actually come to my office ready to tell me off, even though she'd been the one who should have been apologizing.

I wanted to see. Had Kee finally decided to do what she wanted?

Had I finally gotten my girl back?

CHAPTER 37: KEELANI

Alcohol may have given me courage but my irritation with him gave me strength. He'd had those keys in the nightstand this whole time and hadn't told me.

I didn't consider anything except that I was going to chew him out. I stomped out of the suite and down that hallway in hopes he could hear each footstep.

The conference rooms were spread throughout the resort, but I knew he'd have picked the biggest one for his ridiculous meeting.

Of course Penelope was sitting at a desk that expanded across the lobby. She waved to me. "Oh, are you here to see Dex?"

"Yep," I said, and I think I caught a smirk from her. She didn't stop me but waved me right past her so I could shove through the double doors.

I stood there, breathless, my eyes scanning the room for his arrogant ass but instead finding all of them. I saw Armanellis, Bane Black, and the Hardy brothers. All powerful men in black suits. All men I thought were back in their hotel rooms with their wives but instead they sat there discussing something. Except silence filled the room now and on the projector was the man in the Oval Office staring at me.

The fucking President of the United States glared at me on the big screen.

Somehow, I'd let my emotions, my anger, my loss of

control get the best of me. The alcohol drained from my system as embarrassment filled my veins.

What the hell was I doing? Dex Hardy was a man of business, of prestige, of a billion-dollar empire. And I stood there looking crazed in a freaking raggedy old college T-shirt just long enough to cover my ass.

Dex's eyes had widened in probably utter shock at my intrusion and then they dragged over my body from head to toe, pausing at the hem of my shirt. I didn't even have a stupid bra on, I'd been so mad.

"I'm sorry. I—" I whispered, all the fight leaving my body as embarrassment replaced it instead.

"You've got ten seconds to get the fuck out of this conference room."

I took a step back. He was right. God, he was so right. Of course he hadn't thought I'd actually burst into the room.

Although...Penelope had let me right through. She'd even waved me in like it wasn't at all an inconvenience.

"I understand," I murmured, taking a step back in my bare feet.

"Heartbreaker"—he pinched the bridge of his nose—"not you. Never you. Them."

"But I—"

The men had already stood and were filing out past me. Dimitri kissed my cheek and murmured that I should call him *when* I needed him, and he winked at me like he knew this was coming.

Dex was telling the president, "I'll call you back. My fiancée is here."

My jaw dropped as he hung up on him. The freaking president.

Bane kissed my forehead. "We're working on getting that bastard of a stalker, you know that, right?"

No one seemed to think this behavior was outrageous.

As Bane closed the door behind him, I heard, "Now, come sit on my lap because, right now, you're mine."

We stared at each other quietly, the clock on the wall ticking away as if it was counting down the seconds to the bomb between us that was supposed to go off. "You can't tell the president you'll just call him back!" I screeched.

"I just did." He set down his pen and leaned back in the leather chair he was lounging in. Then, he patted his thigh. "Come sit."

"You're indulging me when I'm being ridiculous, Dex."

"When's the last time you were completely ridiculous?"

I stood there in that baggy shirt, not sure I could answer the question. "This isn't like me, and I know that, and—"

"It is like you. You just haven't been given the chance to be you in a long time."

"Well, I can't start now. You can't up and marry a completely unhinged individual. And I think I'm verging on that. I literally..." I shook my head. "I'm happy with you, do you know that? When I thought I'd be miserable, I'm happy and I feel safe to be myself and am completely—"

He chuckled. "Perfect. You're perfect, heartbreaker."

"I'm not. I just got off on a camera for you and burst into your meeting with the president."

"Yeah, and you enjoyed it, didn't you?"

"No. I'm not enjoying this."

He looked me up and down. "The blush on your cheeks alone shows me it's affected you. It's more than just a little foreplay. Don't act like it isn't."

Of course he had to call out how my body rebelled against me, and I couldn't help but snap back. "And I bet my whole Black Diamond salary that me standing here has affected you too. You hard under that conference table of yours?" Welp. Guess the alcohol hadn't completely worn off, and I slapped a hand over my mouth.

He stared at me as his jaw worked, and then he sucked on his teeth before going to his phone to type something in. An alert sounded on my phone too, and I glanced down at the bank notification.

The number of zeros. He'd just dropped a million dollars into my account. "Jesus, Dex. That was a joke. Take the money back," I whispered.

"What for? You won the bet. I'm fucking hard as a rock. Want to come sit on my lap and find out?"

"You're acting like you're for real with this idea of marriage, Dex. You're acting like—"

"Like what's mine is yours?" He shrugged. "It is."

"I need a glass of water or... I need a moment." I glanced around and saw bottled water at the corner on the table. When I picked one up, of course it was ice cold. I pointed to it. "This is over the top."

"I had over-the-top men in here."

I twisted open the lid and took a long drink before I glanced at the door, then the screen, and then at Dex. "I shouldn't be here."

"You should be where I am."

"You won't be saying that after our press release."

"We are only doing a press release after we get married."

I shook my head slowly as I walked toward him. "I'm not marrying you, Dex. We don't know the first thing about being married. We don't even know the first thing about being in a relationship with each other, considering this was all for—"

"Real," he finished for me.

I stared at him as a million thoughts ran through my head. "You're so confident in this. In us?" He shrugged like he already had everything figured out. "How can you be when I don't even know..." How did I explain what I was feeling? "I haven't been able to be me for years, Dex. I don't even know exactly who I am."

"That's what life is about, right? People change every day, and we figure it out every day."

"What if, when I find out, you don't like that person?"

"I know who you are, Kee. Let me be the judge of that. That's fair, isn't it? You walked away from me once without giving me a chance, right? Let me have it this time." His tone was soft, and he didn't get up from that chair to approach me at all. He was keeping himself exactly where he was in case I bolted. He knew I was skittish now.

I bit my lip. "The wedding is still going to be a colossal mess. I've been just texting Penelope the most ridiculous things."

"Looking forward to it."

"It shouldn't be in our hometown where they—"

"It'll be small, right? No one will even know."

"You're not going to give up, are you?"

"I'm never going to give up on us again."

I chewed on my cheek, trying my best not to cry. "I think I might be falling in love with you, Dex."

"Well, good. At least the fall is starting for you. I'm so far down the hill, I need you to catch up at some point. Now, you did interrupt a meeting with the president. Want to say sorry?"

"Sorry." I shrugged because what did I care about one little word.

"Say sorry by wrapping your lips around my cock."

"Doing that in a conference room with your assistant outside, Dex, is—"

"An experience. A rush. A fucking high. Get on your knees. Show your fiancé how sorry you are."

He knew I wasn't going to deny myself experiences anymore. He knew I wanted every single one. I walked up to him and moved between him and the desk. Before I could kneel, he growled, "Actually, I want to see what's under this shirt first."

He lifted it slowly, his hands at my hips as he inched it up to my waist and saw that I hadn't slipped anything on underneath. "I was in a hurry."

"To fuck your future husband."

"To yell at him."

"Want to scream his name instead?" He slid a finger in me fast, and I gasped at how sensitive I still was from getting myself off just minutes ago. "So wet, baby. You came prepared for me, huh?"

"Your ego is getting quite big, Dex."

"Only because I can back it up." He shoved my hips up and back onto the desk, and then he lowered his head. There was no time to brace for how good his tongue would feel over my clit as he twirled it over the sensitive bundle of nerves.

I arched on the table and pulled at his hair. "I'm too sensitive, Dex. I just orgasmed—"

"And you're going to again for me." He slid another finger in and curled them against my G-spot, causing electricity to sing through every nerve in my body. I bucked on the table, my body primed for him in a way I knew I couldn't have done myself.

"You're giving me every orgasm I want to take, heartbreaker. Forever. Your future husband deserves to see you come apart again and again."

I shivered at him claiming that. I told myself I'd discuss it again later with him. For now, I just wanted to live in this moment. Just feel everything I could. "Please," I whimpered, because now I wanted it. I wanted to hit that high with him again and again.

He growled against my sex, vibrating my inner walls so perfectly that my whole body tightened as I screamed his name and came all over his mouth. So fast, like lightning through the night sky, the electricity of his mouth on me caused me to see blinding light.

And still he didn't let up but rather drank in my aftershocks until I was completely relaxed and satiated. I tried to pull him back by his hair, and he hummed low against my core. "You taste sweet as fuck afterward, heartbreaker, like you're leaving me extra dessert to come back for more. I'm never going to get enough of this pussy."

"Dex," I whimpered, and he finally let up, kissing my thigh once and then twice before he sat back and looked at me.

I peered over him and saw how his trousers were tight around his cock. My mouth watered, and I knew I wanted him here, wanted him to lose control, enough that he'd find it worth it always to hang up on the president for me. Our connection was worth it. I scooted off the table and got on my knees before him.

"Kee, I was kidding about the—"

I unbuckled his trousers and held his cock in my hand before he could protest further. Then I said, "Are you going to be as loud as I was when you come in my mouth?"

He hissed when I deep-throated him as best as I could right away. My hand barely wrapped fully around his cock, but I loved the feeling of his piercing against the top of my mouth, loved how he hardened even further as I slid my tongue around his tip. "Fuck, heartbreaker. Fuck. Fuck. Fuck."

Right then, someone knocked on the office door, and Dex didn't do what I thought he might. Instead, he said, "Come in."

I heard the doors open as his hands threaded through my hair, holding me there right as I was about to pull back. Then, I heard Penelope. "Sir, the president is on line one, calling back. Would you like to tell him to hold?"

"He can call back."

There was mirth in Penelope's voice when she said, "Again? Reason being?"

"The woman that's about to be my wife under my desk good enough?"

"Absolutely." Penelope snickered, and I heard her soft congratulations like she thought we'd finally worked through all our problems.

Like me sucking him off under his desk wasn't another one. But I couldn't stop. I wanted him to lose the control he always had so much of.

"You have to stop or I'm going to come down your throat, Kee." Good. He tried to pull me back by my hair, but I leaned forward to take him farther in. "Heartbreaker," he warned, but then his hips jerked forward, and I knew he'd snapped. "That's it. Take my cock down your throat. So sick of being good. I've always loved you bad, anyway. That fuckable mouth was made for me." He thrust his cock farther as he held my head and I moaned. "And only me."

The problem with Dex's declaration was that there was a

letter that had been intercepted for us by the time we left the office. It was in a red envelope.

This engagement wasn't supposed to be real.

If you marry him, I'll be devastated.

Don't you know we belong together? Please.

Break it off. Show me we can be together.

Why have you closed your hotel windows, Keelani?

I can't see you. I need to see you.

CHAPTER 38: KEELANI

His face reddened, his whole body seemed to lock up in fury, and his eyes held malice as he stared at that envelope for hours. I tried to reassure him it was just an obsessed fan, someone who was probably making a joke or had taken their obsession a bit too far.

Still, Dex didn't come to bed that night. He told me he would be in his office working and I knew what he was working on.

The problem with technology was it didn't track letters and those red envelopes didn't have fingerprints on them. Someone had been too careful, but Dex would be more meticulous in his search.

I could see it even when that week rolled into the next and he packed his suitcase for our hometown. He told me to do the same.

"We shouldn't be getting married," I told him, worrying over how tense he looked. Yet, I knew we were too close to the date. I also knew that the record label was running with the story, that Dex wouldn't back down, and that I would have to see this through.

"Of course we should be," he replied. "You want to get divorced in a few months, fine. But this is the plan until you're done with Trinity. What are you so worried about anyway? You can't think being married will be much different than being engaged."

"Well, no. But...this is a huge thing to do. It could be hell to deal with."

"We do huge things for family though right? And you're family. You're mine. I'll go to hell and burn there for all I care. You think I won't?" He stopped what he was doing to stare at me then. He was daring me to disagree.

Silence stretched between us before I finally sighed. "Marriage then. For a little while."

He huffed and went back to work.

***

When the time came, he drove us to the corporate airfield and we got on the private jet.

That's when it started to feel more real. Olive, Pink, and Dimitri passed us in the aisle to go to their seats and Olive murmured for me to check my phone.

"Jesus, what are we doing?" I whispered as I stared at the text she'd sent.

> **Olive: A source at Trinity leaked that Dex has always struggled to right his bad-boy ship. See attachment. They say he's noncommittal and influenced you when you were underage causing destruction to your hometown and you, but he's seeing the light now. You're saving him supposedly.**

"They're dragging you through the mud because of me." I closed my eyes, growling at that, and pounded the top of my phone so the screen would turn off. Then I stared out the

365

window of Vegas getting smaller and smaller as we approached the clouds. "I can't let this happen again."

Dex shrugged at my frustration. "You realize that this time, I'm letting it happen," he said and turned to give me a small smirk. He looked lighter and less stressed now, as if we could relax even though we were barreling toward saying I do when we should have been saying I don't.

"This is serious, Dex." I held up my phone to show him and then started to ramble. "The media outlets are trying to paint you as some man who needs redemption and that's not true. I can't be responsible for that. You should release a statement on your own. You could discredit the label and me if you need to."

"Keelani Hale." He stopped me by dropping my full name. "Do you ever let someone help you?"

"Help me with what?"

"With handling your life. You've done all this for far too long on your own. You know that?"

I huffed at his comment. "So what? I'm used to it. They're ruining your image and twisting mine and—"

"Who cares?" Dex patted my leg and opened his laptop, not at all influenced. "It takes one social media post from us to quell the news anyway. It'll be fine. We're just not giving them anything right now, so they're recreating drama."

"Don't you see how terrible that is?" I shoved his hand off my thigh at the fact he wasn't as offended. I was offended for him. He protected me, watched over me, made me feel freaking free. Yet, they were saying he did the complete opposite. It was wrong. They'd been wrong for years but now I wanted justice. I wanted to rage and act out and release a statement that would ruin Trinity. I didn't care anymore. He was doing too much for me and receiving nothing in return. "And you're spending unnecessary amounts of time on people who are mad I'm engaged to you."

"Are you talking about your fucking stalker, Kee?" he gritted out, his eyes turning dark as he stopped looking at his laptop to glare at me.

"It's merely a fan," I tried. "They're mad I'm not single and—"

"All the more reason to get married," he bellowed. "Don't you see that? I'm not going to let someone threaten my girl."

"Dex—"

"No, Kee. You're *mine*. You can take all the time you want to accept that, but they can't." His jaw worked up and down. I didn't know how to accept it when I was scared to burden him with all this, when I was scared there wasn't a way we'd truly be able to make it after everything we'd been through.

He continued on, "I've started running checks on every celebrity you've talked with in the last couple years. And we should pull a list of people at events who've shown up repeatedly."

"Dex, I promise it's nothing," I told him and squeezed his arm.

He stared at me for a beat and then breathed out like he was trying to dissipate his concern. "Okay, heartbreaker. It's nothing." He rolled his eyes. "Let's focus on the wedding. You iron out everything you wanted with Penelope?"

"I told her we could get married at the courthouse and take some pictures around the gazebo in town, Dex. Nothing big."

He hummed and nodded.

"We can make an easy enough social media post on that. I'm hoping it will squash rumors, like you said."

"Right. We will most likely do an interview too. Mitchell wanted that for the record label."

My gut twisted at him doing another thing he shouldn't have to do for me. "Dex, you shouldn't—"

"I want to," he concluded. "Don't worry, okay? Look, you got your team back there." He waved back at Olive, Dimitri, and Pink. They'd agreed to come. Yet, we didn't invite the rest of Dex's family because I hadn't agreed to this being any more than a sham. I was retreating back to the agreement where I could protect Dex from my problems, from my fame, from stalkers, and from my label.

Thankfully, his family had all been very understanding—supposedly—when Dex told them.

"I could still call Mitchell to see if maybe we could—"

"You're in the air, halfway home. The venue is set." He turned back to Olive and Pink, who were a few rows back in plush seats, drinking and talking over stage sets. "Ladies, Kee thinks we shouldn't go through with the marriage and instead just do a press release. Thoughts on that?"

Olive frowned. "If that's what you want, we'll support you, but the photographers have been vetted and approved. I think the pictures will speak volumes on social media too."

"Personally, I get why you don't want to marry him." Pink smirked at Dex. "But it's the best way to avoid drama with the record label and shut the media up. Just do it."

Pink and Olive went back to talking, and I turned to Dex. "They shouldn't be painting this type of picture, and you shouldn't have to marry me to change it."

"What if I just want to marry you?" Dex stared at me, his green eyes bright.

"I don't know if you're thinking right after seeing that last letter, Dex," I whispered to him now because I knew that letter had sent him into a tailspin. I saw how he'd paced the room after, how he'd stayed up late that night, how he'd bothered the post office again and again before coming to the conclusion that the marriage was an even better idea to deter all my stalkers. According to him, he was now convinced I had a thousand.

"You're marrying me this weekend, heartbreaker." He went back to his laptop too.

That sounded so real. So final. "For the press," I added on quietly.

"Sure, heartbreaker," he murmured. "Whatever you say. If that makes you feel better. You need to relax. Want me to help you?" The devilish smirk I knew now as him thinking dirty thoughts surfaced.

I chuckled nervously but my body reacted. "What? Absolutely not. I'll read," I huffed. I needed to escape from my nerves anyway. I could escape into a book for a bit. I pulled up a book on my phone.

Every now and then, he'd squeeze my knee or look over from his laptop to drag a finger across my cheek. It was every time I was reading a spicy part of the book, and I would swat his hand away.

"Just making sure you're aware of the parts you like, heartbreaker. Highlight them so you can read them to me later."

I bit my lip and nodded because I wanted to do that too much to deny it. "You're almost to book boyfriend status by saying that."

"The goal is to get to book *husband* status." His eyes darkened as my lips parted and then he leaned forward to unbutton and discard his suit jacket. "You know what, fuck it. You need this."

He draped the jacket over my legs. "Why? I'm not cold. It's—"

Suddenly, his hand disappeared under the jacket, and I felt his fingers dip into the waistband of my yoga pants. "No you're not cold. You're fucking hot. I've stared at your ass all day in these pants. And now you're sitting next to me wound up and wet."

"I'm not—" I gasped as he pushed my panties to the side. His fingers slid easily over my arousal.

"Go ahead. Finish that sentence. Tell me you're not soaking right now." He whispered in my ear, "I want to see how well you lie as my fingers slide into you."

Jesus, his mouth was dirty when he wanted it to be. "You can't seriously be doing this right now. Dimitri, Olive, and—"

"They're all at the way back of the plane behind us, occupied with their own shit." He licked my ear. "Be good and quiet and they won't know I'm making you come."

My breathing picked up as my adrenaline rose. All worries dispersed as my pussy tightened in excitement. My body wasn't going to deny itself.

Then Olive asked across the plane, "Kee, you wanted to keep your location quiet until after the wedding, right?"

Her question made total sense, and I knew the answer, but my teeth dug into my bottom lip in an effort to keep from moaning. All I could focus on were his two fingers sliding into me fast and curling up against the walls of my sex, intensifying how close I was to the brink. My clothing clung to me now as heat washed over my body, and I saw how a sheen of perspiration glistened even on my arms.

"Answer your friend, heartbreaker," Dex murmured in my ear.

"Yes, that's great," I said, breathless, but my friend seemed to take that as a good enough answer because she didn't ask me anything further. "So great," I murmured quietly.

"Now, spread your legs a little," he told me, and I listened, complying without any hesitation. "That's right. Let me help you relax, huh? So nervous about a little wedding like you haven't been thinking of marrying me forever. I'm going to be your husband, heartbreaker. And you're going to fucking like it." He slid another finger inside me while pressing his thumb hard into my swollen clit. Then he worked me faster and faster. "You're going to love it, Kee. Say it."

I ran a hand through my tousled hair, trying to keep myself looking normal for my friends behind me, but then I met his hungry gaze. Dex was fixated on me, his pupils dilated, his sight lingering on my lips. Somehow, our connection ignited the fire in me, and I couldn't stop from rolling my hips. There'd always been something primal between us that simmered underneath it all there, something I'd never be able to shake, and in that moment, it took over. He must have felt it, too, because he pulled me close and kissed me as I came. I whimpered softly into his mouth as my pussy tightened around his hand.

He groaned and pulled his fingers from me before he brought them up and commanded quietly, "Open."

I looked at him in question, but did as I was told, tasting my salty cum on his fingertips.

Against my ear, his voice rumbled out, "See how excited your pussy is to have me as a husband? Can't you already tell what you taste like?" He waited a beat. "You taste like you'll be forever mine."

My heart probably fell all the way in love with him at that moment, jumping right off the cliff without being concerned at all with the repercussions.

Could we make it? Could we somehow work through

everything and stay married? My heart was all for the idea, but my mind wasn't as reckless.

I breathed in deep before I asked him, "What if we end up just a memory of each other, Dex? You speak of forever like it can happen. Do you really think—after everything we've been through—we should be walking down the aisle to try marriage when—"

"Who else would you try marriage with? Who else would you want 'just memories' with, Kee?"

I stayed silent as I took in that piercing green gaze of his, so alive with love now when before he'd looked at me with apathy. "I don't want to lose you again."

"You won't because you're marrying me." He said it like it would be the easiest thing in the world. It rolled off his tongue, soft and coaxing. Then he bent down to grab his laptop from his bag again.

"I am marrying you, Dex. For just a little. We can annul it later."

"Hm. How about forever?" He threaded his fingers through mine. Then he assessed the ring he'd put there. "This needs to change."

I chuckled nervously. "It's a beautiful ring, Dex. I don't need—"

"You'll like purple better."

A laugh bubbled up out of me because he was right about that. "It doesn't matter." I was trying to cling to reality, trying not to get my hopes up as I said, "When you marry someone someday for real, Dex, you won't have all this baggage, and you can get them the ring they want."

"We will sift through our baggage for the rest of our lives together. Remember that, heartbreaker. When you meet me at the altar tomorrow, know that if you say I do, it's for forever with me. Not someone else. You'll never be with *someone* else again."

I chewed on my cheek as I stared at him, trying not to give away that my stomach had butterflies flapping wildly in it at that moment. Dex would do anything to protect me, even give his forever away. I could see it in his deep-green eyes, so serious now before he leaned forward to kiss my cheek, softly and tenderly like I might break.

I had to not be reckless one more time for both of us. For him. He didn't need my burdens in his life. I'd seen how the burden of someone else could take a toll. "You know, my dad didn't gamble so much until my mother had problems."

He squeezed my hand and rubbed a thumb over my knuckles. "Okay?"

"I think he just knew. Even when my mom had that stroke. Something wasn't exactly right with her after. It's when he really started to stay out late. He'd come home with news of a lost bet, stumbling around drunk, and sometimes when I'd find him that way, he'd look at me and say, 'You think she'll leave me, Kee?'" Dex kissed my hand but didn't say a word as I thought about that. "Maybe he knew her mind was going even then. He was being left behind by the love of his life, and neither of them could control it. I think it broke him, not being able to help her. I think it still breaks his heart daily."

Dex nodded. "I know it breaks your heart, too, Kee."

I took a deep breath. "Right. So what would you do if you knew you were going to burden someone with your life, Dex? Someone you loved?"

"If I loved them?" he said, his eyes holding mine. And when I nodded, his dimples showed because he knew just as well as me that I was telling him I loved him right then and there. "I'd let them choose, heartbreaker. Let someone you love choose to hold that burden with you."

His words rattled me. The corners of my mouth trembled with unspoken words. My heart warmed over the fact that he wanted me enough to marry me and then cooled over the reality that I shouldn't do it.

He must have seen the anguish, because he kissed me hard and took what he wanted. His hand slid up my neck and pulled me close. I kissed him back with just as much fervor, not sure how many times we would be able to do this. The responsible thing would have been to never do it again. I felt myself starting to spiral out of control, wanting to act out and draw negative attention, but Dex didn't deserve it. He didn't deserve the life I was about to live.

Yet, he murmured, "Remember, tomorrow all you have to do is say I do."

***

When we landed, we were escorted straight to another HEAT hotel, and Dex told me to get some shut-eye as he set my purple suitcase down in one of the bedrooms of the suite. Glancing around, I took in the opulence of yet another one of his resorts. The chandeliers sparkled against the leather furniture, and the down duvet was fluffed perfectly for a good night's sleep.

When Dex started to back out of our room though, I asked, "Are you not coming to bed?"

"It's a two-bedroom suite for a reason, Kee. If I lie next to you, I'll fuck you until you can't walk down the aisle tomorrow."

"Don't be ridiculous. Come sleep with me."

Instead, he stared at me for much too long as silence filled the room. His eyes filled with something close to pain as he frowned.

"What?" I whispered.

"Sometimes I don't know if you realize how strong you are and how vulnerable you are at the same time. It's stunning and terrifying."

"Sometimes I don't think you realize how sweet you are and then how matter-of-fact you are. You can't put everyone in a box, Dex."

"I want to, though. Specifically, I want you in one right next to me."

I smirked at him. "So you can watch me all the time? You already do that."

I got his dimples then. "I won't stop either."

"One day, you'll get bored of it."

"Nope, never." With that, he left me sitting in that big room on the huge plush bed by myself, thinking of marrying him for real even if I knew I couldn't.

Every decision 1 would have to make tomorrow felt humongous even if I knew the venue was small. It felt real even if it shouldn't have been.

CHAPTER 39: KEELANI

The next morning, he was gone, but as I stretched in bed, I got a text immediately.

> **Dex: Morning, heartbreaker. Breakfast is in the kitchen for you. I took that engagement ring off your finger too. You'll get a real one soon. A car will be by to pick you up at 3. People will be at your door soon enough.**

> **Me: People? Only Olive and Pink, right?**

> **Dex: Say I do today. Don't worry about anything else.**

I didn't know how to respond because the man knew I was going to say yes. I just wasn't saying yes to a freaking whole happily ever after when I knew that soon I'd be saying no to the record label, that I'd be turning my life upside down, that I wouldn't know how to take care of everything in my family. But I'd find a way.

I grabbed the food in the fridge and started to heat it up. That was when I saw a small piece of paper next to a box with one single lilac placed over it.

The paper said *Put it on.*

And when I opened the box, a large jewel the exact same colors as lilacs glinted at me.

I stared at it. Then I snapped it shut and set it down to take a deep breath, because I knew what this meant. I looked up to find where the camera was and shook my head.

Immediately, my phone rang.

When I answered, his voice growled into it. "Do I have to come there and see you before the fucking walk down the aisle, Kee?"

"No," I croaked, and then I pointed at the box. "You can't get me things like that when we're not even really doing this—"

"I am doing this. You are too," he told me. Then he whispered out, "What are you so afraid of?"

"I'm going to be a mess."

"I like your messes."

"I'm going to be without a job most likely too. The record label is—"

"They were a terrible label to do business with anyway."

"I ruined you once, Dex. And then you ruined me. We're all broken up and—"

"And so we're putting each other back together." He sighed and then said, "Put the ring on, Kee. Don't worry about anything else."

He always said it so easily, like he had everything taken care of, and finally, I believed him. I believed him more than anyone else in my life. I opened the box back up and stared at it. "Did you line this with security measures too?"

"You'd be proud to know that I did not. I'm also done looking at you for the day. I'll wait until the actual wedding.

That ring there is just the ring you want without any secrets... for now."

"For now?"

"Until you say I do...and then I'm going to ask you exactly what you want, if I can stalk you with your permission." His tone was exasperated, but I could hear his smile. "This agreement between us will be different than before."

"You like control," I reminded him.

"Yes, but with you, I only like it if you allow it," he threw back.

I nodded over and over because I was trying my best not to cry. "I can't get married without my family, Dex."

"Good thing I invited them then." He hung up right as there was a knock at the door.

"What are you doing here?" I whispered out, almost jumping back in shock at my father standing at my hotel suite's door in a three-piece suit. "Dad?" I whispered out in confusion.

"You're getting married, Kee." He frowned at me like I should have known he'd be there, like he wouldn't miss it for the world.

"But no. This isn't real, and Mom needs you at—"

"Mom's at home, but she's getting ready too. She's managing with the nurses. Dex worked out extra accommodations for us, and there's a whole team catering to her every need today. I think she'll be able to make it even if she won't know it's your wedding. You should..." He cleared his throat. "Come by the house too. I... You should see her today, even if it's hard. She should see her daughter in her wedding dress. She'd want that."

"Dad," I whispered, "this isn't a real wedding."

He smiled softly and touched my cheek. "Ah, Keelani. He called me. He's been calling me all week. His voice shook when he asked for your hand in marriage."

"But he can't—"

"He wants us all there." He sighed. "He talked to me again about the finances too."

My heart dropped. Dex would have done just that. He would have tried to fix this when it wasn't fixable. Offering my father money just meant it went down the drain. And suddenly, standing there with him in that moment, I felt anger that I knew my father would take it too. He wouldn't even hesitate.

"He's not helping us with anything financially." I said the words slowly but with emphasis. "You're not taking any money from him."

"Well, now, Kee—"

"Don't start, Dad." I held up a hand and it shook but I still did it. Something in my snapped as I thought of him taking advantage of Dex. "I know you're my dad and I know you love Mom, okay? But what we've been doing... It's not right."

The words tasted like acid in my mouth but a weight lifted from my chest as I let them slip from my lips.

"What's not right?" He frowned as if he was confused. He was daring me to say it because in the past I never had.

"Your gambling. You handling our money like it's an investment when it's not, Dad." My voice shook, but still, I felt like suddenly I knew I had to say them.

"Kee, that's a large accusation. You can't possibly believe that." He huffed, trying again to make me feel guilt and shame for speaking his discretions out into the world.

This time, I threw it back at him though. "What else should I believe? Are you claiming you raised me to be that naïve?"

I saw the moment he realized I wasn't backing down. His shoulders slumped, his eyes turned down. "I've only been trying to help." The man shrank before me. He looked older, more tired, and like life hadn't given him much of a break.

But I had. I'd tried to give him everything for so long. And knowing he would take from a man who'd done nothing lately but comfort me shined light on the fact that he was troubled, that he had a problem. "You're not helping by taking money again and again, Dad. And it's been millions. I've calculated what you've lost to what? Bets? Loans?"

His mouth opened and closed a few times, emotions shuttering across his face. "You don't understand. I lost my job. I was trying to make enough to help your mother."

"We had enough with just what I made." I looked away, hating that I saw hurt in his eyes.

"You're not grateful." He voice broke.

"Grateful?" I frowned at him and tried to control the anger building in me. "How can you even be focused on that right now when I just told you that millions have been lost?"

He searched my eyes again. Moments of silence passed between us before he finally whispered, "It's all I know how to do."

It wasn't a sorry but it was an admission.

And that was a start.

A tear in my eye escaped as he said it. "No, it's not, Dad. You just need help. You can do something else."

He nodded over and over. "I don't know how to leave her and get help."

"We'll find a way," I told him, and then I pulled him in for a hug. We'd all find a way together because family didn't leave family behind.

"He told me that too, you know?" my father said gruffly against my head and then pulled back to explain, "Dex offered to help with the gambling and finances. That's what I was going to say. I want to get well. I want to make things right."

I choked out a laugh that turned to a sort of cry. "I might really actually marry him, Dad."

"As you should. He loves the hell out of you, I can tell. He sounds like me when I met your mom. And you love the boy, don't you?"

"Yes." I nodded.

"Then, let's go to the house when you're ready."

"Just me and you. I don't want to upset her."

"Yeah, just me and you, kid. I'll be ready when you are."

He left me standing there with every nerve-racking thought flowing through my body. I turned back to the ring on the counter. I went over to it and slid it on. It fit perfectly.

Like this was meant to be, forever and ever.

CHAPTER 40: KEELANI

Olive and Pink came by the suite after my father left to help with makeup and getting dressed, but my nerves couldn't be settled even as they told me everything would be just fine.

"She barely recognizes anyone anymore. It was fifty-fifty a year ago when I would see her that she'd recall who I was without having an anxiety attack. She remembers me as a kid, not as who I am now."

"Well, maybe you'll get the good fifty percent this time," Olive threw out there.

"I know I won't." Not everything could go right today.

"Even if you don't, don't you want to try?" Olive asked softly. My friend knew that my heart yearned for this, that I'd wanted it for a whole year.

I nodded, and my friends then worked in silence. The silence was filled with love and comfort though. They would be here for me either way. Dex and Dimitri would too. I'd finally found a family outside of my own who loved me just as I was. It might not have been my record label, but that didn't matter.

The silence carried over on the car ride home too. My father didn't turn on the radio or even attempt to make small talk. He just rolled down the window, and we listened to the breeze of my small town.

No photographers were there, and even if we turned a few heads, most everyone kept to themselves. People of the town protected those in that town, and my father was one of their own.

The sound of gravel under the tires was loud as he pulled into the driveway. I took a deep breath before I said, "Maybe we shouldn't do this."

"She'd never forgive me, Kee. You're her daughter. Her only one." His voice cracked. "And she's your only mother. So, you get to see her on your wedding day."

With that, he opened his door and then rounded to mine to help me out. My dress was unconventional in that it wasn't at all white. It was a light, light lilac color, all soft lace, hugging all my curves. Penelope somehow had taken my request of a purple dress and made it beautiful. I'd made the request in an exaggerated attempt to thwart the planning she was doing, but somehow, she'd known.

It swished now against the grass of our front yard before my father unlocked the door and announced we were home. Both nurses came to greet me then stepped aside so I could see my mother in her kitchen.

She buzzed around, the soft sunlight filtering in through the sheer curtains she'd hung ages ago. The small table she set drinks on was still the same, the fridge the same, the dishes the same.

Her dark hair was thinner, but it seemed they still dyed it for her, the wrinkles on her face more pronounced, her frame smaller. Still, she was beautiful, standing there in a deep-purple dress that fell loosely to her knees. And the melody she hummed was one I knew well. A Caribbean song filled with joy, no sorrow. And all I could do was stand there, completely still, and hum it with her.

There was such a peace in seeing the parent who brought you life and knew how to soothe your every worry through the years standing there where you always knew them to be. Such a comfort settled in a child's soul. My comfort was shaky though. My concern for her memory of me edged in to override that peaceful feeling.

What could I say to the mother I loved who might not remember me at all? Everything felt real. The dress was real. The event location was real. My family was real. And my mother... She was the most real thing there.

And when her eyes finally met mine, following the sound of the person harmonizing with her, I stopped. "Oh, Kee. Your voice always sounded better than mine. Why stop?" She shook her head.

I took one breath at her saying my name, and then another, but it was shaky. Alzheimer's could steal a mind at any moment. "I just came by to say hi, Mom."

"That's a beautiful dress for just saying hi," Her voice drifted off for a moment as recognition seemed to dawn. "Is that a...your wedding dress, Kee?"

"Mom?" I think my heart stopped as I stared at her looking at me.

Her eyes were lucid. They didn't look right through me anymore. They held mine captive, full of love, full of her heart. She rushed forward, and even the nurses moved quickly out of the way as their eyes widened. This wasn't normal for her to remember me. I didn't come around often enough.

Still, her hands held my face as her dark eyes filled with tears. "Tell me it's with Dex."

I choked out a sob as I nodded.

She nodded back. "Of course it is. As it should be. And don't you forget that." Tears fell from her eyes. "I'm so sorry I can't remember always."

How could she apologize for something she couldn't control? She'd always tried to protect me from it when she could. "Don't say sorry. I missed you, and I love you and—" I stopped myself from carrying on, or I'd cry or trigger something. I was so scared to lose her again. It felt like if I didn't make any wrong moves, maybe I wouldn't.

She shook her head. "I'll forget again soon. I know it. No one can control that." I hated that she understood that she was forgetting too. That's what hurt the most, knowing she knew. Watching how the world fell away from her, how she knew everything for a moment, even that she was losing it all, and still she smiled at me, brushed a hand over my cheek and said, "Don't worry. Just live."

She started to hum the melody we always did together, and I hummed it with her. This time, her memories faded quietly, without disruption, without pain, without fear. She turned to my father and said, "The sun's beautiful out there today, huh? I bet the lilacs will bloom soon."

He nodded as he wiped at the tears in his own eyes, and I turned to see a black SUV pull up outside of the house. I pointed to it and mouthed to my father that I would see him later.

Dex must have sent a car for me, knowing we'd need it. I backed out of the room, out of the house I grew up in, and then I cried all the way to the SUV.

I didn't think as I got into the vehicle to look at the driver. My emotions were too jumbled, my heart too full from what had just happened. But when I glanced up to thank the driver, Ezekiel was sitting in a seat across from me.

He gripped my wrist hard and fast. "You lied to me, Keelani."

"Lied?" I whispered out as he jammed a needle into my

arm.

"You'll only be paralyzed for a bit. You deserve it though. You know that."

"What?" I was shocked by the prick of the needle, taken off guard by his boldness. I tried to yank my arm away but his grip tightened to a bruising force. "Ezekiel, you can't—"

"You were supposed to be mine. This engagement was fake. Mitchell told me that."

"I'm not yours." I shook my head, but suddenly it felt heavy and dizzy and like I might be under water.

"You are!" His voice raised wildly, and he shook me in frustration. "I own you. My record label."

"No. What?" Everything blurred together. His words, my words, my thoughts.

"We just need to get back to my place. I couldn't have you sleep with him again. Not like you really were on your wedding night. You belong to me. You've always belonged to me, and he's soiled you. Almost ruined you." He continued to mumble, and I saw how his pupils were so dilated, he wasn't all there. I wasn't either.

"What did you do, Ezekiel?" I couldn't keep my eyes open.

He scooted over to me and pulled me close. Then he pressed my head to his shoulder even as I tried to fight him off. It wasn't any use. I was drowning in heavy water. It was sloshing over my thoughts, dragging me down. Even as I tried to yell, my voice was silent.

Into the night. Into the blackness I went.

HEAT

CHAPTER 41: DEX

"Where the fuck is my wife?" I bellowed, and my voice ricocheted throughout our suite as I swiped a vase off the table and it crashed to the ground.

We weren't married. I hadn't gotten to see her walk down the aisle, but she'd always been mine. No one was going to even try to correct me right now.

"Jesus fucking Christ." Cade typed away as he spoke, trying to track down something with the drones while Izzy sat next to him, typing on her phone. "It's only been five minutes. We're going to find her. She's going to be okay."

I should have never agreed to let her go alone to her parents' house in the first place, even though he'd insisted. Now a damn vehicle had picked her up instead of him driving her back. And I'd been stupid enough not to put a tracker on her ring this time.

Fuck. Whoever had taken her had known.

"I'm hacking Trinity and Platinum Casino systems," I finally said as I sat down, because if the blame had to be on someone, it could be on me.

"Let's all get in their systems," Bane announced over the FaceTime Pink had him on. He was fully on board with breaking every law now.

Pink was wringing her hands. "If you guys don't find her, I'll—"

But Bane cut Pink off. "We'll find her, Pink."

"Pull up all the shareholders," Dimitri said softly.

Dante shook his head. "It's not about investments."

"It's about who has access, and investors always get access." He looked at me imploringly. "Do it, Dex."

It was something in his voice. He knew. Shit, I think I knew. I'd told myself that the man wouldn't, that I'd threatened him enough, that we had enough on him to put him in prison for decades.

Still, all signs pointed to him. I'd wanted to be sure, to be meticulous, to run everything beyond reasonable doubt. I'd had Cade pulling files on him, Bane confirming with our rival casino, and going through all the yellow tape the right way. I hadn't told Kee because she didn't need to know.

I was done doing that now.

I hacked government systems and private corporation files fast. While I was digging, I continued to pull up facial searches of Kee and all my cameras.

"Damn, I think you might be even more fucked-up than I am," Cade admitted as he glanced at it.

All the screens showed Keelani at different times. I was mapping her face, tracking her whereabouts, figuring out her every move. "It's my job to be fucked-up. You'd do the same for Izzy."

"If she was missing, sure. But before I didn't."

"Maybe you should have," I threw back as we all pounded on our keyboards. "Didn't you get my sister kidnapped?"

"Whoa. That's out of line. I got myself kidnapped," Izzy interjected, head down as she worked away. "Give me some credit."

"Izzy, your brother seems to want to fight." He said it to my sister but then his eyes cut back to mine. The devil was in them, ready to unleash on me. I didn't shrink away though like most would have. I lifted a brow and he just grunted out, "You're looking for chaos, brother. I'm not pissing my wife off tonight by handing it to you."

"You're not the one I want to rip apart anyway..." Everyone knew I was volatile in that moment. My voice drifted off as I stared at the different investments on the screen, at what Ezekiel had been doing. Small record labels, different newer businesses we wouldn't pay attention to, had invested in our rival casino. It's how he'd probably gotten access to their drone area. Everything he was doing was under private names that weren't accessible to the public.

Had I just stopped playing by the rules, I'd have found it out before this happened. "Ezekiel invested six months ago." I was already pulling up facial tracking on him as Cade and Izzy worked alongside me.

"He's a block away. Motel. Second floor," Izzy said as she stood up, ready to go immediately. My whole family stood up with her.

"How did you—" Cade looked over, equally pissed and proud that she'd beat him at finding Ezekiel's location.

"Cade, you should know by now, we don't send men to do a woman's job. I'll always be faster than you." She kissed his cheek, but I was already getting up to leave.

"Dex, hold on." Dom stood with me and grabbed my arm. As the oldest, Dom was probably the voice of reason. "Let's call 911 to—"

"Go home. Call the cops. I'm going there myself now though. This is my fight." I shook my head, yanking my elbow from him as I headed toward the door. "And it's going to be messy."

"You can't make a mess," Dante warned, but I was already running out and down the hall. I didn't have time. She'd been gone too long. Minutes felt like hours. Hours could feel like days.

I didn't stop to see who was behind me, but I heard Cade say, "Let us do the rest. You ladies go home. Keep up appearances."

And into the night the Armanellis and Hardys went. My brothers walked beside me, as well as Dante and Cade. No one at the motel even questioned us walking in. No one cared with the run-down setup they had going on. The lighting flickered, and the silence of the night felt stifling.

I'd have rather heard her screaming from inside that hotel than nothing at all. I didn't knock on the thin white door. I kicked it in immediately.

And there stood Ezekiel, pacing back and forth in front of my bride. Her beautiful wedding dress was still on. The color of lilacs. And she looked so peaceful as she slept, as if her stalker hadn't kidnapped her.

Ezekiel's eyes were wild when they jumped to mine. The recognition happened quickly, from the dominance he felt to the fear that filled his veins. "Dex. Mr. Hardy... I flew in to see her. She called me. She just... We wanted some time alone—"

"What did you drug her with?"

"Drug?" He laughed maniacally. "Oh, nothing. She's just asleep."

I turned to Dante. "Check her vitals."

My eyes flicked to my brothers and then to Dante and Cade. "Leave now if you don't want to be involved."

Not one of them moved. Even Dom, who had said we should call the cops before, didn't take a step back toward the door.

Cade cracked his knuckles. "Call one of our doctors. We can't have cops here."

"Oh, yes. There's no need for cops." Ezekiel's eyes widened. "Like I said, I just... She's really mine, you know? She sometimes finds herself straying to other men and—"

My first punch to his face to shut him up was fast and hard but not enough. Still, he fell backwards as he screamed, "What are you doing? Do you know who I am?"

I knew exactly who he was. He was a predator and a kidnapper. I knew he was probably more than just that too.

"How did you get the letters to her? The pictures of her? Want to explain?" I murmured close to his face.

That's when his eyes turned angry, like he knew he was cornered and wouldn't get out. So, he wanted to dig the knife deeper. "I could take pictures of all your wives. They'd probably like it just like Keelani does." His eyes darted to her and then back to me. "Money can buy drones and teams to help with just about anything. The drones aren't trackable from the company I use, and the letters were such a nice touch because you all rely so much on your technology."

"We tracked down that you bought into the casino that allowed you to fly your drone though, Ezekiel. You didn't evade us long enough."

"Whatever." He spit blood on the ground. "So you can have this bitch. I'll keep on doing what I want with the other women who are mine."

Maybe I'd been too meticulous in my life, too Type A. I could put everyone into a category, I knew that. Yet, here, standing in front of this man, I knew right then and there, I was going to stick with putting people in categories.

I'd made up my mind.

There was only one place people like him belonged.

"Women?" I asked quietly because I wanted everyone in the room to understand what I already knew.

"Kee was supposed to be special. I've fucked countless of girls under my labels before. They all squirm and act like they don't like it at first, but they learn. They all belong to me. They can spread their legs for me too, and when I'm done with them—"

It was enough. We'd all heard enough. He wasn't going to hurt another woman again and he definitely wasn't going to hurt my future wife anymore.

I punched him harder this time, hoping I delivered enough pain for him to shut up as he wailed on the floor. I stepped over him so I could keep him from rolling on the floor as I continued to punch him, blood spurting from his nose.

When I pulled back for a second, he screamed, "You're fucking stupid. Do you know who I am?"

I breathed in deep as I looked around the room. My tunnel vision cleared for a moment to take in my brothers staring at me, not one of them with a hint of question in their eyes. They knew.

They were ready. And so was I.

"It doesn't matter who you are." I said, my voice devoid of any emotion. I'd felt the rage and the fear at losing Kee because of him. Now, I felt nothing as he threatened me. I'd feel nothing when he begged too. "We're the men who rule this world. And you attempted to assault the woman I love. For that, you will pay with your life."

"Please," he started the begging sooner than I expected.

All I could do was smile.

CHAPTER 42: KEELANI

A drug can morph your reality, mix up time, and confuse your space. I woke up fighting the arms that were wrapped around me, scared it was Ezekiel.

Scared for my life.

Yet, Dex hushed me right away and murmured over and over, "I got you, Kee. I got you."

When I finally stopped flailing, it occurred to me I was in pajamas, back in my suite, and lying next to him. Every word caught in my throat as I tried to be strong and say something.

His hand hovered close to my face before he softly laid it on my cheek like he wanted me to see him going slow so as not to startle me. "I promise I'll never ever let you go again," he whispered. "I'm so sorry he got that close to you."

This man. He was apologizing when actually he'd saved me. "Is he... Did he—"

"We were there seconds after you passed out. You're fine. He's taken care of." Dex's jaw flexed. "Rest, Kee. I. Got. You."

My eyes drifted closed again. I didn't know if it was the drugs that had been laced in my system or that my body was mentally drained. Either way, I slept into the night only to wake and puke up whatever was in my stomach.

A doctor checked on me then and explained that the effects of the drug I'd been given were much like being roofied. I would be fine, but he recommended rest.

Dex didn't leave my side.

That night, my mind couldn't take on thinking about anything else.

The media, the wedding, everything waited.

It was Dex and me in that room together, him holding my body to his as he whispered over and over, "I got you."

The next morning, I stared at the ceiling for a couple minutes, knowing I had to move forward. I wasn't going to let what happened with Ezekiel control me again. I knew I'd have the tools to work through it. I knew I'd have the people around me to work through it too.

Life sometimes isn't fair and we have to go through hell. Life sometimes is beautiful too in that hellish fire, showing you that you're strong enough and that you have support around you to make it.

I let the tears escape for a minute, and Dex rubbed his thumb back and forth on my chin before he turned my head toward his. "I got you, Kee."

"I know," I whispered. "I'll be okay too. I know I will."

He nodded. "What do you want to do today, heartbreaker?"

"I need to press charges." I wouldn't stand aside anymore. I would fight the label and Ezekiel and do whatever I needed to do.

"There's no need." Dex stared at me with an intense gaze, so intense I knew he wasn't joking.

"How can there not be a need, Dex?" I whispered. "Ezekiel will keep doing what he's done to me to others."

"He won't. I've taken care of it." There was that jaw flex again. "And it's best you don't ask the details."

"That wouldn't be the way to start off a marriage," I said quietly and then looked up at the ceiling again. "Unless we're not getting married now. Which is probably for the best. I can only imagine the media storm that's already—"

"It's all being taken care of," Dex repeated. "And we're still getting married. Don't underestimate the power of the family you're marrying into. We've held off the news, Ezekiel's name will be buried, and no one will ever ask of him again."

I stared at him, trying to read between the lines as he got up to pace in nothing but black boxers. Back and forth, back and forth in front of the king size bed.

He'd worked everything out for me again. And together, I knew we would keep working things out. A sense of calm washed over me as I watched him. I didn't need to know details right then. I just needed to know that we'd always keep helping each other.

We'd be a family. One I'd always wanted. I knew it with my whole heart. "You saved me. And I know you'll keep saving me *when* we're married."

His eyes snapped up and I saw their vulnerability for just a second. "No. If I'm being honest, I didn't protect you. I moved too slow when I should have jumped over every law to move fast. He should have never been able to get near you."

"Dex, that's not—"

"I should have put it together sooner." He paced away, then turned to me with fury still in his eyes.

There was my Dex. Always coming to a final conclusion about something.

I stared at him. "That Ezekiel was crazy? How could we have known he was more than a simple creep?" I tsked. "Don't cement something so ridiculous into your brain. No one could have figured it out."

He hurried over to me as I started to get out of bed. "No. Stay in bed."

"Only if you stay with me," I told him. I didn't ask him more questions. That was all for later. Suddenly, I knew all he needed then was us together.

"I've got a few calls—"

"Work later, Dex. Rest now. With me." That's all we needed to do now. Everything else could wait. Life sometimes needed a pause and we needed to give in and pause it when necessary.

He gave in. We showered together and then he lay with me for hours. He also fielded calls from Olive and his family and our friends. We held off putting anything out to the press because he said he wanted to talk to me when I was feeling more up to it.

Olive and his PR team must have handled it all.

We were off the radar for another day and then I woke to Dex not in bed with me. I heard him in the living room working, so I got up. It was the only time I was alone without him, and I took that time to walk over to my wedding dress.

We'd been so close to me walking down the aisle just days ago and now it hung in the hotel closet where Dex had left it. The lace of it was beaded with beautiful crystals and the lilac color actually shimmered in the sunlight.

I ran a hand over it, but I stopped at the base where there were just four tiny dots that weren't the color of lilacs. They were tiny dots of red. Dark red. Splatters of blood. Just four. No more.

But I knew what had happened. He'd never admit it. None of them would. Yet, when Mitchell called hours later, I also knew exactly what he'd say.

"Ezekiel fell down a flight of stairs." He sounded frantic. "Did you know? He had a heart attack not much later is what they're saying. It's not... Something isn't right. I know it's them,

Keelani. Did those Hardy guys...? What did you do?"

"What did I do?" I waited for the answer. There was silence, and it's how I knew the power had shifted. Gone was my fear of him, and in its place was strength. "Why would I have done a thing to that man, Mitchell? Is there something you'd like to share?"

"No. No. Ezekiel was fond of you though. He said he might want to..."

"He might what, Mitchell?" It was clear that in the past, Ezekiel must have gone to Mitchell for information about me.

He growled into the phone and then his tone turned vicious. "How do you expect me to cover something like this up? How do you expect to right this? We need a new deal, and we need to work on this together to—"

"I won't sign a new deal with you ever," I said without another thought. "You should think long and hard about what you're insinuating and your role within that record label. How many women have you disclosed information about, Mitchell?"

"You little bitch. You're still under contract and I will make your life—"

Maybe I was still groggy. Maybe I wasn't thinking right, but I hung up on him. I'd figure out how to leave Trinity even if I had to go to court, because something was very apparent to me. Dex was willing to risk everything for me, and I was now willing to risk everything for him.

He was at the door seconds later. "I thought I heard you up."

I sighed. "Just ironing out a few things."

He sighed. "Kee, I'm so sick of that record label."

"What?" I narrowed my eyes. "Were you listening to my phone call?"

I got his dimples then. "Your ass knows I was."

"I'm going to have to take them to court and fight to get out of that contract, but I'm going to."

He nodded a couple times before he said, "I definitely think your mother would be proud of you now, heartbreaker."

I smiled at him. "I think she would too." I took a deep breath. "Now, should we talk about the secret in the room?"

His brow lifted.

"If we're getting married, we won't hide things from each other. So, you need to tell me. You did something to Ezekiel."

He cleared his throat and scratched his head. And like a boy being reprimanded, he threw back, "He did something to you first."

"That's... You can't categorize what you did as retaliation." But I couldn't help the butterflies in my stomach at seeing the man I knew I loved acting in the way he always did. Dex had his boxes. He lived with and accepted them fully. "There are consequences for your—"

"For what, heartbreaker?" God, he was smiling so big.

"Is he really gone?" I whispered out.

"If I said he was?"

No secrets between us had me answering, "I'd be lying if I said I wasn't happy I don't have to worry about him anymore." My chin shook though at my next thought. "I'd be scared you'd have to worry about the repercussions."

"One less man in the world to terrorize women is something I won't worry about. I promise you that. We make the laws in this country with the amount of money we make. I know it doesn't seem fair, but it's true."

I looked at the ring on my finger, purple sparkling sunlight back at me in the best way. "It doesn't seem fair that I ever considered that we wouldn't marry, does it?"

He smiled and then slid his phone out to send a text. My phone beeped, and I saw then a group text had been started with him and all of his siblings along with me.

> **Dex: Kee's contract isn't up with Trinity yet. We're getting married for real soon. So you all ready to buy the label so she can do whatever she wants?**

> **Dimitri: Finally.**

> **Izzy: Oh God, yes. I love her new sound. We need to invest.**

> **Dimitri: I'll start moving things around.**

> **Lilah: Let's beg Jax Stonewood to be on a song.**

> **Dom: We'll buy it out by EOD. We'll need a statement to go out.**

> **Declan: This is Evie. I'm so excited!**

"Dex! No," I screeched. "What the hell am I supposed to say to all them?"

"Just say yes. Don't worry about anything else. Just live, heartbreaker. With me, forever."

I stared at my lilac wedding dress hanging there, and his words brought tears to my eyes. "My mom said that to me before she forgot again. Did you know that?"

"Your mother is a smart woman."

"I worry I won't ever be as smart as her most days, that I can't make her proud, that I've lost her. And you with my dad, Dex..." My voice broke, remembering the talk I had with him. "You're taking on a lot being with me."

"No more than I was before I was with you dreaming about being with you." He sighed and stepped up to me to pull me close. "Did she like your wedding dress?"

I nodded.

"Do you think she'd like to see it on you in the spring down by the lilacs in your backyard?"

"Dex... I just want you to know I'm going to be a completely different person soon. A new look, a new brand, and the press might hate me and—"

He cut me off. "You asked me once why I needed you in my home. Not just wanted. Needed. It's because I was dying without you, Kee. Suffocating. Couldn't fucking breathe without you. Is that answer enough? I didn't commit. To *anything*. I haven't loved a woman before you nor will I love another after you. I knew it then like I know it now. I have always loved you, and I hated you for that, Kee." He dragged a hand over his face, and then he got down on one knee. "Only because I couldn't be with you. So, you're wearing my ring but I want you to say it too. Say you'll marry me. Say we belong together. Say yes because I'm asking you now. Will you marry me?"

"You're not telling me?" I whispered.

"I will if you say no, but I'll ask first." His dimples showed. And I knew as I looked at him that was the truth. Dex would always protect me. He wanted to. He needed to. But he'd also take into consideration my requests.

We were a team, and I knew as I gazed at the lilac lace splattered with red, it was the only team I wanted to be a part of. "You know you didn't get rid of all the evidence. If I marry you in that dress, someone might see," I whispered.

"Maybe you and not just someone but everyone, needs a reminder that I'll make the world bleed if it hurts you. Do you get that?" he whispered against my ear.

I grabbed his shirt and pulled him close, crying now because there was no way to stop myself. "Then don't let them hurt me again, because I sort of like the world we're creating."

"Is that a yes? You'll marry me? Be with me forever?"

"Yes... For forever and ever."

EPILOGUE: KEELANI

"It's perfect," I whispered, probably a bit too lost in the picture of Dex and I surrounded by lilacs in my parents' backyard. The sunlight poured on us and glinted off the new gold gate Dex had replaced.

On our wedding day, Dex had even given me a shiny key that opened that gate and a tiny music box. When I unlocked the music box, it slowly opened and played the melody of the song my mother and I always sang together. *For the woman who is Kee to my heart* was engraved on it.

That had only been a few weeks ago, but now I felt the tears streaming down my face and remembered the smell of that fragrant flower as I walked down the grassy aisle on that perfect day.

"Good. Then, they're printing it," Dex said like there was no room for negotiation. He'd been sitting at his new desk within my office at Trinity Enterprises while Olive, Pink, and I sat on the ground, stressing over final approvals for one of the biggest magazines in the world.

He hadn't said a single thing until now. "You want to add your opinion now? We've been talking about this for nearly an hour." I glared at him.

He glanced up from his laptop and gave me his dimples as he smiled. "I have no idea what you all have been talking about for the past hour, but it hasn't only been that. Anyway, I'm hungry for lunch with my wife. You like that one." He nodded at the photograph in front of me. "I can tell. So, go with it."

So easily now, the man trusted my judgment and told me to follow my gut. I did most of the time too because I'd been learning to trust myself.

"He's right. That's the one." I pointed down at the photo.

He nodded and then looked at his watch. "Also, you have a meeting with a new artist in an hour and a half. So what do you want for lunch?"

Olive pushed at the flowers in her hair before she nodded and then stood up from the ground to stretch. "Well, that was easy. Also, you're not doing any appearances for the next month. So, I'm guessing you'll have some time off?"

I nodded softly, not wanting to tell her she wasn't needed.

"Means you're free for a whole month, I guess." Dimitri walked into the office and blurted out what I didn't want to.

"Free? I have a dissertation to write," Olive immediately snarled at him. "My professor has been quite interested in what I've come up with."

"That the same professor who called you the other night?"

"The other night?" I questioned, wondering what evening they were even talking about.

"Yes, Olive." Dimitri smiled. "Why don't you tell Kee about the other night?"

"I... You... Why are you here?" she stuttered out.

He smirked. "I came to discuss the night in question."

"What happened the other night?" I finally asked, because neither Olive nor Dimitri had shared anything with me.

Olive's eyes widened before she grabbed Dimitri's arm. "Let's go."

And before I could ask, they both hustled out of the office.

Pink got up and walked toward the door too. "Pretty sure

they're sleeping together."

"Wait...what?" There was no way. Dimitri or Olive would have said something to me.

"I literally can feel the tension when he walks into the room. You see him too much as a friend, but that man could melt her clothes off with his hot stare." She waggled her eyebrows.

"Oh, Jesus Christ, Pink. Are you meeting up with Bane? Me and my wife are having lunch."

"Yeah, yeah." She waved off Dex's death stare and then pointed to the photos on the ground. "You're making the right decision."

I stared down at my wedding pictures, admiring how we both had so much love in our eyes, how Dex held me close around the waist, and how the breeze pushed my hair back just right. The photographer had captured us perfectly, but the train of the dress was showing. With the spots I could see.

"No one can see what you're worried about." Pink sighed. "I think it's badass anyway."

I shouldn't have worn the dress with Ezekiel's blood on it. The move had been bold, reckless, and freeing. My shoulders relaxed into the feeling. "I know it's the right decision. I'll let the magazine know."

The magazine's focus wasn't at all about Ezekiel. It was about our marriage, our success, and the triumphs throughout our lives. They talked about how love could conquer all. They quoted me saying, "He'd always been the boy who saved me. And I wasn't about to leave behind the man who saved me too." And they quoted Dex saying, "She broke my heart once. I had to make sure she wouldn't again." The magazine got our exclusive interview after Dex and I agreed to only this one.

We'd waited months after Ezekiel's kidnapping to actually

go through with the wedding because there was too much trauma, too much healing to be done, too much of everything.

"I won't rush when I have you forever anyway," Dex had told me. So, we waited.

I finished out my residency in Vegas with special guests flying in to sing with me. They sang my songs, my words, my heart. They made me realize once and for all it's what I wanted to do, that I could make someone shine in the limelight while still enjoying my life out of it.

Owning Trinity allowed for me to do that. Dex and his family buying Trinity allowed that. So, this past month, I'd worked tirelessly to prove to them all I'd exponentially grow the label. I restructured management, leaving Mitchell out of it, and I'd brought on artists that thrived in the limelight. I worked alongside Dex most of the time, because he followed me everywhere—hence him being in my office now.

"So, stamp of approval on that and my work is done here for the week." Pink winked at Dex as she backed out of the office. Right before the door closed, she yelled, "Don't tell Bane I left!"

Dex nestled into my neck as he said, "Why do you always have a million people in your office?"

I chuckled. "Because I'm trying to make Trinity thrive."

Dex's family had been there for me every step of the way, and I would be there for them, by making sure this label wouldn't go under.

Not that any of them truly seemed to care about the success. When Izzy and Lilah called, it was to talk about my mother and how I was adjusting to the shift in my career. They wanted to talk a lot. Clara and Evie did too. They'd become the family I never knew I needed, and maybe in a way, the Hardys had always been that. I just needed to come to terms with it.

Sometimes it's hard to see the sun when you've been standing in the dark for so long. Dex and I were each other's light to find our way back to it. Now, our home was each other, although Dex whispered in my ear, "Do you plan to look at the blueprints of our home soon?"

He was having Dom draw up plans for a perfect ranch in our hometown on land near our parents. Ideally, I wanted to be closer to my mother when I could, but it was clear we'd both be traveling for work for years to come.

I also think Dex might have needed to heal from what had happened so long ago. We'd been home for the wedding, and Gabriella had seen us in a grocery store. I hadn't talked to her much after the accident. I don't think either of us could get past it back then. Our conversations had been stilted as she learned to walk again, and then we simply hadn't called one another much after. I knew she'd gone to college, got married, had kids and was living back in our hometown.

And she waltzed up to us with a trepid smile on her face that day to say, "You're both back!"

She pulled me in for a hug right away and then stared at Dex, worrying her hands even as he nodded and smiled softly toward her. Then he said, "Nice to see you, Gabriella."

She sighed and smoothed the collared polo she was wearing. "I don't think you mean that, Dex."

He frowned. "Of course I do."

She sighed and glanced around fast before she bit her lip. "My husband is walking around somewhere with the kids, but I just have to say...I'm sorry for the gossip I started after the accident."

"Wait. I'm a confused." I narrowed my eyes at her and

put some sauce in my cart. "What are you talking about?" My eyes ping-ponged between them. I saw the shock and then the recognition on Dex's face and the shame on hers.

She took a deep breath. "I egged on reporters and..." She glanced at Dex before she looked down in embarrassment. "I shouldn't have let people run with the story that you were the bad influence. The town painted him to be a villain, and I ran with the story. I was so mad at my luck, at having to relearn to walk, at knowing Dex saved you..."

I started to tell her she had every right to feel angry at her luck, but at Dex? Not at him. Yet, he cut me off. "No worries, Gabriella."

"No worries?" I looked at him with wide eyes.

"I got what I wanted, Kee. I got you in the end. Right?" He smirked at me. The man was ridiculous, I swear.

"Right, and honestly, I know no one could have saved me now. I was young and stupid. We all were. I'll never forgive myself for how cold I was to you when you came to visit. I know you tried to find me in the water."

"It's fine."

Dex tried to stop her, but she shook her head. "No. It's not. You told me you would have given your life for Kee and for me and for Kyle if you could have. I wasn't forgiving then. I'm not really now, either, because there's nothing to forgive."

Dex cleared his throat, but I saw how his eyes sparkled, how he stood so still. His soul needed to hear those words, and I was so thankful Gabriella had been strong enough to say them.

"Also"—she leaned close as she wiped away a lone tear and laughed—"please stop sending checks to me. My husband is starting to think something's going on."

She rushed over to her husband then, who'd just walked

past the aisle, and I stared up at Dex. "You can't save everyone, Dex."

"I can try." He shrugged.

I don't think he ever would stop trying either. He helped me reintroduce myself to my mother, albeit our relationship was much different, but it was still a relationship I wanted. He helped me take my dad to rehab and visited him with me. And now he was here, holding me close in my office, trying his best to help me with my workday.

"Let's look over the blueprints together?" I murmured. "What do you want for lunch?"

"You, Kee." I felt his length against my back.

"My office is not the place for that." I laughed as his tongue dragged across my neck.

"Of course it is. You own the damn place. Let's make use of it."

I couldn't help myself as I rotated my hips so I could get closer to him. "And why is it again, Mr. Hardy, that I own this place?"

"Because you worked your ass off for it."

I smiled at how good he was to me. "Right, but also when the interviewer pressed you on the topic, tell me again what you said?" He lifted a brow. "Go on. I like hearing you say it," I told him, because it gave me butterflies reading it.

"That interviewer was an asshole. He shouldn't have asked why I invested in the company in the first place."

Dex was right. It was the interview that stopped all other interviews, because the man had eyed me up more than once, and Dex had seen him. Then, on national television, he'd insinuated Dex was buying me.

"Isn't it true you made your family invest?"

"I don't make my family do anything." Dex's jaw flexed and right then I knew the man was going off script.

"My good friend, Mitchell, a former manager at Trinity, tells me you weren't very into music. Why buy Trinity Enterprises when it's not the best financial decision? You've been touted as a great investor and one who is pragmatic in all you do. The world-renowned magazine *Financial World* actually is quoted as saying, 'Dex Hardy is structured and ruthless in his categorization of most everything in his life.' So why this company? Your wife really that good, or is she just good in—"

"I recommend you don't finish that sentence about my wife." Dex's words came out in a growl before he'd leaned back and stared at the host. It was a stare so dark and vicious that it took over memes across the world. I loved that stare, but more so, I loved what he said after.

"Tell me again what you said."

He chuckled against my neck as his hand slid up my thigh. "When he asked me why I bought your label, I agreed that I'm pragmatic in all I do and said, 'Pragmatically, no one stands in the way of my wife's happiness. She wanted it, so I bought it. There's no other explanation needed.'"

And that's how I'd chosen to live with him from then on.

Without explanations. Without apologies. Without fear.

But with confidence. With love. And with my Dex.

THE END

For additional content, including bonus scenes, sign up for
Shain Rose's newsletter: shainrose.com/newsletter

ALSO BY SHAIN ROSE

Hardy Billionaires
Between Commitment and Betrayal
Between Love and Loathing
Between Never and Forever
Hardy Billionaires #4 - Fall 2024

* * *

Tarnished Empire
Shattered Vows
Fractured Freedom
Corrupted Chaos

* * *

Stonewood Billionaire Brothers
INEVITABLE
REVERIE
THRIVE

* * *

New Reign Mafia
Heart of a Monster
Love of a Queen

ABOUT SHAIN ROSE

Shain Rose writes romance with an edge. Her books are filled with angst, steam, and emotional rollercoasters that lead to happily ever afters.

She lives where the weather is always changing with a family that she hopes will never change. When she isn't writing, she's reading and loving life.